A Secret and
Unlawful Killing

Also by Cora Harrison

My Lady Judge

A Secret and Unlawful Killing

❋

A Mystery of Medieval Ireland

Cora Harrison

Minotaur Books ⚞ New York

A SECRET AND UNLAWFUL KILLING. Copyright © 2008 by Cora Harrison. All rights reserved. Printed in the United States of America. For information, address St. Martin's Press, 175 Fifth Avenue, New York, N.Y. 10010.

www.minotaurbooks.com

The Library of Congress has catalogued the hardcover edition as follows:

Harrison, Cora.
   [Michaelmas tribute]
   A secret and unlawful killing : a mystery of medieval Ireland / Cora Harrison. — 1st U.S. ed.
      p. cm.
   Previously published in Great Britain under title: Michaelmas tribute, 2008.
   ISBN 978-0-312-37268-2
   1. Women judges—Ireland—Burren—Fiction. 2. Burren (Ireland)—History—Fiction. 3. Law, Celtic—History—Fiction. 4. Law—Ireland—History—16th century—Fiction. 5. Community life—Ireland—History—16th century—Fiction. 6. Ireland—Social life and customs—16th century—Fiction. I. Title.
   PR6058.A6883M53 2008
   823'.914—dc22

                           2008020346

ISBN 978-0-312-58602-7 (trade paperback)

First published as *Michaelmas Tribute: A Burren Mystery* by Macmillan, an imprint of Pam Macmillan Ltd

First Minotaur Books Paperback Edition: December 2009

10 9 8 7 6 5 4 3 2 1

For my husband, Frank; son, William;

daughter, Ruth; son-in-law, Pete, and grandson, Shane,

with all my love and thanks for their help

ACKNOWLEDGEMENTS

It gives me great pleasure to acknowledge, once again, a debt of gratitude to my agent, Peter Buckman, of the Ampersand Agency, for his unfailing support and encouragement, and to my editor, Julie Crisp, whose faith and enthusiasm are all that any author could wish for. She, Sandra, Ellen, Liz, Nicole and many others at Pan Macmillan have become friends as well as colleagues to me in the process of writing these books.

I would, in addition, like to express my gratitude to those, such as Fergus Kelly, Daniel Binchy, Kuno Meyer, among many others, whose research made the fascinating subject of Brehon law available to the general public.

Helpful staff at the British Library allowed me to handle and to leaf through the precious manuscript of over ninety folios written in the mid sixteenth century by Domhnall O'Davoren, of Cahermacnaghten law school and his scholars; many thanks to them, also. It was wonderful for me to see the different scripts, some neat, some slapdash, one obviously left-handed, and to speculate on the varying personalities of the students. It was great to read their comments in the margins, complaining of the bad food, commenting that the week felt so long that it seemed as if it had two Thursdays in it, and making jokes about Sémus and the drink! I felt as though the law school that I had created in my books had suddenly become real.

PROLOGUE

The kingdom of the Burren was then an isolated place, with the Atlantic Ocean guarding its northern and western coast, and the broad sweep of the River Shannon encircling its eastern and southern sides.

Then, as now, it was a place of contrasts: rounded mountains flanked its borders, fertile valleys lay between the mountains and in the centre, on the High Burren, was a broad expanse of shining, bare limestone pavement. Then, as now, it was a land of grey stone, almost black in the winter rains and fogs, but sparkling silver in the sunlight, with tiny jewelled flowers and ferns growing in the grykes between the clints, and in summer the vivid green of the valley meadows was stitched with yellow, pink and purple flowers.

Its people, the Burren clansmen, lived according to the ancient customs and Brehon laws of their ancestors. Their way of life, in this isolated spot, had hardly changed during the last one thousand years, but the end was drawing near. The threat to their traditions was not far away: the city of Galway, with its English laws and English-speaking, Anglo-Norman people, was only twenty miles across the bay.

Nevertheless, it was King Turlough Donn O'Brien, not the ageing Tudor king Henry VII, who still ruled those western kingdoms of Thomond, Corcomroe and the Burren when in the spring of 1509 the elderly *taoiseach* of the MacNamara clan died and the *tánaiste*, his son Garrett, took his place.

On the ancient Celtic feast of *Imbolc*, at the beginning of February, the MacNamara clan gathered outside the old tower house at Carron. Garrett MacNamara, dressed in a white *léine* and a mantle made from pure white lambswool, was led in procession to the cairn, a burial mound covered with small white quartz pebbles, a sacred place to the MacNamara clan. At the foot of the cairn, King Turlough Donn touched him on the head with a newly peeled white rod from the ancient ash tree that grew nearby. In a loud, steady voice, Garrett swore to be the king's vassal in accordance with the ancient Brehon laws, to maintain his lord's boundaries, to escort his lord to public assemblies, to bring his own warriors to each *slógad* and, in the last hour of his lord, to assist in digging the gravemound and to contribute to the death feast.

Then Garrett bowed to King Turlough Donn and encircled the cairn three times sunwise before climbing nimbly to the top of the mound. He lifted up the white rod and held it high above his head. The clan of MacNamara named him in a thunderous shout as *the MacNamara* and Garrett swore to serve his people and to protect them in return for a just rent and a fair tribute. Thus was Garrett MacNamara inaugurated as *taoiseach* of his clan.

No one then could have foretold the murderous events that happened almost eight months later, on the day of the Michaelmas tribute.

ONE

CRÍTH GABLACH (RANKS IN SOCIETY)

Each kingdom in the land must have its Brehon, or judge. The Brehon has an honour price, lóg n-enech [literally the price of his or her face] of sixteen séts. The Brehon has the power to judge all cases of law-breaking within the kingdom, to allocate fines and to keep the peace.

As soon as dawn broke on the morning of Michaelmas, the mist rose over the stony land of the kingdom of the Burren. It clung to the sinuous curves of the swirling limestone terraces on the mountains and filled the valleys with its thick, soft, insubstantial presence; it swathed the crenellated tops of the tower houses and wrapped the small oblong cottages in its feather-light folds; it encircled the walls of the great fortified dwelling places:

3

cathair, lios or *rath*, and rested softly over the stone-paved fields.

Mara, Brehon, or judge, in the kingdom of the Burren, a tall, slim, dark-haired woman, wearing the traditional *léine*, a creamy-white linen tunic, under her green gown, stood at the gate of the law school of Cahermacnaghten and for the fortieth time that morning peered hopefully through the heavy mist. She was expecting her six scholars back from their holiday and not a single boy had arrived yet.

'You might as well stay warm inside, Brehon,' said Brigid, her housekeeper, coming out from the kitchen house inside the law school enclosure. 'The chances are that none of them will come today,' she continued, brushing the drops of mist from her pale sandy-red hair. 'The fog is bad enough here. It will be worse on the hills and the mountains. There's even some frost about: Cumhal said that the grass was white on the north field when he and Seán were doing the milking.'

'I suppose you're right, Brigid,' Mara replied. Normally she could see for miles across the flat tableland of the upper Burren but today she could barely make out objects only fifty yards ahead of her. The small sunken lanes that ran between the fields were blotted out and their red-berried hedges had become part of the grey landscape. There was no sound. Even the swallows, which only yesterday had been chattering busily on the rooftrees of barns and houses, had now fallen silent.

'Why don't you come inside?' urged Brigid. 'They won't come today. Cumhal brought a load of turf in and there is a good fire in the schoolhouse if you want to work there. It's freezing weather.'

Brigid and Cumhal had been the servants of Mara's father

4

when he had been Brehon of the Burren and now served the daughter with the same respect, commitment and fidelity as they had shown to the father. Nevertheless, Mara usually found herself obeying Brigid as if she were still four years old, so she turned obediently to go indoors. Then she stopped. Her quick ears had heard a creaking sound. She started to walk down the road, and Brigid trotted rapidly after her.

'It's just a cart,' said Brigid after a moment.

'It's Ragnall MacNamara, the MacNamara steward,' said Mara.

'Out collecting the Michaelmas tribute for the Mac-Namara, I suppose,' Brigid muttered sourly. 'There was a lot of talk about that last night at the Michaelmas Eve *céilí*. The word was that the MacNamara is not content with the tribute that his clan usually give; he's telling them what he wants from them. Giving them orders, no less!'

'Really!' Mara said no more because Ragnall, mounted on his white horse, was now quite near, but she was astonished. The annual tribute to the *taoiseach*, hallowed and shaped by custom and tradition, was normally conducted with grace and courtesy on both sides. The clansmen gave what they could afford from their year's produce and the *taoiseach* thanked them and promised his favour and protection in return.

She saluted Ragnall with the usual blessing. He muttered, 'and St Patrick,' without looking at her. Obviously he still resented the fine she had imposed upon him at the last judgement day for hitting Aengus, the miller, with a heavy stick.

'I was wondering if you had seen any of my scholars,

Ragnall,' Mara asked him calmly. 'I'm expecting them today, but none has arrived yet. Are the roads very bad over towards the east of the Burren?'

'Bad enough,' he grunted, without replying to her query.

'But you've managed to get around,' she persisted. 'You came over the Clerics' Pass?' Her eye went to the heavily laden cart. She counted seven bags of wheat flour there, each with the milling date, 25 September, and over-stamped with the MacNamara insignia of a prancing lion. This meant that Ragnall had managed to get up the slopes of Oughtmama to take the annual tribute from Aengus. It would have been a pleasure to him, she thought, to watch the miller load the bags of unbleached linen with his precious flour. Wheat grew in only a few favoured spots here in the cool, moisture-laden, stony environment and wheat flour was highly valued.

He grunted again, but still said nothing. He clapped his heels to the sides of his white saddle horse and jerked his head at Niall MacNamara, who was driving the cart, and continued on down the road without a backward glance.

'Did you ever see such a man as that!' exclaimed Brigid, her green eyes flashing with anger at the discourtesy. 'You mark my words, Brehon, one of these days that man will get what's coming to him.'

❊

By mid-afternoon the mist had begun to lift. Suddenly colour, shape and sounds came back to the landscape. The wet flagstones that paved the fields shone with a gleam of silver in the autumn sun, the magenta-coloured cranesbill glowed, beads of moisture dropped from the delicate, drooping heads of the pale blue harebells and the swallows gathered in large chattering flocks.

Twelve-year-old Hugh, the son of a prosperous silver-smith in the Burren, had arrived at the law school around midday, but there was still no sign of the other scholars. Now Hugh was getting restive and uneasy in the company of three adults without the other boys. Mara found him moodily kicking a stone on the road outside her house and cast around for something to make the day seem less long for him.

'Shall we go to the market at Noughaval?' she asked. 'That might be fun. We'll take Bran as well. Bran,' she called, and a magnificent white wolfhound bounded out of the stables, tail wagging vigorously. 'Run in and get his lead, Hugh. We'll walk in case the mist comes down again at sunset.'

Noughaval was a short walk to the south of Cahermac-naghten. It was a small settlement of a few houses, a church and a fine market cross at the edge of the square. The market square was crowded today. It seemed as if every trader in the three kingdoms of Burren, Corcomroe and Thomond had set up stall. Their wares were varied: the usual butter and cheese; fish fresh from the nearby Atlantic waters; leather stalls selling belts and satchels; wool stalls with lengths of rough fustian, honey cakes and hot pies for the hungry; and more-exotic stalls selling silks and laces brought in from foreign countries. In one corner of the square, near to the entrance gate, the O'Lochlainn steward, a big genial man, was collect-ing the annual Michaelmas tribute from the many O'Lochlainn tenants. He was mounted on a tall box so that none could miss him and beside him, outside the market wall, was a cart piled high with sheepskins and firkins of butter and rolled hides of fine calf skin or goat skin.

'God bless the work, Liam,' called Mara and he grinned in answer as he stowed away some silver in his leather pouch before turning to greet her.

'You are well, Brehon?' he enquired. 'The *taoiseach* is over there talking to the O'Brien. He'll be glad to see you. He was saying last night that he was going to consult you about some point of law.'

Mara groaned inwardly. Ardal O'Lochlainn always did want to talk about some point of law. 'Here's some silver for you, Hugh,' she said. 'You go and enjoy yourself while I talk to the *taoiseach*. Bran, go with Hugh,' she added with a quick pat on Bran's narrow hairy head, and Hugh and Bran galloped off through the crowds towards the honey cake stall.

'You are collecting the tribute here at the fair?' she asked Liam.

Liam shrugged. 'It's the easiest way. Let them come to me.'

'I met Ragnall MacNamara out on the road this morning,' Mara told him. 'He must have been out since dawn, his cart was already piled.'

'Well, the MacNamaras don't have too many families here on the Burren,' Liam said dismissively. 'If I were to do that I would be on the road for weeks, going from farm to farm. Besides, the O'Lochlainn likes it best this way: he wouldn't want it to seem as if he were asking for anything; the tribute is for the clan to give.'

Mara nodded. The O'Lochlainn clan had been kings

of the Burren in former days and the unconscious dignity of royalty had descended to the present chieftain, Ardal O'Lochlainn.

'Anyway,' continued Liam with an amused look, 'it's just as well that Ragnall is not here today. It gives his daughter, Maeve, a bit of time for courting. There's going to be trouble about these two,' he whispered, pointing to a young couple in the churchyard. 'The O'Briens and the MacNamaras don't get on too well. Ragnall MacNamara will never agree to a marriage between his daughter and the son of Teige O'Brien.'

Mara's eyes followed his pointing finger. She knew young Donal O'Brien by sight; he and Fachtnan, the eldest of her law school scholars, had become great friends in the last few weeks of the Trinity term. Donal was a hot-tempered boy, inclined to drink too much and to get into fights; probably basically a nice boy, she thought indulgently, just the spoiled only son of a wealthy *taoiseach*. Maeve Mac-Namara she didn't recognize. No doubt I have seen her before, thought Mara, but she was probably one of those girls who had suddenly blossomed into beauty with the dawning of adolescence and now was unfamiliar. She was quite small, but with a pretty, well-rounded figure and a face that, with its wide kitten-like eyes, delicate pink and white complexion and small pointed chin, reminded Mara of a heartsease pansy. Donal was bending over her, holding her two tiny fragile hands in his large ones and looking at her with adoration.

'I suppose the O'Brien wouldn't think it was a good match for his only son,' she said sympathetically, but Liam shook his head.

'No, it's not that at all,' he said emphatically. 'That boy

9

gets his own way about everything; his father would agree, but Ragnall won't consent. He would have to give too many cows to settle his daughter with the son of a *taoiseach*. The man is so mean that he would skin a mouse to get the fat off it.'

'Was it a good evening at the *céilí*, yesterday, Liam?' asked Mara, changing the subject. After all, it was up to Ragnall to arrange a suitable marriage for his daughter. Liam, as she had planned, was immediately diverted.

'The *craic* was mighty,' he said, smiling happily at the thought of the fun and the conversation and the sallies of wit, which would have been accompanied by large amounts of ale and mead.

'No trouble?'

'Ah well,' he said, with a hasty glance in Ragnall's direction. 'There was a bit of a fight between Aengus and Ragnall, again. There's bad blood between those two. The MacNamara should sort it out before it gets any worse. They'll be killing each other if this goes on. And then, of course, that young fool Donal O'Brien had to put his oar in.'

'On Aengus's side?' asked Mara.

'No, would you believe it. And after Ragnall turning him down when he wanted to marry the daughter! I suppose that Donal thought Ragnall might get to think better of him if he spoke up for him. Anyway, he took hold of Aengus, but Aengus flattened him. Donal was pretty far gone in drink, of course. Aengus cleared off after that and the O'Brien steward persuaded young Donal to go home, but I heard that the young fool would not be told and went flying after Aengus.'

'Oh well, as long as no harm was done,' said Mara tolerantly.

'Brehon,' called Ardal O'Lochlainn, making his way through the crowd, which opened up respectfully to allow him to pass. 'You are looking well,' he added with his usual courtesy.

'I'm very well thank you, Ardal,' Mara replied. 'Liam was saying that you might want to consult me on a point of law,' she added, with her usual directness.

'It's just a matter of the MacNamara mill at Oughtmama,' he said. He sounded a little uncomfortable at having to approach the matter without the usual enquiries about health and comments on the weather. 'I just wanted to check with you. My understanding of the law is that no man can alter, without consultation, the flow of a river or stream that goes through a neighbour's land. Well, the stream that turns his millstone goes through my land on the mountain, and now Garrett MacNamara has ordered his tenant, Aengus Mac-Namara, the miller, to divert a few of the other streams on the top of mountain, above my land, so now my stream floods my land from time to time. Has he any right to do that?'

'He should certainly have consulted you and perhaps paid compensation if it has done any harm to your land,' Mara told him cautiously. 'The law is quite clear on that matter.' What a fuss about nothing, she thought. The stream only went through a hundred yards or so of O'Lochlainn land.

Ardal O'Lochlainn's face brightened. 'So can I bring a case against him on the next judgement day?'

'I think it would be better to talk it over with Garrett first,' said Mara hastily, having spotted a disturbance over at the market cross. A fight would break out there soon, she thought, if someone did not intervene quickly.

'And he has done the same thing on the other side, on Teige O'Brien's land,' Ardal continued, oblivious to the commotion behind him. He was a man of single mind. He reminded Mara of a dog she had once, which was so obsessed with digging holes that he would even ignore a rainstorm and stay digging rather than retreat to his cosy bed in the stables.

'I'll consult my law texts and let you know,' she promised and hurriedly made her way to the market cross.

The crowd had gathered around a trader selling linen. He was a small man with a thin face and a back that looked permanently bowed by the weight of his pack.

'What's the trouble?' she asked crisply.

The crowd immediately fell into a respectful silence and parted to allow her to go through. She took a quick glance around. A large roll of coarse unbleached linen was lying on top of an open pack on the ground and beside it a pair of iron shears. The trader picked them up hastily and stuffed them into his pack. Then he began to roll up the linen.

'Diarmuid, what is happening here?' Mara quickly picked out a neighbour of hers, a man she could trust.

'Well, Brehon,' said Diarmuid, his freckled face worried and his sandy brows drawn together with a frown. 'It seems as if a lot of people have got short measure from this man, Guaire O'Brien from the kingdom of Corcomroe.'

Corcomroe was only a mile or so from Noughaval, but the people of the Burren were intensely clannish. The O'Brien clan of the Burren were liked and respected by their neighbours, as were O'Lochlainn, O'Connor or even MacNamara, but it was a different matter with an O'Brien from Corcomroe. Traders from Corcomroe were scrutinized carefully and any small infringements of the laws of weights and measures pointed out instantly. However, there seemed to be more than a small infringement here. There was an immediate chorus of assent to Diarmuid's words. Women were pulling out lengths of linen from their baskets and holding them up in front of her, indignantly clamouring to be heard.

'How is this?' asked Mara. 'The measuring line is here, on the market cross. It is plain for everyone to see. There is the inch line and there is the yard line. Haven't you been using that?' she demanded sharply of the trader. He had the face of a thief, she thought. His eyes were sly and his mouth was tight.

'He pretends to use it, Brehon,' said Áine O'Heynes, 'and then at the last moment he moves the cloth. I was watching him, because when I took the cloth out to show it to my daughter, I thought it looked short-measure so I came back and watched him carefully.'

'Let me have the cloth, Áine,' said Mara, stretching out her hand.

'That was supposed to be four yards,' Áine told her. 'That was what I asked for and that was what I paid for.'

'Measure the cloth for me,' Mara firmly requested, holding it out to the man, Guaire.

He took it from her and held it stretched between his two hands as he lined it up with the stark black horizontal lines on the well-scrubbed base of the market cross. It was almost half a foot short of the four yards.

'I'll throw in an extra foot,' he said hastily.

'You won't,' said Mara severely. 'You will cut a new piece of that same linen and you will make sure that it is exactly four yards in length. Is there anyone else who needs their cloth to be remeasured?'

A crowd of women surged forward and Mara groaned inwardly. She didn't relish the thought of standing there, overseeing, for the next hour. In any case, down the road from the market square she could see a crowd of young men following a trundling cart. The air was still and slightly frosty, and the sound of angry voices carried well. She fixed a stern eye on Guaire and announced clearly: 'Anyone with any further complaint come and find me.'

Rapidly she moved to the outer wall of the market. She could see that the heavily laden cart was accompanied by a man on horseback. Mara narrowed her eyes against the low sun and then tightened her lips. Yes, it was Ragnall Mac-Namara, on his white horse, and behind the cart was a group of men led by a huge giant of a man, an angry man judging by the tone of his voice. Mara stopped and stood very still. Fintan MacNamara, the blacksmith, was a great bull of a man and now he was roaring his disapproval and anger. She could hear his voice clearly now rising over the gruff voices of his supporters.

'You can tell the *taoiseach* that I'm not paying this extra tribute. Why should we pay a tribute to the *ban tighernae*? It's never been done before in the MacNamara clan and if I have anything to do with it, it will never be asked for again. I'll tell the MacNamara that to his face, himself.'

So that was it. Garrett MacNamara was a man in his thirties, who had recently succeeded his father as *taoiseach* to the MacNamara clan. He had taken a wife in the early summer and now the tenants were expected to pay for the lady's expensive tastes. It was strange having an extra tribute

14

for the *ban tighernae*, the lord's lady, but not unknown. Mara took another step forward and then continued waiting, standing in the exact centre of the laneway. She had not seen Garrett MacNamara at the fair, but no doubt he was expected there. Like the O'Lochlainn steward, Ragnall MacNamara would expect to gather some of the tribute from the members of the MacNamara clan who thronged the market and it was customary for a *taoiseach* to come and publicly thank his clansmen on those occasions. In the meantime it might be possible for her to avert a fight by virtue of her authority.

'Tell me what the trouble is, Fintan,' she said crisply as the cart drew near. With one hand she signalled to Ragnall to stop the cart and then turned a listening attentive face towards Fintan.

'Well, this is the way it is, Brehon,' said Fintan in a conciliatory tone. 'I paid my tribute to the MacNamara early this month. He was telling me that he wanted a pair of new gates for his tower house at Carron. I supplied them and I fitted them. Fifteen feet high and ten feet wide, they were.'

'Yes.' Mara nodded. 'I've seen them, Fintan, and they do you credit.'

'Well, as you can imagine, Brehon,' Fintan continued in mollified tones, 'I thought that would be enough of a tribute for any reasonable man, but when I was off at Caherconnell shoeing the physician's horses, Ragnall comes along and takes those four candlesticks from my forge and tells my lad that the *taoiseach* requires them as my tribute for the *ban tighernae.*'

'Let me see the candlesticks,' said Mara. She moved closer to the cart.

The branched candlesticks were at the bottom of the cart

and surrounded by firkins of butter, baskets of eggs, linen bags of goose down and a few large round cheeses. There seemed to be no doubt that the MacNamara was exacting a very big tribute from his clan this Michaelmas. The candlesticks were beautifully made; each one of them branched to hold eight candles. Fintan had probably hoped to sell them to the king, Mara surmised. They were too fine for most people on the Burren.

'And that's not the whole of the story,' went on Fintan. 'He went to Eoin's farm and took three, instead of the usual two, bags of sheep's wool and he took them while Eoin himself was up Abbey Hill. He shouted at Eoin's wife and made her give it, and she with six small children there on her own!'

Mara frowned; it sounded as if Ragnall MacNamara had been unnecessarily autocratic.

'You may take your candlesticks, Fintan, if you wish,' she said grimly. 'They should not have been taken from your forge without your permission. However, you may wish to see your *taoiseach* and talk over the matter with him first,' she added. Garrett MacNamara already had a reputation for bearing a grudge for a long time and Fintan, despite his brave talk, would hesitate to incur his enmity. 'Eoin,' she said, turning to face the tall young farmer, 'since your wife gave the extra bag I cannot authorize you to take it back now. The law says that she has equal rights to the property that you both work on. What you must do, and what I would advise all of you to do, is to send a request to your *taoiseach* to meet you and to lay down the tribute that will be expected of you in the future. If you wish, the meeting can take place today and I will be present to tell you what the law will or will not sanction. Will that content you?'

There was murmur of talk and Mara waited patiently. There was a look of sour triumph on Ragnall's face. Would his master reward him adequately for the hatred that he incurred on the Burren, she wondered, or did the man enjoy his unpopularity? It made her wonder what sort of life that kitten-like daughter of his enjoyed, cooped up with a sour and hated father in the remote house at Shesmore.

'We'll stick together,' announced Fintan. 'I'll leave the candlesticks for the moment – for the moment only,' he warned, bringing his large fist down heavily on the side of the cart. 'And you, Ragnall, tell the MacNamara that we need to meet with him and to talk to him.'

'He will be here at the market soon,' said Ragnall sourly. 'You can tell him yourselves then.'

'Well, that's ideal then,' said Mara firmly. 'I'll wait with you.'

❃

By the time Garrett arrived, the crowd of MacNamara clansmen had grown larger and more menacing. Mara felt irritated with herself. The right thing to do would have been for her to have invited Garrett to come to the law school at Cahermacnaghten and to have talked with him privately before he met with his aggrieved clan. He was a new *taoiseach*, recently married, touchy about his rights and immensely ambitious. He would not take kindly to being told his duty in public.

'Here he is,' said Fintan, his deep strong voice cutting across the market place chatter.

Quickly, Mara moved across to talk to Ragnall. If she were busy chatting to the steward when Garrett arrived then her presence would seem less formal, less of a challenge to an insecure and newly appointed *taoiseach*. Niall MacNamara, she noticed, was no longer beside the cart. Perhaps his duties were over for the day. Perhaps Ragnall would find someone else to take the cart to the tower house at the end of the afternoon. He had the reputation of being a skinflint and he would not want to pay Niall any money over the minimum necessary.

'How's your daughter?' she asked chattily, after a quick glance around to make certain that Maeve MacNamara was nowhere to be seen.

'She's well,' Ragnall answered, sounding bewildered.

'How old is she now?' asked Mara with one eye on the tall figure of Garrett who was now making his way through the cluster of his clansmen. She noticed that he did not greet them with the elaborate courtesy of the O'Lochlainn, or the joking friendliness of the O'Connor, but contented himself with a few curt nods.

'She's sixteen,' said Ragnall after a long pause, in which he managed to convey that the Brehon should mind her own business.

'Sixteen?' Mara was genuinely surprised. 'Well, how time passes! I would have thought she was only about thirteen or fourteen. Is she here today?' she asked innocently.

'No, she has plenty to do at home,' said Ragnall dismissively. 'Now if you'll excuse me, Brehon . . .'

Mara did not move but stood there smiling: Garrett MacNamara had arrived. He looked as if he expected trouble, she noticed, but then perhaps, with his fleshy, protruding nose and his heavily swelling lower lip jutting out from the receding chin, he always did look like a man about to start a fight. He could not have failed to notice the atmosphere of tension and how his clansmen had formed themselves into a solid crowd at his back. He did not waste time greeting Mara, or his steward, but turned and faced them.

'Well?' he asked.

Fintan, the blacksmith, came to the front.

'My lord, we are finding your taxes too heavy,' he said bluntly. 'More has been taken from us in tribute than has ever been taken before.'

Garrett frowned at him and allowed a long silence to develop and to fill the space after the angry words. Several of the clan shifted uneasily and looked as if they wished they had not come along. The reliance of the clan on the leadership and protection of their *taoiseach* was absolute. The *taoiseach* was elected from the ruling kin-group and once elected had great power – unless, of course, there was a rebellion against him.

'The tribute was too low under the rule of my father,' said Garrett eventually. 'He was a very old man and he had made no changes for a long time.'

'And what about my candlesticks?' asked Fintan angrily. 'I had already paid my dues with that pair of gates for your avenue. Ragnall came and took four candlesticks while I was out.'

'Did you do that, Ragnall?' Mara asked innocently. She moved decisively forward and every eye turned towards her. 'Well, in that case, I would say that you put yourself outside the law.'

Garrett turned enquiringly to Ragnall and the steward did not hesitate.

'The blacksmith lies, my lord,' he said. 'He had left instructions with his man to give them to me as the second half of the tribute that was owed by him.'

'What!' roared Fintan. 'I left no such instruction.'

Clever, thought Mara. The man who worked for Fintan, Balor, a distant cousin of his, was as strong as Fintan himself, physically, but mentally he was a child. He would not be able to stand up to cross-questioning. His classification was that of a *druth* and his evidence would not be acceptable in a court of law. However, did a *druth* have the authority to allow the steward to take goods from his master's storeroom? Certainly not, she decided, and intervened quickly.

'This is a case that I must hear at Poulnabrone,' she said firmly. All courts were held in the open air beside the ancient dolmen at Poulnabrone about a mile from Noughaval. 'I will hear the case at twelve noon on tomorrow, Tuesday 30 September,' she went on, raising her well-trained voice so that it carried all over the market-place. 'The case is between Fintan MacNamara, blacksmith, and Ragnall MacNamara, steward. Fintan MacNamara accuses Ragnall MacNamara of taking four valuable candlesticks from his premises without any authority.' She paused and then lowered her voice and looked enquiringly at Garrett MacNamara. 'And the case of the tribute,' she said evenly, 'do I understand you to say that this was a special, one-off tribute that was meant to compensate for some years of underpayment? Will the tribute on Michaelmas next year be the same as before unless it has been renegotiated with the clan?' She paused again, looking at him steadily. To her surprise she noticed a faint sheen of perspiration on his high sloping forehead. Eventually he nodded.

'Yes, Brehon, that is the case,' said Garrett. He pushed his way back through the crowd and mounted his horse. There was a subdued movement from the MacNamara clan that she feared might explode into a cheer, so she added rapidly: 'Go, then, all of you. Go in peace with your family and your neighbours.'

They moved obediently at her bidding, but few left the market-place. Like a flock of starlings that had been scattered by a stone but soon coalesced back into a tight throng of scintillating black, the crowd dispersed but then came together again at the market cross, resentful eyes glancing over towards the impassive figure of the steward, Ragnall, who was carefully counting the silver in the pouch that he wore on his belt.

ᛏᚹᛟ

AN SEANCHAS MÓR
(THE GREAT ANCIENT TRADITION)

*There are two fines that have to be paid by anyone
who commits a murder:*

1. *A fixed fine of forty-two séts, or twenty-one
   ounces of silver, or twenty-one milch cows*
2. *A fine based on the victim's honour price, lóg
   n-enech*

In the case of duinetháide, *a secret and unacknowledged killing, then the first fine is doubled and
becomes eighty-four séts.*

❧

THE MORNING OF 30 SEPTEMBER dawned with a
slight veil of mist, but this soon dispersed in the warmth
of the autumn sun and the sky at sunrise was a brilliant

22

tapestry of orange and gold behind the rounded purple heights of Mullaghmore Mountain.

'You might as well enjoy yourself for now, the two lads from Thomond will be here by mid-morning,' said Brigid, finding Mara busy in her garden an hour later.

But the first arrival from Thomond was King Turlough Donn himself, and he came bringing gifts.

'She's too beautiful!' said Mara, gazing anxiously at the superb Arab mare. It was truly a gift from a king, but gifts often brought a price with them. Turlough was getting impatient; she realized that. He would expect an answer from her soon: four months had now passed since his surprising offer of marriage. She had pondered the matter during the quiet days of the summer, but she still could not make up her mind. She looked up into his pleasant face with those gentle, pale green eyes, which belied the pair of huge, warlike moustaches that curved down from either side of his mouth. A man of warmth and integrity, she thought, a man that any woman would be proud to call a husband. But was she any woman? Her present life was a happy and satisfactory one. Did she want to change it for all that was entailed by being his queen? 'I don't know how to thank you enough,' she continued.

'Well, that half-bred *garron* you gallop around on wouldn't do for a king's wife,' he said gruffly, eyeing her hopefully.

She rose to the bait immediately. 'Oh, who is this king's wife then?' she asked, pretending to scan the Brehon's house and garden, where her neighbour, Diarmuid, was waiting patiently for her. She had inveigled him into breaking a few pieces of limestone for her new flowerbed just before the

23

king arrived. Her eyes surveyed Diarmuid with affection now. He would be the perfect husband for her, she thought. Tolerant, easy-going, he could move in to her house, carry on with his farm half a mile down the road, and she could continue with her busy life as Brehon of the Burren and *ollamh*, professor, of the law school at Cahermacnaghten. Turlough Donn O'Brien, king of the three kingdoms, Thomond, Burren and Corcomroe, was an altogether different matter.

'You know that I want us to get married as soon as possible,' said Turlough, lowering his voice slightly.

He stopped at the distracted look on her face. Mara's quick ear had caught the sound of ponies galloping at breakneck speed up the lane from Noughaval.

Still holding the reins, she moved away from him with a worried frown as she recognized two of her law school scholars once they rounded the corner. 'That's a couple of my boys!' she exclaimed. 'What's wrong?'

'Brehon,' shouted Aidan, as soon as he had caught a glimpse of her.

'Brehon, we saw a man,' shouted Moylan, desperate to get the information in before his friend could speak.

'And he was dead,' screamed Aidan.

'Dead!' echoed Mara. She hastily handed the reins of the new mare to Cumhal, her farm manager, and moved quickly down the road to meet them.

'Slow down,' she commanded as she came towards them. 'You'll kill your ponies; the news will keep for a few minutes. Now jump down and walk them sensibly.' The boys' faces were bright with excitement and both looked perfectly well so her initial worries were soothed. Her mind was clamouring for a name to this dead man, but her instinct, especially when dealing with the dramatic young, was to meet each crisis with calm.

'Take some grass and rub down the poor beasts,' she scolded. 'They're both covered in sweat. You shouldn't have ridden them like that. I'm sure they are tired after your long journey.'

She waited quietly while the two boys tumbled to the ground and snatched up handfuls of the bleached, dry grass from the side of the road and started to rub down the ponies.

'Where did you see the dead man?' she asked, her tone light and casual.

They looked at her, startled by her lack of alarm, and then Aidan said: 'At Noughaval.'

She waited. Moylan would fill in. This was the way they always talked: each taking turns.

'He was in the churchyard.'

'Someone had buried him.'

'Well, half-buried,' amended Moylan. By now there was an interested audience of the bodyguards and the king himself, to whom the boys made rapid sketchy bows before returning to their exciting news.

'Not enough earth to really cover him properly,' said Aidan with relish.

'Some soil had been taken from another burial pile.'

'It was fresh earth.'

'That would probably be from the burial of old Domhnall,' said Mara calmly. Her mind was seething with questions and suspicions, but she would let them tell their story. 'He died on Friday and was buried on Sunday.'

'The shovel was still there, stuck in the ground.'

'We thought it was two new graves, but then we saw his feet sticking out.'

'We were tossing a hurley ball to each other as we were riding along and Aidan missed it. It went over the wall and we got down off our ponies and went into the churchyard. We were hunting for the ball and then we saw the feet under the trees.'

Mara thought for a moment and then decided what to do.

'When you've seen to your ponies properly,' she said in steady, quiet tones, 'go inside and Brigid will give you breakfast and help you to put your things away. Hugh is here already and the others will be along soon.'

The two boys stared at her open-mouthed. 'But you'll need us to come with you. We know where the body is,' said Aidan.

Mara looked back. Cumhal, as always, had anticipated her need and was walking up the road with the horse, and Diarmuid was coming out of the gate. She would have plenty of assistance without Moylan and Aidan.

'Now go inside, you two,' she said.

They looked at each other in desperation.

'We know who it is,' blurted out Moylan. 'We uncovered the face.'

'And he didn't just lie down there and cover himself with soil,' added Aidan with emphasis.

'There's a big lump of dried blood on his forehead.'

'You'd better let us come with you. You'll get a shock when you see him.'

She gazed at them with an air of mild interest and they couldn't resist the final piece of information.

'It's old Ragnall MacNamara,' Moylan announced.

'The MacNamara steward,' said Aidan.

'The MacNamara steward,' echoed the king.

Mara stood very still for a moment. Ragnall was unpopular, many hated him; she had seen that yesterday. But enough to kill him?

'Cumhal,' called Mara. 'Go back and get the cob, and bring the leather litter with you. We need to go to Noughaval churchyard. Now see to your ponies, you two, and then have your breakfast.' She looked at their downcast faces and then took pity on them. Her warm heart could never resist her young scholars. 'You know your ponies are blown,' she said gently. 'You have to see to them, now, and I'm sure that you want something to eat, yourselves. Anyway, you are the first, except for Hugh, to arrive for the Michaelmas term, so you can tell the news to everyone else when they get here and, of course, you two will be important witnesses when I announce the death at Poulnabrone dolmen this noon.'

They knew there was no use in further pleading so they went dejectedly through the great iron gates into the law school enclosure. The door to the scholars' house stood ajar and smoke was rising from the kitchen house. Brigid would give them a good breakfast, avidly listen to their news, see that they emptied their satchels into the chest at the bottom of each bed, and then they would have the excitement of telling the dramatic story to each new arrival. Mara felt she had enough to deal with without their presence.

'My lord, I will have to leave you,' she said to the king.

'I'll come with you,' he said, with a quick gesture of command to his two bodyguards.

'You may need somebody to send on an errand, Brehon.'

27

Diarmuid was at her side. As always, quiet and unobtrusive, he swung his leg over his horse while the king assisted Mara to mount her mare. She smiled her thanks to both while her mind ran through the steps that she had to take. As Brehon she was responsible for all crimes on the Burren and this looked like a case of a secret killing. She looked regretfully back at her garden and at the exquisite flowerbed that she had been making. It was laid out in a series of small diamond shapes, each one outlined by the dark blue strips of limestone and filled with flowers of all the richest autumn hues. There were clumps of cranesbill, their intensely magenta flowers velvet-soft, then a patch of pale blue harebells and then, in the next space, some purple knapweed.

Mara paused for a moment looking at the effect and watching how the colours blurred and merged with each other. She had once seen a stained-glass window in an abbey church in Thomond; the glory of the jewel-bright colours, each in its black-edged diamond, had stayed with her and this was the effect that she aimed at.

'There'll be a lot of fuss and bother from young Garrett MacNamara if someone has killed his steward,' said Turlough. 'Who do you think did it? Weren't you telling me that there had been some bad blood between the steward and the MacNamara miller – what was his name? Aengus, wasn't it?'

'Yes,' she said absent-mindedly. 'I judged the case between the two of them at the last judgement session at Poulnabrone. I fined Ragnall for hitting Aengus a blow on the leg. It was just a drunken quarrel, but the miller was still limping after a month.'

There was another matter troubling her, though she tried

to thrust it for the moment to the back of her mind. The situation yesterday, on Michaelmas Day, at the Noughaval Fair, had been dangerous and perhaps should have been resolved that afternoon instead of being postponed for judgement at Poulnabrone today. Anger had been seething in the MacNamara clan over the unjust tribute imposed upon them, and that anger had focussed upon the steward rather than on their *taoiseach*. She feared that she bore a certain responsibility for this killing. She had made the wrong decision. This happens, she tried to tell herself. She had done what seemed to be the best at the time; nevertheless it was a terrible thought that a death should have occurred because of a failure on her part.

'Don't look so worried,' said the king, watching her affectionately. 'You know you are looking very beautiful this morning. I love that gown – royal purple, just right for you. You don't look a day over eighteen!'

'I'm thirty-six,' she replied tartly, but she couldn't help a quick, satisfied look down at her new gown. The rich purple, over the creamy white of her *léine*, suited her dark hair and hazel eyes and it had been made according to the latest fashion, closely fitting with a row of small buttons at the front, its flowing sleeves caught tightly in at the wrist. The admiration in the king's eyes warmed her, but she had a task to do.

'Cumhal,' she called over her shoulder to her farm manager, who was riding respectfully behind them. 'Go ahead to Niall MacNamara's farm. He was with Ragnall yesterday when they were collecting the Michaelmas tribute. Get him to send a message immediately to his *taoiseach* and then come and meet us at the churchyard. Actually, no,' she amended with a rapid change of plan. 'Tell him to bring his horse and meet us at the churchyard first.' She would have to see the body for herself before she sent for Garrett MacNamara: she could imagine his fury if he were dragged from his tower house at this early hour of the morning because of a wild rumour from two fourteen-year-old boys.

'I'll go for Niall, Brehon,' said Diarmuid, riding forward. 'You may need Cumhal with you and Niall knows me well. His lands march with mine.'

Mara gave him a quick nod and a smile. That would be best. Niall MacNamara, the illegitimate son of Aengus MacNamara, the miller, was a nervous, timid young man. She could rely on Diarmuid to bring him along without causing him any undue worry. And, of course, it still might be just a false alarm so the least fuss, the better. Aidan and Moylan were not the most reliable of witnesses.

❧

It was no wild rumour though. As reported, the body in the churchyard had been left uncovered, a shovel hastily thrown on the ground beside it. The dead face stared wide-eyed at the sky and a cluster of flies buzzed sacrilegiously around the clotted blood on the narrow brow. It was Ragnall MacNamara. Mara bent down and touched the hand. Stone cold. Yes, it appeared likely that he had been killed last night. She sighed sadly. There was something infinitely pathetic about a dead face shorn of all its defences, she thought. In life she had not much liked the man, but in death she mourned him and breathed a prayer for eternal rest for his troubled soul. She straightened up then and walked back to the gate where she had asked the others to wait. Turlough dismounted his horse as soon as he saw her and came to join her, while Cumhal and the two bodyguards stayed at a discreet distance.

'Yes, it is Ragnall, the MacNamara steward, and he is definitely dead,' she said, before he could ask. He took her hand and held it between his own two large warm hands.

'Is there anything I can do?' he asked quietly. 'Do you want me to get Malachy, the physician?'

Mara shook her head. 'He's in Galway. In any case I don't think that there is much that he can tell me. It seems obvious that the blow to the head killed him.'

'Would you like me to go up to the castle at Carron and let the *taoiseach* know about this? I can easily do it on my way back to Thomond.'

She shook her head again. 'You go on with your journey. I'll have Cumhal and Diarmuid here with me,' she assured him.

'You're not going to prefer to accept help from that *bóaire* instead of from me, are you?' grumbled Turlough.

Mara smiled with amusement. She enjoyed Turlough's occasional growls of jealousy.

'It's more fitting for a farmer to be running errands than for a king,' she told him demurely. She felt she sounded like a parody of her housekeeper, Brigid, who always had a keen notion of what was or was not fitting for various members of society to do, but Turlough continued to look at her suspiciously. He had not liked finding her alone with Diarmuid in the garden earlier.

'*Go n-éirigh an bothair leath* [may the road rise up with

31

you],' she said smiling a farewell, and, despite the presence of the bodyguards, she reached up and kissed him on the lips.

'I'll be back as soon as I can,' he said, holding her tightly in his arms for a few minutes. Then he climbed back onto his horse and, followed closely by his bodyguards, made his way down the road towards the east.

Mara stood quietly, her thoughts lingering on Turlough and the complications, as well as the pleasures, that had resulted from his love for her. Her mind strayed back to her first husband; she had sworn never to marry again. Should she remain firm or accept Turlough's offer of marriage? Then she dismissed the matter from her mind. This was not the time or place for speculations of this nature. Now she had to banish them from her thoughts and put all her energies and intelligence into solving this unexpected death.

❧

Niall was the first to arrive. He was mounted on a heavily built workhorse and he thundered along the road from Rusheen well ahead of Diarmuid on his slow-moving cob. Niall had obviously been told that something was amiss and his young, thin face was drawn and apprehensive as he swung his leg over the broad back of the horse and then came slowly across to her. He did not show any shock at the sight of the dead body of the steward, but his lips tightened. Mara noticed that he did not mutter the customary prayer either. She found that strange.

'As you can see, Ragnall MacNamara has been killed,' she said quietly.

32

Niall moistened his lips and opened them as if he were about to say something and then shut them again.

'When did you leave him last night?' Mara asked. She had thought to postpone questioning until after Garrett had been called and the body removed to the church before being decently buried, but often a question when someone is shocked could provoke the truth while time for thought produced only silence. However, she was surprised and puzzled to note how shaken Niall looked. True, he was only in his early twenties, but he must have seen many dead people in his time: the Gaelic custom was to hold night-long wakes after every death and young children were routinely brought to these events.

He raised troubled eyes from the corpse at their feet and looked at her. 'I didn't see him after I left him at the market square, Brehon,' he said. 'You were there yourself. You probably saw me go. I never saw him after that until this very second.'

She frowned. 'But what about the cart?'

'Well, I was a bit late coming back for the cart. A cousin of mine was at my house. He had come all the way from Tuamgréine to see me so I didn't want to rush away. I thought Ragnall would stay until the end of the market. He always likes to make sure that he gets the last ounce . . .' His voice trailed away and his eyes went once more to the silent body on the ground.

'So what time did you come back?' asked Mara.

'The sun was still up . . . well, I suppose it was setting . . . but it was before sundown . . . I remember my shadow being very large on the ground ahead of me as I walked towards

33

the fair,' said Niall defensively. 'There were plenty of people still there. I passed the merchant from Corcomroe, Guaire, on the road when I was leaving Rusheen.'

'And Ragnall had already gone?'

'The cart was there and no one was with it.'

'And his horse?'

'That was gone, too.'

'And what did you do then?'

'Well, I waited for a while and then I crossed over and had a word with Liam O'Lochlainn, the O'Lochlainn steward. He was still on that box of his, collecting the Michaelmas tribute from all the O'Lochlainns. He said that Ragnall had gone some time ago. So I took the cart back to my own place at Rusheen. That had been the arrangement: I would keep it overnight, and then drive it over to the tower house this morning.'

'So it's in your barn now?' Mara asked thoughtfully. 'Did you check it before you stored it?'

Niall shook his head. 'No, Brehon, I just put it in the barn, locked the door, released the dog and then went back indoors. That dog of mine is a great barker; no one could come near the place without him rousing me.' He turned his head as the clatter of horse hoofs sounded on the stony road.

'Here comes Diarmuid,' said Mara. 'You go now, Niall. Just knock on the door of the priest's house and send him over here. Once we have brought Ragnall to the church you must ride as fast as you can and bring your *taoiseach* back here. He will want to make the arrangements.'

She watched him carefully as he hurried across the churchyard. There seemed to be something always rushed and apprehensive about Niall. His early life as the illegitimate son of Aengus, a sour, difficult old man, and his servant, Cliodhna, probably accounted for that. Nevertheless, there seemed to be something unusual about the jerky way that his long thin legs crossed the churchyard, and he waited for a moment, standing with his head bowed, before pulling the bell rope.

'Did you tell Niall that Ragnall was dead?' she asked Diarmuid quietly as he came down the path to meet her.

He shook his head. 'No, I didn't, Brehon. I just said that you wanted to see him and that you were by the church. He didn't ask anything, but jumped on his horse straight away and was off down the road nearly before I had finished speaking.

Almost as if he knew what I had found, thought Mara. Aloud she said, 'Diarmuid, would you be able to spare the time to ride over to Carron and tell Garrett MacNamara about this killing? Would that be asking too much of you? I think I need to speak to Niall and I would like to send Cumhal back to the school as soon as possible. You know what Aidan and Moylan are like, and Enda and Shane will be arriving soon. I don't want to leave Brigid alone with them for too long. I hate to disturb your morning though,' she added, looking dubiously at him. Diarmuid, she knew, would always hasten to carry out her lightest wish and for that reason she didn't like taking too much advantage of his affection.

'No trouble at all,' said Diarmuid briefly, his freckled face lighting up with pleasure. 'I'll enjoy the ride and I'll be glad to do something to help.'

Mara looked after him fondly as he rode down the path, his red-blond hair glinting in the late September sunlight. He was a trustworthy man, she thought, a good neighbour, loyal to his clan and kind to his animals. He lived alone on a farm in North Baur, about a mile from Cahermacnaghten, with only his ferocious dog, Wolf, to keep him company. What a shame that he never married and had a wife and family!

※

Father O'Connor, the parish priest at Noughaval, was an elderly man. As soon as Mara saw him emerge she went hastily to the churchyard gate to break the news to him.

'I'm afraid this is a sorry sight, Father,' she said. 'Ragnall MacNamara has been killed and his body has been left in the churchyard.'

The priest nodded heavily as if such things were a daily occurrence in his life. Perhaps he was so old that nothing now came as a surprise to him. He put the black stole around his neck, followed her and without hesitation knelt on the damp grass beside the body. Quickly he anointed the five senses: feet and hands, the two ears, the mouth, and the nostrils, and then just above the widely opened sightless eyes, murmuring the ancient Latin words.

Mara crossed herself perfunctorily as the priest rose to his feet, but her mind was already busy with the arrangements for the next stage.

'I think, Father,' she said, 'that it would be best if we took him into your church for the moment. He can repose there until we see what the MacNamara says. And of course there is his daughter, Maeve. We'll have to see if she wants to have his wake back at the house, or if it will take place in the tower house.'

'Poor child, poor child,' said Father O'Connor compassionately. 'She lost her mother three years ago and now her father. What a sad thing. She has no brothers or sisters either, to help her bear the burden. It was a late marriage between Ragnall and his wife. Just the one child.'

And where was Maeve? Mara wondered, following Cumhal and Niall as they bore the body into the church. Her mind was working busily. Why had Maeve not informed anyone that her father was missing? Surely she would have noticed and been concerned when Ragnall had not come home that night.

'Would you like me to go and see her afterwards and break the news to her?' asked Father O'Connor, getting out his prayer book as they entered the church.

'No, Father,' said Mara thoughtfully. 'I think I will do that myself.' She said a brief prayer over the dead man and then walked back out to the graveyard. Niall and Cumhal followed her.

'Niall,' she said gently, 'I've changed my mind. I've sent Diarmuid to fetch the *taoiseach*. You and I will go back and check on the cart and then I'll go to Shesmore to see Maeve MacNamara and break the news of her father's death to her.'

Niall said nothing, just looked at her apprehensively. She gave him a reassuring smile and then turned to her farm manager. 'Cumhal, you can go back to the school, all the scholars should have arrived now and Brigid will have her hands full with them.' Despite the serious and tragic situation, her lips curled in an irresistible smile at the thought of the excitement at the law school as Aidan and Moylan told their dramatic story over and over again.

'Yes, Brehon,' said Cumhal obediently. He went towards the cob, and then hesitated, looking questioningly over his

37

shoulder at her. She joined him instantly. Cumhal said little, but when he spoke it was always worth hearing. As he and Brigid had been her father's servants from their youth, there was little they didn't know about the Brehon's business.

'Did you notice that Ragnall didn't have a pouch, Brehon,' he said in a low tone when she joined him.

'No,' said Mara. 'I didn't, Cumhal.'

'His mantle fell back when we were lifting him onto the litter, so that's why I noticed. It had been cut from his belt,' Cumhal continued, still in an undertone, with a quick glance over his shoulder to where Niall was standing, waiting at a discreet distance from them. 'I saw the marks where the leather had been cut. Niall put the mantle back around him before we carried him in. That's why you wouldn't have seen it.'

'Thank you, Cumhal,' said Mara quietly. She returned to Niall and smiled at him. 'One minute, Niall, I must just have a quick word with Father O'Connor.' She went rapidly back into the dim chill of the stone church and knelt beside the priest, her eyes scanning the body lying peacefully on the marble slab.

'I've sent Diarmuid O'Connor for the MacNamara,' she said. 'I am sure the *taoiseach* will take charge of all the funeral arrangements.' She spoke mechanically, deftly disturbing the dead man's heavy outer garment while the priest's face turned towards the church door. Now she could see for herself that Cumhal was correct. Ragnall wore a heavy, broad leather belt beneath his mantle. The belt was black with age and usage but the edges of the tags, which would have supported his pouch, showed almost white. They had been cut recently with a sharp knife and the pouch stolen. After death? Or before death? Impossible to tell, thought Mara, but she was sure of one thing. By late afternoon that pouch would have been crammed full of pieces of silver. It had even begun to bulge by the time she had seen Ragnall in the early morning of Michaelmas. It had been stupid of her to miss the pouch, she thought. It was as well that Cumhal had his wits about him. She looked more closely at the dead body, determined not to miss anything else. The bone of Ragnall's forehead was splintered, but there was also a dark purple bruise above the left ear. Possibly the man was first stunned, fell to the ground and was then killed. She rose from her knees. The priest was oblivious of her, still muttering prayers, whether for himself or for the dead man she did not know. She did not disturb him, but slipped quietly away and joined Niall outside the church.

❊

The journey down the lane towards Rusheen was a silent one: Mara riding ahead and Niall trotting quietly behind her. For the last hour Mara had been too busy to value the present given to her by the king, but now as the horse moved smoothly beneath her she realized the true worth of the gift. This was a gentle mare of superb breeding. The late September sunshine lit the pale gold of her mane and seemed to give her a look of a magical horse, one that had been given by the sun god himself. Mara leaned forward and stroked the narrow head and the small neat ears and the mare turned her head and looked at her with wise understanding eyes.

I'll call you 'Brig', thought Mara. The renowned female Brehon, Brig, had been like a beacon to Mara from her early childhood. Her father had often told her the story of how a young male judge, named Sencha, had delivered an unfair judgement against a woman. Blisters had come out upon his cheeks and they had stayed until Sencha had sought out Brig and the female Brehon had put him right. 'You must not judge a woman as if she were a man,' Brig had said. 'A man brings horses to take possession of a property; a woman brings her goats. A man brings a richly jewelled drinking cup; a woman brings her kneading trough.' So Sencha had gone back and reversed his judgement and the blisters had disappeared.

Mara had always loved that story and had been determined to become as wise a female judge as Brig. Her father had smiled indulgently, but she had persisted with her studies and he had been amazed and proud of the speed with which she learned. She had become an *aigne* (lawyer) at sixteen, the year of his death, and he had left the law school in her hands. When she became an *ollamh* (professor) two years later and Brehon of the Burren five years after his death, she had hoped that her gentle father was looking down at her from Heaven and was happy at her success.

❧

Niall had a small farm of twenty acres about a mile away from Noughaval. As they approached, Mara looked over the hedges with interest. The young man was obviously a good farmer. The fields were brightly green; fat, contented cows cropped the luxuriant growth of late summer grass and neat well-thatched haystacks, each as large as a cottage, were grouped in a sheltered spot near the barn. The stone walls that enclosed the fields were well built and kept in good repair; hedges were neatly clipped and kept thick and stock-proof. The small cottage and the surrounding cabins gleamed with fresh limewash.

'You've a great farm here, Niall,' she told him appreciatively.

'I've had a lot of help from good neighbours,' Niall said modestly. 'Your own Cumhal has always been ready to lend a hand and Diarmuid O'Connor has been like a father to me. Better than any of my own clansmen,' he added with a faint touch of bitterness.

Mara considered this. Niall's was the only MacNamara farm in the south-western edge of the Burren; most of the MacNamara farms were to the east of the kingdom, so it would be natural that Niall's nearest neighbours would be the ones to help him rather than far-off cousins. However, the fact that he was the son of an unacknowledged and secret tie between Aengus the miller and his elderly servant might have something to do with his lack of contact with the MacNamara clan.

Niall MacNamara's dog barked and then wagged a welcome when they came to the gate. Mara bent down to give him a quick pat before following Niall as he unlocked the barn. It was dark and shadowy and smelled of the dry dust of old hay.

'Could you take the cart outside, Niall,' she said. 'We will never be able to check the goods in this bad light.'

She waited while Niall pulled the shafts of the cart and steered it out into the yard. He immediately went through the goods, obviously remembering each tenant's contribution to the lord's tribute. Mara only half listened to him. There was something missing. She had known that as soon as he had begun to lift the bags of wool and the firkins of butter.

'The four iron candlesticks that Ragnall took as tribute from the smithy are missing,' he said when he had reached the bottom of the cart. He searched around the few things left and then looked at her, his face shocked out of its usual ruddy colour.

'Fintan,' he whispered. 'Lord save us, I never would have thought it of him. Why would he do a thing like that just to get back a few scraps of metal?'

There was more than a few scraps of metal involved, thought Mara. All of Fintan's talents as a smith had gone into the making of those magnificent candlesticks and he would not have been able to bear to be cheated out of them. Would that mean that he had killed, though? Mara did not know him well enough to be sure of the answer to her own question. And, of course, the candlesticks were not the only missing goods from the tribute.

'I suppose you noticed that Ragnall's pouch was also missing, Niall, didn't you, when you put his mantle around him?' she said casually.

He looked at her with seemingly unfeigned surprise in his light-coloured eyes. 'No, Brehon,' he said quickly. Surely that must be a lie, thought Mara. Niall had been with Ragnall for most of the day. He would have noted how, piece by piece, the silver would have been carefully stowed away in the pouch. Cumhal had immediately seen that it was missing.

'And yet you put his mantle around him,' she pointed out.

'I m . . . might have done,' he stuttered. His face had gone very white. He stared at her for a few minutes. Even his lips were blanched and bloodless, she noticed. She waited patiently, looking at him enquiringly.

'I was very upset when I saw the body,' he stated finally, after visibly racking his brains for an explanation that would content her.

'I see,' said Mara gravely. 'Well, I think the best thing would be for you to keep the cart here until your *taoiseach* tells you what to do with it.'

He nodded silently, bending down to do the task immediately.

'Not a word to anyone else of this in the meantime, Niall,' she warned as he replaced the goods into his cart. She waited while he wheeled it back into the barn again and locked the door securely. He walked to the gate with her.

'What's my best way to get to Shesmore, Niall?' she asked.

'You'd be quickest if you go through Noughaval church-yard and then down the path between the fields of Ballyganner,' he said. His voice was still low and shaken, she noticed, but he made an effort to steady it before he spoke again. 'When you pass the tower house at Ballyganner, just turn left and take the lane over towards Shesmore. It's a narrow lane, but wide enough for a horse. When you see the farmhouse, you can cross two fields and you'll be there.'

'I'll leave you to go back to the church then, Niall,' said Mara. 'Stay with Ragnall's body until your *taoiseach* arrives.' She clicked her tongue, shook the reins lightly, and the mare responded instantly with a quick glance over her shoulder and a sparkle in her fine eyes.

On arriving back at Noughaval, Mara dismounted at the gate and led the horse through the churchyard, stopping for a moment to look at the spot where the body of Ragnall had lain. She could see the scattered earth where Aidan and

Moylan had uncovered the body. There was very little of it; not enough even to cover the body properly. There was no intent at concealment, then. Surely the murderer could have easily dug a hole in the soft, friable soil that had been continuously reworked over the centuries. Perhaps the murder had taken place when there were still plenty of people at the market square, when the possibility of discovery was too high for a risk like that to be taken. But why cover the man at all? Why not just leave the body lying on the ground after the fatal blow had been struck? Could it be that the murderer could not bear to see the accusing, wide-open eyes of the dead man? Did that show some relationship between killer and killed? And what had been used to strike the blow? Something heavy, surmised Mara, and she looked around, wondering if there was anything in the graveyard that could have been used as a weapon.

Not far from the scattered earth lay a small, roughly fashioned stone cross. It was only about two feet long. It had nothing engraved upon it, but it probably came from one of the many graves dotted around. Holding her reins in one hand, she bent down and picked it up. It was heavy, she thought, but not too heavy to be swung and used as a weapon. One side of it was covered with moss and lichen – that would have been the side facing the north-west, she surmised. However, the vegetation at the top of the cross was broken off, leaving the surface not white, as would be expected, but a rusty brown. For a few minutes she stared at the mark. Her years of experience had taught her to identify this particular stain. It was definitely dried blood. Carefully she placed the heavy cross back on the ground and then stopped as the sunlight glinted on an object loosely covered with soil. She knelt down and sifted the soil, allowing it to run through her hands until her fingers met something. She tightened her hand and then opened it. There was something hard there that sparkled: it was a brooch, still pinned to a torn piece of grey cloth. A piece of a *brat*, a mantle, she surmised, finely woven from the wool of the sheep that filled the mountains and the uplands of the Burren. It was the brooch, however, that held her attention. It was a valuable brooch, made from gold, circular, and in the centre, inlaid into red enamel, were the figures of three lions. The three lions, she thought, inspecting the brooch with its telltale piece of grey cloth still attached, and then turning it over and over in her hand. This was the badge of the O'Brien clan. These three lions snarled from every flag and every banner of the O'Briens. She looked at the brooch thoughtfully and then placed it carefully within her pouch. She hadn't found the answer to her question: only another question. She sighed and then looked around. Yes, there was a gate at the far side of the churchyard.

It was interesting, she thought, as she went to collect her mare, that this secret hidden path, with its high hedges, led from the churchyard at Noughaval to the farm at Shesmore and from there to the O'Brien tower house at Lemeanah.

THREE

CÁIN LÁNAMNA (THE LAW OF COUPLES)

A woman should marry a man of the same status as her father. If she marries a man of higher status, then her father must supply two-thirds of the cattle and the father of her husband need supply only one-third.

The same applies to a man. He should not marry a woman of higher status than himself. If he does, his father has to supply two-thirds of the cattle for the couple and the father of the bride supplies one-third.

᪾

HARA WAS JUST AT the churchyard gate when she heard the clop, clop of Diarmuid's horse. She smiled a greeting before asking: 'So what did Garrett MacNamara say about the killing, then?'

46

Diarmuid chuckled, dropping his reins so that the horse could nibble at a clump of grass by the entrance to the graveyard. 'You wouldn't believe it, but the first thing he wanted to know was what business of mine it was. He wasn't that interested in hearing about his steward's death.'

'What!' For once Mara was speechless.

'Well, you see, he reckoned that it should have been one of his own clan who brought the news, Brehon.' Diarmuid always called Mara, 'Brehon'. Although they had been children together, his respect for her position was enormous.

'And he didn't even thank you for riding all the way up there to Carron in order to tell him?' The outrage in Mara's voice was enough to make the mare, Brig, turn her head to look at her mistress enquiringly.

Diarmuid shook his head. 'I didn't need thanks,' he said quietly. 'I did it for you, not for him.' Absent-mindedly, he bent down and picked a few creamy-gilled mushrooms from the side of the road and placed them in his pouch. No doubt he would fry these over his kitchen fire with a couple of rashers for his supper, thought Mara, feeling suddenly touched by his lonely bachelor status.

'How is Wolf?' she asked. Wolf was a magnificent dog with red-gold fur and a huge head. Diarmuid's cousin, Lorcan, had bred him from a mating between a sheepdog bitch and a wild wolf. Up to a few months ago Wolf had treated all mankind, except his owner, with suspicion, but during the summer Mara had made friends with him and now Wolf adored her also.

Diarmuid looked startled and then pleased. 'He's in great form,' he said. 'You wouldn't believe the company that he is.' He paused, giving her an embarrassed look, and then

47

confessed, 'I often bring him into the house during the evening. That dog can almost talk.'

'I'll come down one evening to see him and I'll bring some of Brigid's sausages with me,' promised Mara, amused at his confession. Diarmuid, like all farmers, tried to pretend that a dog was just a piece of merchandise. Wolf, she guessed, was a substitute for wife and children to this warm-hearted man.

'That'll be nice,' he said; his eyes were full of affection and Mara smiled at him. He seemed to be the one person in her busy life who never looked for anything from her. The people of the Burren respected her and were fond of her, but the clansmen usually had some legal problem for her to address. The boys at the school, her servants, her farm-workers, all brought her problems and questions. The king was beginning to get restless and to want an answer to his surprising proposal last May. It would be very peaceful to visit Diarmuid; they would pass a pleasant couple of hours together, admiring Wolf and talking over old times.

'So is Garrett going to take charge of the wake and the burial?' Mara asked.

Diarmuid nodded. 'The *ban tighernae* tried to tell him that Ragnall's daughter should do that, but I said she was only a child without any near relations. She tried talking me down, but I just stood there. In the end, I said that the Brehon wanted the *taoiseach* to do it. The *ban tighernae* still tried to argue, but Garrett agreed straight away when he heard that.'

'What's she like, Diarmuid? Ragnall's daughter, I mean.' asked Mara. She bent down to pick a sprig of purple heather, but then changed her mind. Let it grow, she thought. The bees were enjoying it. It would only die tucked into her brooch.

'Pretty little thing,' said Diarmuid. 'Quiet girl . . . I don't rightly know if I've ever heard her say anything much except, "yes, Father". She was always working on that farm and she's only a small girl; you wouldn't think that she would have the strength for some of the things that he made her do. He was out being the steward and she was left looking after the farm. I'd say that she had a hard time,' said Diarmuid compassionately. 'You never saw her out having fun with the other young lads and *cailíní*. Ragnall kept her locked up at home. I don't suppose she'll miss him too much, but, of course, you never can tell. Do you know her to see, Brehon?'

'I just saw her yesterday at the fair with young Donal O'Brien. Liam, the O'Lochlainn steward, seemed to think that they were in love with each other.'

'I saw them too,' said Diarmuid meditatively.

'And would you agree with Liam?'

'Oh, yes,' said Diarmuid softly. 'She's in love with him.'

'Do you think that he is in love with her, though?' asked Mara. 'A steward's daughter doesn't seem good enough for the son of a *taoiseach* and, by all accounts, this is a young man with great notions about himself.'

Diarmuid nodded emphatically. 'He's in love, all right,' he said firmly. 'He would carry the clouds for her,' he added in a low voice, almost as if he were speaking to himself.

Mara was silent for a moment. She had never heard the phrase before. She looked at Diarmuid, but he was not looking at her, just gazing into the distance. His face had a lonely, sentimental expression. Was he thinking of young Donal O'Brien and his love for the pretty little Maeve, she wondered, or was he thinking of himself and his twenty years of loyalty to the friend of his youth? She felt sorry for him; she suspected that he had been in love with her all of her life. She remembered his anguish when he heard the news that she was to marry Dualta, a young student at her father's law school, and his disgust when Dualta, contrary to Brehon law, had revealed secrets from the marriage bed in the local alehouse. Without Diarmuid's loyalty to her, she might never have been able to divorce Dualta and to rid herself of an unworthy husband. Would it have been better for her if she had married Diarmuid rather than Dualta? They would have been very happy together and he, she knew, would have taken, as much as was possible, the weight off her shoulders. She dismissed the fanciful thought. Now she would have to deal with the present and make sure that young Maeve and her lover, Donal O'Brien, had nothing to do with the murder of Ragnall MacNamara.

'I'm going down there now,' she said. 'I have to break the news of her father's death to her.'

He looked back at her then. 'Are you going down to visit young O'Brien, too, today? Would you like me to come with you? They say that he has a bit of a bad temper. He always seems to be in some fight or other whenever he visits an alehouse.'

'I think I have plenty of experience in managing bad-tempered young men,' said Mara with a chuckle. 'No, you go back now, Diarmuid, I've taken up enough of your time for today. I'll be around to see you during the next few days.'

❉

The lane to Shesmore was long and winding, with hedges so high that, even mounted on horseback, Mara could not see over the top of them. Being the only farm between Noughaval and Lemeanah it must be a very lonely place for a girl, Mara thought compassionately. Still, perhaps that had added to her attractions for young Donal O'Brien. The kingdom of the Burren was a sociable place, with all the inhabitants taking full advantage of the many fairs and horse-racing events, as well as the four big festivals of *Imbolc, Bealtaine, Lughnasa* and *Samhain*, so Donal would have been meeting all the other young girls continually from childhood onwards. Maeve, with all her prettiness, would have come as a welcome novelty to him if he had suddenly met her one day in the lane that joined the lands of Lemeanah Castle to Shesmore.

Shesmore itself was a prosperous-looking farmhouse, originally a cottage Mara surmised, but with additions so that now the whole was a substantial, L-shaped, two-storeyed building with windows filled with thick opaque glass. Ragnall had obviously done well for himself during his stewardship of the MacNamara clan. Very few people in the Burren had glass in their windows; most were content with wooden shutters and perhaps a piece of linen nailed across the window frame during the summer months.

Maeve was at home; she came out at the sound of the horse hoofs on the well-paved yard.

'Brehon,' she said. Maeve was startled to see her; there was no doubt about that. It took a minute before she added politely: '*Tá failte romhat.*' There was a definite note of wariness in the young voice, despite the routine words of welcome.

'*Dia's Muire agat*,' replied Mara, walking her mare to the mounting-block. She eyed the girl carefully. She bore no apparent signs of sorrow or guilt. There was nothing amiss with the delicate complexion of the pretty face before her, and the wide blue eyes were as innocent as those of a baby.

'Have you been worried about your father, Maeve?' she asked quietly as she dismounted.

The blue eyes – surely there was a shade of purple in them; they were darker than the blue *léine* that she wore – widened even more. 'No, Brehon,' she replied softly and deferentially, 'has he sent you with a message for me?'

Either this girl was innocent or she was a consummate actress. It was impossible to tell which. In fact, there was something slightly over-naive about the last phrase. Did Maeve really think that her father had sent the Brehon, a person of almost as high a rank as the king himself, as a messenger?

'You weren't worried when he didn't come home last night?'

'I thought he probably stayed overnight at Carron,' said Maeve. She didn't look puzzled or enquiring and the perfection of her face was unmarred by any shadow of worry. Mara watched her carefully. Surely by now she should have started to worry, whatever the relationship was between herself and her father.

'I'm afraid that I have very bad news for you, Maeve,' Mara said gently. 'Your father was found dead this morning.'

'What happened?' breathed Maeve and then she turned away, her face closely hidden by her hands, her shoulders heaving.

'No one knows,' said Mara. 'His body was found at

Noughaval. It appears that he was murdered sometime last night.' She put an arm around the girl, but Maeve's face remained resolutely hidden, and she did not respond. Small sobbing noises came from her, but Mara wondered cynically if they were genuine. After a few minutes, the girl pulled herself away and walked over towards the door of the cow cabin, where she seemed to be struggling to regain control of herself. Finally she pulled a handkerchief from her pouch and scrubbed vigorously at her eyes, took a deep breath and came back to Mara.

'I don't know what to do,' she said unexpectedly. Mara was startled; she had expected more questions about the cause of death, enquiries about the murderer or just laments for her dead father, but it sounded as though Maeve were more worried about the practicalities of death than anything else.

'About what?' Mara asked, taking the girl's hand. She was touched to feel calluses all over the small palm and the slim fingers. Diarmuid was right. This girl, despite her child-like appearance, had been made to work hard. It would be little wonder if there were no love lost between Maeve and her father.

For a moment the blue eyes, their clear white surrounds unmarred by grief, nor reddened by tears, looked at her assessingly and then the black eyelashes dropped over them.

'I don't know what to do . . . about his body . . . about the wake . . . I don't know what to do . . .' she stuttered. 'There's no one . . . no near kin.'

That distress appeared genuine anyway. Poor child, thought Mara pityingly. She was glad that she had sent Diarmuid to Carron Castle. He had handled that matter well.

There would have been little point in putting this child through all the difficulties of caring for the dead body and then the long-drawn-out ceremonies of the wake. Garrett owed it to his steward to look after his funeral arrangements. It could be done easily by his household; he had enough servants available to handle this.

'I think you can leave that to the *taoiseach*. He'll manage everything. The wake would be best held at the tower house in Carron and then your father can be buried at Carron Church beside your mother,' Mara told the girl firmly.

Maeve nodded and held her handkerchief to her eyes again. Mara gave a quick glance at the sun to check its progress. There was one other task that she needed to do before riding back to Poulnabrone. It had taken her longer than she had imagined, riding down that very narrow lane. She would probably have been as quick, if not quicker, going round by the road. However, after being the bearer of such bad news, she felt some compunction at leaving the child alone. 'Is there anyone that I could send to be with you?' she asked.

'No,' Maeve replied tonelessly. 'Don't worry about me, Brehon. I'll be all right. Fionnuala is in the kitchen.'

'Would you call her, or shall we go in to see her?'

The girl shot a quick sideways glance at her. There was something slightly odd about the expression, not sorrow – there appeared to be little genuine grief there; her face seemed defensive rather than grief-stricken. There was also a shade of impatience in her look, almost as if she wished that she could be left in peace to do what she had to do.

'Fionnuala,' she called and when an elderly woman appeared at the door, Maeve moved quickly over to her.

'Fionnuala,' she said, 'the body of my father has been found in Noughaval churchyard.'

Mara looked at her with interest; she was sure that she hadn't mentioned the churchyard to Maeve.

'God bless us and save us,' said Fionnuala. She crossed herself, but there was something perfunctory about the gesture and her eyes were wary as they looked at the Brehon.

'I think you had better take Maeve indoors,' said Mara mildly. 'She's had a bad shock.'

'Yes, of course,' replied Fionnuala, and there was nothing false about the motherly way that she put her arm around the slight figure of the girl. Mara felt relieved. At least she could leave Maeve in her hands with an easy conscience.

'I'll need to find the road to Poulnabrone,' said Mara. 'I suppose if I strike across the fields there towards the west I'll meet it.'

'Yes, Brehon,' said Maeve. 'The road is just two fields away. I'll open this gate for you,' she said hurriedly, moving out of Fionnuala's arms and rushing over. Obviously she wanted to get rid of the Brehon as soon as possible. Mara wondered why, but perhaps it was natural. Perhaps she wanted time to grieve privately. Many people handled sorrow like that. 'You'll find a gap just straight across the field,' Maeve continued, 'that will take you into the second field. The gap is open at the moment so you'll have no trouble.'

Mara thanked her, mounted her mare and went through the gate. It was strange that no further questions had been asked, she thought. However, grief can rob a person of their wits; she had often witnessed that. She rode steadily across the field to the gap at the far end and then looked back over her shoulder. There was no sign of Maeve or Fionnuala so no doubt they had gone into the kitchen. Mara hoped that this Fionnuala was a motherly person. She might well be more of a parent to Maeve than that strange, bad-tempered man, Ragnall MacNamara.

The second field Maeve had described seemed to have been abandoned; it was very overgrown with hundreds of hazel bushes sprouting from the grykes between the slabs of stone. The bright purple flowers of the field bugle were everywhere underfoot and the pale cream faces of the burnet rose twined around the hazel stems and raised their small pretty flowers to the sun. Ragnall should have cut down this hazel scrub and then put a few goats in here, Mara thought impatiently. She wondered why the steward had neglected this piece of land so much. However, the farm was probably only a small part of his income as he would, of course, receive a portion of all the rents and tributes which he collected each year on behalf of the MacNamara *taoiseach*. It was a big farm, nevertheless; too big, thought Mara, for Maeve to be able to inherit it all. The Brehon law was strict about that: land must be kept within the kin-group and the clan. Unless Maeve married a cousin, she could take only land enough to graze seven cows as her dowry. That would mean about twenty acres of this good grazing land of the High Burren.

Mara got down from her horse and led her carefully through the clustering twigs and small branches; she would not risk a tear to the golden hide of her finely bred mare. As she pushed her way through the thickets she could hear the small tan-coloured hazel nuts crunch beneath her feet. The foxes and the pine martens would have a great feast here and plenty of nourishment to get them through a hard winter.

By the time that Mara eventually reached the road, the sun had already moved well out of the east and was approaching its September zenith. However, she did not turn north towards Poulnabrone – if she were late, she knew that the people of the Burren would wait courteously and patiently for her – she turned towards the south and towards the new tower house of Lemeanah.

Teige O'Brien, a first cousin of King Turlough Donn O'Brien, had built Lemeanah soon after he had become *taoiseach* of the O'Brien clan on the Burren. It was a four-storey-high tower with doors set into the outside walls of the third and fourth floors, ready for a new extension to be built sometime in the future. It was the biggest tower house on the Burren, built in a magnificent style, which Mara was sure that Garrett MacNamara envied. Smoke poured from its chimney, and servants and workers bustled in and around the small cabins that surrounded it. On the north side of the tower house was a field with some stallions galloping about whinnying loudly, and Mara's mare raised her head as if to answer them.

'Hush, girl,' said Mara, hurriedly stroking the golden neck. Quickly she dismounted. Her sharp eye had caught sight of a flash of blue on the top of the wall. She narrowed her eyes against the sun. Yes, it was Maeve climbing into the field near the tower house. Apparently she had gone by a quicker route than the way she had sent Mara. She had not gone for comfort from Fionnuala, but had come to her lover. Was it for comfort or to prepare him for the Brehon's visit? Mara did not know the answer to that question.

Someone else had seen that flash of blue also. A tall young man had vaulted the wall near to the tower house and was striding rapidly across the field, ignoring all of the playful young stallions, and making directly for the girl in the blue *léine*. Mara waited patiently for a few minutes to give a chance for the news to be passed on, and then she mounted again, riding sedately down the road, with her head turned away from the young couple and towards the stony fields opposite.

By the time that she reached the gates of Lemeanah, the two had disappeared from the field. Mara thought that Donal might have come to meet her, but there was no sign of him. He had obviously not inherited the courtesy of his father, Teige, she thought; he must certainly have seen her as she rode down towards the tower house. Or perhaps he had his own reasons for not encountering her. However, she had little time to waste if she was going to get to Poulnabrone for noon, so she refused the offer to dismount from a servant who came running to the gate, and sent him instead to find Donal O'Brien. There was a flash of puzzlement in the eyes of the man; he found it strange that she should ask for the son rather than the father, but he did not dare question the Brehon so he straight away went in search of his young master and Donal appeared several minutes later.

His mantle was not torn; Mara noticed that immediately. It was made of finely woven grey cloth, but then most people on the Burren wore grey made from the wool of the mountain sheep. These produced the most rain-resistant wool and that was important here on the edge of the Atlantic where rain showers swept in almost continuously. Perhaps he had another mantle, though. A family of this wealth could easily afford two or even three cloaks for the son and heir of the family.

'Ah, Donal,' she greeted him, looking closely at the handsome, sullen face. 'I thought I saw you in the yard. I want you to pass on a message to your father. Ragnall MacNamara has been killed and I will be making an announcement at Poulnabrone at twelve noon.'

'Yes,' he said, his eyes refusing to meet hers. 'The news came a while ago. My father has already gone up to Poulnabrone.'

So Maeve's mission was unnecessary, thought Mara. Or perhaps it was more to tell her young lover that no awkward questions had been asked by the Brehon. She wondered how to deal with this young man. Perhaps being direct would be the best method.

'I saw you with Ragnall's daughter, Maeve, at Noughaval market, yesterday,' she said rapidly.

His face paled slightly, but then he nodded.

'I understand that Ragnall had refused permission for any betrothal between you and Maeve,' she continued. 'So what happened when he turned up at Noughaval yesterday? That would have been a surprise to you; you would have expected him to be on the road all day and I suppose so he would have been if the fog had not been so dense. He must have decided to turn back when he reached the sea.'

Donal said nothing, but a spark of anger smouldered in his eyes. Was it anger against her or against Ragnall? Mara wondered.

'So what happened when he arrived?' she asked abruptly.

He licked his lips, thought for a moment and then explained hurriedly: 'Nothing happened. When we saw him, Maeve and I went away. I took her home to Shesmore and then I came back here.'

'What time did you arrive home?'

'Mid-afternoon,' he said, after a moment's pause for thought. That would be about right if he had done what he said, thought Mara. Either he was telling the truth or he was quick-witted enough to tell a plausible lie.

'Did anyone see you arrive home?'

He licked his lips again. His dark eyes were wary. 'No,' he said. 'No one was about. Everyone was either at the market or else out in the fields. I went up to my room and I stayed there until suppertime.'

That would be fairly unlikely, thought Mara. An active young man, and a beautiful afternoon with the golden September sun warming the fields . . . Surely he would have gone out with his dogs and his horse if he had no tasks. However, it might be possible. The boy was obviously very much in love and miserable at the denial of his request by the father of his sweetheart. Perhaps he did lie on his bed and brood. Or perhaps he did come back and then go out again She decided rapidly on her course of action. It would be best to surprise the truth out of him now, if possible, before he had time to think up a story.

'You lost your brooch,' she said, delving into her pouch and producing it.

He held his hand out instantly.

'It is yours?' she asked, still retaining it in her own hand, but angling it so that he could see the three tiny lions enamelled in red.

He hesitated then, and a look of fear came into his eyes.

'It is yours, isn't it?' she persisted.

He made no move to take it from her now. His dark eyes

were hooded by a fan of downcast black lashes, so she could not read their expression, but his mouth was tight.

'Any of your servants will know whether it is your brooch or not,' she told him bluntly.

'Where did you find it?' he asked. He was looking at her now, but his expression was guarded. His young face looked suddenly aged and wary.

'Where did you lose it?' she countered sharply.

He shifted his position so that his face was no longer lit by the sun but was shadowed. The wariness had intensified.

'I lost it somewhere,' he said hesitantly. 'I don't know where I lost it, exactly. We were hunting . . . myself and the three O'Lochlainn lads . . . We were hunting foxes with a pack of dogs. We took the dogs and we went out after foxes.'

'And did the O'Lochlainns help you to search for your brooch?' she asked with an air of concern which rang to her ears as showing a satisfactory degree of friendly interest.

'No.' He replied to this promptly as if he had guessed that the question would be coming. 'I didn't realize that I had lost it until I came home.'

'And where were you hunting?' asked Mara.

He shrugged. 'Can't remember really – it was a few weeks ago – all over the High Burren, I think . . . You know, from Slieve Elva over to Carron.'

She considered this. 'Did you go through Noughaval?'

'Yes,' he said eagerly. 'Yes, we went through Noughaval.'

'What about the churchyard? You didn't go through the churchyard at Noughaval, did you?' she asked, looking at him keenly. It would be strange for a hunt to go through the churchyard. There was a great respect for the bodies of the dead on the Burren. Even if the hounds went through the churchyard, the riders would usually circle outside calling off their dogs.

He hesitated for a moment and then bowed his head. 'No,' he said. 'We didn't go through the churchyard.'

Mara allowed the silence to linger for a few moments before turning the mare's head towards the north.

'I must go now,' she said. 'I will see your father at Poulnabrone. Are you coming too?'

He shook his head. 'No, Brehon,' he said warily. 'I have tasks to do here.'

After Mara had ridden through the gatehouse and had turned her mare's head towards the north, she turned back. Donal O'Brien was still standing, very still, in the spot where she had left him. He looked, to her, like a man who was bearing a heavy weight of anxiety on his broad shoulders.

FOUR

Berrad Airechta

(court procedure and judgements)

A court shall be held in a place that is sacred within the kingdom. That is to say it should be by a great rock, known as the Brehon's chair, *or on the top of an ancient mound, or beside an ancestral burial place.*

THE FIELD AROUND THE dolmen of Poulnabrone was full of people when Mara arrived. It was almost as if the birds of the air had carried the news of the secret and unlawful killing of Ragnall MacNamara. It would have been natural for the MacNamara clan to be there, she had appointed this time to hear the case about the blacksmith's candlesticks, but the other three clans, the O'Lochlainns, the O'Connors and the O'Briens were there also, in strong numbers. With one of the rapid weather changes so customary in the west of Ireland, the sun had disappeared and the sky had turned the colour of polished pewter. There was no wind, but the atmosphere held the ominous promise of a storm to come. The air had turned chill, but no one in that huge crowd moved.

The ancient dolmen with the four upright stones and the jagged tip of the soaring capstone was silhouetted against the leaden sky, dwarfing the humans who surrounded it. It had been the burial mound of the ancient inhabitants of the Burren and then the hallowed place where the people of the kingdom came to hear the judgements and pronouncements of their king and of his Brehon. Mara had already been Brehon of the Burren for fifteen years, but when she spoke at Poulnabrone she never failed to feel thrilled and yet humbled by the strength of the tradition in this sacred stony place.

Cumhal, her farm manager, was there, as he always was whenever he was needed, and he took the mare from her as soon as she dismounted. The six scholars, neat in their white *léinte* and polished leather sandals, were lined up beside the dolmen. Mara smiled at them as they bowed to her. There was an air of suppressed excitement about them; judgement days were often tedious, filled with small wrangles over boundary stones and cattle trespass, but this one would be full of drama. However, she was glad to see their faces were grave. She always insisted on the highest level of decorous behaviour in public, but inside, she knew, they were bubbling with anticipation. As her scholars they would be closely involved in the investigation. What an exciting start to the Michaelmas term for them.

'Brehon, this is a terrible, terrible thing to happen.' Garrett MacNamara pushed himself through the crowd followed by a tall, brown-haired man, who stood affably behind him, looking around at the crowd in a friendly fashion. Mara recognized this man instantly although it was a while since she had seen him.

Murrough, the younger son of King Turlough Donn, greatly resembled his father. He had the same light green eyes, the same war-like moustaches curving down from either side of his mouth, the same brown hair, though his father's was greying. However, the son looked quite different to the father in his dress. While Turlough wore the *léine* and *brat* of his ancestors, Murrough was dressed in the latest English fashion of skin-tight hose and very short velvet doublet barely reaching to the top of his legs. He looked very out of place, thought Mara, in this assembly of clansmen. The O'Brien clan, in particular, viewed him with a certain disdain; Teige O'Brien, with a broad grin on his face, was whispering behind his hand to his cousin, Cian, the silversmith.

Mara came forward to meet the young man. 'Murrough!' she said. 'You are well? And your family, also?' She did not enquire about his father; Turlough, she knew, was not getting on well with this son, though previously Murrough had always been the favourite, and still was, she suspected, despite his infatuation with all things English. She wondered briefly whether Murrough knew of his father's hopes to marry Mara, Brehon of the Burren, and what he thought of it. However, their relationship had always been warm and friendly and she was pleased to see that there was a beaming smile on his face as he greeted her and asked after her family.

'Do you think you can handle this affair?' he asked teasingly.

Mara smiled at him sweetly, raising her dark eyebrows in

a look of polite enquiry. She always enjoyed his wit and his sense of fun.

'Handle?' she asked in a puzzled tone of voice.

'This is a very serious matter,' he said with an amused glance at Garrett. No doubt Garrett had been pouring out his thoughts to the king's son.

'Every death is a serious matter,' said Mara gravely.

'Oh, the death, that, of course,' said Murrough, his green eyes dancing with mischief, 'but there is also a matter of stolen goods, a pouch full of silver; not just an ordinary theft, but a theft from a *taoiseach*.' Again, he gave a quick amused glance at Garrett.

'The law makes provision for all theft, and for all cases of serious injury and of death,' said Mara evenly, ignoring the irony in his tone. She did not wish Garrett to feel that he was being laughed at by this boy. Without waiting for an answer she addressed Garrett.

'I agree, Garrett, this is, indeed, a terrible matter. There is no doubt, I think, that Ragnall's death is a secret and unlawful killing, but I will make the announcement now and call for evidence.' She moved a little closer to Garrett, deliberately turning her back on Murrough, and said in a low voice: 'Of course the people were called to Poulnabrone to hear this case between Fintan, the blacksmith, and Ragnall, the steward, but now that Ragnall is dead I think we can let this matter drop, do you agree? Ragnall had no right to take those branched candlesticks from Fintan's man, Balor; the whole of the Burren knows that Balor was classified as a *druth* and, as such, he could not have had the authority of his master to give the candlesticks. I assure you that is the legal position.'

She waited calmly, looking up at him. Garrett was a tall man, who looked more than his thirty years. He was staring down at her with his prominent gooseberry-coloured eyes and furrowing his brow. He would look better with the hairstyle of his youth, she thought. The English fashion for hair curled back, on him, revealed an abnormally high, white forehead which had until recently been covered with the Irish *glib* (fringe). The height of his forehead seemed to accentuate the size of the huge fleshy nose and the heavily swelling lower lip. An unattractive man, she thought, despite his fine English-style clothing, and yet, he was reputed to have married well. Slaney, his wife, came from one of the most important families in Galway and bore the reputation of being a magnificent specimen of womanhood.

'Balor?' he queried.

She nodded. 'Yes, the bastard son of Aengus the miller, Niall's younger brother,' she said calmly. 'I classified him myself. I can assure you that the law is quite clear on this point. Ragnall had no right to remove those candlesticks without the permission of their rightful owner. I think that the easiest thing would be just to give them back quietly, don't you?'

Eventually he nodded reluctantly.

'Good,' she said. 'I'll tell Fintan that he may have them back.' She had no notion of revealing that Fintan had possibly already removed the candlesticks. She waited for a moment to see whether Niall had told his *taoiseach* about the missing candlesticks, but he made no answer, just nodded his head again. It was good that Niall had kept that matter to himself, she thought. There was going to be trouble enough over this secret and unlawful killing; she did not want any more. She moved towards her traditional place, just beside one of the huge upright stones of the dolmen. Fachtnan, the eldest scholar at the law school, handed her a scroll and she raised it. Instantly silence fell.

'*Dia's Muire agat,*' she said in the traditional greeting and back came the answer: 'God and Mary and Patrick be with you.'

'I, Mara, Brehon of the Burren, announce to you that a killing took place of the steward, Ragnall MacNamara, at Noughaval on the evening of the feast of Michaelmas.' She paused; a little ripple ran around the crowd with those nearest repeating her words so that those on the outside of the crowd could hear.

'I now call on the person who killed the steward, Ragnall, to acknowledge the crime and to pay the fine. Ragnall's honour price as a steward is half the honour price of his lord, Garrett MacNamara, so it is the sum of seven *séts* or three and a half ounces of silver. The *éraic*, or body fine, for an unlawful killing is forty-two *séts*, or twenty-one ounces of silver. The whole fine, then, is forty-nine *séts*, twenty-five ounces of silver, or twenty-five milch cows.'

There was no sound; no one moved and no one spoke.

'For the second time, I call on the person who killed the steward, Ragnall, to acknowledge the crime and to pay the fine of forty-nine *séts*,' said Mara. She waited, surveying the crowd, but no one stirred.

'For the third time, I call on the person who killed the steward, Ragnall, to acknowledge the crime and to pay the fine of forty-nine *séts*,' said Mara, but she knew by now that no one would reply.

'As soon as forty-eight hours have passed since this

killing took place,' she continued, 'I will declare it to be a case of *duinethàide*, a secret and unlawful killing. The *éraic* will then be doubled to eighty-four *séts*. Add to that the victim's honour price of seven *séts* and the fine will then be ninety-one *séts*, forty-five ounces of silver, or forty-five milch cows.' She waited for a moment, now she could hear a low murmur of conversation. Heads were turned, one to the other. This was a huge amount of cows for any single individual to be able to afford. The whole *fine* (family group) would have to come to the rescue of the murderer. She held up her scroll again, and again silence fell.

'I will now take evidence about this case,' she said. 'First, I call upon my two scholars, Aidan and Moylan, to give evidence as to how they found the body.'

The two boys managed a more coherent account than usual, she thought. They even managed not to interrupt each other. While she kept a respectful face turned towards them, her eyes were busy scanning the crowd. The O'Lochlainn's clan was there in almost full strength, she thought, as she saw them grouped around the tall figure of Ardal, their *taoiseach*, a fair number of O'Connors also, and plenty of the O'Brien clan. All of the MacNamaras, of course, that could be taken for granted – or were they all there? Suddenly her attention sharpened. Quickly her eyes went from face to face, all faces were concerned, all grave, but none bore any sign of sorrow, she thought. This was what had alerted her to look for the miller from Oughtmama; she had been looking to see what emotion Aengus MacNamara showed at the news of his enemy's death.

But Aengus MacNamara was not there.

'Has anyone else any evidence to give,' she asked, after

she had thanked the two boys. Silence greeted her. She had not expected anything of importance to be volunteered. Every tongue would be guarded in this public place. No one would want to implicate a friend, a neighbour, a relative, or a member of the clan. These enquiries would have to be made quietly and privately and the truth would have to be discovered as soon as possible for the sake of everybody in the kingdom. For over fifteen hundred years they and their ancestors had lived by this system of justice that relied on the goodwill and the co-operation of the clans to keep the peace within its community. The truth would have to be acknowledged here at Poulnabrone, the fine paid, and then the community could go on living at peace with their families and their neighbours.

'Fachtnan,' she said when the crowd had begun to disperse, 'do you see Aengus the miller anywhere?'

'No, Brehon,' said Fachtnan, standing on a nearby rock, brushing his rough curly dark hair out of his eyes and scanning the closely massed MacNamara clan. 'He doesn't seem to be here. Would you like me to ask Fintan Mac-Namara, the blacksmith? He's his cousin.'

'No, I'll talk to him myself,' said Mara. 'Would you ask him to come over, Fachtnan?'

Fintan came willingly. When she had seen him yesterday at the head of the dissident clansmen he had looked like an angry bull, his dark eyes sparkling with rage and his broad chest lifting with the long breaths he sucked in, but his eyes were peaceful now. He was looking tidier than usual, she thought. He had shed the blacksmith's leather apron, and his high-coloured face was cleansed of the usual spots of soot, though it still bore the scorch marks and scars of old burns.

A hard trade, thought Mara, though a highly valued one, as no community could manage without its blacksmith. Fintan was busy from morning to night with making, mending and repairing. Every house and every farm bore examples of his work, but nothing she had ever seen previously was as fine as that magnificent set of candlesticks. She had only glimpsed them briefly in the bottom of Ragnall's cart, but they had stayed in her mind. Each candlestick had been moulded in the shape of a gnarled oak tree with the branches springing from it. Every branch ended in a cluster of perfectly formed oak leaves and this cluster held the candle in its midst. A wonderful piece of work, a piece of work to be prized by its maker: but would he have killed to recover it from the clutches of the greedy steward?

'Your scholar said you wanted me, Brehon,' said Fintan. His voice was habitually hoarse and rough, but was there a shade of truculence in it today?

'Yes, Fintan, I was looking around for the miller, Aengus MacNamara. Have you seen him today? Fachtnan tells me that you are his cousin.'

Fintan smiled, though there was still a wary look in his dark eyes. 'The Burren is full of my cousins, Brehon,' he said. 'I'd be hard put to lay my hand on all of them. Even Ragnall, God have mercy on him, was a sort of cousin of mine.' He turned around and scanned the crowd. Mara eyed him sharply. There was something unnatural in his words and movements. She had once seen a group of players enacting a miracle play on a cart outside Noughaval church. The way that Fintan scanned the crowd reminded her of one of those players. The gesture of lifting his right hand to shield his eyes against the few watery gleams of silvery light in the

71

sky, the way that he turned his whole body slowly from side to side, the slightly raised left hand, all reminded her of a player. Instantly she felt certain that Fintan knew that Aengus was not among the crowd, and that for some reason he did not want to reveal that he had noticed the absence.

'No, Brehon,' he said eventually, after a quick sidelong look at her face. 'No, I don't seem to see him. Perhaps he is busy at the mill.'

'Perhaps,' said Mara, her voice placid and non-committal. It was unlikely, she thought, that Aengus was so busy that he would not have come to the meeting to discuss the Michaelmas tribute. He would have known about that, she was sure, even if he had not heard of Ragnall the steward's death. She looked at Fintan thoughtfully.

'Did Aengus know of Ragnall's death?' she asked mildly.

He winced noticeably and glanced around him with a look of desperation, like a bull at bay.

'I don't know, Brehon, I haven't seen sight nor sound of the man for days,' he said. He was sweating heavily, she noticed, but that could be normal. He was a big, heavily built man. The MacNamara clan would have been discussing the matter among themselves before she arrived and, having noticed the absence of Aengus the miller, would have speculated about his possible guilt. She decided to release him; she would get no more from him now, she knew.

'Thank you, Fintan,' she said. 'You'll want to be getting back to your work. I'll drop in on you one day. I'd like you to make an iron bench for my garden. I'd like to have it over by my holly hedge. I was thinking the other day that a black iron bench would go very well with the white flowers that I have growing there.'

'I'd be delighted, Brehon,' he said, a relieved smile coming over his face.

'I was wondering about a design of holly leaves on the back of the bench. I got the idea when I was looking at the oak leaves on your candlesticks. They are so beautiful, these candlesticks,' she continued innocently.

His face changed. She expected him to look angry, but anger was not what the expression showed: it was fear.

'Ah well,' he muttered. 'I'd better be getting back now. I think that *himself* wants a word with you.'

The *taoiseach*, Garrett MacNamara, was sailing majestically towards her, the crowd parting and then closing up again in his wake. Mara noticed that Murrough had now left him, had mounted his horse and was trotting off towards the east. She gazed after him with pleasure. On horseback, he made a fine figure of a man. She could understand how proud Turlough was of this handsome youth. Perhaps Murrough would soon be back in favour again now he had returned from England. His visit there, in the company of his father-in-law, had upset Turlough badly. I'll have a word with Turlough, she thought, this breach between father and son was pointless. Murrough, like most young men, wanted the freedom to choose his company and his ideas. At the moment, English customs and way of life were new and interesting to him and, of course, he did love to tease his father. Mara was sure that things would soon settle down if Turlough ignored him. She turned back to face the other man.

'Ah, Garrett,' she said briskly. 'You wanted another word with me.'

It was obvious that he was full of words, she thought. She could see them bubbling up inside him.

'You know your own business, Brehon, of course,' he began and then looked startled when she interrupted him to agree firmly: 'Of course.'

He sucked in a long breath through his flaring horse-like nostrils and started again.

'It's just this affair with my poor man, Ragnall,' he continued. 'I understand that the candlesticks that were given as tribute by the blacksmith, Fintan . . .' he paused for breath and she interrupted him quickly.

'The candlesticks were not given by *Fintan*,' she said. 'They were given by Balor, Fintan's servant, whose classification is that of a *druth* and as I explained to you, that is illegal. A *druth* cannot make any contract and cannot, therefore, pay tribute.'

'Yes, yes,' he said hurriedly. 'I understand that, Brehon. I just wanted to mention to you that the candlesticks are now missing from the cart. Niall MacNamara has just confessed that to me when I questioned him.'

'So I understand,' said Mara calmly. Now will come either a blunt accusation that Fintan murdered Ragnall, or else a sly insinuation that this was what must have happened, she thought. He surprised her, though.

'I just wanted to say that I want no more said about the matter of these candlesticks,' he said hurriedly. 'If people knew that the blacksmith had secretly taken them back, they might think Fintan had something to do with Ragnall's death and I'm sure that is not true. He is a hot-tempered man, but not one to commit a crime like this against one of his own *sept*.'

Mara's heart warmed towards him. Garrett might be pompous and overbearing, but deep down he had the instincts of a *taoiseach*. He would not want to see one of his clan accused of this crime. She smiled cordially at him.

'Garrett, you can be sure that I will conduct my investigation of this murder as carefully, and thoroughly, as possible and that my thoughts on this matter will remain, as always, silent until I come before the people of the kingdom at Poulnabrone and tell the truth of the matter,' she asserted solemnly. He seemed impressed by that and bowed his head silently, but as she turned to leave him he recovered his self-possession.

'There was another matter that I wanted to mention to you, Brehon,' he said. 'One of my men told me that there was a merchant there at the fair who was cheating the people. His name is O'Brien, Guaire O'Brien, from Corcomroe. Niall MacNamara, who drove the cart, told me that he came up to Ragnall and was asking him all sorts of unnecessary questions and was trying to sell him some linen.'

'Yes?' queried Mara. Of course, she thought, Guaire O'Brien is an outsider from the adjoining kingdom of Corcomroe. Everyone, whether MacNamara, O'Lochlainn, O'Connor, or even O'Brien, would be glad to pin this crime on him. For Garrett this would be a much better solution than to have the murder pinned on one of his own clan. She waited patiently, but said no more.

He looked slightly disconcerted for a moment and then recovered his flow of words. 'Of course, I wouldn't want to tell you your business, or anything like that, Brehon, but it might be a good idea for you to have a word with this Guaire O'Brien.'

'I assure you, Garrett,' Mara answered gravely, 'that I will talk to everyone who can give me any information. The killing of a man is always a crime against the community and the law that regulates it. A secret and unlawful killing is doubly abhorrent and the truth must be uncovered as soon as possible.'

I'm beginning to sound as pompous as he, she thought with amusement, but she kept a straight face as he nodded uncertainly.

'Well, I won't take up any more of your time, Brehon,' he said, beckoning with a lofty air of authority to his servant to bring up his horse. 'We'll be holding the wake for poor Ragnall, may God be good to him, tomorrow night at the castle. I will see you there,' he stated.

'Yes, indeed,' said Mara, thinking with an inner sigh of the many hours in every year which she had spent at wakes. These were huge ceremonies that went on for hours in the evening, or, more often, all night, before the burial. It was time that she could ill afford from her busy life as *ollamh* of the law school and Brehon of the kingdom. It had to be done, though: the community had to mourn the passing of one of their members with all due ceremonies. She watched Garrett ride away and then hastened to join her scholars, who were walking ahead with her neighbour, Diarmuid.

'And we spent all night on the Great Lake,' Shane was telling Diarmuid. Shane was the son of the hereditary Brehon to the O'Neills, the ruling clan in northern Ireland. His home was at Dungannon Castle in Ulster. 'And I caught a trout as big as this.' He opened his hands to the width of his slim ten-year-old chest and then widened them a bit more.

'As big as that!' gasped Diarmuid. He was good with all of her boys, but had a special fondness for Shane.

'That's nothing,' scoffed Moylan. 'I went shark fishing and caught a shark and it was as big as Fachtnan.'

'All by yourself?' queried Mara with an eye on Shane's downcast face.

'Well no, there were a few of us,' admitted Moylan, 'but I helped to cut it up. We roasted some shark steaks on the sand. You should have tasted them, Diarmuid. They were *iontach*!'

Mara smiled. She could see that *iontach* was going to be the word for the season; it had been *ar fheabhas* all through the Trinity term.

'Well, now, I don't think I've ever tasted shark steaks,' said Diarmuid modestly. 'But I'm a great man for trout,' he added with a smile at Shane.

'I went to the *Lughnasa* Fair at Killorglin,' boasted Aidan. 'You should have seen the girls there!' He gave a long, low whistle, whether to indicate extreme beauty or extreme availability was uncertain, but Mara decided that she would not pursue the matter. Let him boast afterwards in the privacy of the scholars' house.

'And what about you, Enda?' she asked. 'What did you do on your holiday?' It was strange that Enda was not already shouting Moylan and Aidan down with his own holiday stories.

'Oh, this and that,' said Enda briefly. 'Mostly helped on the farm.' He had grown up this holiday, she thought. Before the summer holidays he had been noisy and troublesome; now he seemed rather quiet and withdrawn.

'So did I,' said Fachtnan. 'Actually my brothers and myself were building a watermill to pulp down the flax. It was great *craic*, but we didn't really get it working that well. I'd like to go up and have a look at the mill at Oughtmama, some Saturday, Brehon, if that is all right.'

'Yes, of course,' said Mara mechanically. Once again her thoughts went to Aengus, the miller of Oughtmama. Why was he not at Poulnabrone today? Could he know anything about the murder of his fellow clansman and his enemy, Ragnall MacNamara?

FIVE

URAICECHT BECC (SMALL PRIMER)

A gobae, *blacksmith*, or bangobae, *woman black-smith, has an honour price that is fixed at seven séts. This does not increase even if he (or she) attains the grade of ollamh.*

TRIAD 148

There are three essentials in the world:
  1. *The womb of a woman*
  2. *The udder of a cow*
  3. *The moulding block of a blacksmith*

&oe;

'WE'LL SET OFF EARLY for the wake at Carron because I want to call in at the forge on the way and see Fintan the blacksmith,' said Mara, late on Wednesday afternoon. She surveyed her scholars seated on their stools in the schoolhouse. They still looked fairly neat and tidy after their day's hard work at their studies, she noted thankfully. They would not need a change of clothing before they went.

'Fachtnan, go and ask Brigid for some buttermilk and some oatcakes for you all before we set out,' she said. No doubt they would get plenty of cake pressed on them at the wake; such was the custom at even the humblest of households. However, they looked tired and something to eat now would refresh them. The study of the Brehon law, with all of its complexities and its huge reliance on oral memory, was a hard, demanding life. Children were usually sent to a law school like hers at the age of six or even five and they remained there until they passed their final examinations at an age between eighteen and twenty-one. Mara's grandfather and great-grandfather had been Brehons for the O'Lochlainn clan, but her father, Séamus O'Davoren, had become an *ollamh*, professor. He had tired of the life of a dependant with, as the law texts put it, *a seat at the board and a bed by the fire*. So when he had inherited some property from a distant cousin he had set up the law school in the ancient fort of Cahermacnaghten, and Mara, as his only child, had inherited it when he died, soon after she had qualified as a lawyer. She had been sixteen years old then – too young, many thought, but not one of the four young scholars who had been at the law school in that year of 1489 had been removed from her care and since then the school had prospered. Five years later she had become Brehon of the Burren and had balanced the two roles with energy and commitment. Her scholars had always profited from her willingness to

80

involve them in all the practical aspects of the legal problems in the kingdom of the Burren.

The six scholars had put away their books and pens and were looking at her enquiringly. The corners of her mouth twitched with amusement. She had noticed how their tired faces had lit up with keen flashes of interest at the mention of Fintan MacNamara's name.

'Is Fintan a suspect then, Brehon?' asked Enda politely. He had definitely grown up since last term, she thought. There had been a time when he had been quite a problem but now he seemed to want to work hard and to achieve success in his studies. He had grown even taller during the three months of outdoor life since the end of the Trinity term in June. Soon he would top Fachtnan, who was two years older. A good-looking lad, she thought fondly. With his blond hair, his tanned skin and his very blue eyes he was unusual in the west of Ireland where black or red hair and white or freckled skin seemed to predominate.

'I don't care for the word "suspect", Enda,' she said. 'At least not spoken aloud,' she amended. She always tried to be as honest as possible with her scholars and there was no doubt that, mentally at least, she was already forming a list of suspects. 'Now what should we consider to help us decide who would be likely to commit this murder?'

'Motive and opportunity,' said ten-year-old Shane, brushing his black fringe out of his eyes and sitting up very straight as Fachtnan put a cup of buttermilk into his hands.

'Well, Fintan had a motive because Ragnall had taken his candlesticks without permission,' said Enda. 'Hugh told us all about it. Everyone at the market knew about that.'

'And he probably had opportunity because the forge is

not too far from Noughaval market,' said Fachtnan thoughtfully, licking some crumbs from his fingers.

'So he is a suspect,' said Enda triumphantly. 'I'm just using that word in the privacy of the schoolhouse, Brehon,' he added rapidly.

Mara allowed herself a smile. She was glad to see that Enda, despite his new-found seriousness, was still irrepressible. All of the scholars had sworn an oath on the Bible that very morning to keep silent in public about all matters concerning the legal affairs of the kingdom and she knew that would be in the forefront of their minds now. The law year started on the feast of Michaelmas and she always began the year with this solemnity. They would need reminding from time to time during the year, but not now when the words of the oath would still be ringing in their ears. During all her years at the law school, Mara had only known of one person who had broken that oath.

'What are you going to ask him, Brehon?' asked Fachtnan.

'I think that I must ask him what he knows about the missing candlesticks,' said Mara. 'If he has them, then there is no problem; the MacNamara wants him to keep them. He wants no more trouble about them.'

'Enda could beat a confession out of him,' said Moylan slyly. 'Do you remember the caves and how he—'

'Shut up,' said Enda, his smooth brown skin flooding with an angry flush.

'That was when he was younger,' said Mara firmly. The episode in the caves had taken place only last May, but she knew that, to the young, five months was an eternity. Enda was now seventeen; then he had been only sixteen. To him there would be a world of difference. Hopefully he would be steadier and more reliable this year. Already she had noticed a great change in him. An idea came to her and with her usual impulsiveness she immediately acted upon it.

'Enda is now the senior scholar in this law school,' she said with solemnity. 'Fachtnan will be my assistant this year.' She smiled affectionately at Fachtnan who was running his fingers through his bushy dark curls, his honest face looking bewildered. He had not passed his final examination yet – Latin was his weakness – but there was no reason why he should not act as her assistant before he qualified as an *aigne*. She would pay him what she had paid her previous assistant and she was sure that he would never let her down. He looked quite staggered. It was typical of his easy-going, modest nature that he had never thought of anything like this even though he was now nineteen years old.

'Thank you, Brehon,' he said eventually, though he still looked puzzled.

'Thank you, Brehon,' said Enda radiantly. He cast a triumphant glance at fourteen-year-old Moylan.

❋

Fintan, the blacksmith, lived on the road between Noughaval and Kilcorney. The place was called *Lios na nGabhain*, its name revealing the fact that smiths had lived and worked here for hundreds, and perhaps thousands, of years. It was a bare, open spot on the High Burren – a flat tableland of fields paved with great stone clints, broken into irregular squares and oblongs by the flower-filled grykes. No trees, not even bushes, grew there. On winter days it was a bleak, cold spot, but now, in autumn, the ground was glowing with pale blue harebells, bright magenta cranesbills, radiant little yellow suns of the carlines and tiny purple flower heads of the scented thyme, all set against the background of sparkling-white limestone flagstones. The air was crystal clear and the mountains gleamed silver in the sunlight.

There was smoke coming from the forge as Mara, with her scholars riding demurely two by two behind her, approached Fintan's home. No doubt he was making up for lost time during the day and then he would go to the wake later in the evening. She had relied on that. Most people found that the drink flowed faster and that tongues were less inhibited as the evening wore into night.

Balor came to the door enquiringly when she dismounted. He was a huge young fellow, one of Aengus the miller's two illegitimate sons. It had been kind of Fintan to take him on at the forge when his own father had found him too tiresome and without the judgement and skill necessary to work the mill. Balor was immensely strong. He was carrying a heavy iron gate now as if it were the weight of one of the harebells that were sprinkled through the grass. He opened his mouth apprehensively when he saw her and backed away, still carrying the gate.

'Master,' he shouted. He cast an anxious look towards the forge and was obviously waiting until Fintan appeared before saying anything else. He was probably about eighteen, she thought, casting her mind back. He had been the son of a middle-aged woman who worked for Aengus at Oughtmama. She had died in giving birth to this late and unexpected arrival.

Mara greeted him gently and was glad to see that none of her boys sniggered or averted their eyes. Hugh gave him a shy smile and Shane, with the usual unselfconsciousness of a ten-year-old, called out a brisk blessing.

'Take the Brehon's mare,' said Fintan coming out of the forge, a large blacksmith's hammer in one hand. Mara had begun to dismount as soon as she saw him coming and signalled to the boys to do the same. Balor backed away nervously, but Fachtnan, with no fuss, took Mara's mare and held both sets of reins in one large capable hand.

What was wrong with Balor? Mara was puzzled. Obviously he could not be frightened of horses: he worked with them every day of his life. She watched him carefully from the corner of her eye. He had given her a quick, nervous glance but then had sidled up to Fachtnan. He was now stroking Mara's mare with every appearance of appreciation and enjoyment.

'Balor is frightened of you, Brehon,' whispered Shane, looking up at her, and she gave him a quick nod.

'Just go and talk to him for a minute while I talk to Fintan,' she murmured. There was something badly wrong with Balor and Fintan's eyes looked wary.

'I thought I would drop in on the way to the wake at Carron, Fintan,' she said briskly. 'This is just a quick sketch of the way I would like the bench to look. Do you think that it looks possible?'

Fintan took her hasty sketch in one large sooty hand and studied it carefully. Mara waited patiently. From behind her she could hear Shane's high, light voice and Fachtnan's lower deeper tones. They were talking to Balor about her mare and Shane was telling him about it being a present from the king. Balor seemed relaxed now. She even heard him say: 'She's mighty,' which was obviously high praise from him.

'Yes, Brehon,' said Fintan eventually. 'I think that would work out very well. The only problem would be with the holly leaves – if they are to look natural, then you would have to have the prickles sticking out and that would be uncomfortable for your back. I think it might be best if I made two wreaths, perhaps made them to look like moss, and had the holly leaves sunken into them.'

Mara nodded. This man is an artist, she thought. 'That sounds wonderful, Fintan,' she said. 'I'll leave it entirely in your hands. I know you will make me something that I will love.'

She moved to go back towards her mare and then turned back: 'Oh, Fintan,' she said in her usual clear carrying tones, 'your *taoiseach* is happy for you to have the candlesticks. I have persuaded him that Ragnall had no right to take them in your absence.' Although she was not looking at Balor she could not miss the convulsive start that he gave.

'That's good,' muttered Fintan.

She said nothing, but waited. The boys stopped talking, also, so there was silence for a moment. Fintan looked around and then seemed to gulp.

'I mean it will be good to get them back,' he said.

Mara raised her eyebrows. 'Oh,' she said, 'the *taoiseach* understood that you already had them. They were not in the cart.'

'Well, I don't have them,' said Fintan defiantly. He did not, noticed Mara, look at Balor when he said that. She tried to see Balor's expression, but he had his face turned away and he was blowing gently into the mare's nostrils.

'You're sure that they weren't returned, one way or another?' she asked quietly.

86

'You can come in and look, Brehon.' His tone was respectful, but there was an underlying note of truculence in it.

'No, Fintan,' she said firmly. 'I will tell the MacNamara that you don't have the candlesticks. It's for him to make enquiries now.'

❧

'Did you believe him, Brehon?' asked Enda as they all dismounted to open a gate and take a short cut to Carron across the fields.

'I'm not sure,' said Mara honestly. 'What did you all think? You were watching.'

'He was sweating,' observed Moylan.

'So are you,' said Aidan.

'I'm not,' contradicted Moylan.

'He's not, that's just grease on Moylan's nose and forehead,' said Shane. 'It's too cold to be sweating.'

'But Fintan works over a hot fire,' said Hugh.

'Yes, but he wasn't sweating when he came out,' argued Enda. 'Moylan's right. He started to sweat when the Brehon asked him about the candlesticks. I think what happened was that he went back and had a quarrel with Ragnall and biffed him. He might not even have meant to do it, but once he had done it, he took the candlesticks.'

'How did Fintan get Ragnall to go into the churchyard?' asked Shane. 'Ragnall must have been in the churchyard when he was murdered. No one could have murdered him in front of all of the people at the market.'

'That's easy,' said Enda scornfully. 'He just hung around until Ragnall went in of his own accord to ... Well, you know,' he finished with a quick glance at Mara.

Mara considered this. Of course, that was the most likely way that things had happened. It was unfortunate, but true, that most people at the Noughaval market used the church-yard, with its sheltering trees and bushes, as a private place to urinate. Up to now, she had assumed that Ragnall had withdrawn into the churchyard to meet his murderer. If it were true that it was just by chance, then the killer might possibly be Fintan. He would be a man who would find it hard to judge the strength of a blow. But would he have picked up the stone cross? Wouldn't he be more likely to use his own powerful fist?

'How were the candlesticks stolen then?' she asked. 'The cart remained in the same place, in the corner of the market-place, until Niall MacNamara arrived to take it away.'

'What about Fintan getting a few people to help him?' asked Shane. 'Three or four of the clan could have stood around the cart to hide someone else who could slip the candlesticks into a bag or something.'

'Yes, no one would have taken any notice of Mac-Namaras around the cart,' said Enda enthusiastically. 'I vote that we consider him a suspect . . . in the privacy of this field, of course,' he added hastily.

❦

There was a stream of people on horseback, or on foot, winding their way up the hill towards the MacNamara castle when they arrived at Carron. Mara noticed the tall figure of Ardal, *taoiseach* of the O'Lochlainns, beside the small round figure of Teige O'Brien. Teige's son, Donal, was not with them, she noticed. It was a couple of months since she had visited this castle, the home of the chief of the MacNamara clan, and she looked at it with interest. There seemed to be very little difference on the outside; it was still rather grim with its tiny windows and its castellated roof. The limestone blocks in the walls were carelessly hewed and were irregular and propped up by numerous small stones. It was no wonder that Garrett's new wife desired to make changes.

The small entry passage, with the guard's chamber leading off it, still looked the same as well. There was no new oaken furniture, nor wall hangings to soften the cold grey of the stone. The spiral staircase had been hollowed with the tread of many feet, and the icy chill in the air of this late September evening moistened the stone walls with winding rivulets of condensation.

The great hall, however, glowed with the warmth of braziers filled with orange and black heaps of burning charcoal. These walls were covered almost entirely with painted leather hangings, and a new dais had been built at the top of the hall with a magnificent oak table running the length of it. The benches on either side of the table were covered with heavy linen cloths and at the head of the table were two magnificently carved oak chairs, heaped with velvet cushions. The new wife, Slaney, had certainly begun to make an impression on this run-down castle of her husband's. Mara looked around her with interest, but of Slaney herself nothing was to be seen. Rumour told that she spent much of her time in Galway, visiting her family and inspecting goods from merchants.

The body of the steward, Ragnall, was laid out on a trestle table at the far end of the hall, away from the braziers and the rich furniture. His face showed a strange brooding dignity in death which he had not displayed during his lifetime. There were no mourners beside the body. On a bench by the wall, his pretty little daughter Maeve, encircled by Fionnuala's motherly arm, held a linen handkerchief to her eyes from time to time, but the handkerchief seemed to be quite dry.

Then the priest from Carron took out his rosary beads and others in the hall joined in. There was a movement and shifting in the crowd as all the servants and men-at-arms in the castle stepped forward. Mara glanced guiltily at her scholars. She had forgotten to remind them to take their beads and only Fachtnan seemed able to produce the circlet from his pouch. Aidan took something out and showed it to Moylan. However, even from a distance, it looked to Mara more like a fishing spool than a rosary and Shane was stifling a giggle behind his hand. Mara sent them a warning glance, but then forgot them as she noticed the tall, dark-haired figure of Donal O'Brien standing behind one of the pillars in the upper portion of the hall. So he was here after all! His eyes were fixed on his beloved Maeve and his face seemed full of pain.

Mara watched him intently. Did he look like that because he couldn't bear to see the girl cry, or was there some other reason for the look of brooding sorrow? Could it be guilt? Perhaps he felt that he should have protected his beloved's father against an assault. Or did he commit the murder himself? Was that, perhaps, the only way that he could get his heart's desire and marry the girl that he loved?

'Brehon, you are very welcome.' Garrett came sailing up fussily, waving a servant to bring mead and another to bring a stool.

'We won't stay long, Garrett,' said Mara, touching her

90

lips to the mead and then holding it in her hand. Its honeyed sweetness was not to her taste. She preferred the subtleties of a good French wine. 'We've just come to pay our respects to Ragnall.'

'There's a good crowd here,' said Garrett, with the satisfaction of a host who has put on a successful feast.

'Aengus the miller isn't here.'

'No, he isn't.'

There had been a slight question in Mara's voice, but Garrett had not picked that up so she continued. 'Are you expecting him?'

'Oh, of course,' said Garrett readily. 'But he will probably be in a bit later. It's a fair journey from Oughtmama.'

'You don't think that the trouble there was between them is keeping Aengus away?' asked Mara, looking at him closely.

Garrett looked startled. 'Surely not,' he said in a pious tone. 'The man is dead; no grudge travels beyond the gates of death, Brehon.'

Mara accorded this pompous aphorism a moment's respectful silence before continuing.

'By the way, Garrett,' she said, lowering her voice. 'Those candlesticks that are missing; well, Fintan declares that he has not got them.'

Garrett raised his bushy eyebrows with an expression of disbelief. He looked around. The priest had finished the rosary and everyone was rising to their feet, looking around for something to eat and drink. Men and women servants hurried to and fro with trays. Garrett beckoned and Niall MacNamara came hurrying over.

Mara studied him with interest. He bore little resemblance to his brother Balor, or even to his father Aengus. Of

91

course, Niall must have been born at least five years earlier than Balor. Aengus had been kinder to his elder son than to Balor. Though he had never acknowledged him openly, he had not denied the relationship and had given him some land near Noughaval. Niall had done well with it.

'Niall, the candlesticks were definitely missing from the cart, weren't they?' questioned Garrett.

Niall nodded firmly. 'And they could not have been taken from my yard,' he said quickly. 'The cart was locked into the barn and the dog was loose in the yard outside.'

'And you thought that Fintan must have taken them when you saw that they were missing?' persisted Garrett.

'It did come into my head,' said Niall uncomfortably, with an awkward, shamefaced glance at Mara.

'Fintan says he did not take them,' stated Mara.

Garrett gave her a quick glance and then turned back to Niall. 'And did Fintan, or anyone else, come to your house or yard that evening?'

'Not a soul nor a sinner,' said Niall promptly. 'We went to bed early and I only unlocked the yard when the Brehon came back with me that time to see the cart.'

'So the candlesticks must have been taken some time at Noughaval market when there was no one with the cart,' said Garrett. 'Who could have done that?'

'Unless it was that cheating linen merchant, Guaire O'Brien from Corcomroe,' said Niall. 'If Fintan says that he didn't, then he didn't. I'd trust Fintan to tell the truth always.'

I trust no one to *always* tell the truth, not even myself, thought Mara. There will always be an occasion when a lie serves the purpose better than the truth. 'I must leave you now, Garrett,' she said smoothly. 'My scholars and I will say a prayer for the deceased and then we must depart. There is much to be done.'

From the corner of her eye she could see Moylan making urgent signs to one of the servants to bring them some mead, so she rapidly swept her scholars up and had them on their knees in front of the open coffin in a couple of seconds. As her lips moved automatically with the well-accustomed words of the prayer for the dead, her mind focussed on the problem ahead of her. If it were a hasty blow triggered by anger and resentment, then the normal practice would have been for the crime to be admitted and the fine paid.

Who had killed Ragnall?

And why was it kept a secret?

And where was Aengus?

Was it embarrassment, because a man he had quarrelled with was now dead, that had kept him hidden in his mountain home?

Or was there a more sinister reason?

SIX

CRITH GABLACH (RANKS IN SOCIETY)

*A taoiseach has an honour price of fourteen séts.
He should have a retinue of six persons on state
occasions. He has a wife of equal rank to his own
and five horses, including a saddle horse with a silver
bridle. His house must contain at least eight bed
places.*

☙

THE BURIAL OF RAGNALL MACNAMARA, steward to
the MacNamara clan on the Burren, was a magnificent
affair. It was as if Garrett had spared no effort to impress the
importance of the MacNamara clan on those who attended.
The morning of Thursday 2 October was dry and frosty and
filled with the sweet chirp of speckled fieldfares. The midday
sun shone with a clarity that turned the black sloes in the
hedgerows into mysterious purple jewels and set a few red
butterflies flirting among the flowers in the grykes. The scent

94

of the last stalks of frothy meadowsweet in the ditches sweetened the air.

Ragnall was laid to rest in the little mossy churchyard of the stone church of Carron. It was no morning for death, thought Mara, and all the trappings of white horses groomed and hung with gold and silver, all the lines of men-at-arms and the wild music of the pipes and the cries of the professional keeners seemed to diminish rather than honour the dead man. The pipes finished and then the MacNamara bard stepped forward and spoke the words of the lament to the gentle notes plucked from a small harp. The last notes of the harp now faded away and the bard was silent. And then the horn sounded. The slow, mellow notes, sad and yet defiant, filled the air. Then came the voice of the priest intoning the words of the great psalm: '*De profundis clamavi ad te, Domine.*'

Mara looked around. This would be the moment for tears and sobs, but there was no trace of any sorrow from the MacNamara clan. Even the dead man's daughter just dabbed at her eyes in a perfunctory fashion.

'Aengus MacNamara is still not here, Brehon,' whispered Fachtnan in her ear.

Mara's eyes searched the crowd and then she nodded slightly. It was true; there was no sign of Aengus. She would definitely have to go up to Oughtmama. There was something very wrong. It was unheard of for a man not to attend the burial of another clan member.

The last handfuls of earth were thrown down onto the coffin lying quietly in its two-fathom-deep hole. Mara waited until the crowd began to stream towards the gates and then she beckoned to her scholars. She had hoped to get back and have an afternoon's teaching, but her duty now was to investigate this murder. It was nearly three days since Ragnall was killed and she was no nearer to a solution than she had been on the morning after Michaelmas Day.

'Fachtnan,' she said, once they were all gathered around her, 'I am putting you in charge of the scholars for the afternoon. You all have plenty of work to do. Hugh and Shane, I expect you to have memorized another twenty wisdom texts and then you can do that Latin translation which I prepared for you. Enda, you know what to do. I'm very pleased with that work you did for me yesterday. Aidan and Moylan, I want you to write up an account of that illegal entry. Make sure that you quote from the judgement texts and the wisdom texts.'

'Yes, Brehon,' they all chorused. She watched them mount their ponies, stayed for a moment to note that they were riding sensibly and quietly across the stone-paved fields and then went to untie her own mare.

'Brehon,' came a familiar voice from behind her and with an inward groan she turned. She had thought she might escape, but he had been too quick for her.

'Yes, Garrett,' she said pleasantly.

He looked shocked, she thought. His high sloping fore-head was wet with sweat and his face had lost its colour. With him were Malachy, the physician, a distant relative of her own, and Malachy's daughter, Nuala. Mara smiled a greeting at Malachy and Nuala, but did not speak to them; it was obvious that Garrett had something of importance to say. He was beckoning urgently at a small bald-headed man who instantly abandoned the cluster of clansmen who sur-rounded him and came hurrying to his *taoiseach*'s side.

'Brehon,' said Garrett, 'this man, Maol, has brought me some terrible news. I don't know what is happening, but Aengus the miller has been found dead by his mill at Oughtmama.'

'Dead!' echoed Mara.

'Drowned dead,' said Maol with relish.

'Drowned!' said Mara incredulously. The mountain stream that powered the mill was fast-flowing, but it was very shallow; a child could hardly have drowned in it.

'What happened?' she asked, turning her eyes towards Malachy.

'It was I who heard the news first,' said Nuala. 'Maol MacNamara from Oughtmama came running up the road. He had taken a cartload of oats to the mill yesterday and couldn't find Aengus, so he thought he was at the wake and when he went to the wake himself he didn't see Aengus, and then when he went back to the mill this morning Aengus still wasn't there, so he started to search for him. He found him lying in the stream. He went for Father.'

'I went up there straight away,' said Malachy, 'but it was no good, the man had been dead for days.' He hesitated, with a quick glance at Nuala.

'I suppose he had begun to decompose,' said Nuala calmly, her brown eyes alert and thoughtful. Nuala was a tall girl for barely fourteen; a pretty girl with her skin tanned to a deep brown and her glossy black hair neatly braided into two long plaits.

'I must go up there,' said Mara with immediate resolution. 'Malachy, will you come too?'

'And me,' said Nuala firmly.

'Not you,' said Malachy with equal firmness.

'I'm your apprentice,' said Nuala. 'I need to go where you go. That's how I learn.' With a quick movement she hitched up her white *léine*, allowing it to blouse over her leather belt, and had swung herself onto the back of the pony before Malachy, always slow to speech, could think of anything to say. She moved on down the road and then stood, obviously waiting for them.

'I'll get some men and the priest,' said Garrett. 'They can bring a cart up to take the body back.' He stopped for a moment as if a thought had struck him. 'Do you think it was suicide?' he said to Malachy in a shocked whisper.

'I don't know,' said Malachy indecisively. 'It would be difficult to tell. The body was attacked by wild animals – foxes probably. I don't want Nuala to come,' he said with sudden energy. 'Will you tell her, Mara? Tell her not to come.'

Mara pretended not to hear. He irritated her slightly. Nuala was immensely intelligent, far more so than her rather slow-thinking father. She had set her heart on being a physician, she studied long hours with little help. If she felt she should see the dead body, then she should be allowed. After all she had seen her own mother die in agony almost two years ago. She had brains, courage and confidence; her father should not hold her back just because she was not the son that he had longed for.

Garrett, too, was staring at her, indecision wrinkling his high bare forehead.

'Brehon,' he said in a low voice, 'if this is suicide . . . then I shouldn't take the priest, should I? Aengus can't have a Christian burial. He'll have to be buried quickly at the crossroads.'

Mara looked at him coldly, trying to keep her fury and disgust at bay. 'I should not make any assumptions about this death, Garrett,' she said. 'I would bring the priest to say the last prayer over him and have the poor man buried in the faith of his forebears.'

She waited for no more, but crossed over to where her farm steward, Cumhal, held her mare.

'Would you like me to come with you, Brehon?' he asked when she had mounted. As usual, he seemed to know what she was going to do as soon as she knew it herself. She suspected that he was one of those people with very sharp hearing and quick instinctive reactions. He would have read the story in the faces around her. 'Or would you prefer that I go back to the law school?' he added.

'Go back, Cumhal, if you will,' she said. 'I've left Facht-nan in charge, but it might be an idea if you kept an ear open. Aidan and Moylan can be a bit of a nuisance at times. I think Enda will be all right now; he seems determined to work hard this year, but the other two need an eye kept on them.'

'I've plenty of wood that needs to be chopped,' he said obligingly. 'I'll do it in the yard outside the schoolhouse. That way, Fachtnan will know I'm close at hand.'

'Thank you, Cumhal,' said Mara. She smiled affection-ately as he trotted away; he was as sturdy and reliable as the cob that he rode. She often wondered how she could manage her busy life if she didn't have Cumhal and Brigid.

Mara patted Brig and urged the mare on to a slow trot through the graveyard path. Father O'Mahon, she was glad to note, was climbing onto his horse. Despite his doubts, Garrett must have asked the priest to accompany them.

But why those doubts? she wondered, as she quickened her pace once she had reached the stony road to Oughtmama. Why should Garrett think that Aengus had committed suicide? Why not an accident?

But if it were neither an accident nor suicide, could there be any connection between those two MacNamara deaths, in the one week, of Ragnall, the steward, and Aengus, the miller?

SEVEN

DI CHETHARSLICHT ATHGABÁLA

(ON THE FOUR DIVISIONS OF DISTRAINT)

There are eight signs of a good mill:

   1. *A fast-running stream of water*

   2. *A sluice gate to control the water in case of floods or drought*

   3. *A chute of elm wood*

   4. *A floor of stone*

   5. *A wheel of eight paddles of alder wood*

   6. *Two millstones of heavy stone*

   7. *A shaft of elm wood*

   8. *An honest miller*

OUGHTMAMA WAS A SMALL settlement in a deep valley on the side of the mountain to the east of Clerics'

Pass. A steep lane led up to it from the road and Mara could hear Garrett, Malachy, the two MacNamara clansmen, Eoin and Maol, and also Father O'Mahon, dismount from their horses when they reached the steepest part. Her mare showed no signs of distress, so she rode on and caught up with Nuala.

'Your father is worried about you witnessing Aengus,' she said bluntly. 'He has been dead for a while and animals have attacked the body.'

'I'm not a child,' said Nuala rebelliously. 'This is a good opportunity for me to learn. There's so much that I don't understand about bodies. You can't learn everything from scrolls and Father doesn't write down much. My great-grandfather wrote the most, but his handwriting is hard to read and some of the words are in old Gaelic.'

'Well, if you feel sick, just move away quickly,' advised Mara in a matter-of-fact manner. The girl was right. She had to learn. Her father had wanted to marry her off this month; if he had had his way she would be bearing a child next summer and that would be more injurious to her. Mara sympathized with Nuala's ambition to be a physician. She herself was the only woman Brehon in the whole of Ireland. It would be great to have a woman physician as well, in the kingdom of the Burren.

Oughtmama had originally been a monastic settlement. It had probably dwindled away gradually with the competition from the Cistercian monks just across the valley in the abbey of Our Lady of the Fertile Rock, and now no monks inhabited its ancient stone buildings. It was a favoured spot: a small valley, filled with rich soil, in the fold of the mountain, open to the south, and well sheltered from the east, west

102

and north. There were still the ruins there of the ancient churches – two of them within the old enclosure wall and one outside. At one stage Aengus had inhabited the abbot's house, a handsome two-storey building of well-cut limestone, roofed with Liscannor stone slates, but in recent years he had used one of the small houses kept for passing visitors in the days when it was still an abbey.

'That was the ladies' chapel.' Mara indicated the small ruined building outside the walls. 'The monks didn't like women within the enclosure so they built a chapel out there for those sinful creatures.'

Nuala giggled. 'If I had been around at that time I would have gone straight to one of the ones on the inside.'

'You probably would,' said Mara, but already her eyes were going towards the mill, which was the only working remnant of the monastery where once the long-dead monks had tilled the land and ground the corn. It was a small mill, powered by the stream that ran swiftly down from the mountainside and turned the paddles on the great wooden shaft, causing them to ceaselessly spin.

The wheel was turning merrily when they came and they could hear from inside the small building how the millstone was turning round and round. There was even a slight smell of over-heated stone.

Garrett was the first of the men to arrive. He went swiftly into the building and the sound ceased.

'Where's the body?' asked Nuala.

'We should have waited for Maol MacNamara,' said Garrett coming out, his face flushed with the heat from the stone. He looked downhill. Eoin and Maol were a long way back, walking slowly up the slope beside the heavy cart.

Ahead of them Malachy plodded on his heavily built horse and Father Mahon kept pace with him. Mara dismounted from her mare and looked around. The grass was still lush and very green; obviously the frost had not reached this sheltered valley.

'There's no sign of Aengus,' said Garrett in an irritated tone. 'Perhaps Maol was mistaken. He's—'

'He's here,' called Nuala, her clear voice showing no sign of emotion. She had hitched her pony to the post, had gone upstream and was standing just where the stream burst through from the mountain land which was held in common between the O'Brien and the O'Lochlainn clans.

Mara tied the bridle of her mare to a nearby tree and went up rapidly. Aengus MacNamara was there all right. The body had been mutilated by foxes, but that was not what made her draw in a long breath.

Where the stream ran down from the mountain and into the mill land at Oughtmama someone had placed a gate, a sluice gate. In its usual position it allowed the stream to flow unhindered but it stopped any sheep from trespassing. A flock of sheep had gathered there, perhaps waiting to be fed, Mara had surmised when she had noticed them first, but now as she approached there seemed to be something about them that reminded her of the mourners at the grave-side in Carron. There in front of them Aengus the miller lay, full length, stretched out in the water, his neck trapped under the gate, with his body in MacNamara land and his head in O'Lochlainn land and his sightless eyes fixed on the sky above.

'God almighty,' breathed Father O'Mahon, whether as a

prayer or an exclamation, Mara did not know. She turned to look at him and met Malachy's troubled eyes.

'We'll have to get him out of here,' said Malachy. 'I left him so that the Brehon could see exactly where he was. Here are Maol and Eoin. Stand back, Nuala.'

'His neck is trapped under the gate,' said Father Mahon huskily.

Ignoring her father's instruction, Nuala hitched her *léine* well up above her knees, knelt down on the soft grass and examined the dead face intently. Reluctantly Malachy put his satchel on the ground, came over beside her and bent down.

'Did he drown?' asked Nuala. 'Can you tell by his face?'

'No,' said Malachy grimly. 'But we'll be able to check for that in a minute.'

But who put him there? thought Mara. She said nothing, just watched Malachy's face as he studied the corpse.

'Help me to get him out,' said Malachy to Eoin.

Together they dragged the swollen, sodden body from under the gate and laid him on the grass. The smell was atrocious, but no one moved. Father O'Mahon approached, laid the holy oil on the forehead and then on the eyes, nostrils, ears, mouth, feet and hands, anointing each of the five senses in turn. Then he stood back, looking stricken and suddenly very old, and murmured the prayer for the dead.

'Wash your hands, Father,' said Nuala. 'Wash them above where the body lay. The water is still pure there.'

'What do we do now?' asked Garrett in a low voice. He looked from Malachy to Mara. His confidence seemed to have deserted him. Mara almost felt sorry for him. Two violent deaths of members of his clan within the one week would set tongues wagging. There was still a very primitive belief in 'luck' among the people of the Burren. The aura of 'bad luck' could attach itself to a man and he would never be fully trusted or liked after that. Garrett's father had been a benevolent, respected and well-loved *taoiseach*; his son would be judged all the more critically because of that.

'Was it suicide?' asked the priest, looking at Malachy.

Malachy shrugged. 'Impossible to tell at this stage; the man has been dead for days.'

'Could you examine him for any signs of blows or bruising?' asked Mara crisply. Malachy, as well as she, had a duty towards the dead man now. They had to discover the truth about his last lonely agony.

With an expression of distaste Malachy approached the body. He turned it on its back and instantly Nuala knelt on the grass beside him, her lips tightly closed, but her large brown eyes alert and intent on the task. Mara bent over also. The back of the head seemed to be uninjured to her eyes, but the front of the neck was badly marked and the head was almost severed from the body.

'Was he strangled, do you think, Malachy?' she asked after waiting for a few minutes.

'Could be,' said Malachy. 'If he were, it would be impossible to tell after this length of time, but I would think that this damage to the neck came from the pressure of the gate. He may have been unconscious when it was placed on him, but I don't know if he was dead. What would be the point, anyway, of putting him there in the stream if he were dead beforehand?'

'The gate can be lifted easily, Brehon,' said Maol in a low voice. 'The O'Lochlainns take their sheep out that way when they are sending them to the market. This is the quickest and easiest route for them. They have had the right-of-way here from time immemorial.'

A great phrase: '*from time immemorial*', thought Mara as she stood up to examine the gate. Brehon laws, also, had been in existence from *time immemorial.* They were the means that the community used in order to live at peace with their neighbours and their clans. Though not a religious woman, she breathed a quick prayer that she, the present-day representative of these laws, might be given the insight to solve these crimes and to restore peace to the people of the Burren.

The fittings for the gate had probably been made by Fintan, or perhaps by his father, or even his grandfather before him. They were a fine example of the blacksmith's art, strongly made and fitting the wooden gate like a glove. She stood in the stream and lifted the gate with her hands. It moved readily up, and then crashed down when she let it go. She climbed back out again. Her boots and the bottom of her *léine* were soaking wet, but it had been worth it. She knew now how Aengus could have met his death. And yes, suicide was a possibility. It would have been easy for a strong man like Aengus to have held the gate in his muscular arms, above his shoulders, and then lain down. Hopefully the weight had broken his neck so that he died instantly rather than through the long suffocation of drowning. She turned and went back to Malachy.

'Is there water in the lungs?' she asked.

He tightened his lips, but made no objection, just seized the body, rolling it over on its side with the head facing down. A small amount of liquid trickled out.

'He didn't drown,' he said curtly. 'The weight of the gate probably broke his neck and killed him.'

'It must have been suicide,' said the priest bleakly. 'Why should anyone do a thing like that to a man when it would be just as easy to strike him over the head – quicker and easier – or else strangle him with a rope?'

'He was a strange, melancholic man,' said Eoin, shaking his head sadly. 'He'd hardly give you the time of day when you brought the flour to be milled.'

'But why put the gate over his neck?' asked Garrett, looking anxiously from face to face. 'Wouldn't that be a strange thing for a man to do to himself?'

'You'd be surprised.' Father O'Mahon nodded his head knowledgeably. 'I've seen suicides where a man put the noose around his neck, then tied his hands together before jumping off the stool. They are afraid in case, by the mercy of God, they will have second thoughts.'

But the 'mercy of God', according to his earthly inter-preters, will condemn a man to eternal damnation for this deed, thought Mara, trying to keep her rising irritation at bay.

'Do you think that he committed suicide then, Father?' asked Garrett respectfully. 'Would you refuse him burial in the churchyard?'

'It could have been murder,' said Mara coldly. 'It was obviously not an accident, but it could have been a cold-blooded murder, arranged to look like suicide.'

'He had nothing much to live for,' sighed Eoin. 'He just

worked from morning to night. He said to me once that he wished he had married and had a proper son of his own to follow him and to help him at the mill. You see, he was never really sure that Niall was his son. He didn't look a bit like Aengus and, what was more, he didn't look a bit like the mother either. There was quite a lot of talk about that. It put Aengus off the boy, and then, of course, the other poor fellow, Balor, him being a *druth*, well, Aengus could have no pleasure in him.'

'He was a sad, poor man.' Maol wagged his bald head solemnly. 'His only pleasure in life seemed to be going to church. He went to Mass at the abbey every single morning of his life. Even went to vespers most evenings.'

'I suppose when you haven't much to live for, then death seems the only way out,' agreed Eoin.

Father O'Mahon nodded sadly. His face was set in stubborn lines and Mara knew that he had made up his mind. Poor Aengus would be buried at the crossroads at the bottom of the hill – just as if he were a dead sheep or cow. Garrett would go along with this; it would be quicker and easier than another elaborate funeral. And then there was the state of the body to be considered. It would be an urgent matter to get it quickly underground.

'What do you think, Brehon?' asked Garrett.

Instantly a compromise solution came to Mara.

'Only God knows the truth about this death,' she said solemnly. 'I think we should leave the final verdict to Him. We should bury the body now in the old churchyard here between the two churches.'

She looked around; there was still doubt on the faces of both Garrett and the priest, so she hurried on. Once everything was organized, there would be no room left for argument. Her voice took on a tone of crisp authority.

'Eoin, you and Maol go into the mill and get a board to place him on. You'll find some spades there, also, and you can dig the grave while we are preparing the body. Nuala, come with me and we'll see if we can find some old sacks to wrap him in.'

Eoin and Maol gave a quick sideways glance at their *taoiseach*, but he made no move to stop them, so they set off downhill towards the mill. Garrett and Malachy followed them, glad to get away from the stench and to be doing something practical, thought Mara, though she doubted whether Garrett would lose his dignity to the extent of actually digging the grave.

'We'll leave you to your prayers, Father,' she said. 'Come, Nuala.'

'You think it is a murder, don't you?' asked Nuala softly as they made their way down through grass-covered remains of ancient buildings.

'I think it might be,' said Mara, 'but I'm not sure.'

'Strange isn't it, two deaths in the week – they must be related,' stated Nuala with the conviction of the young and the self-confident.

❊

The mill was a two-storey building made from wood. It was dark and dusty inside after the clear bright air outside. It took a moment for Mara's eyes to see around. She had not been inside it since she was a child and had ridden with Cumhal to buy flour from the miller. The stream flowed under the mill via a chute that directed its flow against the paddles of the mill wheel. The weight of the water turned the wheel, which had a central shaft that went up through the ceiling into the upper storey and was attached directly to the upper millstone. When the mill was working then the upper stone would turn, grinding the grain, but now all was silent, except for the sound of the water and the swish of the paddles.

Beside the main chamber downstairs was a small store-room, and the four men appeared from this. Malachy had a shovel and spade in his large capable hands while Maol and Eoin were carrying a board. Mara looked around. There were no sacks of flour standing on the shelves at the far end of the room, though large baskets of grain stood waiting to be milled. Ragnall must have taken, as tribute, all of the sacks of flour that Aengus had already ground when he called at Oughtmama on that foggy Monday morning, surmised Mara. Did that mean that Aengus was killed on the following day? On the Tuesday, perhaps? Or perhaps on the same day, even? She stood back to allow Garrett, followed by Eoin and Maol, to go out, but then touched Malachy's sleeve to detain him.

'What do you think would be the day of death, Malachy?' she asked as soon as the others were out of earshot.

'Well today is Thursday . . .' he said reflectively. 'Monday at the latest,' he said then with more decisiveness than she expected from him.

'The body had only just begun to decompose,' observed Nuala sagely. 'There was a very warm sun yesterday, remember.'

Malachy nodded. 'The days were warm,' he said. 'But that was balanced by the couple of cold nights and then of course the flowing water would have kept it cool. No, bearing all these things in mind, it could have been Sunday. Yes, I would think it was Sunday.'

'That's probably impossible because Ragnall took seven sacks of flour as tribute from him on Monday morning,' said Mara. 'It must be Monday afternoon at the earliest. I don't think even Ragnall would have just helped himself. Aengus had quite a reputation for violence.'

Malachy shrugged. 'I would be pretty sure that it was Sunday,' he said. 'After all, the sacks might have been left there on the shelf and Ragnall could have just taken them if there was no sign of Aengus.'

'It's possible, I suppose,' said Mara doubtfully.

And then, as Malachy hastened to join the gravedigging party, she remembered the quarrel on Sunday between young Donal O'Brien and Aengus. What had happened? Donal had galloped after Aengus, had followed him home? Something about impressing Maeve with his championship of his father ... She must ask Liam, the O'Lochlainn steward, for the whole story.

'Would these do to cover him?' asked Nuala. She had gone into the depths of the shadowy interior of the mill and appeared carrying some old clean sacks. Aengus was obviously a tidy, careful man. The sacks had been washed, folded neatly and put away for reuse.

'I can slit them' continued Nuala. 'I found a good sharp knife in there on a shelf. That will do it.' She busied herself for a few minutes and then produced three slightly ragged, large squares of linen.

'These will do very well,' said Mara absent-mindedly. Her eyes were fixed on a single sack of flour in a dark corner beside the mill wheel. 'Open the door as far as you can, Nuala,' she said, narrowing her eyes to look at the bag. Yes, she could read it properly now and she was not mistaken. The sack had the milling date, 25 September, stamped on it, seven days previously, she noted, but what was strange was that it was over-stamped with the MacNamara insignia of a prancing lion. Ragnall had seven bags of flour in his cart on that foggy Monday morning when she met him. She remembered thinking that an odd number like seven was strange; she would have expected six or eight. She bent down and examined the sack carefully. Obviously Ragnall had stamped it. This meant that it would have been placed in the cart, sealed and stamped.

'Why had it been taken out again?' she said aloud with a puzzled frown. 'Ragnall must have taken it as part of the tribute.'

'Look, it's torn,' said Nuala, and Mara's eyes followed the direction of her pointing finger. The sack was made from coarsely woven, unbleached linen and it had obviously been washed and reused many times – too many times: a thin trickle of flour was spilling out from a spot where the threads had begun to split. Mara looked at it thoughtfully, her agile mind raking through various possibilities.

'We'd better go,' said Nuala after a minute. She was glancing anxiously out of the open door. 'Father O'Mahon is pacing up and down. I don't think he is happy about burying Aengus in consecrated ground, even ancient ground like this. They all think it was suicide, except for you.'

Mara roused herself. Whatever the truth was about that lonely and agonized death, she felt sure that it was not suicide. She would have to do this one last thing for Aengus.

He had been a religious man in his life; in death his body should not lie at a crossroads and his soul condemned to roam, forever excluded from the heaven to which he had prayed so ardently. He would have the last rites from the Church that he had believed in so fervently.

'Is that the knife that you found on the shelf?' she asked, seeing it in Nuala's hand. 'Let me see it.' There was a glint of something from the hilt that made it unlike a miller's knife. She took it from Nuala's outstretched hand and gazed at it, noting the stains of dried blood on the blade and on the hilt. It was a fine knife, a hunting knife, too long for general use and too fine for a miller. It had a few jewelled stones embedded in the hilt and an enamel oval set well inside the silver. And in the centre of that oval were the three lions of the O'Brien crest.

'No,' she said evenly, 'no, I really don't think that it was suicide.'

EIGHT

MACHCSLECHTA

(SECTIONS ON THE RIGHTS OF SONS)

There are three sons who can inherit their father's goods: Mac Aititen, a recognized son, Mac Óige, a son of a pure woman (chief wife) and Mac Aldaltraige Urnadma, a son of a betrothed concubine.

❦

'SO WE NOW HAVE two deaths to account for,' said Mara. Her six scholars sat very straight on their stools and their eyes were bright and concentrated. This was much better than Latin. She went on slowly and carefully, trying to sort out her own ideas as well as explaining the complicated situation to them.

'Ragnall MacNamara, the steward, was killed probably late on Monday evening,' she said. 'He was killed in the churchyard beside Noughaval market. Aengus MacNamara, the miller, was killed two miles away at Oughtmama. His time of death is uncertain, but Malachy the physician thinks it could not be later than Monday. In fact, he thinks that he was killed on Sunday. The body was badly decomposed.' She frowned at the quick ripple of excitement as Moylan and Aidan looked at each other with wide eyes. 'There is a possibility that Aengus committed suicide,' she continued. 'He drowned in the stream that powers the mill; his neck was trapped under the sluice gate.'

'Could it have been an accident, Brehon?' asked Enda.

Mara shook her head. 'No, that would be impossible. He must have been a strong man: after all, he spent his life carrying sacks. If by any chance he put his neck under the gate then he could easily have lifted it up. He either committed suicide or else he was murdered,' she added bleakly, remembering the swollen body with the water trickling from the gaping mouth.

'Why go to all that trouble to kill a man?' asked Fachtnan. 'Why not just hit him over the head or stick a knife in him?'

'Perhaps the murderer wanted it to look like suicide,' said Shane eagerly.

'There's some people coming,' said Moylan. 'Lots of them . . . listen!'

Mara went to the door of the schoolhouse and opened it. There seemed to be a large company of men riding down the quiet road that ran from Noughaval to the law school at Cahermacnaghten. She stood waiting and then glimpsed the familiar heads of the king's bodyguards over the hedge.

'It's King Turlough Donn,' she said over her shoulder to

her scholars. 'He must have heard the news. I think you should all go and have your supper now and we will talk about this tomorrow. Remember, though, don't speak of anything that you have discussed here, except among yourselves. Shane, run over to the kitchen house and tell Brigid, will you?'

Brigid would be in a fuss, she thought as she went to the gate. She would like to have had some notice if the king were coming to supper, but Mara felt a great wave of joy sweep through her at the thought of seeing him again.

'My lord,' she said formally, looking up into his pleasant open face, 'you are very welcome.'

The king swung himself off the saddle with the quick agile movement of a man who has spent much of his life on horseback and advanced with wide-open arms.

'Mara!' he said, kissing her fondly, while his bodyguards rode into the law school enclosure. 'You were expecting me?' he asked, a query in his voice.

'No,' said Mara frankly, 'but you are as welcome as the swallows in April.'

'Didn't Garrett MacNamara tell you then? I told him to tell you. We are inaugurating his *tánaiste* [heir] tomorrow. I thought I, Fergal and Conall,' he jerked his thumb at the two bodyguards, 'would stay here in your guesthouse and the rest of my men would be billeted with Garrett.' He glanced around to make sure he was not overheard and then said tenderly, 'I take every excuse to enjoy your company.'

'Though, of course, you are desolate at missing an evening in the company of Garrett and the well-born Slaney,' said Mara with a straight face. She spoke quietly, but at the same time she also gave a quick glance around to make sure that no one could overhear her. Only with Turlough could she allow herself to joke about Garrett and his wife; with everyone else she always preserved a veneer of impartial friendliness towards all of the people in the Burren.

Turlough chuckled. 'Oh, I do miss you when I am away from you,' he said. 'Why can't you make up your mind to marry me and leave this place and live with me in Thomond! I know what it is; it's those wretched boys. You don't want to leave them. Why can't you bring them with you, set up a law school in Arra. The place is big enough, goodness knows!'

'I'll think about it,' promised Mara with a smile. Their courtship had settled down to a good-natured teasing and enjoyment of each other's company since his surprising offer of marriage last May – perhaps he, no more than she, did not really desire any great change. It wasn't just the law school that she would miss if she went as his queen to Thomond; she knew that. She had been Brehon of the Burren for fifteen years now and she did not feel that she wanted to give up that position or to leave the gleaming limestone pavements and flower-filled grykes of the Burren for the monotonous fields of rich grassland in east Thomond.

'It's strange that Garrett didn't tell you,' said Turlough, reverting to the affairs of one of the three kingdoms he reigned over. 'What an odd man he is! After all, you, as Brehon of the Burren, have to be there for the inauguration.'

'He's had a lot on his mind,' said Mara quietly. 'Have you heard that there has been a second death in the Mac-Namara clan?'

'A second death!' exclaimed Turlough.

'Aengus, the miller, was found dead yesterday on the day of the burial of the steward,' continued Mara. 'I thought that

Murrough would have told you. He was at Carron that day, or so I heard.'

'That son of mine never bothers communicating anything with me,' said Turlough, his impatient tone belied by the indulgence in his eyes. 'He's too busy with his English friends, riding in and out of Galway and spending more time with his father-in-law over in Kildare than he spends with his own father in Thomond. And look at the way he dresses! It's no wonder that my own clan don't like him much. I suppose they are afraid that if he became king he might sell out to the English. They say that the O'Neill is thinking of doing this. I must say that I'd be happier if Murrough saw less of his father-in-law and spent less time crossing over to London in his company.'

'Murrough's young,' said Mara consolingly. 'He'll get over this nonsense, especially if he and Eleanor have a son, soon.'

'No sign of that at the moment.' Turlough brooded for a moment and then his face cleared. 'After all, he is only young; you're right. I suppose I committed a thousand follies myself at that age.' Suddenly he swung around to face her. 'So what's this about the miller then? Another death?' he said abruptly as if the words had only just reached him.

'I'm afraid that it was murder,' said Mara. She thought about it for a moment and then repeated 'murder', in a firm tone. She would not voice Garrett's fears about the miller's death being suicide to anyone, when she was convinced he hadn't died by his own hand. She told Turlough briefly of the whole affair and he nodded.

'Could there be a connection?' he asked. 'Two Mac-Namaras: the miller and also the steward; it would seem strange if there was not a connection. You say that there was bad blood between the two men. You had to judge a case between them at Poulnabrone, isn't that right?'

'That's true,' said Mara. 'I haven't begun my enquiries properly yet. That could be the connection . . .'

'But there is something worrying you, isn't there?' asked the king, eyeing her closely. 'Come on, I know you. You're holding something back.'

'There is one other thing that connects the two murders,' said Mara slowly. 'There was a brooch found in the earth that covered Ragnall, the steward, and there was a hunting knife found in the mill.' She stopped for a moment and then continued. 'I think that the brooch and the knife may belong to the same person.'

'And who is that?' asked Turlough, sitting on the low stone wall beside the road and absent-mindedly shredding a piece of golden vetch.

Mara glanced around. There was no one within earshot, the two bodyguards, Fergal and Conall, in the enclosure, were surrounded by the noisy crowd of scholars, Brigid was flying over to the vegetable store at the far side, Cumhal was driving the cows back to pasture after the evening milking and the road to Slieve Elva was empty.

'The brooch belonged to young Donal O'Brien and I think the hunting knife might also,' she said quietly. 'It has the O'Brien crest set into the knife and you know that crest may only be used by the *derbhfine*.'

Turlough whistled. 'Teige's boy?' he asked.

Mara nodded. Teige O'Brien was Turlough's first cousin and therefore part of the *derbhfine*. The *derbhfine* was the family group descended from the same great-grandfather.

Anyone within the *derbhfine* could become *taoiseach* or king of the clan. Mara had known that Turlough would not like this news about his cousin's son. There was a family connection and also bonds of friendship and liking on both sides. Teige was a very loyal supporter of his king.

'What could the connection be between young Donal and two of the MacNamara clan?' Turlough asked, his face serious and concerned.

'Brigid is in a state,' said Mara, avoiding the question, and looking down the road where her housekeeper was bursting out of the gate. Brigid always walked quickly but this time she almost flew, her lips were compressed and the linen covering that she wore over her sandy-coloured hair was all askew.

'My lord,' she said shrilly, when she had come within shouting distance. 'My lord, I did not know that you were coming and I have nothing fit for you to eat in the place at all.'

'What had you planned to give to the lads and myself, Brigid?' asked Mara soothingly. She didn't care; let the king eat what they were going to eat. He should have let them know that he was going to come.

'I was going to do the usual Michaelmas supper for them, Brehon,' said Brigid, turning her distraught gaze on her mistress. 'Since the lads were not here on Michaelmas Day I thought I would leave it until Friday. Cumhal has lit the fire in the yard and there is a small pig roasting.'

'I knew I smelled something good,' said Turlough heartily. 'One of my favourite meals! Nothing like roast pork at this time of year with the nights turning frosty.'

'I could make you a good wine sauce and perhaps an

apple sauce as well and then there are some roots,' said Brigid, mentally turning over the contents of her larder. Her face was beginning to lose its worried lines.

'And I can find a good flagon of wine,' said Mara. Personally, as long as the food was acceptable, she thought that wine was the most important part of the evening meal. 'We'll have a cup of wine in my house, Brigid, while we're waiting. Send one of the boys for us when you are ready.' She wanted to discuss the two killings with Turlough and also to find out what he thought of Garrett MacNamara's new heir. In the house they would be private; in the yard of the enclosure there might be a dozen ears listening in to the conversation.

❉

'Anyway, how are your family?' asked Turlough, as together they strolled down the road towards the Brehon's house. 'How's your lovely daughter Sorcha? Is she well? And her husband? And the grandchildren?' He, like she, seemed to decide that it was best to postpone the discussion of the serious affairs of the kingdom until they were in the privacy of her home. If it were indeed young Donal O'Brien who was responsible for one, or both, of the murders, then the affair would be very grave.

'They're very well,' said Mara lightly. 'I spent a fortnight with them in Galway in August. It was lovely being there with them all. Domhnall and little Aisling seem to grow every time I see them. Domhnall is reading very well now,' she boasted.

'I suppose that you will be having Domhnall at the law

school soon,' said Turlough, opening the gate and standing back to allow her to walk up the flagstoned path towards the front door.

'I don't think so,' said Mara, casting a quick glance towards her new flowerbed with the jewelled shades of pink, purple, blue and magenta blending together in a rainbow of colour. She stopped for a moment, ready to show it to him, and then, with a glance at his worried, preoccupied face, she walked on. Now was not the moment, she thought. 'Sorcha would like to keep him with her until he is eight,' she continued, 'and I think she is right. Some of these children come here too early. Brigid and I do our best, but most of them would be better off with their mothers until they are a bit older. Enda, now, he came when he was eight and yet after a year or so he was as good as Fachtnan in almost every subject, and Fachtnan had been studying since he was five. If they have the ability, they learn quickly.'

The east-facing room in the Brehon's house was dim and shadowy after the bright slanting brilliance of the sunset outside. Mara lifted down the tinder box from the shelf above the fireplace, struck a light and lit a couple of candles. They blazed up quickly, filling the room with the honeyed smell of warm beeswax. She took one candle and held it to the pile of dry pine cones in the fireplace and within seconds their warm spicy scent dominated the smell of wax. This room was always at its best in the evening: the heavy oak bench, stools and table gleamed with the splendour of dark gold, and the fire brought out the rich lights from the depths of the red velvet cushions and curtains. Mara looked around her with satisfaction, but the king's face was still full of gloom as he sank down heavily on the cushioned bench by the fireplace.

'What on earth would possess that boy to do a thing like that?' he muttered. 'He has everything in front of him. Teige wanted to make him his *tánaiste*; I was happy, there's no one else, really, that is fit. The *fine* would have gone along with it, and so would the *sept* and the clan.'

'I think that he is in love with Ragnall's daughter,' said Mara. Just as well to let him talk out the whole business now, she thought. He'll enjoy his dinner better then. 'But the father was against any talk of marriage.'

'The father was against the marriage? The girl's father! Never! That would have been a wonderful match for the girl. You don't mean Teige, do you? Teige is completely besotted by that boy. He would have refused him nothing.'

'But Ragnall did,' said Mara dryly. 'Apparently, he said no. The O'Lochlainn steward, Liam, said that Ragnall was too mean to supply sufficient cows with his daughter, but it may have been something else.'

'Brehon!' came Shane's high, excited voice. There was a thud of flying sandals on the flagstoned path and then a loud hammering on the door. 'Brehon, Brigid says that the meat is ready now. We are going to give the champion's portion to King Turlough. We all agreed.'

Mara got to her feet with a smile. 'You are highly honoured,' she said, hastening to open the door before it was battered down. 'Every Michaelmas the scholars vote for who is to get the champion's portion.'

'The shoulder, my favourite part of roast pork,' said

Turlough beaming. Shane and Hugh were waiting at the door and he playfully tried to knock their heads together.

'Quick, run,' he said. 'Don't let Fergal or Conall take it before I get there.'

'It was Fachtnan's idea,' shouted back Shane, as they scampered down the stony road ahead of them.

'I am very worried about this, Mara,' said Turlough in a low, confidential tone as they followed the two young boys down the road. 'Teige is a great supporter of mine, one of the best within the *fine*, apart from my boys, of course. I wouldn't like any trouble to come to him. In fact, if anything were to happen to Conor, my eldest – and you never know, he gets these fevers, my physician is worried that it is the wasting sickness – if anything were to happen to him, then Teige would be the choice of the clan for *tánaiste*. Murrough doesn't seem to take their fancy, as I told you, and I'm not sure that I blame them. However, if there was some disgrace to his son, if he were shown to have murdered an old man like Aengus, or even the two of them, miller and steward, Aengus and Ragnall . . .'

Turlough stopped and kicked a wayside stone with such force that it flew over the wall and startled a few sheep, which bleated indignantly and moved away into the centre of the field.

Turlough gave a short laugh and then continued. 'They might just look to appoint another of my cousins, Mahon O'Brien, the brother of the abbot, and I can't stand that sanctimonious idiot.'

'But why not Murrough?' asked Mara. 'I can't believe that wearing English clothes and a few jaunts to London makes that great difference to a man. He would continue to uphold our way of life, wouldn't he? I've never heard him say anything against Brehon law, have you? He wouldn't want to replace that with English law, would he?'

'I don't think I've heard him express an opinion,' said Turlough impatiently, 'but that's not the point . . .'

'That is the point, though,' said Mara quickly. 'If Murrough will rule his kingdom by our ancient laws, then he will be a good king.'

'It's not just that. Even though he's my own son, and he's a great fellow, I must say that Murrough is too much in the pocket of the Great Earl, too keen on English ways. Perhaps the *derbhfine* is correct. Teige, and possibly his son after him, would be more likely to keep the kingdoms in their Gaelic ways. But not Mahon! I couldn't stand that.'

He glanced at her keenly, but she did not respond. Justice was her affair; let the king order his political power base as he wished. It was her task to find the murderer of those two men and to apportion the fine. She might have been appointed by the king; but she was appointed to administer the kingdom according to her own judgement and according to the laws that had been laid down over hundreds of years, rather than be influenced by clan politics. The law had to be above all of that.

Turlough looked at her again and there was a measure of amusement as well as impatience in his glance. He understood her well and he knew that she would be inflexible in all matters to do with the law. If Donal O'Brien were guilty of murder, he would have to confess his deed to the people of the kingdom at Poulnabrone and pay the fine.

'I know what,' said Turlough so loudly that the heads of

the two bodyguards swivelled around and they both moved to join them at the gate. He waved them back impatiently and then continued in a penetrating whisper.

'This is the most likely way it happened. Aengus murdered Ragnall and then got sorry and committed suicide. That's it. The case is solved. You need do no more.'

'Perhaps you're right,' murmured Mara with a slight smile lifting the corners of her lips. 'Now come and have your champion's portion.'

The sun had set by the time the supper was ready and the ancient enclosure within the ten-foot-wide walls of Cahermacnaghten was full of leaping shadows. The fire burned brightly and the whitewashed walls of the schoolhouse, the guesthouse, the scholars' house and the kitchen house gleamed orange in the light from the flames of the bonfire. Cumhal had stoked it with great ragged branches of sweet-smelling pine and the scent almost overpowered the savour of the succulent roast pork stuffed with branches of rosemary from Mara's garden.

When King Turlough appeared there was a loud cheer from all of the scholars and from his own two bodyguards and amid cries of 'the champion's portion' he was ushered to the front while his platter was ceremoniously filled with a huge hunk of shoulder meat and liberal helpings of roast parsnips.

Mara watched and was surprised to find that her eyes filled with tears. Turlough was so at home here amongst her boys. If only he had been a humble farmer, and not the king of three kingdoms, they could perhaps have settled down happily together. But the facts could not be changed. He was King Turlough Donn, descendant of the High King, Brian

Boru, ruler of Thomond, Corcomroe and Burren. As his wife, she would have to be by his side at his table, would have to journey around with him; the duties of a queen would occupy hours of every day. How could she give care to her scholars, teach them, manage the affairs of the Burren if she had to spend most of her time in Thomond? Unfortunately, each had too much to lose: he, his kingship, and she, the position of Brehon of the Burren. And, perhaps, my hard-won independence, as well, she thought wryly, thinking of her first marriage to the unworthy Dualta.

'Go and collect the flagon of wine and the two wine cups from the table of my room,' she said, having beckoned over Fachtnan. He sped off instantly without a backward glance at the fun and she looked after him gratefully. He was such a nice boy. That was certainly a diplomatic idea of his to have the king take the champion's portion. From the time of Mara's own youth the champion's portion had been awarded to the scholar who had achieved the most during the past year, and it had often caused much heart-burning and jealousy.

'Here's your platter, Brehon.' Enda smoothed his blond fringe from his eyes and presented her dish of roast pork with the air of a man of the court. She accepted it with a smile. It seemed only yesterday when he had been a charming, blue-eyed eight-year-old and then a gawky, troublesome adolescent and now he was beginning to seem like an adult. Time passed so quickly these days, she thought with a pang. Before she knew it she would be old. Should she accept the king's offer, be his wife, and have companionship into her old age or carry on here as Brehon of the Burren and *ollamh* to the law school of Cahermacnaghten?

The scholars were lining up for their food now that the bodyguards had received their portion. Mara took the wine from Fachtnan and joined Turlough, who was perched on Cumhal's chopping block gnawing happily on an immense bone.

'You don't have to finish all of that. You could always slip it to Bran when no one is looking.' Surreptitiously she dropped some of her own pork on the ground by the great wolfhound that lay patiently beside her.

'What!' He was outraged. 'I've never left anything unfinished in the course of my life: not an enemy nor a bone. This is delicious. Oh good, they've brought my wine, though I suppose I should be drinking mead with this, shouldn't I?'

'You can drink mead, if you wish, but you'll drink on your own,' she said, handing him his cup and savouring her own wine contentedly. It was an excellent wine from Bordeaux. Sorcha's husband, Óisín, imported barrels of wine and sold it to the rich merchant families of Galway. Two or three times a year he brought a barrel over for her. Mead was homemade from fermented honey and too sweet for her taste.

'The MacNamara may, in fact probably will, be consulting you about the mill, tomorrow,' she said quietly. The boys were making an immense amount of noise, all shouting and laughing and poking new branches into the bonfire. They could talk with as much privacy here as in her sitting room.

'What about the mill?' he asked, his mouth full of roast pork.

'Well, the mill was the property of Aengus. His grandfather purchased it after years of successful farming. It's not the property of the *taoiseach*.

'Nothing to do with Garrett, then.'

'No,' she said hesitantly.

'But?' he queried.

'Aengus wasn't married and there was no near relative,' she said evenly.

Turlough swallowed a mouthful and then whistled.

'Well, you know the law better than I do, but I would say that if Aengus had no family, then the mill reverts to Garrett as clan property. Lucky!' He whistled again, sounding like one of the teenage lads.

'I didn't say he had no family,' said Mara quietly. 'He was reputed to have two sons.'

'Acknowledged?'

'Well, yes and no,' said Mara hesitantly.

The king smiled. 'That doesn't sound like you. You're always so sure.'

'It's not a matter that anyone, except the man himself, and his God, could be sure about. The law is, of course, as always, quite plain and simple on this matter. If the son is acknowledged by the father then his rights of inheritance are as solid as if the parents had married.'

'And did Aengus not acknowledge these two sons?'

'Not in so many words,' said Mara thoughtfully. 'The youngest, Balor, is extremely like the father in appearance, but he is classified as a *druth* and as such would have no rights to an inheritance even if he were the son of a legitimate marriage. The elder, Niall, is quite unlike the father in appearance and I have heard it said that he is unlike the mother also. The mother is dead, and I didn't really know her, not to remember, so I couldn't say for sure.'

'And Aengus denied paternity?'

'Not to me,' said Mara, 'but again, I have heard that he expressed doubts. The mother was a servant working at the mill.' She chewed a piece of roast pork thoughtfully. It was beautifully cooked with crisp crackling on the outside and the pale meat succulent, but her taste was more for beef. She swallowed some more wine and nodded in appreciation. Generally, she preferred the wines of Burgundy, but this really was excellent.

'So the fellow himself, this Niall, he claimed to be the son, although Aengus denied it, is that it?'

'It's not as straightforward as that,' said Mara, putting down her cup and taking a piece of linen from her pouch to wipe her hands. 'It—' she stopped as a tall figure came running over from the bonfire.

'Would you like some more, my lord?' asked Enda respectfully. 'And, what about you, Brehon?'

'No, thank you, Enda.'

'Yes, please, and tell Brigid it's delicious,' said Turlough at the same moment.

Mara waited until Enda had gone back to the bonfire carrying the two empty platters before continuing. 'It was always assumed on the Burren that both Niall and Balor were the sons of Aengus. It was an open secret that he was sleeping with his servant. Aengus bought a piece of land for Niall near Noughaval and gave it to him as a present. I am certain of that. I myself drew up the lease. It was enough land to give Niall the status of an *ocaire*, small farmer, though previously he had been described as a servant boy. I think that if I were to judge the case at Poulnabrone I would give the verdict that Aengus had never publicly contradicted the widespread assumption that Niall was his son and that his purchase of the land went far beyond anything that a master would do for a young servant. No, I think that Niall was the son of Aengus, and I think that Aengus did believe him to be his son.'

'So now Niall inherits the mill?'

'Yes,' said Mara. 'At the moment, that is the way that I am thinking. Whether Garrett likes it or not, Niall inherits the mill.'

NINE

TUAITHI (ON THE DIVISIONS OF THE
KIN IN THE KINGDOM)

The fine (kin group) is divided thus:
  *The gelfine (bright kin), the descendants on the
  male line of the same grandfather*
  *The derbhfine (true kin), the descendants on the
  male line of the same great-grandfather*
  *The iarfine (after kin), the descendants on the
  male line of the same great-great-grandfather*

ઉઉ

THE CASTLE AT CARRON, home of the MacNamara,
was transformed when Mara and Turlough, followed by
the bodyguards and the six scholars, arrived at midday on
Saturday. The ugly, poorly built, exterior walls were hung
with great linen banners proudly displaying the MacNamara
crest of the prancing lion. Fluttering pennants, in the English

style, were placed on either side of the magnificent iron gates, and horn-players and drumbeaters lined the path up to the old oaken door. The clan had gathered in great numbers, standing around braziers of burning charcoal in the inner courtyard, or waiting under the boughs of the ancient ash tree near to the cairn where the inauguration ceremony would take place. A hum of excitement had begun as soon as the king was sighted and fervent blessings and greetings were called out as they made their way through the massed throng.

'Wait here,' said Mara to her scholars as she and King Turlough handed over their horses to a servant, then walked up the path and in through the wide-open door.

For once the draughty ground-floor entry passage was warm and welcoming with braziers of sweet-smelling pine burning in every corner. In honour of the occasion, great efforts had been made to brighten the worn stone spiral staircase: thick candles of scented beeswax were flickering in each small embrasure and newly woven MacNamara banners hung from the curved ceiling above their heads.

At the door of the great hall, Slaney, the new wife of Garrett MacNamara, stood to receive her guests. She was a tall, heavily built woman, about thirty years of age, guessed Mara, gazing at her with interest. Slaney had a high colour, sapphire blue eyes, a wide sensual mouth and a pair of well-displayed, enormous breasts. She had come from a very wealthy merchant family in Galway and was dressed in the latest English fashion, her skirt broad under the hooped width of the farthingale and her hooded headdress stiff with jewel-encrusted embroidery. A haughty, arrogant woman, thought Mara, and wondered why Garrett had gone outside his own clan and any of the other clans in the kingdom in order to marry this large and domineering person. Slaney, she noticed with a flash of amusement, gave the simplicity of the Brehon's attire and uncovered hair a contemptuous glance and then turned her attention to the king.

'My lord,' she said in English, 'you do us great honour.'

Turlough stared at her disapprovingly and made no reply. Mara suppressed a smile. Was this Slaney stupid? Surely she should know by now how bitterly opposed the king was to anything English. Slaney, however, gushed on in her breathless, high-pitched voice.

'Prince Murrough is here already,' she said sweetly as she beckoned to her star guest, who came forward reluctantly, his eyes full of amusement. Mara concealed a smile. Father and son faced each other for a few moments, rather like a pair of rival stags about to lock antlers.

'*Prionsa*, she calls you, and you not even a *tánaiste*,' said Turlough tauntingly, eyeing this son, so alike, and yet so unalike.

Mara sighed. It was typical of Turlough, of course, but it was not very politic for father and son to be continually airing their differences in public. It was especially silly since she knew with great certainty that this son was the apple of his father's eye. Poor Conor, though an earnest, hard-working man and a very good son, was never as beloved as Murrough, who had inherited his father's looks and charm. She gave Murrough a warning glance now and then turned her attention to her hostess.

'You have made some wonderful changes here,' she said kindly to Slaney, and armed herself for a boring ten minutes of hearing about Flemish tapestries and the high cost of linen in Ireland.

However, Slaney's eyes left hers immediately and widened in horror and disbelief. Mara turned and looked over her shoulder to see Niall MacNamara coming up the steps.

'What is that man doing here?' hissed Slaney to one of the servants, speaking fluent Gaelic to Mara's amusement. 'That man has no right to be here.'

Then she pushed the servant aside and confronted Niall herself.

'This is for the *derbhfine* only,' she said coldly and then as he stopped and stood still in the middle of the stairs, a quick flush of embarrassment mantling his face, she flapped her hand at him as if shooing a chicken away, turned her back and seized 'Prince' Murrough by the sleeve of his elaborate silk shirt, drawing him over towards the fire. Mara gazed after her with interest. To suddenly engage in a quarrel with a clan member and then to abandon her most important guests: what very poor manners towards the king and his Brehon! And why was Slaney so anxious to impress 'Prince' Murrough and to show the world that she was on his side in this apparent quarrel between son and father? After all, as Turlough had pointed out, it was Conor, not Murrough, who was the *tánaiste*, heir, to the kingdom, and Turlough himself was hale and hearty and looked set to live for many more years. If Murrough did ever inherit the throne, Slaney would probably be an old woman by then and well beyond looking for favours from the ruling family of the three kingdoms of Thomond, Corcomroe and Burren. Was there something else? speculated Mara, gazing after the couple with interest. Was perhaps Slaney romantically interested in Murrough? He was certainly a dashing figure. She had always felt his charm herself. She looked carefully at the two figures. There seemed to be a certain attraction between them, she thought. They were certainly very aware of each other, standing closely, almost touching but not quite, eyes locked for a moment and then self-consciously pulling away and surveying the room as Slaney's husband, Garrett, came out from an inner room.

Well, well, well, thought Mara. Now this is interesting. Slaney has only been married to Garrett for less than three months and already she has found herself another man. Turlough will be amused at that.

'Look at him,' spluttered Turlough now, staring angrily at his son. 'Look at him, dressed up like an English man. Look at his doublet and his short mantle and that indecent tight hose. Soon he'll be shaving off his moustaches and growing a little pointed beard.'

'Have a cup of mead,' said Mara beckoning to a servant just as Garrett came rushing up, his high-foreheaded face flushed with embarrassment. He had obviously seen how his wife had left the king without the basic courtesy of offering him something to drink. He took the cup from the servant and proffered it on bended knee.

Turlough received it with a grunt, but then patted Garrett on the shoulder as the first swallow of the honeyed drink slid down his throat. He was not a man to stand on his dignity or to bear a grudge. Garrett stood up looking relieved and then made a signal to an elderly man by the fireside.

'My lord, may I present Cormac, elected by the clan to be the *tánaiste*,' he said.

The previous *tánaiste* had not died but had become so crippled with old age and infirmity that he had resigned his position and asked the clan to elect a new heir to the *taoiseach*. This Cormac, a cousin of the previous *tánaiste* and of Garrett, did not look as if he would last too long either, thought Mara. He must be sixty, at least, though he looked more.

'You'd think that Garrett would have got the clan to select his own younger brother?' whispered the king, after he had greeted Cormac. Mara did not reply, though she knew the answer to the question. Garrett would be hoping that this old man might last until a son of his recent marriage became old enough to be elected as *tánaiste.* A son to succeed the father; this English custom was beginning to come into Ireland. Garrett's younger brother, very keen on long sea voyages for trade and adventure, was a man only in his early twenties. If he became *tánaiste*, then Garrett's eldest son, as yet unborn, might have little chance to be the next *taoiseach* of the MacNamara clan. That thought reminded her of Turlough's eldest son.

'Where is Conor?' she asked. 'I would have thought he would be here today. Is he away?'

Turlough's face clouded. 'He's not well and that's the truth of it. He hasn't been well all of the summer. He's getting a lot of fevers and he is getting thinner and thinner. First they thought that the house on the island at Inchiquin Lake didn't suit him, but he's been no better since he moved out of that. I'm worried about him. I've had physicians from all over the country to come and look at him and they give him this and that, but none of it makes any difference.'

With that, he moved abruptly away and began to talk to Teige O'Brien, his cousin. Mara gazed after him. He did look worried. The wasting disease that attacked many young men and women seemed to have no cure and if that was what ailed Conor, then his father was right to be anxious.

By now, despite the noticeable lack of food and drink, people in general were beginning to enjoy themselves. Most of them, anyway, Mara thought, turning her eyes thoughtfully towards Niall MacNamara. He must have decided to ignore his hostile reception because he had now reached the top of the stairs and was huddled into an obscure corner of the hall; in England he would be reckoned a bastard, but here in Ireland? She took tiny sips of her mead, trying to look as if she were enjoying it, while her dark green eyes studied Niall intently, taking in his unaccustomed finery. He had an obviously new mantle and it was pinned with a shining silver brooch. Slaney, of course, was right. This hospitality in the castle would be for the *taoiseach*'s immediate family, only important outsiders like the wheelwright, the blacksmith and the miller would normally expect to be invited. Did Niall think that since his father was dead, he had inherited his father's privileges? He did not look as if he were enjoying his victory. No one spoke to him and his face was tense and nervous. Mara nibbled some hazel nuts meditatively and wondered about him.

'Clear the room.' Garrett was bustling around getting servants to move the crowd to the sides of the hall. It seemed as if the meagre allowance of mead and food for the privileged guests had now come to an end. 'Make way for the king,' he said fussily. 'Move back everyone. My lord, and you, Brehon, would you follow me.'

Garrett went awkwardly down the narrow twisting staircase, bowing his head to avoid the trailing banners, Mara and Turlough followed him and behind came Slaney with 'Prince'

Murrough. When they reached the door there was a great cheer from the MacNamaras waiting patiently in the chill of this early October day. They surged forward to gather under the pale yellow leaves of the huge ash tree, leaving a wide pathway for their *taoiseach* and their king. Turlough gathered his mantle more closely around him and then he strode forward to take his place on the raised platform of heavy stone slabs beside the cairn, the inauguration place of the MacNamara clan on the Burren. Mara stood on one side of him and Garrett on the other. Slaney and Murrough mounted the platform also, but stood at the back, whispering to each other.

'By the power devolved on me from my great ancestor, Brian Boru, and from his sons and his grandsons, I, Turlough Donn O'Brien, King of Thomond, Corcomroe and Burren, son of Teige, son of Turlough Beg, son of Brian, son of Mahon, son of Murrtough, son of Turlough, true descendant of the *derbhfine* of Brian, son of Cinnéide, now inaugurate Cormac MacNamara as the new *tánaiste* of the MacNamara clan here in the Kingdom of Burren.'

The mellifluous Gaelic sentences flowed on and the clan stood reverentially silent until he finished. Then their *taoiseach* left the platform, took Cormac by the hand and brought him to the king and formally presented him as the duly elected *tánaiste* for the MacNamara clan in the kingdom of the Burren. The cheers were fairly muted, thought Mara, as Cormac the *tánaiste* knelt cautiously, his ageing joints audibly creaking, and placed his hands within the hands of his overlord King Turlough Donn O'Brien for the ceremony of *imbas*. And then Garrett knelt and paid homage also. This time the cheers were definitely very half-hearted. Garrett seemed to have made himself unpopular in the last few months. Perhaps with a different and less ambitious wife, things might have been different for him. His father had been a popular man and this would have influenced the clan to elect the son as the successor and also to warm towards him. Garrett had his chance; now it looked as if he had lost the goodwill of the MacNamaras on the Burren.

'My lord,' said Garrett, still on his knees before his overlord, 'we of the clan of MacNamara have two more matters to settle. There have been two deaths during the last week. Ragnall MacNamara has died and left no son, just a daughter.'

He stood up and looked around. There was a ripple of movement in the crowd as heads turned to see whether Maeve MacNamara was present and then turned back again when she was not discovered. Mara noticed that Teige O'Brien took a long searching look around the crowd. What did he think about his son's fancy to marry the daughter of the MacNamara steward, she wondered.

'There is no other near relation of the dead man,' continued Garrett, 'so I ask that the land be returned to the clan to be used where necessary.' His eyes found his wife, who had moved slightly forward, and then he looked back again at the king. Slaney took another step forward so that now she was definitely part of the group.

'The Brehon will tell us the law about this,' said Turlough Donn with a slight frown. 'There must be provision made for the girl. How old is she?'

'She is sixteen years old and she will shortly be married,' said Slaney, speaking in Gaelic so that all could understand. 'Maol MacNamara is anxious to marry her and he could be granted a portion of the land. The *taoiseach* is in favour of this match and has already given his permission.' She cast a quick stern glance at her husband and he bowed his head obediently.

'The law is that, where there is no male heir, a female heir should be given enough land to graze seven cows and the dwelling place that is her home,' said Mara dryly. She fixed Slaney with a long cold look. What business of hers was this? Slaney had been born and brought up in Galway and had lived under English law. She could not be expected to know Brehon law, but she could hold her tongue until she knew the customs of her husband's land.

She waited for Slaney's prominent blue eyes to drop before hers before she continued. 'Maeve herself, as she lacks a father, will come under the protection of the king. I would be happy to deputize for you, my lord,' she said to Turlough, wishing that she had fixed this up beforehand.

'That's settled then,' he agreed heartily as Mara breathed a sigh of relief. She should have known that he would not let her down. 'Maeve MacNamara gets land fit to graze seven cows and the dwelling house. And the Brehon, in my name, will order her marriage as she thinks fit.'

'But, my lord,' said Slaney in her sweetest manner, 'surely the chief of the clan can be relied upon to look after this fatherless young girl.' Once more she spoke to the king in English and once more Turlough Donn turned a blank face towards her and then looked at Garrett for an explanation. Garrett flushed and cast an uneasy glance at his wife.

'What the *taoiseach*'s wife is saying, my lord . . .' began Mara, and translated Slaney's remark slowly and carefully. There was a little ripple of appreciation from the crowd. They were enjoying this; the *ban tighernae*, Slaney, was not popular amongst them. She gave the remark a moment to sink in and then added: 'But, of course, the law is quite clear. The king now has the responsibility for Maeve MacNamara; her land and her dwelling house go with her into any marriage which is arranged for her. The rest of Ragnall MacNamara's land goes back into clan land, and will, no doubt, be allocated by the *taoiseach* to a deserving young man.' Or else used to furnish Slaney with all the fine goods which would allow her to boast to her merchant relations in Galway of the splendid marriage she had made. Mara looked quickly at the king and saw her own thoughts in his sceptical eyes. He nodded quickly and she finished: 'This is the law of the king.'

Garrett looked uneasy. Slaney began to whisper in his ear. The king stared at him with an expression of disbelief in his eyes. Though Turlough was the last person to stand on ceremony this still must strike him as very strange behaviour. After a moment he grew impatient.

'Is that all?' he asked. 'Perhaps we can return inside. The day is becoming cold.'

'My lord,' said Garrett after a pause while he licked his lips and glanced nervously at his wife. 'There is another matter. Aengus, the miller, died; whether by his own hand or by another's no one can tell. He was not married and had no immediate family so I ask that you confirm that the mill, and the land around it, goes back to the clan and its *taoiseach*.'

'My lord,' said Niall, hastily pushing himself to the front of the crowd. 'I am the son of Aengus the miller and as such I claim my father's property.'

'Aengus was not married,' repeated Garrett pompously, staring at this insignificant member of his clan.

'My lord, I was born of the union between Aengus and his servant, Cliodhna,' persisted Niall.

'The church frowns on such matters,' said Slaney. Her Gaelic was fluent and perfect when she chose to speak it.

'There is no evidence that you are the son of Aengus,' said Garrett dismissively. 'Eoin!' he called, his voice rough and peremptory. As Eoin came forward reluctantly, Garrett seized him by the arm and held him face to face with Niall.

'What was that you said when we found Aengus's body?' he demanded. 'You spoke then about how Aengus was depressed because he had no son to follow him in the mill.'

Eoin's face was dark red and he was obviously disconcerted by this public challenge.

'Were you quoting the words of Aengus the miller, or just general gossip?' intervened Mara.

'Just gossip, Brehon,' said Eoin. He looked relieved and then averted his gaze from the indignation in Garrett's face.

'Has anyone heard Aengus publicly acknowledge Niall as his son?' Garrett's voice was loud and determined.

There was an awkward silence. No one found the courage to speak and to incur the wrath of the *taoiseach*. The clansmen looked from their *taoiseach* and his *ban tighernae* to the king and then back at the face of their Brehon. Slaney took a quick step forward, but was waved back by an imperious gesture from Turlough.

'Niall,' said Mara, taking a step forward so that she was now in front of Garrett. 'Did Aengus the miller acknowledge you as his son?'

'Yes, Brehon,' said Niall eagerly. 'Even when I was young he told me that he would look after me if . . .' His voice tailed away.

If ... what? wondered Mara; but, she supposed, there would always be an 'if' with a dour suspicious character like Aengus. If the boy behaved himself, if he were docile and helpful around the mill, if he did not anger his father ... This condition did not mean that he was not the son; in fact, it made it more likely. Why should Aengus worry about looking after the son of a mere servant woman if there were no special relationship?

'And then years ago, when you were eighteen years old, Aengus purchased the land at Noughaval for you?'

'Yes, Brehon,' said Niall. His face brightened. 'He purchased it from the profits of the mill and gave it to me on my eighteenth birthday. He told me that I had been a good son to him, but that there was not enough work for two men at the mill,' he ended defiantly.

'I drew up the lease myself,' said Mara. 'That certainly was my understanding. Although nothing was written down, I do remember Aengus saying that he wanted to make provision for you.'

'But you say nothing was written down about a relationship,' said Slaney sharply. Whenever she spoke in Gaelic her voice seemed different, harsher and more that of a country-woman than her previously refined Galway tones.

'True,' said Mara, 'but Aengus paid a good sum of silver for this farm. He bought it from the O'Lochlainn. I remember the occasion well.' She went ahead, speaking slowly and carefully. Though inwardly wishing that this dispute had not arisen on the occasion of the inauguration, she made her voice slow and authoritative and kept a stern eye on Slaney.

'The O'Lochlainn said to Aengus that it was a good farm and a productive twenty acres and, to the best of my recollection, Aengus said: "Well, I would like to see the lad settled. It was not his fault that his mother was never married." I think if this case is to be tried at Poulnabrone,' she added, 'then I would call upon the O'Lochlainn as a witness. I'm sure that he will remember the occasion.'

'So if this case were to be heard at Poulnabrone what would be your verdict, Brehon?' asked the king, eyeing her closely.

Mara waited for a moment while she considered her words. The air seemed very still and very quiet and then she realized that the swallows, whose high-pitched *veet vit* sounds had been the background to the whole summer, had now finally departed across the sea. Soon winter would come. Already the beauty of the summer flowers was fading and the sharp chill of winter was beginning to grip this land of harsh grey stone.

'My lord,' she said formally, addressing herself to the king, 'if this case did come for judgement at Poulnabrone I would call on witnesses who had known Aengus the miller and Niall MacNamara. Niall, himself, would then have time to call his witnesses and to make good his claim to be the son of Aengus. I cannot say what my judgement would be once I heard all of the evidence.' That was not what she had said to him in private, but it was all that she was prepared to say in public.

'But perhaps it does not need to go as far as that,' persisted the king. 'Perhaps you could tell the *taoiseach* now what your opinion at the moment is. I'm sure he wants to do the right thing by this member of his clan. Perhaps this matter could be settled now for the sake of unity in the clan.'

'All I can say now,' said Mara slowly and gravely, 'is that

I have never heard Aengus deny his parenthood of Niall, and of Balor. The fact that he paid for a farm to be given to Niall is, to my mind, evidence of a closer tie than that of mere servant and master. My opinion, now, at this moment, without having heard the evidence, is that Niall was the son of Aengus and as such, unless there is an objection, he has the right to, as the law puts it, *"uncover his father's hearth and take possession of his father's lands and goods".'*

She waited for a moment, looking directly at Garrett. It seemed to her as if the entire clan, gathered around, held their breath. She was conscious that this might be a crucial moment in Garrett's relationship with his followers. Some show of generosity now would make up for the mistakes of the past few months. His eyes avoided hers and looked towards his wife. She looked back at him stonily, her bright blue eyes seeming to grow even more prominent with rage. Garrett glanced up at the dilapidated castle. Mara could see him mentally assess the amount of repairs that it needed and then he returned his gaze to hers.

'I object,' said Garrett harshly.

Mara nodded briefly. The king beside her made a sudden violent move and sighed impatiently. She could imagine his thoughts. Turlough was a man of great generosity himself and this evidence of a mean and grudging spirit in the *taoiseach* of a clan would be abhorrent to him. However, Garrett was within his rights, and the law would, as always, be even-handed in its judgements. This would be a hard-fought case. Because of his wife's extravagance, money was suddenly all-important to Garrett. But the mill itself would be important for Niall. It would make him prosperous and it would also make him respected within the community. Mara made up her mind. There was no more to be said at this time and in this place.

'In that case,' she said gravely, 'the matter cannot be settled here today. It will tried at Poulnabrone next Saturday at noon. Witnesses should be brought by both sides to the dispute.'

She cast one look at Niall's stricken, blanched countenance. Suddenly the picture of him driving the cart on that foggy Michaelmas Day came to her. Malachy had put the time of death as Sunday, but conceded that it could have been Monday. She understood his difficulty. Hot sunny days and cold frosty nights and the fact that the body lay in the fast-flowing mountain stream made the time of death hard to estimate. Perhaps Aengus was still alive on Monday. Who had collected those sacks of flour from the mill at Oughtmama? Was it Ragnall, or was it Niall who went in to fetch the sacks? And if it were Niall, did he meet his father Aengus? Were there hot words between them? Did Niall lose his temper and perhaps see this way of getting rid of his father and inheriting his lands and his mill?

'I won't stay for dinner,' she murmured to the king. 'I feel I should leave now. I should not take further hospitality. I must not appear to be on Garrett's side when I hear this case on Saturday.' She ignored his indignant face – he would not enjoy the company of Slaney and Garrett, and of his son, without her presence, but she could not help that. He, like she, was bound by his position in life. She crossed the platform to where Garrett stood while his wife still whispered in his ear.

'I will bid you farewell now, Garrett,' she said. 'I have much to do and can not spare any more time. Cormac, I wish you all the blessings and a long life to enjoy your new position. *Slán leat*, Slaney.' And then, without waiting for a reply, she signalled to Fachtnan and he quickly rounded up the other scholars and took the bridle of her mare, holding it steady for her to mount.

'You wouldn't have got much to eat anyway,' she said to her indignant young scholars once they were riding down the road. 'I bet the dinner would have been nothing compared to what you get at Cahermacnaghten. When we reach Caherconnell you can gallop ahead and ask Brigid to cook you some of her sausages. Then you'll have the rest of the day to yourselves to play hurling, or whatever you want to do. Fachtnan, will you ride with me? I want to call in at the forge on the way home.'

'Fintan won't be at the forge, Brehon,' said Enda. 'He was at the inauguration. I saw him there in the courtyard. He'll stay for the dinner.'

'I know,' said Mara. 'That's why I am going this afternoon.'

Ten

Do Breathaib Gaire
(Judgements of maintenance)

The fine (kin group) is obliged to care for those who are handicapped in their minds or their bodies.

The guardian of a druth (mentally retarded person) is responsible for his offences in the alehouse. Missiles thrown by a druth do not require compensation. Anyone who incites a druth to commit a crime must pay the fine himself.

ॐ

'Fachtnan, will you ride ahead of me,' said Mara as the two of them turned down the quiet deserted lane that led from Caherconnell to Noughaval. 'I don't want Balor frightened; he seems nervous of me and you will be able to reassure him. Just chat to him until I arrive.'

If that were Enda, she thought with a smile of amusement, there would be fifty questions and surmises, but Fachtnan just nodded his head of rough brown curls and galloped off. She slowed down her mare and walked her along the rough surface of the lane. The sun had come out and was pleasantly warm on her face. A light wind from the Atlantic stirred the bleached seed heads of the grasses and rippled through the nodding pale blue harebells. The hedgerows were laden with dark red haws and the blackberries glistened fat and luscious amongst the orange and yellow glow of the bramble leaves. There were still some red and green fruits between the ripe black ones. These might never mature now, thought Mara. All the signs seemed to point to an early, hard, cold winter.

She could hear the rise and fall of Fachtnan's voice interspersed with the slower, deeper tones of Balor as she neared the bend in the lane just before the forge. They seemed to be having an amiable conversation. Quietly she dismounted, leading the mare slowly towards the forge.

'*Beannacht Dé leat,*' she said pleasantly to Balor. He had a hunted look in his eye and he cast a quick glance over his shoulder as if he were about to escape. Swiftly she bent down and picked up the mare's forefoot, holding it out towards him.

'Has she got a stone in her foot?' she appealed to him.

He couldn't resist that. He was obviously a man who loved horses. He came to her side, chirruped to the mare, taking his time to gentle her, but she knew him instantly and nuzzled his neck. He produced a small red apple from his pocket and offered it to her and she crunched it delicately. He took the foot from Mara, handling it carefully in his enormous blackened hands, probing with the sureness of a surgeon around the shoe, and then shook his head with a puzzled expression.

'No, no,' he said.

'She's all right?'

'She's mighty,' he said, looking at the mare lovingly.

'Just trod on a stone for a moment, perhaps,' said Mara. She was not sure whether he understood, but he nodded immediately.

'Not sore now,' he added, after a minute's more probing. Perhaps he was not as slow as Aengus the miller had made out when he brought him to Poulnabrone a few years ago. She wondered whether Aengus had been unkind to him. The work here with Fintan among the horses would have perhaps slowly built his confidence. She stood next to him and joined him in petting and caressing the mare.

'Balor,' she said after a minute, looking at him gently and speaking slowly. 'Did you take the candlesticks from Ragnall?'

He carefully put the mare's foot back on the ground and then looked at her with panic-stricken eyes. She felt slightly ashamed, but this matter had to be cleared up.

'It doesn't matter,' she said, making her voice as reassuring as she could. 'They were belonging to Fintan so you took them from Ragnall and you brought them back. That was it, wasn't it?'

Slowly he nodded. Fachtnan patted him encouragingly on the back.

'The Brehon isn't cross,' he said carefully, as if he were talking to an eight-year-old. 'Tell her what happened.'

Mara held her breath. The candlesticks were of little

concern to her, but it was possible that Balor might hold some other vital pieces of information.

'I took 'em from cart,' he muttered, looking at her shyly.

Mara nodded in a matter-of-fact way. 'When Ragnall had gone into the churchyard.'

'They were master's candles,' he said beseechingly.

'Yes, of course,' she answered soothingly. 'And they were lovely. Did you help to make them?'

He nodded proudly. 'Hammered the iron,' he said.

'And was Ragnall a long time in the churchyard?' she asked. 'Was he talking to anyone?'

She wasn't sure whether he understood her, but then he turned his back to her and whispered hoarsely in Fachtnan's ear.

'Yes, I know,' said Fachtnan, 'that's what he went in to do, but the Brehon just wants to know, did he talk to anyone when he finished.'

'Just Donie,' said Balor.

'Donal O'Brien, from Lemeanah?'

'Yes, young Donie . . . not anyone from our clan.'

Mara drew in a deep breath. This was worrying. It certainly needed investigating.

'Tell your master that the candlesticks are his, Balor,' she said. She thought of uttering a few legal rules about not helping yourself from another man's cart, but decided not to bother. 'You're a good worker, Balor,' she said. 'Your master is lucky to have you.'

He smiled happily then. He chuckled to himself. 'Master went back to give him a good wallop,' he said, his enormous toothless mouth grinning.

'After you brought the candlesticks home?'

'Yes, he say: "*good man yourself, Balor*", and he go down road.'

Mara nodded slowly. This evidence was not evidence that she could use in a court of law, the man was classified as a *druth*, and classified as such by herself. However, it did seem to put Fintan MacNamara, the blacksmith, back into the picture again.

When she looked back, she could see Balor happily carrying huge logs of wood to stoke the fire. He seemed to have forgotten his fright. He was probably quite child-like and was glad that the matter was now discovered and was off his mind. It had been a worthwhile visit for both of them. Though she took little pleasure in the knowledge that Donal O'Brien might well be the last person to have seen Ragnall MacNamara alive, the sooner the truth was found, the sooner the community could settle down again. King Turlough would be upset but that could not be helped.

'Fachtnan, you go back to Cahermacnaghten and have your dinner,' she said. Tell Brigid I may be late. I am going down to Lissylisheen to see Ardal's steward and then I will probably ride on to Lemeanah Castle.'

❊

The O'Lochlainn tower house at Lissylisheen was set in the middle of an open field, three storeys high, plainly made from well-cut limestone blocks. It was a solid, unpretentious tower, kept in good repair. Mara could see where some work had been recently done to the stone roof slates and there was new pointing between the stones on the northern side. The flagstoned yard in front of the house was swept clean and the stone wall around the enclosure was well built and carefully maintained. What a pity that Ardal didn't marry again, thought Mara. It seemed a shame that he had no sons to enjoy this fine property.

'Do you want the *taoiseach*, Brehon?' A man cleaning out one of the stables came running to hold her mare, while another hovered ready to summon Ardal.

'No, I won't trouble him,' said Mara. 'I just wanted to have a word with Liam, the steward. Is he anywhere near?'

'Liam is in the barn, Brehon. Will I get him for you?'

Mara thought for a minute. Her natural politeness made her unwilling to interrupt for too long one of the busiest days of the year, when the O'Lochlainn steward would be storing and recording all the Michaelmas tribute. However, if she went into the barn then she would have to speak to Liam in front of many ears. If she stayed where she was then she could ask a private question or two.

'Ask him if he could spare me a minute,' she said, putting her hand out to stroke the tiny fronds of a maidenhair fern in the crevice of the gate pier, but making no move to dismount.

The man went running and in a few moments, large and affable as ever, Liam emerged from the barn, shielding his eyes against the low brilliance of the setting sun.

'You're well, Brehon?' he enquired. 'You'll come in and have a cup of ale? Something to eat?'

'No, I won't, Liam,' she said. 'I just wanted to ask you about Ragnall on Michaelmas Day. You remember? You saw him at Noughaval Fair?'

'Yes, indeed,' said Liam, hastily rearranging his smiling features to an expression of solemnity.

'Do you remember seeing him leave the fair and go into the churchyard?'

'He may have done,' said Liam, his face expressing the hope that he might not have to go into any embarrassing details about Ragnall's visit to the churchyard.

'Did you see young Donal O'Brien go after him?' asked Mara bluntly.

Liam paused. A quick expression of something that she could not quite read flitted across his face. Then he nodded.

'He may have done,' he said slowly, and then, more quickly, 'of course he might have just been going home to Lemeanah Castle by the back route.'

Mara nodded. Unlikely, she thought. She had been over that route herself and it had nothing in its favour. There were better and more straightforward ways of getting to Lemeanah.

'They're in a lot of trouble up there in Carron – the MacNamara, I mean,' commented Liam. 'I hear the miller is dead, also. Someone was talking about it last night. Maol is supposed to be the man to be the new steward; no one knows who will be the new miller.' He eyed her with interest. Undoubtedly he would have heard about the dispute between Niall and his *taoiseach*, Garrett. She wasn't going to talk of this, but it would be no harm to probe Liam a bit about Niall. She waited, saying nothing, just glancing around at the horses on the well-drained fertile fields. Liam, she knew, could not keep silent long. He was an affable man who enjoyed the sound of his own voice.

'Shame, though,' he continued after he had waited a courteous minute for a comment from her. 'Everyone thought that it would be Niall. The whole of the Burren knew that he was the son of Aengus. Mind you, it's not a surprise that Maol would get the steward's job. They say that Ragnall had promised his daughter's hand to him and the stewardship was probably promised at the same time. Ragnall would have wanted to keep it in the family. He wasn't getting any younger. The job would have got too much for him sooner or later.'

Well, I mustn't keep you talking, Liam,' said Mara courteously. 'This is a busy time for you, I know. The tribute has been good this year?'

'No complaints, no complaints at all,' he said expansively. 'Mind you,' he added, 'the O'Lochlainn would never be one to complain. He's a great man to look after his people and to be just to all. Whatever the clan can afford to give; that will be welcomed by the O'Lochlainn.'

And with this compliment to his own *taoiseach*, and perhaps a sly swipe at Garrett, the MacNamara *taoiseach*, Liam strode back to the barn, calling a cheerful blessing over his shoulder. Mara waited until he had gone, pondering her best route to Lemeanah. She wondered whether to return to Noughaval, but that would mean either going past the forge again, alarming Balor, or else going through the dense hazel scrub around Shesmore. In the end she decided to take the road towards Kilfenora and then to turn east. In doing so, she would encroach upon the kingdom of Corcomroe, but Fergus, the Brehon of Corcomroe, would be the last man to worry about a thing like that. She would mention it to him the next time that they met. There was, of course, no law to forbid a professional person like herself from entering another kingdom, though the farming community were supposed to keep to their own kingdom, unless on days of fairs or festivals, but generally she preferred to keep to her own territory.

Lemeanah Castle, or tower house, looked very peaceful as she cantered up the road towards it. A few boys were playing outside the surrounding cottages and a couple of little girls were picking some of the late blossoms of a tall purple loosestrife from the hedgerow.

However, as soon as she approached the castle, someone in the gatehouse immediately challenged her. In the past, before the kingdoms were united under Thomond, the largest of the three kingdoms ruled over by King Turlough Donn O'Brien, this would have been the borderline between the kingdoms of Corcomroe and Burren and tensions still showed in the guards on both sides of the border. Lemeanah Castle was just inside the border of the kingdom of the Burren, and the original *cathair* of Lemeanah had been built by the O'Lochlainns to defend the border against the O'Connors.

'Mara, Brehon of the Burren,' she announced, and there was instant deference.

'The *taoiseach* is at Carron Castle at the inauguration of the MacNamara *tánaiste*,' said an earnest young man. 'Is there anything I can help you with, Brehon?'

'Is Donal O'Brien here?' asked Mara.

'He is indeed, Brehon,' said the earnest young man, his brow clearing of the anxiety of dealing with a Brehon on his own. 'Will you come in and have a cup of ale while I find him?'

'No, I'll wait here,' said Mara firmly and watched him run up the path while she turned over in her mind what she would say to young Donal. This was a difficult situation. It certainly looked as if Donal O'Brien may have been the last person to see Ragnall MacNamara alive. But did he kill him?

'Your knife,' she said, instantly producing the knife from her pouch the moment he arrived.

The shock was immense. When she had shown him the brooch, he had immediately stretched out his hand for it in quite an unconcerned way, but now he actually took a step backwards as if she had slapped him across the face. His sunburned face turned a sickly yellow; under his tan, all the blood had drained away.

'Where did you lose it?' she asked gently.

He stared fixedly at her as if he feared to drop his eyes.

'When you were out hunting?' she asked. 'Did you lose it the same time that you lost your brooch?'

She thought he was going to agree, but then his eyes hardened.

'It's not my knife,' he said rapidly.

She let a pause linger while the shouts of the children echoed off the high stone wall of the tower house.

'Whose is it then?' she asked bluntly. 'Your father's, your uncle's?'

He said nothing. He knew well that only members of the *derbhfine*, of the kin group descended from the one great-grandfather, had the right to use that form of the O'Brien crest.

'Show me *your* knife,' she said after a minute.

He put his hand to his pouch and hesitatingly took out a knife. It was an ordinary blacksmith's knife with no engraving, no crest; it was the sort of knife that every farm lad would carry. It was not the knife of a *taoiseach*'s son.

'And that is your knife?'

'Yes,' he said sullenly.

'And you have had no other?'

'I did have one, a *derbhfine* knife,' he said reluctantly. 'But I lost it sometime ago. I didn't want to bother my father about it. I didn't want any lectures about carelessness so I just got Fintan to make this one for me,' he added, trying to force a note of conviction into his voice.

Unlikely, thought Mara. Everything about him, from his fine leather boots to the gold torc that he wore around his neck, spoke of a man who always made sure that his possessions were of the finest quality. He wouldn't be afraid of his father, either. Turlough had said that his cousin Teige gave the boy anything that he wanted.

'And when was that?'

He hesitated. 'About a month ago,' he said.

'And Fintan made it for you?'

'Well, no, now that I think, that was just an old knife that I had when I was younger.'

'I see,' said Mara and waited until he had drawn a perceptible sigh of relief before she pounced again.

'Tell me about Michaelmas Eve,' she said and watched him keenly.

'Michaelmas Eve?' he repeated, staring at her. He looked horrified.

Mara nodded. The boy was in a state of nerves. Her heart sank. It did seem as if he were guilty. Had he killed Aengus? Or Ragnall? Or both?

'Yes, at the *céilí*, the evening before the Michaelmas Fair. You had an argument with Aengus?'

'He was jeering at Ragnall, taunting him with having to pay a fine.'

'And you intervened, on Ragnall's side? Why was that?'

'Because he was Maeve's father,' said Donal with a simple dignity that impressed her.

'You hoped he would yield and allow the two of you to marry if you stood up for him and took his part.'

'Yes, I suppose so,' Donal said, sounding a little unsure. He smiled then. It was an attractive smile; it lit up his whole face. 'I was a bit drunk,' he confided, with all the assurance of a man whom women, young or old, found irresistible.

'And you followed Aengus home?'

'No.' He sounded quite indignant.

'Where did you go?'

He shrugged. 'Can't tell you,' he said. It sounded so like a small boy, that she found it hard to keep a smile from lifting the corners of her lips.

'Tell me at Poulnabrone, then,' she said casually. 'In front of the people of the Burren.'

That scared him. He looked incredulous, as if he could not believe that anyone could be so cruel. He was spoiled all right. Probably no one had ever said 'no' to him or made him face the consequences of his actions before.

'Well, if you want to know, I came over to Shesmore to see Maeve,' he confided. 'Old Ragnall was drinking fit to burst and I thought it would be safe for an hour or two. Fionnuala knows all about us. She would keep watch and let us know if he were coming.'

'And Maeve will be able to bear witness to that?'

'Of course,' he said. And now he was blithe again. He was young, rich, privileged, and the greatest obstacle to the marriage that he wanted so badly had now been removed.

'Then let us go and see her,' said Mara. 'Get your horse.'

With a lordly gesture he called for his horse and when it came swung himself into the saddle like a man without a care in the world. Mara had said no more while they were waiting, but she had observed him very carefully. He looked quite at ease now, a little scornful, a little amused.

❋

Maeve was at home and came out into the yard as soon as the clatter of the horses' feet sounded on the cobbles. Donal swung himself to the ground, threw the reins over the post and immediately took her in his arms. Mara stayed on her mare, looking at them both. There was no doubt that they were in love. She envied them. It must be a wonderful thing to love so wholeheartedly, not to weigh up reasons for and reasons against. They were an attractive young couple. If the boy proved to be innocent, there would be no objection to this marriage. The king had given the matter into her hands, and she thought she would enjoy seeing their happiness.

Gently she moved her mare a step forward.

'Maeve,' she said, and the girl disentangled herself while Donal gazed adoringly at the small flushed face.

'You remember last Sunday, Michaelmas Eve?' asked Mara. She watched carefully to see whether a look was exchanged between them, but Maeve kept her wide round eyes fixed on Mara.

'Yes, Brehon,' she said demurely.

'In the evening, did Donal come here to Shesmore?'

This time there was a faint hesitation and a quick glance at her sweetheart's face, but that was surely natural. She would be embarrassed about entertaining a young man when her father was not at home. She cast down her long eyelashes over her pink cheeks and said, 'Yes, Brehon.'

'And how long did he stay?'

'A couple of hours, Brehon. He was helping me with the cows,' she added primly.

'So, was it dark before he left?'

Maeve nodded her head with just the faintest touch of hesitation. 'Yes, Brehon,' she said after a few moments.

'What time was it?' asked Mara. She knew that there would be little chance of Maeve knowing the time. Most people took their time by the sun, or by the bells from the abbey or from the cathedral at Kilfenora. Few bothered with a candle clock. However, the question gave her an excuse to call another witness, so as soon as Maeve shook her head wordlessly, Mara called out: 'Fionnuala, would you come out for a moment?'

The stout middle-aged woman appeared at the doorway. 'Yes, Brehon?' she asked enquiringly.

'Can you remember what time your master came home on Sunday night, Michaelmas Eve?'

'I'd say it would be a couple of hours after sundown, Brehon,' said Fionnuala readily.

'And did anyone else come that evening before your master arrived?' asked Mara casually.

This time Fionnuala looked at her young mistress. It was just a quick glance, but undoubtedly some message was passed. Fionnuala turned back to Mara.

'The young master, here, he came for a while,' she said carefully. She nodded her head towards Donal.

'And no one else?'

'No one else, Brehon.'

'And Donal left before your master arrived.'

Fionnuala smiled. 'Yes, he did, Brehon. He went down the lane to Lemeanah as soon as I saw the light from a torch coming from Noughaval.'

Mara nodded. It might or might not be true, but that was the story that they had, all three, decided on. 'I'll leave you now, Maeve,' she said. 'Don't you trouble about escorting me, Donal; I'll take the path back to Noughaval. I'll come and see you again in a few days' time, Maeve.'

Perhaps the news would be good, then, thought Mara as she rode slowly along the narrow pathway that led to Noughaval. Perhaps she would be able to give permission for Donal O'Brien and Maeve MacNamara to be betrothed. If, as it appeared, Donal had been with Maeve for the evening, then he was probably not guilty of the murder of Aengus. But what about the murder of Ragnall? Was he guilty of that? Mara sighed impatiently. Every time she thought of one murder it seemed to get tangled with the other. Was there any possibility that the two deaths were not connected?

Whether connected or not, neither death would leave a great gap in the community. They would not be mourned. The sons of Aengus and the daughter of Ragnall would perhaps be far better off without a father. Nevertheless, the law demanded that the crime should be acknowledged and reparation made. If it were Donal that had killed Ragnall, then a fine would be paid to his daughter and recompense made. But would a daughter marry the man who had killed her father?

However, if it were Niall who had killed his own father,

Aengus, then the crime of killing one of the same blood would be deemed so horrendous that the law would demand that he be banished from the kingdom and condemned to a lonely and terrible end.

ELEVEN

BRETHA CRÓLIGE
(JUDGEMENTS OF BLOODLETTINGS)

Fingal (kin slaying) is the most serious crime that can be committed. No fine can be paid, nor no recompense made, by someone who has killed a member of his immediate family. The murderer is banished from the kingdom by being placed in a boat with no oars and sent to drift out to sea.

❦

'YOU DESERTED ME YESTERDAY,' whispered Turlough as she came and knelt beside his burly figure in the top pew in the church at Noughaval.

'Why aren't you at Mass at Carron Church?' she whispered back, piously etching a cross on her forehead, lips and breast with one thumbnail.

'Couldn't stand another minute of Slaney,' mumbled

Turlough behind the two immense hands which cupped his face. 'I told herself and Garrett that you had invited me to dinner. Murrough was staying on, of course, so she didn't care if I stayed or I went. You won't believe this, but . . .' he said, removing one hand from in front of his face in order to whisper hoarsely in her ear, 'I think she's making sheep's eyes at that son of mine.'

Hmm, thought Mara. If Turlough, always the most innocent of men, had noticed the situation between Slaney and Murrough, then things were getting very obvious. Had Garrett noticed anything, she wondered, as they all rose to their feet while Father O'Connor ambled out from the vestry behind two spry young altar boys bearing lighted candles. Was that, perhaps, why Garrett was so keen to get every lucrative piece of property into his own hands? Was this his only way of keeping the stately Slaney as his own? Murrough had a wife, but she had borne him no sons and he just might seek a divorce from her and marry Slaney. Yes, she decided, Garrett had noticed and this was why he was behaving so stupidly and alienating his clan. He was desperate to load Slaney with all the ostentatious wealth that she felt her origins demanded.

'*Introibo ad altare Dei*,' came the quavering voice of Father O'Connor, and as she sank to her knees Mara gave a rapid glance around the church. Yes, the tall figure of Ardal O'Lochlainn was there just behind them. She made a quick note to see him after church. This is the wonderful thing about the weekly duty of Sunday Mass, she thought enthusiastically, as she devoutly beat her breastbone and joined with the rest of the congregation in the muttered '*mea culpa, mea culpa, mea maxima culpa* . . .' It was such a great opportunity for everyone to get business done that might otherwise take hours of walking or riding between far distant farms and enduring hospitable offers of ale and honey cakes.

As she rose to her feet for the recital of the Gospel, she had another quick glance around the little church. Yes, Niall was there. She must see him also. And so was Fintan, the blacksmith, with his wife and children and the enormous figure of Balor beside them, balancing a wriggling small son of Fintan on his wide shoulders. She would have to ask Fintan about that second encounter with Ragnall on Michaelmas Day. After having spoken to Ardal, she would leave Turlough with him, she planned, while she did her business and then they could ride back down the flowery lanes at a leisurely pace that would give Brigid time to plan a meal fit for a king. Mara smiled to herself. Cumhal and Brigid were at the back of the church with the six scholars and Mara was absolutely certain that at the same time as suspects, motives and opportunities were racing through the mind of the mistress, the mind of the housekeeper was busily reviewing the contents of her larder and her storeroom. Yes, indeed, this weekly Mass was a great institution.

❧

'Ah, Brehon,' said Ardal as she made her way towards the tall, red-haired figure of the O'Lochlainn *taoiseach* as he stood on the steps outside the church. 'I was hoping to have a word with you.' He walked away from the crowd, courteously ushering her in front of him, but at the same time making clear that he wanted privacy. 'You remember I spoke to you on Michaelmas Day about the dispute between myself and the MacNamara over the streams on lands above Oughtmama?' he said.

Mara sighed. She had enough to do without presiding over Garrett and Ardal's quarrel over the water that flowed down from the mountain. Here in the west of Ireland rain fell on two days out of every three in the year. Surely water wasn't that important!

'Well, I had a visit from the MacNamara two days ago. He wanted to know if, now that Aengus MacNamara is dead, I was interested in buying the mill at Oughtmama from him?'

Mara's eyes suddenly snapped wide open in astonishment. This was extraordinary. That mill had been in the hands of one of the MacNamara clan for hundreds of years. Why on earth should Garrett try to sell it? And what about Niall? She frowned thoughtfully.

'Did you understand him correctly?' she asked. 'It wasn't the land above it, the land on the mountain, that he wanted – just so that there was no trouble about the streams?'

Ardal shook his head. His blue eyes were anxious. He was a man who would guard his clan's lands and property with his life, if necessary. This move of Garrett's would be incomprehensible to him.

'No,' he said. 'No, it was the mill itself. He even named a price. He wanted to be paid in silver, not in milch cows or by any exchange of land. He just wanted silver.'

'And what did you say?' asked Mara cautiously. The silver would not be a problem to Ardal, she thought. Unlike most people on the Burren, unlike even the O'Connor, he would have silver. He traded his horses in Galway and exported them overseas and the merchants in Galway paid in silver.

'I asked him what Niall felt about this,' said Ardal in a low voice. He cast a quick glance around. Niall was standing not far away, obviously hoping to speak with either the O'Lochlainn or the Brehon.

'And what did he say?'

'He said Niall had nothing to do with it. He said that Niall was not the son of Aengus, that Aengus had never acknowledged him, that Aengus had no *derbhfine* left alive, so therefore the mill reverted to being clan property and as such could be sold by the *taoiseach*. He was very anxious to get the matter settled, but I told him that I would have to speak with you before even thinking about it.'

'But would you like to buy the mill?' asked Mara.

'I would indeed,' said Ardal vigorously. 'It's great land up there and there are some very good houses left since the time of the monastery. In fact, I thought Garrett was going to do something about those buildings before now – they would be clan land, nothing to do with Aengus, though he was allowed the use of one as a living place. In fact, Garrett himself told me that Slaney had great plans to repair the abbot's house; she was always going up there, he said.'

'What would he have wanted it for?'

'Well, I think perhaps to have it for the next steward. Ragnall was getting too old for the position and Garrett was thinking of having Maol as steward and leasing him the house and some land. Anyway, the sale, so far as I was concerned, would be for the mill itself and the old abbey lands around it, including the buildings on them. I got the impression that Garrett would like to get rid of them. If Maol marries Ragnall's daughter, Maeve, then they would occupy the house at Shesmore of course.'

'So you'd like to buy and he'd like to sell,' mused Mara.

'I think I could do better with the mill,' said Ardal. 'Aengus wasn't a good man as a miller. He liked his own company; he didn't welcome people. A lot of the farmers took to doing their own grinding. If I had it, I would put in someone friendly and hospitable. I have someone in mind. I would do up the abbot's house as his *ban tighernae* planned and then use one of the small buildings as an alehouse. There could be two prosperous businesses there – a mill and an alehouse – and the valley would be a great place for the mares and foals. Even though the MacNamara is asking a high price, it still could be very worth my while.'

It would be, too, thought Mara. Ardal had brains and he was a hard worker. The O'Lochlainn clan were lucky to have him.

'There's only one thing that worries me,' said Ardal, his eyes going to the figure of Niall who still stood silently waiting. 'I would not like any man to be wronged, even if he is not a member of my own clan.'

Mara nodded. Now was the moment to ask her question. 'Do you remember when Aengus bought that small farm from you, here at Noughaval?'

'I do indeed,' said Ardal readily.

'What was your impression of the relationship between Aengus and Niall, then?' asked Mara. It was a hard question to ask of a man who had just seen a new and exciting business proposition open up before him, but Ardal was an honest man. She knew that he would give her an honest answer.

'I thought he bought the farm because Niall was his son,' said Ardal without hesitation and Mara smiled with pleasure.

It was good to know that she was not wrong about him: Ardal O'Lochlainn was straight and honourable.

'My memory is that nothing was put down about a relationship in writing, but that was also my impression,' she said cordially. 'Could you check the deed, Ardal?'

'I've already done so,' said Ardal. 'There is nothing about a relationship there.'

'I see,' said Mara. 'Well, I have promised Niall that I will hear the case at Poulnabrone. He may wish to call you as a witness. Would you be willing to testify?'

'I would be willing,' said Ardal firmly.

'I'll tell him that. I want to have a word with him.' She cast a quick glance over her shoulder. Turlough was obviously coming to the end of civilities with Father O'Connor. 'Go and entertain the king for a few minutes, would you, Ardal. I just want to see Niall.

'Wait for me for a moment, Niall, I must have a quick word with Fintan,' she said as she passed him. He looked very unwell, she thought. He had the look of a man who had not slept. His skin was pale and puffy and there were black smudges under his eyes. Fintan saw her coming and left his wife and family and joined her. She wondered whether Balor had told him of his confession, but Fintan looked relaxed and happy, pretending to roar at a small daughter that ran after him.

'Balor said you were looking for me yesterday, Brehon,' he said. 'Was it about the bench?'

'Oh, I was just passing, Fintan,' said Mara. 'I was coming back from the inauguration of the new *tánaiste* at Carron Castle so I thought I'd stop at the forge. My mare was going lame so I got Balor to have a look to make sure that there was nothing wrong. He said she was fine, and he proved to be right.'

'He's a great lad with horses,' said Fintan genially. 'Well the bench is coming on good, Brehon. I think you'll be pleased with it. Drop by any day, whenever you have the time and, if you like it, myself and Balor will bring it over in the cart and set it up in your garden.'

'That will be lovely,' said Mara. 'Oh, and Fintan, there was something else that I wanted to ask you about. Do you remember when you went back to talk to Ragnall again on Michaelmas Day? Was there anyone with him? He was still in the same place, just near Liam, was he?'

Fintan was silent for a moment. She could see his mind running through explanations for his return, but then he just said simply: 'He wasn't there, Brehon. He was in the church-yard, talking to young Donal O'Brien. I was going to wait, but then I decided to leave the matter. After all I had the . . .'

He stopped abruptly and Mara smiled. 'Yes, you had the candlesticks back by then, didn't you? So you decided, like a sensible man, to leave matters alone.'

Fintan looked embarrassed, but relieved. 'So you've heard that,' he said with resignation. 'I should have known that Balor wouldn't have been able to keep a secret for too long. I went back. I was still in a bit of a temper, but then I calmed down. And like you said, I had the candlesticks back, so I just went home again. That was the way of it, Brehon. There were lots of our clan there. They'll all have seen me. You can ask anyone you like. No one will be able to say that they saw me go into the churchyard.'

'Can you remember what time it was, then, Fintan? Had the bell gone for vespers, yet?'

'No, Brehon, it hadn't. I heard it just as I was going back in through my own gate.'

'Well, Fintan, that's all I wanted to know,' said Mara. 'I'll be along one day to see the bench. I'm sure I'll be very pleased with it.'

She watched him rejoin his family and swing his little girl onto his immense broad shoulders. Turlough and Ardal were deep in conversation, so she walked over towards Niall.

'Niall,' she said, 'on Michaelmas Day was it you that collected the sacks of flour from the mill?'

He hesitated and then nodded. He looked at her fearfully.

'And Aengus gave them to you?' No one could be sure, not even she herself, of the time of Aengus's death, so the question should not strike him as strange.

'No, Brehon, he wasn't there.'

'So how did you know what to take?'

His face cleared. 'I was talking to him at the festival, in the alehouse, the night before. He told me that he might be at Mass at the abbey when we came, but he would leave the sacks by the door.'

'And who took back the damaged sack?'

He looked surprised, but answered readily. 'Old Ragnall himself did that, Brehon. He was riding behind the cart and he saw the trail of flour spilling out from the damaged sack. The lane is narrow there, so he told me not to bother trying to turn the cart. We hoisted the sack onto the saddle of Ragnall's horse and he walked back with it to the mill.'

'I see,' said Mara. So Ragnall had gone back to the mill alone. Had he seen something there? Was the murderer of Aengus hiding when they arrived with the heavily laden cart creaking up the lane and the sound of men's voices? And did the murderer then emerge, only to be seen by Ragnall?

'And did Ragnall say anything when he came back?' she asked, voicing her thoughts.

Niall thought for a moment. 'I don't remember, Brehon,' he said doubtfully. 'He might have done.'

'Well, Niall,' she said briskly. 'I will be judging your case at Poulnabrone on Saturday. In the meantime, I suggest that you gather as many witnesses as you can who will be able to testify if Aengus ever spoke of you as his son, or ever implied that you were his son. Now I must leave you, Niall. I see the O'Lochlainn steward over there and I want to have a quick word with him.'

She left him looking rather glum and disheartened. With his mother dead and nothing written down, it was going to be a difficult case, she thought. Generally a *taoiseach* would be expected to know something like this and his witness would be very important. But in this case the *taoiseach* was new to the area and was hostile to Niall's claim. In fact, thought Mara, this *taoiseach* was desperate for money and would do anything to obtain it. His testimony would not be reliable. His marriage might depend on him getting some extra silver.

❧

'Brehon, you're looking well,' said Liam as she joined him.

'What a lovely breezy autumn morning, Liam,' said Mara. Usually she didn't bother discussing the weather, but she did not want the O'Lochlainn steward to see anything of significance in her query. He was a great man for collecting gossip from all corners of the kingdom and then airing it in the alehouse. She would talk about the weather and try to find an opening into which she could insert her question.

'Mackerel sky, not long wet, not long dry,' he said, eyeing the clouds above. 'You see the look of the sky over there, over the Aran Islands. I wouldn't be surprised if we have a shower before nightfall.'

'Well, we've had all sorts of weather this week,' said Mara seizing the opportunity. 'What with the fog on Michaelmas Day, or did that start on Michaelmas Eve? Niall was telling me that it was misty that evening at Noughaval, was that right? I wasn't at the Michaelmas Eve *céilí* myself; I was busy preparing the scholars' work for the Michaelmas term.'

'No, no, it was a lovely evening,' said Liam. 'But Niall wasn't there. I remember noticing that. What with him living so near, I would have expected him to be there. No, we had a good time that evening. After Aengus and Ragnall had the row, you remember I was telling you about that ... and it was then I looked to see if Niall was there – I thought he might stand up for his father since Donal O'Brien was standing up for old Ragnall – well after all that *comhrac* was over and Aengus and Donal had gone, a group of us took our ale outside and it was almost like summer again.'

'It must have been another day he was talking about then,' said Mara briskly. She had her information now so she might as well depart. 'Are you waiting for the O'Lochlainn, Liam? King Turlough is coming home with me for dinner so I'd better collect him now, or else Brigid will be complaining.' Turlough was starting to look bored, she thought. He liked his conversation with a little more savour than the earnest Ardal could provide.

❋

'So tell me all the gossip from Carron Castle,' she said as they both started to ride along the road from Noughaval to Cahermacnaghten. 'What was the stately Slaney up to with your son Murrough? Don't tell me that they were rolling in the hay, or kissing and cuddling in the barn.'

'Well, of course, they were careful in front of me,' said Turlough with an appreciative chuckle. 'They wouldn't want to take any chance that I would carry tales to Murrough's wife.'

'You wouldn't do that – about your own son!'

'Serve him right. Still, I don't suppose that I would. I don't like her much, Eleanor, I mean. She's too like her father, Gearóid Mór, the Earl of Kildare, as he calls himself these days. The whole family is in the pocket of the English. He is always popping over to London to see Henry VIII. That son of mine would like an earldom, also. He'll make sure that no talk of Slaney ever gets to Eleanor's ears. He will want to keep on the good side of the Earl of Kildare.'

'Slaney would love to be married to an earl,' said Mara maliciously. 'I was wondering if she were thinking of divorcing Garrett and marrying Murrough. Well, if Murrough is not for her, I wonder whether she has any hope of getting Garrett to become an earl. Perhaps we'll see herself and Garrett trotting across to Kildare one of these days.'

'Garrett! That fellow is just a *sóerchéile*, a vassal, of mine. I'd stick a sword in him if he betrayed me like that,' shouted

Turlough so loudly that a donkey, which had been enjoying a heap of small red crab apples under the hedge, came running up and stuck his head over the wall with an alarmed hee-haw. Turlough gave a sudden shout of laughter, the donkey tossed his head with an even louder bray and the two bodyguards who were following at a discreet distance came galloping up, full of alarm.

'All right, all right,' said Turlough, looking slightly embarrassed. 'Nothing's wrong. It's the Brehon's fault,' he added. 'She was making a joke about a donkey and then up comes another donkey to enjoy the fun. Ride ahead, lads. Tell Brigid we are on our way and I am starving.'

'So how's your murder case going?' he said as the bodyguards, with a few uneasy glances around, rode on down the road towards the law school.

'Complicated,' said Mara. 'You see, if Malachy could even tell me which one was killed first, I would have something to go on. It seems unbelievable that there should be no connection between two deaths within a few hours of each other and each man belonging to the same clan.'

'What could the connection be though?'

Mara drew her mare to a halt and Turlough did the same, looking at her enquiringly. 'Let me think,' she said. 'Let me draw a picture, that's the way my mind works best.' She stopped for a moment, her mind shifting through the confusing facts, placing them in order, discarding some and putting others to one side, for the moment. Turlough watched her affectionately, his green eyes alert and interested.

'Let's take this for a possible story,' said Mara slowly. 'It's Monday morning, a foggy, cold morning. Aengus is in his mill; the murderer is there also. He wants to murder

Aengus. He creeps up on him with his knife, or perhaps it is a heavy stick. He knocks him on the head, or slits his throat – the second I think.'

'Why?' asked Turlough.

'Because that would be a reason to put the gate over the man's throat – it would hide the wound.'

'Why bother?'

'Wait a minute,' she said. 'Don't interrupt me. I'm just feeling my way in the dark. The murderer kills Aengus, carries his body outside, and places it under the sluice gate in a clumsy attempt to make it look like suicide. The sluice gate falls down on the man's neck, probably breaking it.'

'And then?'

'And then,' she said triumphantly, 'Niall comes in, sees the bags of flour for the Michaelmas tribute all lined up by the wall, takes them out one by one and places them in the cart, turns the cart and goes back down the lane.'

'Why was Ragnall murdered then?'

'Well, Ragnall was a mean man and as he followed the cart he saw a tiny trickle of flour coming from a hole in one of the sacks. They could not turn the cart in that lane – it's only about six foot wide the whole way down the hill, so Ragnall loaded the sack onto his own horse, went back and saw the murderer, perhaps heard a sound, went out and saw him putting the body under the sluice gate.'

'So the murderer murders Ragnall.'

Mara nodded.

'But not until the evening, not until sundown at the Michaelmas Fair. Why the wait?' Turlough questioned.

'Well, that makes sense,' pointed out Mara. 'After all, Niall was there, with the cart. He couldn't tackle two men.'

'And why did Ragnall say nothing if he did witness a murder? Was he planning blackmail?'

'That I don't know,' said Mara. 'My picture is fading now. You were interrupting too much.'

'Not at all,' said Turlough with a grin. 'I'm just teaching you to think sensibly, and not to go off on wild flights of fancy.'

'The other picture, of course,' said Mara, ignoring this, 'is that Aengus was actually killed on Sunday night, after the Michaelmas Eve festival. Now that . . .'

'Brehon.' Shane was running up the road, his black hair blowing in the fresh wind from the west. He stopped abruptly and gave a quick bow to the king. '*Tá failte romhat, a thighernae*,' he said quickly and then turned to Mara. 'Brehon, Brigid sent me to tell you that the Brehon of Corcomroe and his wife are waiting to see you. Oh, and Hugh and me are helping to baste the roast goose while Brigid is making the apple sauce. Brigid says to tell you that the goose will be ready in a wee while,' he finished, lapsing into his north of Ireland dialect, as he made another quick bow, turned and fled back down the road.

'Roast goose!' said Turlough reverentially. He was a man who worshipped his food and Brigid always laid her best in front of him.

'Fergus and Siobhan MacClancy,' said Mara in tones of despair. Fergus was a nice, kind man, who had been very good to Mara, taking on the duties of Brehon of the Burren when her father died and then influencing the king, Turlough's uncle, to appoint Mara herself as a Brehon. Mara was fond of him, but he was never good company and Siobhan was an immensely boring woman.

She could see them now. They were standing at the gate of the Brehon's house, looking eagerly up the road.

'We smelled the goose all the way up the road,' shrilled Siobhan. And then she saw the king. She bowed reverentially. '*Dia's Muire agat, a thighernae*,' she said respectfully and Fergus's quiet voice echoed his wife's.

'I just wanted to see you, Mara, for a minute about this affair of the merchant Guaire O'Brien, but I won't interrupt your Sunday,' he said.

'No, no,' said Mara forcing herself to be hospitable. 'You must stay and have some dinner with us. There will be plenty of goose for us all. Brigid always cooks too much of everything.' The scholars would be disappointed, she thought. There would be few leftovers after this meal. Fergus, despite his frail looks, was a good trencherman and Siobhan's stout frame openly proclaimed her love of food.

'Well, if you're sure,' said Siobhan with a cursory show of reluctance. 'Shall we go inside, my lord, while Fergus and Mara talk business? Brigid has a lovely fire in the sitting room.'

Turlough gloomily followed Siobhan indoors. Mara found it hard to suppress a smile. His expression was so like that of a small boy denied a treat. She turned to Fergus.

'Guaire O'Brien?' she questioned.

'Yes, the linen merchant, from Kilfenora, I understand he was at your Michaelmas Fair.'

'That's right,' said Mara. 'He was in a bit of trouble for giving short measure.'

Fergus nodded grimly. 'So I understand. That was not all, though. He got very drunk that night at an alehouse in Liscannor and he was stabbed by a Frenchman who got back onto his boat before he could be caught.'

'I see,' said Mara, wondering why Fergus was telling her all of this. This was a Corcomroe affair and outside her jurisdiction.

'The thing is,' said Fergus, 'when we returned Guaire's pack to his widow; I went with it myself because this pouch, that was at the bottom of the pack, puzzled me. It was full of silver and it didn't seem likely that it was belonging to Guaire. Anyway, when I opened it and showed it to the widow, she said she had never seen it before.'

He reached into one of the saddlebags that hung on either side of his ancient horse and produced a pouch, adding, 'Look, the thongs have been cut. I brought it over to show you as I heard that he had been at the Michaelmas Fair here at Noughaval that day. Do you recognize it?'

Mara looked at the heavy leather pouch, blackened with age and with hard usage, and then she looked at the startlingly white ends of the slit thongs and she nodded.

'Yes,' she said. 'I know who it belonged to.'

'Well, perhaps you can return it to him,' said Fergus placing the pouch in her hands.

'I can return the silver,' she said slowly, 'I know who the silver belongs to, but the pouch belonged to another man and he has been in his grave for the last two days.'

TWELVE

CÓRUS FINE

(THE REGULATION OF THE KIN GROUP)

If a man is unable, through poverty, to pay the fine for a murder or other serious offence, then his fine (kin group) must pay it.

However, if the offender dies, then no payment need be made.

⸙

'So it looks as if one of the murders is solved already then, Brehon, is that right?' said Enda, in the tones of one who feels himself hard done by. He had obviously been looking forward to putting his keen brain to work on solving the double murder.

'It looks a bit like that, Enda,' admitted Mara. At the end of a long day of hard work she had taken pity on her pupils and had allowed them to put away their books and to sit grouped around the fire to discuss the two murders that had taken place in the community. Enda had looked very tired, he had been working until very late the night before in the schoolhouse, and the two younger boys had been yawning, but now all faces brightened.

'Will Guaire's widow have to pay the *éraic* to Ragnall's daughter, Brehon?' asked Fachtnan in concerned tones. 'That will be hard on her if she has ten children.'

Mara smiled slightly at him, appreciative of his humanity and concern for the widow and orphans while she deplored his lack of law knowledge.

'She won't, will she, Brehon?' said Shane eagerly. 'I'm sure she won't.'

'Can anyone remember the saying of Fíthail?' asked Mara, looking around.

'"*Marbhaid cach marbh a chinta*", every dead man buries his offences,' said Enda promptly.

'So that means that even if Guaire killed Ragnall, his widow is not responsible for his crime,' said Shane. 'That's the law, isn't it, Brehon?'

'He did kill him, bird brain,' said Aidan.

'Has it been so declared at Poulnabrone?' asked Mara, fixing him with a cold eye.

Aidan squirmed slightly, taken aback by the formal words.

'No,' he mumbled, 'but it's obvious, isn't it?'

'*Post hoc* is not *propter hoc*,' said Enda with the lofty superiority of someone who has just attained the ripe age of seventeen. 'And that means "*after which*" isn't the same as "*because of which*",' he added in a patronizing way to Aidan.

184

'The fact that Guaire had the pouch after Ragnall was found dead doesn't mean that Guaire killed him.'

'Perhaps Guaire stole the pouch from the dead body,' said Hugh unexpectedly. He seldom took part in these discussions, relying on ten-year-old Shane for a lead in most things. Possibly he just lacked confidence. His mother's death earlier in the year, on the day of his twelfth birthday, was a great shock to him. Mara gave him an encouraging smile.

'That's a very good point, Hugh,' she said. 'It might have happened that way.'

'Guaire could have gone into the churchyard to, well . . .' said Aidan eagerly.

'To relieve his bladder,' prompted Mara.

'That's it,' chimed in Moylan, 'to . . . Anyway, he might have seen the dead body of Ragnall stretched out there on the grass and the pouch full of silver.'

'So he slit the straps and shoved the pouch under his mantle and came out and jumped on the mule and rode off towards Liscannor.' Shane's voice was excited.

'It's more likely that Guaire was the one that killed him,' said Fachtnan. 'I think if you found a man stretched out dead on the grass of a churchyard, the first thing you would do is to give a shout. He wouldn't keep silent, would he? He wouldn't have just gone up and started poking around to see if there was something that he could steal without saying a word.'

'You're forgetting that he had done very badly at the fair,' said Hugh. 'I know that; I saw his face after the Brehon made him give new lengths of linen to everyone that he had cheated. And after that no one went near him. He would have felt that the fair was hardly worth going to. He might have wanted to come home with enough silver to have made it worth his while to have gone to the Noughaval market. He would know that Ragnall was wearing a pouch full of silver. Anyone at the fair would have known that.'

'I think Guaire would probably be a more likely murderer than Donal O'Brien,' said Fachtnan. 'I can't see Donal committing a murder.' He and Donal were friends and Fachtnan's honest young face looked very troubled. Mara sympathized with his feelings, but her experience told her that almost anyone could commit murder if the circumstances were right. Fachtnan, as far as she knew, had never been wildly and passionately in love in the way that Donal O'Brien was at the moment. It was quite likely that Donal might have made a last appeal to Ragnall, hoping that his support of the old man in the argument between him and the miller the evening before at the Michaelmas Eve *céilí* would have gained him approval, and then, if Ragnall refused him once more, perhaps turning away in disdain, Donal could have picked up the stone cross in a fit of rage and brought it down on Ragnall's head.

But, of course, it could have been Guaire. The picture of Guaire, packing his goods, including all the unsold, too-short lengths of linen, then taking his mule and perhaps tying it up to the gate pier so that he could pay a quick visit to the churchyard before setting out on the route to Kilfenora – that picture was almost irresistible. Guaire could have gone into the churchyard, seen Ragnall, snatched up the stone cross and killed him. It would all have taken only a few seconds, including the removing of the pouch. Alternatively, of course, he could have found Ragnall already dead, wondered whether to raise the alarm and then settled on a quick snatching of the well-filled pouch. On the whole, though, Mara was inclined to agree with Fachtnan. The likelihood was that Guaire O'Brien from Corcomroe had killed Ragnall. His reputation was bad and he had both motive and opportunity.

If that were what happened, then Turlough would certainly welcome it. His last words to her before he departed after dinner were, 'Let me know if there is any further news about young Donal O'Brien.' The support of Donal's father, Teige, was of great importance to Turlough.

'Go and have your supper now,' she said to her scholars. 'And if the field is not too wet, then you can have a game of hurling afterwards.'

She accompanied them to the door of the kitchen house. 'Don't worry about supper for me, Brigid,' she said, putting her head in the door. 'I'll have a few oaten rolls and some cheese later on. I think I'll go down to Fintan's place and have a look at the bench he's making for me.'

'Would you like me to saddle your mare, Brehon,' said Seán, putting down his knife and cup of ale and rising respectfully to his feet.

Mara considered the matter for a moment; she enjoyed walking, but her mare would welcome a trot along the road and Balor would be delighted to see the horse again.

'Yes, I think I will ride, but there's no hurry,' she said. 'Finish your meal first.'

Brigid gave Seán a quick, irritated glance when he sat down and looked like continuing to munch his enormous hunk of bread, so he instantly rose to his feet again. Brigid slapped down a pan on the iron grid and muttered something under her breath. Mara looked at her with amusement. Brigid was quick thinking and energetic and Seán was slow and lazy. However, today Brigid seemed even more impatient than usual. Her sandy hair was sticking up wildly where she had run her fingers through it, her normally pale face was flushed and her green eyes looked stormy. Of course, usually Cumhal kept the peace between Brigid and Seán.

'Cumhal's not back yet, is he?' asked Mara with a quick glance around the kitchen. Earlier in the day she had sent Cumhal to Garrett with the pouch full of the silver from the Michaelmas tribute.

'No, he's not, Brehon,' replied Brigid. 'I've been expecting him. Perhaps they delayed him at Carron Castle.'

'Probably they gave him a meal,' said Mara reassuringly. There had been a slight note of anxiety in Brigid's voice and even now she looked slightly sceptical at Mara's explanation. She was not one to worry needlessly about her husband, who was a strong, courageous man, so her anxiety communicated itself to Mara. Two men had been killed during the last week, perhaps because of this Michaelmas tribute. Cumhal should have been back long before. She should have ordered him to take Seán with him, as a guard. Still it was possible that Garrett and his wife would be so overjoyed at the safe return of the silver that perhaps they would be more generous than normal and ply Cumhal with food and drink. Or perhaps Cumhal had decided to do some job before returning. He was the farm manager and he was his own master so far as anything to do with the farm was concerned. As long as he had got safely to Carron Castle, there would be no need to worry about his return journey.

It was time that these two murders were solved, thought

Mara impatiently as she waited by the mounting block at the gate, gazing at the hedge across the road. October was now well on its way. Soon it would be *Samhain*, that festival that marked the dying of the year. The leaves were already beginning to fall from the hawthorn bushes, leaving the dark red berries dangling from tiny bare stems. The rough farm hedge was a thing of beauty that evening, with the hundreds of tiny silken webs woven between the black hips of the burnet roses and the stiff berry-laden stems of the hawthorn. The webs glistened silver with the moisture in the air. The spiders must have done these this morning; the night had been too wet for such fragile threads to survive from the day before. Even as she watched, a flock of linnets, the feathers on their breasts and heads still flushed with the summer rose-coloured hue, swooped down to feed from the berries, their three-clawed feet breaking the webs, before scattering in a panic as Bran, her wolfhound, came bounding out, ahead of Seán and the mare.

'I'll take Bran, Seán,' she said. 'He'll enjoy the run.' She mounted her mare and crossed the road, lingering for a few moments by the hedge. Yes, already a few spiders were busy repairing the damage to their webs. She watched them for a moment, admiring how unerringly the gossamer threads from their bodies formed the complicated wheel-like pattern, all leading to where the juicy fly could be trapped in the centre. This was what she had to do now: see the pattern and trace back the filaments that could attach the murderer to the murdered.

As Mara trotted down the lane to Noughaval, the memory of the worried look in Brigid's eyes reproached her. She was responsible for maintaining the king's law in this kingdom of the Burren and a miasma of surmise and suspicion would soon poison the usually friendly and relaxed community. Fachtnan was right of course. It would be convenient if Guaire O'Brien, an outsider from Corcomroe, were responsible for one of the murders, but that still left the mystery of the miller's death to be solved.

'*Herself*'s here, Master!' came Balor's gruff voice when she appeared at the forge. He dived inside. For a moment she wondered if he feared the wolfhound, but he was back almost instantly, dangling a heavy iron bench from one hand, his huge face split in an ear-to-ear smile. Fintan followed him and both watched her face eagerly and beamed at her cry of delight. The bench was beautifully made, broad and comfortable with plenty of space to seat two people.

Mara dismounted from her mare, handing the reins to Balor. She lingered for a moment looking at him. It gave her great pleasure to watch the happiness in his face as he stroked the narrow, well-bred head of the mare and blew softly into her nostrils. Then she crossed over to the bench and examined all the details. The strips of iron that formed the seat were as smooth as silk and the armrests were shaped into ovals, each one large enough to hold a cup of wine. The back swooped up and down in two noble curves and the pair of holly wreaths, suggested by Fintan, nestled within the centre of a spiral beneath each curve. There were even tiny berries amongst the holly leaves.

'It is beautiful, Fintan,' said Mara. 'I never imagined that it could look as good as this.'

He beamed with pleasure and Mara spent another minute examining the bench before adding: 'Oh, by the way, Fintan,

I wondered if you had seen the merchant Guaire O'Brien at the fair on Michaelmas Day? You remember that time when you went back and you saw Ragnall in the churchyard talking to Donal O'Brien?'

'That would be the linen merchant, from Corcomroe, Brehon?' asked Fintan with a puzzled look. Obviously the news of Guaire's theft and his death that night had not spread to the Burren yet.

'That's the one,' said Mara, noticing that Balor was looking at his master in a worried way. He was devoted to Fintan and, even though he might not understand many words, he was sensitive to any atmosphere. She smiled at him again and stroked the bench appreciatively, her fingers tracing the intricate spirals of iron. He joined her, still holding the reins in one hand and patting the iron with the other, almost as if the bench were a horse that would welcome his appreciation.

'Yes, I did see him, Brehon. I think he was packing up, then,' said Fintan pondering. He was quite untroubled by her query. 'Yes, he was. I remember thinking that mule of his was a bit small for the load of linen he was putting on its back. I'll tell you who might have seen more, though: Liam O'Lochlainn. He'd see everything, standing up on the great big wooden box of his. He's a great man to notice things, too. You should hear all his stories in the alehouse. You should go and see him, Brehon, on your way home.'

'I'll do that then, Fintan.'

'We were wondering about painting the bench, Brehon,' said Fintan. 'You can see it has had its first coat of paint, black just like you wanted. We'll give it a second or third coat before we bring it over to you. The thing is, that Balor here has got it into his head that he wanted to do the berries in red. What do you think?'

Mara hesitated for a moment. She liked the simplicity of the black iron bench, but one look at Balor's eager face made her quickly come to a decision.

'Red for the berries would be beautiful,' she said smiling at Balor. 'Red is a lovely idea.'

'Well, Balor will do it for you then,' said Fintan. 'He's a great hand at doing the small delicate bits. I always leave that sort of thing to him. You'd be surprised how good he is at painting.'

'The school cob!' exclaimed Balor turning his head towards the east.

'That must be Cumhal,' said Fintan. 'Balor knows the sound of all the horses around here. Yes, it sounds like that cob of his. I know the way he bangs his feet down on the road. Run out to the road and tell him that the Brehon is here, Balor.'

Balor quickly shambled out and bellowed, 'Whoa!' Mara and Fintan followed. Bran wagged his tail and ran ahead of them. The cob and he were great friends. Cumhal slowed his pace and then reined in the cob.

'I'll see you when I come back, Cumhal,' said Mara. 'I'm just going to ride over to Lissylisheen now.'

Cumhal looked uncomfortable, and she added, 'All is well?'

'Yes, Brehon,' he said. He still looked ill at ease so she watched him narrowly and saw him give a quick glance at Fintan and Balor.

'I'll just wait and go along a stretch of the road with you, Brehon,' he said carefully.

Mara was about to tell him to ride on, that Brigid was worried about him, but something in his expression checked her.

'That will be nice,' she said affably as she waved a farewell. Cumhal said nothing until the two men had returned to within the forge and even then he spoke in a low voice.

'Brehon, there was a bit of trouble up in Carron.'

Mara shielded her face from the western sun and turned to look closely at him.

'At the tower house? What happened?'

'Well, when I arrived at the gatehouse with the pouch, the MacNamara himself came out. I thought he would just take it and thank me. But he took me into the hall. And he started to weigh out the silver.'

'To *weigh* it?' asked Mara incredulously, her voice rising. 'From the pouch!'

Cumhal edged the cob a little further over onto the grass verge to make more room for Mara to ride on his left side. Then he lowered his voice even more. 'And then the *ban tighernae* came in and she started doing it, too.'

So Slaney herself came to check the contents of the pouch, no doubt to see how much she had to spend on the latest improvements to her husband's property. For once, Mara was speechless.

'I think that's Niall coming down the road with his blue cow and calf,' said Cumhal with an alert ear for the usual sounds of the country. 'We'll just pull the horses in at this gate until he passes. She's a bit nervous-like, that cow.'

What on earth did Garrett hope to find out by weighing the silver? wondered Mara as she automatically smiled at the plump little calf and greeted Niall. He didn't look too well, she thought, but her mind was too full of the extraordinary behaviour of the MacNamara and his lady wife to wonder about Niall.

'They were taking out all the leases from the big chest in the hall and looking at them and making lists of what had been paid in tribute last year and of what was given, who would have paid silver,' continued Cumhal, clicking his tongue at the cob who had just found an inviting piece of grass on the far side of the gate.

'So they were looking at the leases, then,' said Mara thoughtfully, reaching out to pat the cob who had obediently forsaken the interesting grass and was now plodding determinedly towards home and stable and evening meal.

'That's not all, Brehon,' said Cumhal. His tones were hushed and embarrassed. 'They say that not all the silver is there. There should have been more. They want to see you, Brehon. They want you . . .' here he hesitated, but seeing that Mara's enquiring gaze did not waver, he continued bravely. 'The *ban tighernae* said that she wanted an explanation from you, and the *taoiseach* agreed with her. They want you to come and see them tomorrow morning.' His voice was distressed and embarrassed and he avoided her gaze. She understood him well. He had served the father, and then the daughter, and every fibre of fierce Gaelic loyalty was given to her. Any insult to her would be of grave importance to him. He and Brigid would die for her, and she had to remind herself continually not to underestimate the strength of that allegiance. She smiled grimly as the picture of Slaney's stately

194

figure, summoning her to Carron, came to her. No one else in the whole kingdom of the Burren would treat the Brehon, the king's representative, with such discourtesy. Mara pulled up her mare and stayed standing in the middle of the road. Cumhal stopped also and sat pulling the cob's ears and looking at the distant slopes of Slieve Elva. Bran looked enquiringly from one to the other.

'Well, well, well,' said Mara lightly. 'Do you know, I think I will do just that. I'll go and see them and put them both right about a few things. Cumhal, would you take Bran back to Cahermacnaghten? I think I will pay the MacNamara and his wife a visit today. I don't want to waste the lads' time tomorrow; they need their schooling. I'll ride up to Carron this evening. I'll be back before dark. Go with Cumhal, Bran; good boy.'

'I'll take Bran back and then I'll come and ride with you,' said Cumhal firmly. 'You don't want to be going up there on your own. It wouldn't be fitting.'

'Oh, nonsense,' said Mara firmly. 'You've had a long day, and I don't suppose they gave you anything to eat while they were busy weighing silver and consulting ledgers. You take Bran back and have your supper and keep an eye on the lads for me. No, you go now, Cumhal. I'll be fine.'

After they had gone Mara waited, standing quite still on the road, until she was sure that Bran was going happily with Cumhal. Her mind was busy. She didn't care in the least about Slaney's rudeness. She would soon put her straight on the sort of behaviour that should be shown to the high office of Brehon. No, that was not what made her thoughtful. Suddenly Garrett MacNamara was revealed as a man who was so desperate for silver that he would even offer a discourtesy to the Brehon – someone whose honour price was lower only to that of King Turlough Donn himself. No one else in the Kingdom of the Burren would have done that.

The day was turning chilly and Mara cast a worried eye over her shoulder as she galloped her mare along the road towards Carron. The western sky was ominous with wild slashes of silver behind the soft black down of the clouds. There might be a storm in a few hours. She had no desire to accept any hospitality from the MacNamara and his unpleasant wife. However, there was a road going all the way along the valley from Noughaval to Carron and her mare was fit and in a mood to enjoy a flat-out gallop. She would just say what she had come to say and then depart immediately. There would be a couple of hours before sundown. If it rained, it rained. Mara was philosophic about that. Anyone who lived in the west of Ireland was used to the rain and her *brat*, or mantle, with its combed woollen surface, made a rainproof and windproof covering.

She wasn't the only visitor coming to Carron Castle on this late afternoon. As she approached the tall, gloomy tower house, she heard the sound of another horse galloping fast towards her. Mara slowed her mare, as the road was narrow at this spot. She would wait until the horse passed before turning up through the magnificent iron gates, presented as a Michaelmas tribute by Fintan.

However, the other horse slowed also, and as the rider approached Mara saw who it was and schooled her face to present a grim appearance.

'Slaney,' she said with a nod of acknowledgement, but omitting the usual greetings and blessings. She deliberately

crossed the road in front of Slaney and her horse and proceeded up the avenue in front of the *ban tighernae*. She was
pleased to notice from a quick glance over her shoulder that
Slaney had looked quite taken aback and seemed content to
follow the Brehon meekly up the avenue. Neither spoke until
they reached the courtyard in front of the great oak door.

'Find someone to take my horse,' said Mara in tones of
cool command. Slaney was looking very flushed and ill at
ease and, to Mara's surprise, even slightly guilty. A man
rushed out from the stable and then looked from one to the
other uncomfortably. Mara walked her horse to the mounting block and held out the reins to him. He came instantly
and meekly took the reins while she dismounted.

'Murty,' shouted the stableman and a boy rushed out and
started to lead Slaney's horse to the mounting block while
Mara hung on to the stableman's hand for longer than usual,
ensuring that Slaney clambered awkwardly down without
assistance. Mara turned away from her and addressed the
stableman.

'Fetch the MacNamara,' she commanded. 'Tell him that
the Brehon wishes to speak to him.'

He rushed off to the barn, looking alarmed. Garrett was
doubtless counting over the tribute in there, as he appeared
in a minute followed by bald-headed Maol. No doubt Maol
was being taught the steward's duties.

'Ah, Garrett,' said Mara. 'I wish to speak to you. Shall
we go inside?'

A quick glance passed between husband and wife, but
neither spoke. Both followed her meekly in through the door
and up the steep winding staircase to the hall above. There
was no fire in the hall and the room was damp and chilly. A

197

large chest, full of scrolls of parchment and sheets of vellum, stood in the centre of the room, its lid thrown back and its contents untidy and jumbled.

'I've received an extraordinary message from my farm manager, Cumhal,' said Mara, looking from one face to the other. 'He said that you had *summoned* me. Can this be correct?' She was pleased to notice that the right degree of astonishment and incredulity sounded in her voice.

'No, no,' stuttered Garrett, but Slaney was made of sterner stuff.

'That is correct,' she said defiantly. The flush had faded from her face and her prominent blue eyes were hard as pebbles.

'Oh,' said Mara icily. It annoyed her that the statuesque Slaney was so much taller than she. She looked around the room. There was a carved chair, luxuriously padded with red velvet cushions, placed beside the empty brazier. Mara crossed the room and sat on it. Now Slaney and Garrett were left standing awkwardly together in front of her like a pair of scholars waiting to receive a scolding.

'Tell me what the problem is,' she said.

Garrett looked at his wife and she did not fail him.

'The problem is that we don't think there is enough silver in the pouch,' she said aggressively. She seemed to have recovered completely from her earlier embarrassment. Mara raised an eyebrow and continued to stare at her.

'We would just like an explanation of how the pouch came into your hands.' Was there, perhaps, a slight emphasis on the words *your hands*? wondered Mara.

'Oh, didn't Cumhal tell you?' she said with an air of surprise. 'You should have asked him,' she continued.

'Yes, yes,' stuttered Garrett, but once again Slaney interrupted him.

'If you could just tell us the whole story, Brehon,' she said, trying to make her shrill, high-pitched voice sound soft and sweet.

'Guaire O'Brien, the linen merchant from Kilfenora, was killed in a fight,' said Mara evenly. 'He was in an alehouse in Corcomroe. When the Brehon of Corcomroe heard that there was a pouch full of silver in the dead man's possession he went himself to the widow. She confirmed that the pouch was not belonging to Guaire. The Brehon was told that Guaire had been at the Michaelmas Fair in Burren so he brought the pouch to me. I confirmed that it was Ragnall's pouch so I sent Cumhal over to you.'

'You looked inside the pouch?' Slaney's question was delivered with the speed of a cat pouncing on a fleeing mouse.

Mara allowed a long silence to fill the chilly room before she replied.

'The Brehon of Corcomroe opened the pouch, showed me the silver. If he had not done so, I would have sent the pouch over to Shesmore so as to return it to Ragnall's daughter. No doubt you have returned the man's personal private property to Maeve by now. Perhaps that's where you were coming from?' she added to Slaney, knowing that the woman had been riding from the opposite direction. Garrett was mumbling something about Oughtmama and the mill when Slaney cut across him again.

'Of course, neither of us would suspect either you or the Brehon of Corcomroe of tampering with the money,' she said with the sweet air of one who is too innocent to believe any evil.

'Of course not,' said Mara coldly.

'It's just that we feel the full sum of the tribute was not contained in the pouch,' continued Slaney.

'I can't help you with that,' said Mara. She put her two hands on the carved arms of the chair and made as if to rise.

'Oh, but you can,' said Slaney quickly. 'The MacNamara and I believe that Guaire O'Brien must have removed at least half of the silver and left it, probably at his house and in the care of his wife, before going to the alehouse. We want you to see the Brehon of Corcomroe and make arrangements for the missing silver to be returned. If it is not done within two weeks, then I understand that the Gaelic custom is for a blood feud to be declared.'

'A blood feud!' echoed Mara allowing her voice to rise until it was almost as high as Slaney's own. She didn't need to act astonishment, though. For a moment she was completely flabbergasted. She turned to Garrett, who was looking worried and embarrassed.

'Garrett, you were born and brought up here. I know that you have spent several years away, but you must know the laws of the kingdom better than that. You certainly can't declare a blood feud over a case of suspected theft. And I must tell you, Garrett . . .' now she allowed all of her fury to sound in her voice '. . . that I personally think that pouch is probably as full now as it was when Ragnall wore it less than an hour before his death.'

'We've been looking at the amounts in the ledger books,' said Slaney. 'We've added them up. Not enough silver is here in the pouch.'

'Yes, but,' said Mara impatiently, 'amounts are often stated in silver – I do this myself for fines, sometimes, but the fine can be paid in anything worth that amount of silver. You have a barn full of flour and honey and skins and everything else that the clan have managed to find for you. You will soon begin to learn of the customs here,' she added, deliberately allowing a note of condescension to sound in her voice.

'There didn't seem to be enough silver, though,' said Garrett, his voice soft and apologetic as if to try to make amends for his wife's belligerence.

'I can't help you with that,' said Mara flatly. 'Did you order Ragnall to write down amounts given as soon as he received them?'

'No,' muttered Garrett. 'I suppose he just went on doing things the way he did them when my father was alive.'

'And there was never any trouble then,' stated Mara. 'As far as I know,' she added struggling to retain a feeling of impartiality.

'Well, what happens now, then?' said Slaney impatiently. 'Do you try the case at Poulnabrone? If this were Galway, the woman, the wife of this Guaire O'Brien, would be arrested and thrown into prison and brought before a court. Surely there is something that you can do, even in a place like this.'

Galway! thought Mara. They don't even have a law of their own there, but have to ape English laws. Imagine throwing a poor unfortunate woman into prison and probably torturing her, just because of some silver!

'There is no case to be heard,' she said aloud, her voice flat and authoritative.

Slaney stared at her, open-mouthed.

'You mean you refuse to hear the case.'

'I am giving you my professional opinion that there is no case to be heard. No one knows how much silver was in the pouch. It looked fairly much as it looked when I saw Ragnall at Noughaval. If you have no further evidence, then there is no case.'

'Well, what can we do then, if we are refused justice by you?'

'You can come and fast from food for several days outside my gate if you think that you have not been fairly treated,' said Mara dryly, with a quick glance at Slaney's voluptuous figure. 'The law gives you that right and the custom was often used in the past. If you fast for three days and three nights outside my gatepost, then King Turlough himself will hear your case against me.'

Mara allowed a minute's silence while she enjoyed the expression of horror on Slaney's face. Then she rose to her feet quickly and flashed a bland smile at both. She could not afford to have dissension in her kingdom, she reminded herself. 'I'm sure that when you think about it, you will see that you must drop this matter,' she said soothingly. 'Now, alas, I must leave you. The affairs of the kingdom keep me too busy for long visits.'

'You will have a cup of wine before you go,' stammered Garrett. She noticed that his face had gone very pale. The mention of the name of King Turlough Donn had probably frightened him.

'No, I won't,' she said. 'Brigid will have my supper waiting for me.'

They hadn't asked her to supper, she noticed, but Garrett now made quite a ceremony of calling for her horse and he himself handed her into the saddle. The light was fading as she walked her mare slowly across the courtyard and she noticed that the barn was now illuminated with an orange gleam from many lanterns. Figures moved within, stacking bales, salting meat and emptying sacks into bins. It looked as if a large tribute from a fairly minor clan had been exacted. Why were Garrett and Slaney now so anxious about a few ounces of silver?

Thirteen

Míashlechta (sections on rank)

A taoiseach *should have many servants.*

Foremost among these is the steward. He is the man who collects the tribute, arranges the work of the other servants, and who looks after the food and drink and sleeping places in his lord's household.

A steward's honour price is half the honour price of the taoiseach.

朶

What a shame that Turlough was not there; he would have enjoyed that, thought Mara, allowing a laugh to ring out as she galloped along the narrow valley that carved its way through the Aillwee Mountain. The wind was gusting strongly from the west, blowing back the hood of her *brat*, but the picture of Slaney fasting before her gate in order to obtain justice was enough to keep her in good humour.

'I'd better send Cumhal with a letter to Turlough,' she muttered. As overlord, the king should be aware of the danger towards the peace of the region posed by Slaney's plans of a 'blood feud'. Now she was half sorry that she had put the hearing of Niall's case forward to the following Saturday. The sooner the whole situation of the mill was resolved the better.

The trees were bending and straining in the wind by the time that she reached Caherconnell. For a minute she hesitated. There was no doubt that the weather was worsening. Overhead came the harsh squawking of gannets and kittiwakes taking refuge inland from the Atlantic storm. The wind was so strong that it almost seemed to be snatching the breath from her lips. Perhaps the sensible thing to do would be to stay the night with Malachy. He and Nuala would be delighted to see her. Brigid wouldn't worry; she would assume that her mistress had spent the night with Garrett and Slaney at Carron Castle.

However, it had not begun to rain yet and there were only two more miles to go. The mare was pressing on strongly. Her Arab blood gave her stamina and courage. She tossed her head and looked back at her mistress and then galloped on. In any case, thought Mara, I have too much to do to waste any more time. I must get home tonight and I must devote the whole of tomorrow to these two murders. Mentally she began to sift through the possibilities. Suddenly it seemed to her as if she could solve it as she would solve a tricky piece of law. The affair was intricate, but the visit to Slaney and Garrett had cleared her mind and allowed her to concentrate on the essentials.

The pace was exhilarating; she always loved the west

wind; loved to feel the salt on her lips, and the strong rush of wind blowing through her coiled and braided hair seemed to clear her mind. She would take each case separately and solve each one and then she would see what the connection was, she resolved.

'Motive and opportunity,' she said aloud to a startled pine marten emerging from a slot in the stone wall, carrying a large rat in its mouth. She wished it well as it darted back into the shelter of the wall. She hated rats and the pine marten was very beautiful with its cat-like face and its enormous bushy tail. Winter was coming on and the wild creatures of the Burren would soon face their annual struggle for survival.

The storm was getting worse. The sky to the west had turned to the blue-black colour of the sloes on the blackthorn bushes on either side of the small lane. Now she half regretted not seeking hospitality at Caherconnell. A brilliant spiked line of lightning flared up ahead of her and for the first time the mare slowed her pace. Two minutes later thunder rolled its solemn drumbeat. The rain began to fall in great sheets of water, blowing directly into their faces and hissing on the slate-black clints in the fields. The mare put back her ears.

'Easy now, girl, easy,' murmured Mara. To her left was the tall, grey, crenellated outline of Lissylisheen tower house. Without hesitation she turned the mare's head towards the gleam of light coming from the courtyard. Instantly a man emerged from the stables, a slit sack covering his head from the worst of the rain. Another man raced towards the heavy front door and hammered on it. It was opened in a second; the first man took her horse and Mara ran towards the hospitable door. A minute later she was inside.

'Brehon, you're very welcome! Come in. Come in. Are you wet?' Ardal came clattering down the stairs.

'Hardly a drop,' said Mara, slipping off her *brat* and shaking a few raindrops from the tightly curled outer surface. 'This faithful companion of mine has kept the rain off me for nearly twenty years now.'

'You wouldn't believe it, but I sell quite a few of these to England,' said Ardal, taking it from her. 'Irish mantles, they call them there. They fetch a good price. I find it's a great use of the wool and, of course, I have about a couple of thousand sheep these days grazing up on the Gortclare Mountains, up above Oughtmama.' He carried her *brat* into the guardroom and hung it carefully near the fire. 'Come upstairs. You'll have some supper? Liam is here. We were talking of you a few minutes ago, and wondering how you were getting on.'

Liam was standing at the window gazing out at the storm when Mara entered the hall. It was a smaller room than the one in Carron, but much cosier, she thought, with a large fireplace now filled with burning logs of scented pine. The table was black with age, but gleaming with polish, each point of candlelight reflected in its glistening surface. The walls were plastered and newly limewashed and a couple of large wolfhounds dozed by the fire.

'You are well, Brehon?' asked Liam, his voice as resonant of good living and fine drinking as was his large comfortably covered frame. 'We saw you turn in as we were looking out. You just got here in time. Look at that storm now!'

'I hear I'm just in time for supper,' said Mara joining him and looking out at the pewter sky streaked with silver. Once again the jagged lightning zig-zagged down. They waited in silence and then eventually came the explosion of the distant clap of thunder.

'It's moving away,' said Liam. 'That'll be over in a couple of hours.'

'Have a cup of wine, Brehon,' said Ardal hospitably. 'You'll enjoy this. It's a good wine. I bought it from your own son-in-law, Sorcha's husband, in Galway. You sit by the fire here and Liam will entertain you while I go and make sure that they have a good supper to put before you.'

Mara took the proffered cup and settled down on a cushioned chair by the roaring fire. Liam came and lowered his massive form into the seat opposite. They were on good terms, the O'Lochlainn and his steward. Liam had the air of being very much at home here within the walls of Lissylisheen tower house. He turned his beaming smile on her and threw a few more logs onto the fire.

'You're out in bad weather,' he said.

'I've been up to Carron to see the MacNamara,' she said, sipping the wine. Yes, it was a good wine, rich with the fruity taste of the Rhône valley wines.

'Didn't get supper there, I warrant,' said Liam with a knowing chuckle.

Mara smiled, drank some more wine, but did not comment. She had been Brehon long enough to realize that her lightest word was wafted immediately through the whole kingdom of the Burren and that the greatest significance was placed on her utterances. Only with Turlough would she allow herself to joke about Garrett MacNamara and his wife.

'We have a good roast saddle of lamb for you, Brehon,' said Ardal coming back in, followed by a manservant who laid the trenchers on the table and placed a sharply pointed eating knife beside each place. Another servant bearing a flagon of wine followed him and together they went to and fro, spreading the table with bowls of rosy red apples and baskets of crusty small loaves of bread.

'Lovely,' said Mara happily. Normally she preferred beef, but the O'Lochlainn lamb, fed on mountain herbs, was always tasty and her ride through the storm had given her an appetite. She sniffed appreciatively as the large joint was carried in.

'Sit here, Brehon,' said Ardal, pulling out a chair and carefully placing a soft, velvet cushion on it. He poured some more wine into her cup and then took up a long sharp knife and began to cut well-shaped slices from the meat.

'We were talking about old Ragnall,' said Liam taking the left-hand side of his host and handing bread across to her. 'I was just saying to the O'Lochlainn that it seems amazing that he is dead. I can see him there at the fair, sitting on that horse of his, waiting for the clan to pay the tribute. Any news yet of his killer?'

'Not yet,' began Mara and then she stopped. She stopped partly because the servants were bringing in small jugs of creamy garlic sauce and more iron dishes piled high with turnips, and roasted apples, but also because something had struck her about Liam's words. She chewed a piece of tender sweet-tasting lamb and swallowed some wine before she identified the full significance of what he said.

Yes, of course, Ragnall's horse, where was that horse? Now she could remember the scene clearly. Niall had his own horse to pull the cart. When they arrived at Noughaval Fair, Niall had unhitched his horse and taken it back with him to his own farm, no doubt so that the animal could be fed and watered and rested after his strenuous morning. But Ragnall had stayed, mounted on a horse, a white horse with a wall eye, Mara remembered.

'What happened to the horse?' she asked, looking keenly at Liam.

He was taken aback: she could see that.

'I wouldn't know, Brehon,' he said staring at her blankly. 'What did happen? Has no one found it?'

'Not that I have heard,' said Mara. She watched them both. This had surprised them.

'Did he take it into the churchyard with him?' asked Ardal, holding a piece of lamb on the end of his knife. Liam finished chewing his before he replied.

'Do you know, I think that he did,' he said in the end. 'If I remember rightly, he just rode in there through the gates.'

'Seems strange to take his horse in,' remarked Ardal. He seemed about to say more, but then hesitated.

'My young lads think that he probably went in there to urinate,' said Mara blandly.

'Well, yes,' said Ardal, looking slightly embarrassed.

'You'd've thought he would have got some youngster to hold his horse for him,' remarked Liam, ladling a few more slices of lamb onto his trencher.

'He had a nasty temper that horse,' said Ardal. 'I remember someone offered me a foal with that breeding and I refused it. It may have been that Ragnall was not able to leave it with a boy in case it bit him. I wonder that we haven't heard about it though. My land stretches all around Noughaval. I would have been told if anyone found a horse straying.'

Mara swallowed some of her wine and shook her head to the offer of turnips. The affair of the horse would have to be solved but in the meantime she might as well glean as much information as possible.

'Of course, he may have gone in there to meet someone, to talk to someone,' she said thoughtfully. 'You said you saw him talk with Donal O'Brien, Liam.'

'Yes, but Ragnall was the one that went into the church-yard first and then young Donal O'Brien followed him in,' said Liam.

A question hovered on Mara's lips about the linen merchant but she decided not to ask it for the moment. After Slaney's talk of a blood feud she had no desire to start any speculation that it might have been Guaire O'Brien who killed the MacNamara steward. She turned to Ardal.

'So you're running two thousand sheep on the Gortclare Mountain, are you, Ardal?' she asked, picking a fresh apple from the bowl and munching it appreciatively.

'Yes,' he replied, looking at her keenly, 'on my land above Oughtmama.'

This was the second time that he had mentioned Ought-mama so she was not surprised when he added hesitantly, 'I suppose the MacNamara said nothing more to you about selling the mill to me.'

'No, he didn't,' said Mara dryly. 'I don't know yet that it is his to sell. Niall declares that Aengus was his father and that he was acknowledged as the miller's son. As you know, I am going to try the case on Saturday at Poulnabrone.'

'We were just talking about this before you came, Brehon,' said Liam with an encouraging look at his *taoiseach*.

'You see, Brehon,' said Ardal tentatively, 'I was wondering

whether, if it is shown that Niall was the son of Aengus and if he does inherit the mill, then . . .' He stopped for a moment and then finished. 'Well, Liam here suggested that I might be able to buy the mill from Niall. I've set my heart on having that mill now and I wouldn't care what it cost me.'

'I'm not sure about whether you could do that,' said Mara cautiously. 'The situation is complicated. I've been looking into the year books from a while back and it looks as if the mill was clan property at one stage and then the *taoiseach*, that would have been some sort of a cousin of Garrett's grandfather, sold it to the father or grandfather of Aengus.'

'So it definitely belonged to Aengus,' remarked Liam triumphantly. He put down his knife and leaned across the table.

'Yes,' said Mara slowly. 'It belonged to Aengus, and to his father before him, but the circumstances are slightly complicated. There was a *banna* on the property.'

'But tribute was paid,' said Ardal eagerly. His blue eyes sparkled. He loved the law. The more intricate a matter was, the more it interested him.

'Yes, tribute was paid. It had to be paid every Michaelmas – the amount was not specified. The phrase used was "fair tribute". That's in a lot of old leases. This is where the tribute is different from the English law about taxes. English taxes always specify the amount to be paid. But to go back to the mill . . . After tribute, all revenues from the mill were to belong to the miller, but the *banna* specified that the mill was to be used for the good of the clan and the clan was to have preferential use of it.'

'I see,' said Ardal. He looked somewhat downcast. Obviously the idea of owning the mill had gripped him. She could just imagine, looking around the neat, well-cared-for room and remembering the carefully groomed O'Lochlainn land and livestock, that Ardal would have made a great success of the mill at Oughtmama.

'So the mill would be no good to us even if Niall was willing to sell, is that what you're saying, Brehon?' asked Liam. She was surprised to notice how frustrated he looked.

'I was just thinking that if the MacNamara himself offered you the mill then you could perhaps claim that he had given up the *banna* on the property,' said Mara thoughtfully. 'It's a complicated legal problem, though. I would certainly have to consult King Turlough Donn on this matter.'

'But you think it might be possible, Brehon,' pressed Liam. 'I'm sure that the king would abide by your advice.'

I'm sure he would, thought Mara, but her policy was always to defer to the king's judgement in public. It was a ploy that she found very useful in order to postpone a decision.

'Well, we'll have to see,' she said vaguely, draining her cup and sitting back in her chair. 'Of course, you don't know whether Niall would be willing to sell to you, or not, so I suggest that you wait until after the judgement at Poulnabrone on Saturday. King Turlough himself may attend.'

'I would say that Niall would sell,' said Ardal thoughtfully. 'I don't think that he was ever too interested in the mill. That was probably why Aengus bought the farm for him. He's a good man with the cows, Niall. Mind you, I'd say Aengus was not an easy man to work for. Poor Balor was willing, but Aengus terrified the lad out of the few wits that he has.'

'Why don't you build a mill for yourself?' queried Mara. 'Why does it have to be the MacNamara mill? I can imagine there would be a lot of trouble about that. It has been in MacNamara hands since time immemorial.'

'There's no suitable river on O'Lochlainn land,' said Ardal. 'All those streams up in the mountains are just trickles. It's only by combining them that enough flow is got to work the mill. Running water is valuable around here. You know what this place is like: plenty of rain, but no rivers.'

'Of course,' said Mara. 'I hadn't thought about that. You're right, of course.' The O'Lochlainn clan owned most of the land in the kingdom, but the Burren limestone seemed to swallow up the water and hold it underground. There was only one river in the kingdom that would have sufficient flow to turn a water wheel and that was in the hands of the MacNamaras.

'We could perhaps have a word with Niall before Saturday,' suggested Liam. 'Would you be agreeable to that, Brehon? We've always been on good terms with Niall. We lend him a neighbouring hand from time to time.'

'I think it would be best not,' said Mara decidedly. 'If you are going to give evidence of belief in Niall's paternity, Ardal, then it would look as if Niall might have bribed you by offering to let you purchase the mill. Surely it can wait until after Saturday?'

'Of course, of course,' said Ardal hurriedly. He was a very courteous, sensitive man and Mara could see now how he was hunting in his mind for a subject of conversation that would close the matter of the mill. 'It was a good day at the Michaelmas Fair, Brehon, wasn't it? Did you see much of it?'

'Yes, I did,' said Mara. 'It turned into a lovely afternoon, didn't it?' Ardal had given her the opportunity to slip in the question that she wanted to ask Liam so she turned a smiling face towards him, saying, 'I suppose the fair went on well into the evening?'

'Yes, after the foggy start it turned into a lovely day, thank God,' he replied. 'I don't think a single one of the merchants packed up until nearly sundown and even then most of them carried on with the *craic* in the alehouse.'

'Even Guaire O'Brien, the linen merchant?' she queried with a light laugh. 'I would have thought he would have gone straight home after Áine and a few other women had dealt with him.'

'No, no, he stayed to the end of the fair. I don't suppose he did much business, though, once he had cut the right lengths for everyone. No, I saw him go at sundown.'

'So he didn't have a chat with Ragnall in the churchyard, did he?' asked Mara.

'No,' said Liam slowly. The gleam in his eye showed that he understood her question, but he repeated, 'No, Ragnall went into the churchyard on his horse a good half hour before Guaire packed his linen up. I remember seeing the cart unattended for quite a while. I kept expecting to see Niall come along any minute with his own horse to pull the cart away.'

'And Niall came as Guaire was leaving?'

'A bit after, I'd say. Guaire was one of the first to pack up. I didn't actually watch him go myself, I was too busy organizing our own men to get the O'Lochlainn tribute properly stowed onto the carts. Then, as I said, we all went

215

into the alehouse. Rory, the bard, had a new song, and Roderic was there with his horn, and, all in all, we made a great night of it.'

'Another cup of wine, Brehon?' asked Ardal hospitably.

'I won't, thank you,' said Mara. She got up and walked over to the window. The two men joined her. The rain had ceased.

'You can see I was right,' said Liam. 'You find that at this time of the year. The storms just blow in from the Aran Islands and then they blow themselves out.'

'Liam is a great man for the weather,' said Ardal, smiling appreciatively at his steward. 'You can always get a forecast from him. We never start the haymaking until he gives the word.'

'I think I should get back now, Ardal,' said Mara. 'I need to prepare some work for my scholars; I have a busy day ahead of me tomorrow.'

I must go to Shesmore first thing tomorrow morning, she thought as Liam clattered down the stairs to order her horse to be brought round. Her mind went back to the picture that Liam had drawn of Ragnall, still mounted on his white horse, going into the churchyard. What had made him get off his horse? And what had happened to the horse afterwards?

'Thank you, Ardal,' she said aloud. 'That was a lovely meal and it's always a pleasure to be in your company.'

'The pleasure is all mine, Brehon,' he said with his usual grave politeness, but his face did not look too happy as he accompanied her down the stairs and helped her onto her horse. Liam joined him. The last view she had of them, as she looked back before turning into the Cahermacnaghten road, they were both still there on the doorstep, both still staring solemnly after her.

Once out of sight of the two of them, Mara slowed her mare to a steady walk. She needed time to think. Obviously this business with the mill was of great importance to Ardal. He was that sort of man. He had set his mind on something; he had planned out his whole course of action; he had calculated the expenditure of time, energy and resources; he had decided that it was worth doing.

But why was Liam wearing an angry flush? And why was he rubbing the knuckles of his clenched fists together in the manner of a man who had been frustrated in an ambition?

FOURTEEN

Bretha Nemed Toísech
(Judgements of privileged persons)

A man may rise from his position in life by several means. If he is a farmer and he does well he may buy land and from being an ocaire become a bóaire. If he is a servant, such as a steward, or a herdsman, he can only rise by accumulating silver and setting himself up as a briugu, hospitaller. To be a briugu, a man should have the wealth of one hundred cows, a 'never-empty cauldron' and a fine house, built of stone and near to a public road.

HARA HAD GONE ONLY a little way down the road when a familiar deep-toned bark rose up. She smiled. Diarmuid was still nervous of taking his dog, Wolf, out, but from childhood onwards he had always obeyed Mara. *Take him out of that yard and among people*, she had ordered, so he compromised by taking the massive, half-wolf, half-sheep dog out at night and in bad weather. In that way, he did not meet too many people, but could still assure Mara that he had been trying to socialize him.

'Take Wolf into the field, Diarmuid,' she called now. 'My new mare, Brig, hasn't met him yet and she might be alarmed. Wait for me and I'll join you. We'll walk down to your place together.' She waited for a minute until she heard the sound of the metal gate clang and then she shook the reins and the mare responded instantly.

She would enjoy a walk with Diarmuid and Wolf, she thought. It would clear her head of all the puzzling features of this double murder. The clouds had now blown away from the moon, the road was flooded with light and the air was clean and fresh.

There was someone else out walking on the road. As she came near to the law school she could see a blond head moving rapidly down the road ahead of her.

'Enda,' she called and he turned and came back to her.

'Having a walk?' she asked.

He nodded. In the moonlight his face looked pale and his eyes were circled with black shadows.

'I felt as if my head was going to burst if I studied any more of *Bretha Déin Chécht*, so I came out to get some fresh air,' he said with a tired yawn.

'Don't work too hard,' she said gently, studying his face. He puzzled her this term. He had always done well in the past with the minimum of effort. He was one of those lucky boys blessed with brains and a superb memory and up to now he had seemed determined to get as much fun out of his time at law school as possible. However, this term he had gone at his books as if he could not waste a single second.

'Is something wrong, Enda?' she asked.

He gulped. It was almost as if he were trying to gather up his courage, though he had always been very much at ease with her and with all other adults in his life.

'Brehon,' he said, 'I was just wondering . . .'

'Yes,' she said encouragingly.

'I was just wondering if I could take my final examination this year when Fachtnan does,' he said, the words coming out in a quick rush as if they were words that he had practised many times before. 'I know I'll only be seventeen,' he added quickly, before she could answer, 'but I really would like to try. I'll work hard.'

Mara considered the subject. There was no reason why he could not try. She would not have agreed last year when he had been silly and troublesome, but now he seemed suddenly to have grown up.

'Is there any particular reason for this?' she asked, looking at him closely.

He looked around and then lowered his voice. 'My father is having a spot of trouble, Brehon,' he said. 'The murrain has hit his cattle.'

'I see,' said Mara. The murrain was a serious disease for cattle. Every farmer dreaded it. This accounted, perhaps, for the change in Enda this term.

'When did it happen?' she asked. 'Was it during the summer?'

He nodded. 'Yes,' he said in a low voice. 'It was terrible. They have all had to be slaughtered and he is planting flax on the land.' He hesitated for a moment and then said: 'He told me that he didn't think that he could afford my law school fees next year.'

'I see,' said Mara. She had a feeling of compunction towards Diarmuid waiting patiently in the soaking wet field, but she had to sort this matter out quickly. It was probably the silence, the darkness and the privacy of the empty road that had made Enda open up to her.

'Well, I think you could certainly attempt your final examination this year, Enda,' she said calmly. 'You would have a very good chance of passing it if you go on working as well as you have been doing, but in any case you need not worry. There is a fund here at the law school, which was set up by the king to cover the fees for any promising student in need of it and it is not being used at the moment, so you may have it for the rest of your time here with me. Tell your father when you go home for Christmas that there is no need for him to pay the fees for the Hilary and Trinity terms; the fund will cover these and next year, if necessary.'

And that, she thought, feeling rather pleased with herself, came out very well. She was sometimes amazed by her own ability to tell a convincing lie. It was perhaps a pity that she had mentioned the king, but she would warn him not to give her away if Enda attempted to thank him. Turlough was a very compassionate man and was always very interested in her young scholars. He would probably insist on immediately setting up this imaginary fund.

'No, don't worry about it,' she interrupted the boy's gratitude. 'Now take Brig in for me, will you; ask Seán to look after her and feed her. Oh, and Enda,' she called after him as he was leading the mare through the gate, 'ask Brigid for some sausages for Diarmuid's dog and bring them straight out to me.'

Without waiting for an answer she walked rapidly down the road and called over the hedge, 'Bring him out, Diarmuid.' Normally she approached Wolf with a sausage in her hand, but she thought by now she need not bother. She opened the gate and they came out in a burst of compressed energy, Wolf ahead, towing Diarmuid who was clinging on to the chain lead.

'There's my boy,' said Mara affectionately. She bent down and stroked the massive golden head, fearlessly reaching beneath the ferocious jaws to scratch the soft hair under his chin. 'You're a lovely boy, aren't you, there's a good Wolf, now don't put your muddy paws on my good gown.'

'Someone's coming,' said Diarmuid nervously. His grip tightened on the leather handle of the chain.

'Now, Diarmuid, you're not doing the right thing at all,' scolded Mara. 'You must get him used to people. When you pull him back like that you are sending a message that there is danger. You must tell him that people are not to be feared or hated. Give him to me. Enda,' she called out, 'stand still and as the dog comes near, you just put a sausage on the ground. Diarmuid, give me the lead. No, give it to me. I'll manage him. Come on, Wolf, there's a good boy. You'll like Enda. He's fond of dogs.'

What Enda's thoughts were about this, she did not know, but she walked resolutely up the road, with Diarmuid on the other side of the dog, his hand stretched protectively out, ready to snatch the lead at the first opportunity. Enda, she was pleased to note, was following her instructions, standing very still at the side of the road. As they neared him, he threw the sausage on the road, saying calmly: 'Here you are, Wolf.'

'Good boy, Wolf,' said Mara encouragingly. 'Just throw another one, Enda.' While Wolf was gobbling down this sausage, she moved quickly so that now she was side by side with the boy. Wolf looked up abruptly. A slight growl began in his throat but Enda forestalled it by dropping another sausage. This time Wolf wagged his tail slightly. Then Enda held out a sausage in a steady hand and Wolf took it from his opened palm.

'Good boy, Wolf,' repeated Mara. She walked rapidly on before Wolf could change his mind, calling over her shoulder, 'Well done, Enda, that took courage. Don't study any more tonight, like a good boy. A tired brain doesn't work so well. Now, Diarmuid,' she said, as she handed the lead back to him, 'that's what you should be doing. Make the dog see that you trust him and that you trust the people around him.'

'Yes, Brehon,' said Diarmuid meekly and Mara felt a twinge of conscience. Why should she lecture the poor man about his own dog? I suppose it's all gone to my head, she thought, with a moment's unwonted humility; I am surrounded by people who are continually saying 'Yes, Brehon' and 'No, Brehon' and regarding everything that I say to be of huge importance. It's just as well that I have Turlough to laugh at me and to keep me in my place!

Diarmuid's house was a typical *bóaire*'s establishment – a house of twenty-seven feet long with two rooms: a warm and cosy kitchen with the peat fire glowing in the hearth and a bedroom beyond. Wolf went straight to the ancient knotted rug before the fire and lay down there as one who was quite at home. Mara followed and took her place on the cushioned settle on the left-hand side of the fireplace. Little had changed in that room since the days of her childhood when Diarmuid's father and mother had still been alive. On the top wall, above the fireplace, there still hung a collection of St Brigid's crosses, made from twisted rushes and most of them faded to a pale parchment colour. A few smoke-blackened joints of ham hung from the rafters, turning slowly in the draught from the fire, and the painted wooden shutters were closed over glassless windows. The dresser, built by Diarmuid's father, still stood against the bottom wall of the room and the same unchanging collection of pewter mugs and candlesticks stood upon its dark, polished surface.

'Don't bother with any ale for me, Diarmuid,' she said briskly as she saw his hand go to the flagon that stood on the floor beside the dresser. 'I've just been dining with Ardal O'Lochlainn at Lissylisheen and I couldn't eat or drink another thing. But have some for yourself,' she added hastily, noting how obediently he replaced the stopper on the flagon the instant that she spoke.

'No, I won't bother,' said Diarmuid sitting on the three-legged stool opposite to her.

'I remember the two of us sitting here, side by side, on this old settle,' said Mara with a smile. 'Your mother used to give us oatcakes spread with honey. I used to love them.'

'I've got some here now,' said Diarmuid jumping to his feet and bringing over an oatcake, liberally spread with honey, before she could stop him. Mara accepted it, not liking to mention that she now hated anything so sweet.

'Do you still keep bees?' she asked, holding the platter in her hand and wondering how she could avoid eating it.

He shook his head. 'No, I gave my last lot to young Niall when he set up as a farmer. He gives me pots of honey from time to time. I don't need much. Niall does well with them. He sells the honey at fairs.'

'He's become a very good farmer, hasn't he? It's surprising really as he was brought up to the milling business. Do you think that he will go back up to Oughtmama if he gets the mill?'

Diarmuid shook his head. 'The word is that his *taoiseach* doesn't want him to have it.' He carefully avoided looking at her as he said this, kneeling down to tend the fire, and she took the opportunity to slip the oatcake to Wolf. Dear Diarmuid, she thought affectionately, he was being very careful to show that he wasn't trying to get information from her. However, she had no such compunction. He would be one man that Niall would certainly talk to. She said nothing, just held her hands out to Wolf allowing him to lick the stickiness of the honey from her fingers and then gently scratching the soft downy fur behind his large upright ears. Diarmuid got up from the floor and sat back again on his hard wooden seat. And still Mara waited for him to be the one to speak.

'Niall was saying to me that if he did get it he would stay on at Noughaval, but sell the mill and the lands and the old abbot's stone house to Liam,' he said after a minute.

'Liam!'

'Yes, the O'Lochlainn steward.' Diarmuid seemed surprised at her astonishment.

'But why would Liam want a mill?'

'Well, according to Niall, one of the cowmen at

Lissylisheen told him that Liam has been egging on the O'Lochlainn to buy the mill ever since the MacNamara *taoiseach* offered it to him.'

'Garrett MacNamara offered the mill to the O'Lochlainn!' exclaimed Mara in tones of well-feigned amazement.

'Oh, yes, hadn't you heard that?' returned Diarmuid. 'They say that Garrett MacNamara has overspent himself and that he is in the hands of money-lenders in Galway. The word is that he is desperate for money.'

Mara was silent. Amazing how matters which she had considered to be secrets, locked within her breast, were actually being discussed over the hedges and in the fields of the kingdom! Though, when she thought about it, it was not so surprising. Life was lived mainly out of doors and voices carried. Liam and Ardal, no doubt, had been discussing this matter for days. Perhaps the whole kingdom had by now worked out the solution to these two murders that troubled her so much.

Suddenly she felt sick of the whole affair. She leaned past Wolf, threw a sod of turf on the smouldering fire and smiled at Diarmuid. She wished that she could relax and just enjoy an evening's gossip with an old friend. They could chat together with Wolf lying on the mat between them and turning his large noble head from one to the other as the conversation flowed and ebbed. Perhaps this could have been her life if she had married Diarmuid instead of her fellow student, the stonemason's son, Dualta. Perhaps this could still be her life. Dearest Diarmuid, he would make an excellent husband, but . . . Mentally, she shook herself. She was Brehon of the Burren and she had a job to do. She could not afford to waste this opportunity of a talk with someone who, simply and honestly, would tell her all that he knew. Diarmuid was a man that everyone would confide in. She was not a silly girl, musing about her lovers, she reminded herself sternly; she was thirty-six years old and a woman with great responsibilities.

'Tell me all about it,' she said, and her voice was calm, friendly and detached. 'Why on earth should Liam want the O'Lochlainn to buy a mill?'

Diarmuid chuckled and stretched out his legs to the fire, leaning his back against the warmth of the chimney wall. 'When did Liam ever want anything to happen unless it was to benefit himself? Only the birds in the air know how much he has salted away for himself. He's been steward to the O'Lochlainn clan for the last forty years. Never took too much off anyone, mind you. It was just a matter of a little present here and a little present there, a sheaf of oats, a flagon of ale, a bit of silver, but over the years it has all been mounting up. Of course it helps that Ardal O'Lochlainn and his father, Finn, before him, were not the type to be counting. The tribute was something that the clan gave and were thanked for and there was no looking into it and no questions asked. The O'Connor is the same, but this new young *taoiseach* of the MacNamaras is a very different matter. The word is that the clan don't like him. Who knows what might happen next?'

'And now Liam wants to be a miller?' Mara decided not to discuss the MacNamara problem any further. And she was still puzzled by the news that Liam was the one who wanted the mill. Aengus was probably not too much younger than Liam, but he had been a stringy, active man who had been doing the work for most of his life. She couldn't see Liam heaving sacks around and running up and down the stairs of the mill. In any case, his honour price as a steward would be higher than that of a mill-owner.

Diarmuid shook his head with a smile. 'No, not the mill,' he said. 'Liam would have no interest in the mill. He'll buy it, perhaps, and put someone in and charge a rent, or else perhaps it is the O'Lochlainn himself who wants the mill. No, what Liam had in mind was the big stone building there, the old abbot's house. He was going to have it repaired and he was going to set himself up as a *briugu*.'

'A *briugu*!'

'Well, Liam loves company. He'd even hope to entertain the king himself once he got everything set up. It would be a great place for a hospitaller, there at Oughtmama. It's just off Clerics' Pass and all the merchants travelling along that road from Galway to Burren or Corcomroe or Thomond would be inclined to stop and stay the night there or at least have a drink and a meal.'

'I know that. Yes, it would be a good place. I just wondered if Liam could possibly be rich enough to be a *briugu*.'

'Oh, he's rich,' said Diarmuid wisely. 'And, of course, he has no family. Never did marry! There's no point in him dying rich and then his money just going back into the clan. That's the way that he would look at it. He would want to enjoy his last few years. He must be sixty now if he's a day. If the O'Lochlainn buys the mill, then he would put in a miller and perhaps an inn for the ordinary people to come and drink their ale, and Liam would be there with his finger in every pie. He would love it. It would be a substitute for a wife and family for him.'

'I wonder why he hasn't anyone,' mused Mara. 'He would have been a handsome fellow in his youth before he ran to fat. I'm surprised that he didn't marry.'

'It happens,' stated Diarmuid. He stretched out a hand towards her, and then hastily withdrew it and placed it on Wolf's head. 'I thought I would get married myself once, but . . .' He raised his eyes and looked at her. 'It didn't work out for me then, but I sometimes wonder if it could work out for me now.'

It was as near to being direct as anything that Diarmuid would ever say to her; Mara understood that. She knew that he would not wish to appear presumptuous: that he, a farmer, would seem to be putting himself forward as a husband for the most powerful woman in the kingdom. He would also, she thought, not want to jeopardize the warm friendship that existed between them by embarrassing her in any way. All those thoughts went through her quick brain in a few instants and in that time she realized that she could not offer this man, who had loved her faithfully and for so long, a second-best marriage, a marriage for companionship and convenience. She rose to her feet, placing her hand for a second on top of his and then withdrawing it.

'Ah, Diarmuid,' she said compassionately, 'I don't know any woman in the world who would be good enough for someone like you.'

FIFTEEN

AN SEANCHAS MÓR
(THE GREAT ANCIENT TRADITION)

If there are no sons to inherit from a father, then a daughter is known as a banchomarbae *(female heir) and is entitled to a share in his goods. She inherits all of his personal goods, but only land of the amount suited for an* ocaire, *or small farmer, and this land reverts to the kin-group after her death. However, if her husband is a landless alien, such as a Briton, then the land passes to her sons.*

&⅋℘

'CUMHAL, COULD YOU SPARE a man to take a letter to the king at Arra?' said Mara after breakfast on Tuesday morning.

'Yes, of course, Brehon,' said Cumhal promptly, putting

down the axe with which he was attacking a cord of fire-wood. Cumhal always chopped wood first thing on autumn and winter mornings. Mara suspected that it was his way of warming himself for the day, and also keeping out of Brigid's path as she bustled around the kitchen house, cooking breakfast for the scholars and for the farm workers. Brigid's temper was always fairly lively first thing in the morning.

'The king is not at Arra though, Brehon,' continued Cumhal, mopping his brow. 'I think he is at Lemeanah.'

'Oh,' said Mara. She was surprised. It had certainly been Turlough's plan to go straight home when he had left her on Sunday afternoon. Perhaps he stopped at Lemeanah to discuss young Donal with Teige and then was persuaded to stay the night. 'How do you know?' she asked. It was amazing how Brigid and Cumhal between them always managed to know in minute detail everything that happened on the Burren.

'I met the *mac an rí* [king's son] outside the gates at Carron,' explained Cumhal. 'He asked how you were, and he told me that he was riding down to join his father at Lemeanah.'

'Well, that's good, then, if the king's there; that will only take half an hour,' said Mara. 'You might send Seán,' she suggested as Brigid's voice rose to a shriek urging Seán to keep out from under her feet.

❋

The scholars looked rather forlorn when they came into the schoolhouse after breakfast and saw a heap of work awaiting them.

'I'm afraid that I will have to leave you this morning,' said Mara. 'Fachtnan, you will be in charge, and, Enda, I know you will give him all your assistance.' Enda, she was pleased to note, sat up straight and opened his books with a resolute air.

'I will be back around noon, or if not then, well, very soon after. I'll certainly be back before you finish eating your dinner and then I would like you to help me. I want you to ride around the Burren. I have a list of everyone that I saw at the fair, and Hugh will be able to add to that list. Fachtnan, I will give the list to you, and when all the scholars have finished their work then you and Hugh will be able to go through the names and each scholar can spend the afternoon interviewing these people and getting their memories of the Michaelmas Fair, and in particular,' here she paused and looked around at the six young faces in front of her, 'in particular,' she repeated, 'you must note their memories of Guaire, the linen merchant from Corcomroe. Liam, the O'Lochlainn steward, thinks that Ragnall had already disappeared from sight before Guaire left. If that is true, then Guaire may not have been responsible for his murder.'

'But could Liam be sure?' asked Shane shrewdly. 'After all, the walls of the churchyard are pretty high.'

'Liam was standing on a box,' said Hugh. As the only member of the law school present at the Michaelmas Fair, he now considered himself as an authority on this murder case. Even the older boys had been cross-questioning him on the details. It had suddenly given him the confidence in himself that he had lacked previously.

'And Ragnall was on a horse, you remember him on his big white horse, Hugh? Well, Liam says that he rode the horse into the churchyard.'

'No horse when we went into the churchyard on Tues-

232

day morning,' said Aidan alertly. 'And we were the ones that found the body.' He gave an aggressive stare at Hugh.

'And we looked all round the churchyard to see if the murderer was hiding behind the gravestones,' said Moylan, with the nonchalant air of one who would happily capture a few murderers before breakfast.

'We'd definitely have seen the horse.'

'And he wasn't a quiet horse, either,' said Hugh judicially. 'He was always tossing his head and neighing. He even tried to kick at Bran when I passed Ragnall at the Michaelmas Fair. I'm the only one of you that has been near that white horse,' he said, looking back at Aidan, with innocent blue eyes widely opened.

'Well, where did the horse go then, Brehon?' said Aidan, turning disdainfully away from his junior.

'I don't know,' admitted Mara. 'I thought I would go down to Shesmore today and see if it had returned home.'

'Wouldn't Ragnall's daughter have sent you a message, Brehon?' queried Fachtnan. 'I'm sure that she would have done that.' He blushed slightly as he said the words. He would, perhaps, have seen Maeve with Donal O'Brien. She was a pretty girl. Fachtnan would not like to believe any harm of such a girl.

'Perhaps she and Donal killed her father,' said Enda enthusiastically. 'Then they would have hidden the horse, wouldn't they? Could that be a solution to Ragnall's murder, Brehon?'

'Perhaps we should come with you to Shesmore, Brehon,' suggested Moylan hopefully. 'We could sneak around the stables and see if the horse is there and then confront them with the evidence.'

'It mightn't be safe for you to go on your own, Brehon. Donal O'Brien might be armed and dangerous,' said Enda gravely. Normally these days he treated Aidan and Moylan with disdain, but now the hope of solving this murder made him close ranks with them.

'Anyway, no one would notice us poking around in the stables and they'd notice you. You couldn't make up an excuse to look in the stables, but we could,' said Aidan, in the tone of voice of one who knows that his argument is irresistible.

'No, I don't think so,' began Mara and then she stopped. There was something to be said for Aidan's idea. 'I think,' she continued slowly, 'that I'll take Hugh and Shane with me. They are too young to be conducting investigations like the rest of you, so they can work in the afternoon. You are quite right, Aidan, thank you for pointing it out. Two young boys could easily go unnoticed into the stables, where I would be observed. So go and get your cloaks, you two.'

She ignored the groans from Aidan and Moylan as she went out of the schoolhouse. The scholars had to work hard, especially in their last few years at law school. There was an immense quantity of law texts to be memorized; their Latin had to be as good as their Gaelic; their skills in rhetoric and debating had to be polished and even their handwriting had to be perfect before they could be admitted to the elite body of lawyers, and perhaps, later, become a Brehon. All this could only be accomplished by constant hard work.

Seán, she noticed, as she crossed the yard to where Cumhal was standing holding her beautifully groomed mare, was only just setting out. It was no wonder that he annoyed Brigid. She saw Cumhal glaring at him and smiled to herself.

'You could keep an eye on the scholars, Cumhal,' she said in a low voice. 'I'm taking the two little ones with me, but Aidan and Moylan may give Fachtnan a bit of a hard time and . . .' she stopped, hearing Seán's deep slow voice from the other side of the hedge.

'Why don't you have a word with the Brehon about this, Niall? She's in there in the yard at the moment.'

There was a murmur of voices and then the sound of two horses trotting down the road. Mara took the bridle from Cumhal's hand and walked her horse across to the gate of the law school enclosure and looked out. Niall and Seán were going down the road towards the crossroads. She could hear the sound of their voices, though not the words, and it seemed as though Niall kept company with Seán and turned right at the crossroads, going towards Carron, or Lemeanah, rather than continuing on towards his own farm at Noughaval. Could he want to see the king? she wondered. He had been looking very unhappy every time she had seen him recently. She felt somewhat hurt that he had not confided in her, but it was his right to speak to the king directly and she knew that Turlough would be gentle and kind towards him. In any case, she was certainly not going to chase after him, so she shrugged her shoulders and turned back to smile at her two eager young scholars bursting out of the door of the scholars' house and leaping onto the backs of their ponies.

'We wore our second-best cloaks, Brehon,' said Shane as they joined her. 'I thought it would be a good idea if we are going to be nosing around in the stables.'

'We've made a plan,' said Hugh, as they clattered down the road beside her. 'We decided that we would ask if there were any puppies or kittens around. Even if Maeve doesn't

235

know, then we could just go poking around the barns and stables, pretending that we are looking for them.'

'Hugh says he's sure he'll recognize the horse,' said Shane. 'He says it's a big white horse with a wall eye.'

'Will we tell you straight out if we see him?' asked Hugh.

'Better not,' said Mara.

'We could have a signal,' said Shane eagerly.

'Wink at you,' suggested Hugh.

'That's too obvious,' argued Shane. 'I know. We'll say that we've found a baby swallow in the stable, or barn, or wherever the horse has been hidden.'

'It's too late for baby swallows,' stated Hugh. 'I saw all of the swallows flying out to sea from Drumcreehy on the Sunday before we came back to school. We won't see swallows again until next summer.'

'That's the point,' explained Shane. 'As soon as we say that, the Brehon will tell us that we must be wrong and then we can tell her to come and see and she'll come and she'll be surprised to see the horse.'

'That's a good plan, Shane,' said Hugh approvingly. 'What do you think, Brehon?'

'I think you have worked it out very well between you,' said Mara. They were a sweet pair of children. She felt very maternal towards them. They never fought or challenged or criticized each other in the way that the older boys did. I would miss them all terribly if I gave up the school to become Turlough's wife, she thought. It was all very well for Turlough to pour scorn on her idea of a marriage of fourth degree, but perhaps that was what would suit her best. A marriage of fourth degree, whereby a man visited a woman but did not have her in his house, would work well for both of them. Turlough, of course, disapproved. This type of marriage normally took place between a man and a woman of much lower status. Ardal O'Lochlainn, so gossiping tongues related, had contracted a marriage of the fourth degree between a fisherman's daughter in Galway and himself. Ardal visited her from time to time and no doubt they were very happy. There was no real reason why the same arrangement should not work for Turlough and herself. As for status, she cared little about that; the people of the Burren would accept the position once she explained her reasons to them.

✻

When they arrived at Shesmore, Maeve was there to meet them. The steady clip clop of the horses' feet, the jingling of the harness and the high-pitched chatter from the two boys may have brought her out of the house, surmised Mara. However, Maeve's cheeks were red and her breathing was rapid as if she had been running. And the girl's boots were covered in clay, Mara noticed. She glanced carelessly down the lane that led to Lemeanah. Yes, after the rain of the previous evening, its churned-up surface was glistening with mud and puddles.

'What a lovely morning after the storm yesterday,' exclaimed Mara as she swung herself from her horse. She looked around, admiring the way the autumn sun lit up the pale yellow of the hazel leaves and the gold of the newly thatched roof of the farmhouse. Hugh slid from his pony and took the reins from her hands and then he and Shane proceeded to tie the ponies and mare to the rail.

Maeve said nothing, so Mara talked on, giving the girl a

few minutes to recover her breath. 'I had to take refuge at Lissylisheen yesterday evening. Even though I would have been home in ten minutes, the storm was too bad to risk staying out in it.'

'Yes, I heard that you were there,' murmured Maeve. She pulled at her blue *léine* from where it had been kilted by her belt and smoothed it down so that it covered her boots.

'There are a few things I would like to talk over with you,' said Mara, looking around at the empty yard. 'Shall we go inside? Hugh and Shane, you can go and play in the meadow over there, if you wish.'

'Let's go and see if there are any puppies around, Hugh,' said Shane. Mara had to conceal a smile; his voice sounded so natural.

Maeve hardly seemed to notice his words; she seemed to worry more about trying to conceal how muddy her boots were than about the activities of the two young boys. She led the way into the house and Mara followed her, marvelling at how tiny the girl was: ten-year-old Shane was almost as big as she.

'The king has been discussing your situation with me, Maeve,' she began as soon as she was seated. 'I'll explain a little about the law of inheritance to you first of all and then we'll discuss your future. The position is that you will retain twenty acres of land for yourself and also the dwelling house. I would advise that you keep the twenty acres nearest the house. If you marry,' Mara smiled as she saw the quick blush spread over Maeve's face, and continued, 'perhaps I should say, when you marry, you could put a tenant into this property if you wished or else, of course, you and your husband could live here. The thing you must remember is that this land is yours for your lifetime only. After your death it goes back to the clan.' She went on to explain the law of holding land, but she knew that Maeve was not listening.

'Will I be allowed to marry the man I want to marry?' The voice was sweet and low, but the eyes were determined.

'The king has placed your marriage plans in my hands,' said Mara. 'If I approve of your choice then you will be allowed to marry.'

'Oh!' There was a note of surprise in the girl's voice. She must have imagined that she would be her own mistress once her father was dead.

'So who do you want to marry?' asked Mara indulgently.

'Donal O'Brien,' whispered Maeve, her eyelashes making a fringed crescent of black over her flushed cheeks.

'And does he want to marry you?'

This time a tiny smile tugged at the corners of Maeve's red lips. She said nothing and Mara laughed.

'Yes, I'm sure that he does,' she said. 'I saw him with you at Noughaval on Michaelmas Day. He's a handsome fellow, isn't he? I thought he looked magnificent in that grey mantle.'

Maeve's eyelashes flew up and her blue eyes looked startled, even slightly indignant. 'No, Brehon,' she said. 'Don't you remember? Donal was wearing his best purple mantle.'

'Of course he was,' said Mara, shaking her head and trying to give the impression of a forgetful old lady. 'Of course you're right. He was wearing a purple mantle.' She wondered whether to ask about a brooch, but then the image of Donal on that afternoon suddenly came to her mind. His purple mantle had been carelessly draped over one shoulder, not pinned tidily with a brooch. There was a moment's silence as both pictured in their minds that handsome young man at the fair. He had looked as though the weight of the world were on his shoulders, thought Mara. But why? And why was an O'Brien *derbhfine* brooch, with a piece of torn grey woollen cloth still attached, found on Ragnall's body?

'Will I be allowed to marry him?' breathed Maeve.

'That depends on a few things. I will have to talk to the young man's father. And also I will have to see if he is a fit person to marry you. Just a few enquiries now will save a lot of heartbreak later on. I don't want to see you married this year and divorced the next.'

'That would never happen,' said Maeve with a secret smile.

'It happens,' said Mara bluntly. 'I was married at fourteen and divorced by the time that I was seventeen. I thought my husband was perfect, but I was wrong. He turned out to be a lazy, worthless braggart, so I divorced him.' She smiled at the outraged expression on Maeve's face and got to her feet saying, 'Well, I'll have to take a look at this young man and see whether he is good enough for you. Now I'd better go and find my two young men.'

Shane and Hugh were emerging from the stables when she came out with Maeve.

'You haven't got any baby swallows, Maeve,' said Hugh loudly with a meaningful glance at Mara.

'Swallows?' queried Maeve, looking puzzled. 'You don't get swallows in October,' she explained with a maternal glance at Hugh. His red curls, his innocent blue eyes and his freckled, small-featured face always seemed to evoke affection in the women of the Burren.

'No, I didn't suppose you'd find any,' mused Mara, her eyes on the muddy surface of the lane. 'Well, we'd better be off, lads. We're going down to Lemeanah Castle.'

On the way down, she noticed several horseshoe prints in the wet clay. A big horse had been taken, or ridden, down the lane since last night's rain. It was a pity that Liam had been there last night when she speculated about the horse. No doubt he had made some sort of excuse to call on Maeve that morning and find out about it. However, if the horse had been moved this seemed to point to some sort of guilt on the part of Maeve and Donal O'Brien, so perhaps it was just as well that Liam was such an inquisitive, gossipy man.

❈

'Whew, what a stink,' said Shane as they came near to the castle.

'They're dyeing the wool black in the yard,' said Mara. She could smell the pungency of the iron and the sharp acridity of the bearberry leaves over the familiar odour of wet wool.

'Shall we do the same trick about the swallows?' whispered Hugh.

'Good idea,' said Mara, her attention on the fields to the side of the castle. One of them was full of young stallions, but, in the field beside it, a solitary horse neighed unhappily. He was a striking-looking horse, white with black smudges on his sides.

'Could you fetch Donal O'Brien to speak to me,' she

said to the man from the gatehouse, who came running up when he saw visitors at the side gate.

'Won't you come in, Brehon?' The steward joined them; no doubt he had seen them from the window.

'No, I won't, Barra,' she said. 'I hear that the king is at Lemeanah so I don't want to interrupt his talk with the O'Brien. Just ask Donal O'Brien to come out here and talk to me for a few minutes.'

As soon as he had gone in, she nodded to Shane and Hugh and they tied up their ponies and went into the yard, asking loud questions about the dyeing process. She hoped that they would not soil their white *léinte*; that black dye made from iron and dried bearberry leaves would stain any surface and was almost impossible to remove. However, she had more important things on her mind, so she tied the mare's reins to the pole, picked a red apple from the heavily laden tree above it and walked over to the gate of the field. The black and white horse looked at her hopefully; the grass of the field seemed to be cropped low and turning into the bleached pale fawn colour of winter months. The horse would not find much to eat there and he was a big horse.

'Here, boy,' she said, leaning over the gate and holding out the sweet-smelling apple.

He came trotting up immediately and she retained the apple for a minute while she carefully examined the broad sides of the animal and then looked into its eyes. From behind she heard the light footsteps of a young man running up. The horse lifted its head in an alarmed way, but then turned its attention back to the juicy apple. Mara handed over the apple, heard the horse crunch it, wiped her hands on a piece of linen from her pouch and then turned around.

'You've ruined that horse, Donal,' she said. 'The dye won't come off until he sheds his coat in the spring. Maeve could have got a good price for him if you had left him alone. He's much too big for her to ride; he'll have to be sold.'

Donal stopped abruptly and flinched almost as if she had hit him across the face. For a moment he looked as young as one of her own scholars.

'It's no good trying to wash him, and if you clip the dyed patches, he'll only look strange and perhaps catch cold.' She kept her face serious and her manner casual as she turned back to the horse again.

There was a moment's uncertain pause and then he rallied. 'I don't know what you are talking about,' he said belligerently, 'that horse is a new piebald, bought by my father.'

'Oh,' said Mara, turning back to face him. 'Perhaps I'd better have a word with your father, then. Let's hope that he didn't pay too much for this horse; those splodges of black look very strange to me. I never saw a piebald look like him before.'

Donal cast a quick involuntary glance at the windows on the third floor of the tower house. And her eyes followed his.

'Yes, of course, he is talking to the king up in the hall, isn't he?' She now looked at him steadily and challengingly and his eyes dropped before hers.

'You'd better tell me the truth,' she said, leaning back against the gate. 'It's Ragnall's horse, isn't it?'

He thought for a minute and she did not hurry him.

'The horse came back to Shesmore while I was with Maeve on the evening of Michaelmas Day,' he said eventually. 'It came running down the lane from Noughaval. I caught it and I put it into the stable.'

'What time was this?' asked Mara sharply.

'It must have been soon after sundown.'

'And you didn't think to look for Ragnall?'

He didn't answer and she allowed her voice to sound shocked.

'Surely that would have been the normal thing to do. The man was not young. He could have had a fit or something. Or it could have been an accident.'

He bowed his head. 'I suppose you're right,' he said and then added awkwardly, 'Brehon.'

'So why didn't you?' she asked.

He shrugged. 'Well, you know what things were like. Old Ragnall wouldn't allow me near Maeve. I had to sneak every opportunity that I could. We, neither of us, wanted to see her father arrive; I thought he must be having a few drinks and had forgotten to tie up his horse . . .' His voice tailed away and he gave an embarrassed cough.

'So you put the horse into the stable and then you went home, is that right?'

'Well, a bit later,' confessed Donal.

'How much later?'

'I'm not sure, Brehon, I can't tell,' said Donal. 'A couple of hours, I suppose. Fionnuala came out and told me that I had better go.'

'And why didn't Maeve tell me that the horse had returned?' asked Mara.

'Once we heard the news, once she heard that Ragnall had been killed, she was afraid that you might think that I had something to do with the murder. If the horse had been missing, then it would seem more likely that some thief had killed him.'

'And she had no interest in catching her father's murderer?' Mara watched his face carefully. He looked indifferent. He didn't care, and probably she didn't care either. There seemed to have been little affection between father and daughter. She waited for a minute before adding: 'Perhaps her father's murderer is you. Is that why Maeve had no interest in finding out the truth about his death?'

He looked shocked. 'She wouldn't think that of me!'

'And why was the horse moved down here to Lemeanah?'

'Liam was chatting to Maeve about your visit to Lissylisheen. You know what an old gossip he is; he always likes to show that he knows all the news. He said to Maeve that you would be looking for it, and then we thought we would be in trouble because we didn't tell you about it earlier,' he said awkwardly, obviously concocting a story as he spoke. He looked at her appraisingly and then continued. 'I thought of taking it to Lemeanah. Then I got the idea of disguising it.' He cast a disgusted look at the white horse and kicked the gate moodily. 'I seem to have made a mess of everything.'

'Yes, you have,' she said robustly. 'You've certainly given me strong cause to suspect you. There have been two murders here in this kingdom and the thread of my enquiries seems to lead, in each case, to your name. Perhaps you killed Aengus on Sunday night, on the eve of Michaelmas – it may have been as the result of a drunken fight, but the crime was not acknowledged so therefore it is still classified as *duinethaoide*, a secret and unlawful killing. And then next day you killed Ragnall. Again the crime was not acknowledged, so again it was a *duinethaoide*. What do you say to that, Donal O'Brien?'

'All I can say is that I am not guilty of these two murders,' he replied with a steady courage that surprised and impressed her. 'There were people other than me who might have wished the death of either of these men,' he went on after a moment, speaking slowly and carefully and looking at her earnestly. 'I had no real quarrel with Aengus; I was drunk, but then I cooled down after I left the alehouse. As for Ragnall, he was the father of the girl that I love. Why should I kill him? Sooner or later, he would have seen that it was a good match for his daughter and he would have realized that she wanted the marriage. I would have got my father to talk to the king and the king would have talked to the MacNamara. It would have worked out in the end.'

He was fluent, articulate, brave and quick thinking. He was also a man very much in love and a man born and bred of a warrior race, a man who would kill without compunction. She wanted to believe him, but there remained a doubt.

'Go and fetch my two boys,' she said after a minute. 'They are poking around your barns and stables looking for baby swallows. Tell them they won't find any swallows in October. It's a mistake to spend too long searching for something that doesn't exist.'

He turned to do her bidding, looking bewildered, but wary of asking for an explanation. He had reached the gate to the yard when she called after him.

'Donal, did you see Niall MacNamara today? Did he come here to Lemeanah?'

He looked surprised, but answered readily. 'No, I didn't. You could ask Barra, but I've been around most of the morning and I certainly didn't see him.'

SIXTEEN

CÁIN LÁNAMNA (THE LAW OF COUPLES)

A chief wife must be under the law of her husband unless he fails to carry out the obligations of marriage.

However, a wife of the fourth degree may choose whether to be under the law of her husband, or the law of her kin.

The wife of an infertile husband may leave him temporarily (if she does not choose to exercise her right to divorce him) so that she may become pregnant by another man.

❦

'SO YOU SEE, THAT if Conor ... well, if anything happened to Conor, then the clan might want Teige O'Brien as the *tánaiste*, as my heir,' said Turlough gravely.

'I see,' said Mara, leaning forward to poke the fire. The

247

small chunky sods of turf had collapsed into a pile of softly glowing, copper-coloured ash. She reached in the basket and threw a few more lumps on top. Logs gave a hotter, brighter fire, but on a wet night in early October she loved the strong, sweet, pungent smell of peat. She watched for a moment until the dark brown fibres began to blaze up into bright red sparks and then she sat back.

'No, I don't see,' she said energetically. 'If Conor is your *tánaiste* now and there is a worry about his health, then why not Murrough after him: Murrough is your son, also. Why won't the clan be happy with him?'

Turlough sighed. He stirred impatiently, walked across to the table, poured himself another cup of wine and then sat down again opposite to her, moodily sipping the wine and looking steadily out through the undraped window. She glanced around, following the direction of his gaze. There was a faint watery gleam of moonlight; the rain was over now, blown eastwards by the fresh winds from the Atlantic. The day would be fine tomorrow. That was the way it went on this western seaboard, one day wet, one day fine: the weather and the sky and the landscape continually changing and shifting between light and dark. She sometimes thought that it made for a quick-witted, alert and flexible people, used to taking each day as it came, without bothering themselves by too much fruitless planning.

Mara looked back at Turlough. She could sense the trouble behind his eyes. Murrough was the son that looked like him, the son that was brave, warlike and handsome; Turlough would have liked Murrough to succeed him, but Turlough was a man of principle. He would keep to the ancient ways. It would be for the clan, and, above all, for the *derbhfine*, to elect the *tánaiste* if Conor died. He poked the fire and then turned to her.

'The clan don't like him,' he said bluntly. 'I'm not surprised. He is too English for them. They would be afraid that if he became *taoiseach* the O'Briens would end up, like the Kildares, in the pocket of this young king, Henry VIII, as he calls himself. The *derbhfine* won't go outside the wishes of the clan.'

'The Kildares were originally English,' pointed out Mara. 'It's quite different with the O'Briens. They are Irish: breed, seed and generation. Murrough is young; he'll get over all this English nonsense. He can't be a true O'Brien and not feel the pride in his lineage. What is Kildare to him? Or even this Henry Tudor? Murrough is the descendant of Brian Boru. The laws and the traditions of the Gael must be important to him. If I were you, I would say nothing now. Leave matters alone. With the help of God, Conor will live and prosper and the question about the new *tánaiste* will only come up when you are in your gravemound.'

Unlikely, she thought, as she was saying the words. Conor seemed to waste away daily. There was little that the physicians could do for him. However, she hated to see Turlough so filled with gloom and disappointment, and people did sometimes recover from the wasting sickness.

He roused himself at her words. 'Now if we got married and had a son,' he said, smiling affectionately at her, 'then he would be quite perfect, the apple of his father's eye, and if I live for another twenty years, he could be my heir.'

'I'm too old for sons,' said Mara.

'Nonsense, lots of women have sons at thirty-six. He could have my looks and your brains and then he would be a very fine young man.'

Mara smiled. For a moment the thought was sweet. Perhaps the maternal emotions aroused by Hugh and Shane yesterday had lingered with her and had made her feel that it would be a wonderful thing to have a son. Did the wise female judge, Brig, famed in the wisdom texts – she who reprimanded the young male judge for expecting a woman to behave like a man when taking possession of her lawful dues – did Brig have children? she wondered.

'I've had my child,' she said lightly. 'Sorcha is twenty-one now, would you believe it!'

'And you were managing a law school when she was only two years old,' pointed out Turlough.

'I had Brigid,' said Mara. 'And of course, she was a good little girl, Sorcha.' This child, this son, would be of royal blood, descended from the great Brian Boru himself, she thought.

'I could rebuild Ballinalacken Castle,' he said eagerly. 'That's an O'Brien possession and it's within an arrow's flight of Cahermacnaghten. We could live there for half the year and you would have only a short ride to the law school every morning.'

She thought about that for a moment. Ballinalacken Castle was familiar to her, built on a high crag, a dramatic shadow against the western sky on the road to Corcomroe. A wonderful place to live, she thought. Up on the turrets, there, you would feel as if you could touch the stars. Perhaps a marriage of the fourth degree where each retained independence could suit them both well. She had mentioned it once, but Turlough had been horrified. He had felt that such a marriage would demean her high office. Perhaps she could bring it up again some time.

'We're straying off the point,' she said with an effort. 'You've been talking with Teige O'Brien about the possibility of becoming *tánaiste* if anything, God forbid, happens to Conor. What did Teige have to say about this?'

The gloomy look returned to his face. 'Of course, he wasn't surprised. There had been a few approaches made to him already. He's a good man,' he admitted. 'He would be an excellent choice. It's just that with a strong, healthy, brave son of twenty-two, and being in good health myself, I would have liked Murrough to be chosen if anything happened to Conor.'

'And Teige was pleased? Of course, he has a grown son, also, so it would be likely that young Donal would be his *tánaiste* after you are gone. It would be a great prospect for him.'

'Actually we didn't talk too much about that. He could probably see that it was painful to me. We were talking about young Donal. Teige wanted to know whether the marriage with Maeve MacNamara would be approved and I told him that it was in your hands.'

'Oh, yes,' said Mara sceptically. 'And I suppose you told him that I was bound to approve.'

'Well, I did say that I didn't think there would be a problem,' admitted Turlough. 'There won't be, will there? I can't believe that that boy had anything to do with Ragnall's death. It's nonsense. Why should he? All he had to do was to make enough of a nuisance of himself to his father and his father would have come to me and then the whole matter would have been worked out.'

Mara considered this. He had almost repeated Donal's words to her earlier. Of course, there was a lot of truth in it. Perhaps the young man had nothing to do with those two deaths. She felt her spirits rise. She had liked Donal O'Brien. He was probably over-indulged by his father, but there was something very appealing about him. After all, that brooch she had found had a piece of grey woollen cloth attached, and Donal had undoubtedly been wearing a purple, not a grey, mantle on Michaelmas Day.

'At the same time, I don't think Maeve should rush into this marriage,' she said aloud. 'It will do neither of them any harm to wait a little while and to be sure of their feelings. Maeve has led a strange life cooped up there in Shesmore. I was telling her that, at seventeen, I divorced the man that I adored when I was fourteen.'

'You didn't tell her all the details, did you?' teased Turlough. 'You didn't tell her how you stood up before the people at Poulnabrone and calmly told how he had gossiped in the alehouse about the details of your love-making in his bed.'

'No, I didn't tell her that,' admitted Mara serenely. 'I might do, though. To tell you the truth, I just used that as an excuse. Of course, there is a law that says the husband who tells what went on between his wife and himself between the sheets may be divorced, but the fact was that I was sick of him. He was an idle braggart and no match for me.'

'You should have married again,' said Turlough with conviction. His eyes were on her and she felt her face flush.

She leaned forward to poke the fire again and then went over and opened the window to cool her cheeks.

'We were talking about Donal O'Brien, and the possible marriage between himself and Maeve,' she said with a smile, walking back to her seat.

'I'll leave all that to you,' said Turlough impatiently, 'now let's talk about something more . . .'

'Would you like anything else to eat, my lord?' queried Brigid, pushing open the door after a perfunctory knock. Outside was Cumhal with a covered lantern and Turlough's two bodyguards, obviously keen to get their king into the guesthouse inside the high wall of the law school enclosure.

'No thank you, Brigid,' said Turlough, rising to his feet obediently.

'The king will be out presently,' said Mara serenely. She shut the door in their faces. It annoyed her sometimes that Brigid and Cumhal were so against any closer link between their mistress and the king that they seemed to be acting as bodyguards to a young virgin's virtue. The decision was going to be hers, and hers only, she thought. In any case, the sight of Cumhal had reminded her of something.

'Did you see Niall yesterday?' she asked.

'Niall?' replied Turlough. 'What Niall?'

'Niall MacNamara, Aengus's son. You know, the young man who was brought up at the mill. He was riding down towards Lemeanah. I thought that he was going to see you?'

'No, he didn't come to see me.'

'Strange,' mused Mara. 'He went in that direction. I assumed that he was going to see you. Still, I suppose he might have turned left at the cross. He could have been going to Caherconnell to see Malachy. He would be unlikely to be going to Carron after the reception that he got there when he showed his face at the inauguration of the new *tánaiste*. Slaney certainly made her feelings clear on that occasion. Turlough, you don't think that there is any chance that Garrett has got himself into the hands of money-lenders in Galway, do you?'

'What makes you think that?' asked Turlough with a quick frown. Mara knew how much he hated English ways. A money-lender, even money itself, was anathema to him. He saw no reason why the old ways, where men bartered their surplus goods, should not continue to prevail.

'It's just that Garrett seems very desperate for money,' said Mara. 'He seems determined to do Niall out of his proper and expected inheritance of the mill and he tried to take Ragnall's daughter's rights of property and land away from her. And he even tried to accuse me of taking some silver from old Ragnall's purse.' Then she told the whole story of her visit to Garrett and Slaney.

Turlough looked more cheerful. It had done him good to take his mind off Conor and Murrough. 'Perhaps you're right. Perhaps Garrett is desperate for money in order to keep hold of his wife. What did he marry that woman, Slaney, for? I'd have found him a nice little wife who would have kept her mouth shut and done what she was told.'

'So that's the sort of wife that you would like?' asked Mara demurely.

'You'd better open that door, or they will be thinking that all sorts of things are going on in here,' whispered Turlough, his green eyes twinkling with fun. 'You're a woman with a reputation, you know.'

'It's your reputation that you are worrying about,' whispered back Mara. She allowed another minute to elapse before opening the door, saying at the same time, 'Well, my lord, as Fíthail says, "*A rigne is messu don gaís*", the worst of wisdom is its slowness.'

'I couldn't agree more,' said Turlough, after a moment's startled silence. 'Good old Fíthail,' he said warming to the task. 'You can always rely on him to come up with something useful. I keep a copy of his sayings by my bedside.'

'So do I,' said Mara gravely. Brigid, she thought, had a sceptical air, though the three men looked impressed.

The night was startlingly bright when Cumhal, bowing deferentially, opened the front door. All of the clouds were suddenly blown away and in the immense darkness the sky was blazing with stars, the moon lying in the middle of its soft black expanse like a silver platter on the black polished surface of an oaken table.

'I'll walk over to the guesthouse with you,' said Mara. 'I need to fetch something from the schoolhouse.'

'You lads go on ahead,' said Turlough to the two body-guards. 'There's light enough for us to see by this moon, the Hunter's Moon we used to call it.' He waited for a moment until the bodyguards, followed by Brigid and Cumhal, were out of earshot, before continuing in a low voice. 'I remember, on my eighth birthday, my father took me out hunting at night for the first time and there was a moon like that. And funnily enough, today is my birthday and here's the same moon again.' His voice seemed full of emotion.

'You should have told me,' said Mara. 'We would have had something special for you this evening.'

'Every hour with you is special,' he said softly. 'But that was why I wanted to be with you this evening. Teige wanted me to stay another night, but I told him I needed to talk business with you. I wanted to be with you on my forty-ninth birthday; I'll be fifty next year. My father died two days after my eighth birthday. He was only twenty-seven years old. You will think about our marriage, won't you? We would be very happy together. You need give up nothing that is important to you. I have plans about that.'

She thought he might say more, but he didn't; just walked by her side, his hand holding hers, his arm pressed against her shoulder. They moved apart at the gate to the law school enclosure and then walked quickly across the yard to the guesthouse, she leading and he following. He kissed her briefly at the door, but did not respond to the traditional blessing.

When the door had closed behind him, she turned to Brigid and Cumhal.

'Lend me your lantern, Cumhal,' she said. 'There are a few things that I need to do in the schoolhouse. The king has given me some ideas about this troublesome affair. Sleep well,' she added, taking the covered lantern from his hand and noting that there was a new candle inside its little chamber made from translucent horn. 'And may God and His Blessed Mother and the Blessed St Patrick guard you and keep you safe through the night.'

The schoolhouse was still warm and a large willow-basket of turf stood beside the fireplace. She threw on a few sods. The night was frosty and once she began to read, she would not notice the cold creeping into the little house.

Fachtnan, Enda, Moylan and Aidan had done a good day's work, she thought, lifting, one by one, the neatly written scripts from the pile on her desk. Enda had even tabulated his under the headings of WITNESS, TIME, PLACE, WHO SEEN. She sat for a long time studying the notes and writing other notes on a spare leaf of vellum. She had forgotten about Maol, living there so near to the mill at Oughtmama.

Everything was beginning to seem clearer to her and she didn't like what she was discovering. She went to the wooden press where her copies of law manuscripts were kept. Her father had collected many of these and she knew that she was lucky to have them. She lifted one after another until she found the one that she wanted, *The Great Book of Duniry*. She leafed through the pages until she came to the right place; she made a note and then turned back to the beginning before putting the book away. At the bottom of one page was written, in the same square minuscule script as used by the scholars at the Cahermacnaghten law school almost one hundred and fifty years afterwards:

One thousand, three hundred, ten and fifty years after the birth of Christ to this night and this the second year since the coming of the plague to Ireland, I have written this in the twentieth year of my life. I am Hugh, son of Conor MacEgan, and whoever reads this, let him offer a prayer for my soul.

She never read these lines unmoved. How long had Hugh MacEgan, of that great law family, the MacEgans, survived the plague within the crowded houses of the walled city of Galway? Mara had often breathed a silent prayer for the young man who had written those words on a Christmas night. Tonight the words made her think of the other vulnerable young men whose lives touched hers: of Niall, the illegitimate son, who had expected to inherit a prosperous mill; of the three young O'Briens – Conor, dying of the wasting sickness, Murrough, his brother, who might now never be king, Donal, their cousin, so desperately in love – of her own scholars; of her little grandson in Galway; and perhaps ... she allowed herself to dream for a moment ... of her own son, yet unborn, who could one day be king of Thomond, Corcomroe and of her beloved Burren ...

SEVENTEEN

URAICECHT BECC (SMALL PRIMER)

A physician has an honour price of seven séts. He is expected to apply herbs, to supervise diet and to undertake surgery. There will be no penalty for causing bleeding, but if he cuts a joint or a sinew he has to pay a fine and he will be expected to nurse the patient himself.

A banliaig, woman physician, *is a woman of great importance to the kingdom.*

❦

'AS SOON AS YOU have finished your breakfast, you'd better get your ponies. I want you all to come with me to Oughtmama,' said Mara, putting her head around the kitchen house door early next morning. After reading Enda's notes last night, she knew that she should visit the place again. She needed to look carefully at the mill and the surrounding buildings, and their young eyes and insatiable curiosity would be a great help to her. In any case, she had promised Fachtnan that they should visit the mill. 'Brigid, could you . . .' She tried to continue but was interrupted by wild cheering, in which even Fachtnan joined. She waited for a moment, smiling. She loved to give them pleasure and they had all worked very well yesterday, without supervision.

'. . . put some oat scones and honey cakes and some ale in a basket,' she finished. But her housekeeper had already gone to the shelves and was taking down some of her stores.

'Shane and Hugh, you butter these scones,' commanded Brigid. 'Aidan, get that buttermilk from the scullery. Enda, ask Cumhal for a couple of flagons of ale. Fachtnan, you go and get a pair of leather satchels for everyone. That will be better than a basket, Brehon. They can hang the satchels from the sides of their ponies,' she explained.

'I'll leave it to you, Brigid,' said Mara meekly. 'Come and tell me when everything is ready, Fachtnan. I'll be in the schoolhouse.'

She could still hear the excited voices as she went indoors, but once she had Enda's script from yesterday in her hand she forgot about them and was startled when Enda himself put his head around the door.

'Fachtnan said to tell you we're almost ready now, Brehon,' he said. 'Fachtnan is just putting a new bit on Shane's pony. She's been chewing it and it might break if she starts to run going down that steep hill from Oughtmama. Shane's not strong enough to hold her if that happens, Fachtnan says.'

'Yes, I'll be out in a minute,' she said absent-mindedly. She knew that she could rely on Fachtnan and Cumhal to make sure that the boys were safe on their ponies. 'Enda, just a minute. You put here that Maol met Niall on Oughtmama hill on Sunday evening and told him that Aengus was not there. You're sure that he said Sunday?'

'Yes, I am, Brehon,' said Enda confidently. 'You'll see from my notes that I asked everyone about Sunday and Monday. Maol definitely said Michaelmas Eve.'

Odd, she thought. She distinctly remembered that Niall had spoken of meeting Aengus at the alehouse in Noughaval on Michaelmas Eve and yet Liam, also, had said that he wasn't there. She had asked Niall how he knew which bags of flour to take for the tribute and he had replied that Aengus told him where to find them when he met him at the alehouse in Noughaval. So why should Niall lie? Surely he could have said that he met Aengus at Oughtmama.

'You say here that Maol mentioned that it was just about the time that the abbey bell rang for vespers?'

'That's right, Brehon, and I'm sure of that, too. I didn't write this down, but Maol said that he mentioned to Niall, when he met him, that Aengus had told him that he would miss vespers for once because he was going to Noughaval for the Michaelmas Eve festival. Niall said that it didn't matter and he continued to go on up the lane.'

'Well, we'd better go,' said Mara, moving the fact about Niall to one shelf in her mind. 'I'm sure Shane's pony is ready by now.'

'May we ride ahead, Brehon?' asked Aidan when Mara and Enda joined them.

'Sensibly, of course,' he added hastily, when he saw Mara's dubious face.

'We'll wait for you at Caherconnell,' said Moylan.

'I think,' said Mara, 'that we will all ride down to Noughaval first. There are just a few questions that I would like to ask Niall. You can ride on ahead there if you like, though I can't see that you can go all that much faster than my mare.'

However, she reined in the mare and allowed them to gallop ahead. There were times when their high spirits needed to be allowed to spurt up and be dissipated in a burst of fun or speed or excitement of some kind. She had plenty to think about anyway, so she went at a slow trot down the lane, her mind busy with questions.

Had Niall been there at Oughtmama when Aengus came back from the alehouse? Did he meet his father? If so, why did he lie about it when he spoke with her? Had there been any sign of young Donal O'Brien?

'There's nobody here, Brehon,' shouted Aidan as she rounded the bend leading to Niall's farm at Noughaval.

'Are you sure?' she called back. It would be early in the morning for Niall to have left his farm. It was not long after daybreak and there would surely be a few cows to milk, eggs to gather and barns to be mucked out.

'The dog is locked up,' called Shane. 'We could hear him barking the whole way as we came. If Niall was out in the fields, he would take his dog with him.'

'And the cows haven't been milked yet,' said Aidan knowledgeably. Aidan was the youngest son of a prosperous farmer in west Thomond.

'He can't have gone to Kilfenora and left the cows unmilked,' observed Enda, another farmer's son.

'Fachtnan, would you ride back and tell Cumhal. He could send one of the men round to make sure that Niall is all right, and perhaps to see to the cows if he can't find him. Don't rush, Fachtnan, we'll ride on and wait for you at Caherconnell, though you'll probably be there as soon as we if you come by the valley road from Cahermacnaghten.'

※

'Perhaps you should call in at the forge, and see if Fintan has seen him, Enda,' said Mara as they trotted along the lane between Noughaval and Caherconnell.

Enda was only a minute inside the forge before he emerged shaking his head.

'No, neither Fintan nor Balor has seen him since yesterday morning,' he said as he swung himself with agile grace onto the back of the pony. 'Fintan said that Niall was on his way to Carron when he met him then. He saw him come back a couple of hours later.'

Fachtnan was already at Caherconnell when they arrived. He was standing at the gate, chatting to Nuala.

'Where are you all going?' asked Nuala. There was a trace of wistfulness in her voice. It was a shame, thought Mara, that Malachy didn't have another few medical scholars. Nuala could do with some company from young people of her own age.

'What are you doing with yourself today?' asked Mara.

Nuala sighed heavily. 'Nothing much,' she said listlessly. 'Father has gone to a childbirth case in Carron. It's Seán Ruadh's son's new wife. Father didn't want me to come. He said that the house was too small. It's probably because he thinks that the girl is going to die. He doesn't like me to be around if someone is dying. He thinks I'm still a child.' And she heaved another sigh.

'Well, you are only fourteen,' said Fachtnan gently. He was always very kind to Nuala and Nuala worshipped him. Mara had an unspoken hope that one day they might make a match.

'Why don't you run inside and ask Sadhbh if you can come with us to Oughtmama?' suggested Mara. 'We will be back before Malachy comes home probably, but if we're not, Sadhbh will tell him that you're with me.'

Nuala was back in a moment, her eyes shining, accompanied by Malachy's motherly housekeeper, who was carrying a small linen bag and a flask.

'I've got some honey cakes and a flask of buttermilk for her, Brehon,' she said. 'She tells me that all the lads have got their dinner with them. Aed is just getting the pony from the stable. He'll be here in a moment.'

'I'll put these in my satchel,' said Fachtnan promptly and Nuala glowed with pleasure, her dark brown eyes blazing with excitement.

'You have a lovely day for your ride,' said Aed cheerfully, as he brought out the pony. Fachtnan took the reins from him and helped Nuala carefully up onto the saddle. Mara and Sadhbh both beamed. Aidan nudged Moylan and smirked.

'It is a beautiful day, Aed,' responded Mara. 'Isn't it, Aidan?'

'Oh, y . . . yes,' stammered Aidan, trying to wipe the grin from his face. He gave a hasty glance around and tried to look appreciative. Mara was always endeavouring to teach her pupils to admire the beauties of the Burren.

And it was a beautiful day. The overnight frost still sparkled on the grass, and scarlet rowanberries and crimson haws glowed in the sunlight, their vivid gloss contrasting with the deep, soft, matt pink of the spindle tree fruits and the powder blue of the blackthorn sloes. The broad clints of limestone paving appeared almost silver and the leaves of the ancient oak tree above their heads were turning from green to a clear bright yellow.

'You and Nuala ride ahead, Fachtnan,' directed Mara. 'Enda, you ride in between Shane and Hugh. Moylan and Aidan, you can ride just behind me and keep a look out for carts. You can warn us if anything is coming and then we'll all pull in onto the grass.'

The wonderful thing about the Burren, she thought, as they made their way through the valley and then turned up towards Carron, was that the stone was everywhere. Unlike Thomond and Corcomroe, where roads were muddy tracks after every shower of rain, the roads of the Burren were hewed from solid bedrock stone and they made for easy riding. She loved the way that the noise of the hoofs made a merry ringing sound, and the young voices and the laughter were music to her ears. At this moment, she thought happily, I would not exchange my life with anyone in the world, not even with the Queen of England.

'Fachtnan,' she called out, 'what is the name of the Queen of England?'

'I don't know, Brehon,' he called back. He didn't sound as if he cared too much. He was pointing out to Nuala some minute red and gold finches flying down the road. The birds almost seemed to be flying wingtip to wingtip, so close were they to each other. Each tiny beak held a fluffy piece of thistledown and the gold on their wings flashed in the sunlight.

'It's Katherine, isn't it, Brehon?' asked Enda. 'I seem to remember the king telling us that. The Earl of Kildare was going over to London for the young King Henry VIII's wedding on the eleventh of June, he said. The king was telling us all about it at the end of the Trinity term.'

'I remember,' said Mara.

'And she was originally the wife of Henry's eldest son, Arthur,' continued Enda. 'Did she and Arthur get divorced, Brehon?'

'No, they don't have divorce over in England; he died, perhaps of the wasting sickness,' said Mara. And then she thought of Turlough's son, Conor, but quickly she moved the thought from her mind. She had long practised the art of thinking only of what she could remedy. There was no remedy for Conor, she surmised, if even the son of the King of England could not have been saved.

They passed Carron Castle while Enda was still enlightening the younger scholars about King Henry VIII.

'Only eighteen and he's a king,' whistled Aidan. 'Lucky!'

'So they don't have our rule of *the eldest and the most worthy*, Brehon, do they?' asked Moylan.

'No,' said Mara over her shoulder. 'In England, if your father is king, then you become king the very second he dies. Even a tiny baby can be a king.'

They found this very funny and she sympathized with their amusement. In the Irish society a king was expected to be warlike and to lead his clan from the front. Enda continued to lecture Shane and Hugh about the differences between Brehon and English law, but from behind her she could hear Aidan and Moylan, amid raucous bouts of laughter, swapping details of Turlough's instructive talk to them

266

about the English way of life. From the phrases such as '*arse-hugging breeches*' and '*bulging cod pieces*' she surmised that Turlough had been enjoying himself.

As they approached Oughtmama, Mara hurried them past the small farm where the sight of Malachy's horse, still tied to a tree, showed that the unfortunate fourteen-year-old wife of the sheep farmer was still struggling to produce a baby.

'It's the next left turn, Fachtnan,' she called. He and Nuala were so busy chatting that she thought it was quite likely they might ride past the lane to the mill and thereby amuse Aidan and Moylan even more.

'I've never been to a water mill,' said Shane, when they arrived at the ancient former monastic site. 'How does it work, Brehon?'

'Enda will tell you,' said Mara, dismounting from her mare and tying the reins to a handy branch.

'I'm just going to show Fachtnan where we found the body of Aengus,' said Nuala, swinging her long brown legs over the pony's back. Although Sadhbh made sure, now that Nuala was fourteen, that she wore the customary full-length *léine*, normally she had it kilted at the waist with her leather belt so that it seldom came much below her knees.

'We'll come too,' said Aidan promptly, with a nudge to Moylan.

'No,' said Mara. 'I need you two. My eyes aren't as good as yours. I want to search the grass around here. I don't know what I am looking for exactly, but if you find anything that looks as if it shouldn't be there, then bring it to me. It could be anything like a piece of cloth, or a brooch or a knife – anything at all. Fachtnan and Nuala, you do the same up by the sluice gate. When we've done that, we'll search the mill house, but Enda, Hugh and Shane, you keep a good look out, also.'

Nuala and Fachtnan went up to the sluice gate, Moylan and Aidan seized a stick each and started vigorously stirring the grass and Enda made for the mill house, explaining to Hugh and Shane, 'The water goes in that chute there and it turns that paddle wheel, do you see it? And up these steps in the next storey are the two millstones. Do you remember the eight sayings of Fíthail?

'*"Around what is a household established,"* said his son to Fíthail.

'*"That's easy. Around a steady lower millstone,"* said Fíthail.

'*"Tell me, what is the lower millstone of a household?"* said the son.'

'*"That's easy. A good woman,"* said Fíthail . . .' chanted Hugh obediently.

'Brehon,' screamed Shane.

'What is it?' Mara immediately abandoned Aidan and Moylan and went running across the short thick grass. She passed rapidly through the wooden door and then stopped.

Enda and the two young boys were huddled just inside the door. Mara followed the direction of their horrified eyes.

There on the wooden floor, stretched out, with an ominous, clotted lump of blood on his temple, was Niall MacNamara.

'He's dead,' whimpered Hugh.

Mara looked at the body on the floor. Niall did look dead. Above his head was a large ragged hole in the wooden ceiling; the shaft that rose up from the paddle wheel was cracked in the middle. One half was still sticking up, but the other lay, exposing the jagged edge of its split, on the floor. And beside Niall were two immense stone wheels, one of them broken in half.

'The millstone has killed him,' said Aidan.

It was obvious what had happened: once the shaft had broken, the weight of the two millstones had brought them crashing down through the flimsy wooden floor in the second storey. One of them had hit Niall a glancing blow on the temple.

'What broke the elm-wood shaft?' asked Moylan.

'Was Niall lying there on the floor when the shaft broke?' whispered Hugh.

'Was this an accident, Brehon, or another murder?' queried Enda.

Mara ignored the questions that poured from the boys. Quickly she crossed the floor and knelt beside the body spreadeagled on the floor. She reached out and touched the outstretched hand. It took a moment before her brain registered what she was feeling.

Niall's hand was not cold and lifeless; it was cool, but not cold. Mara moved her finger and found the wrist. There was a faint throb there; a faint beat of life.

'You and Hugh, go and get Nuala,' she said urgently to Shane. 'Enda, get on your pony immediately and fetch Malachy. He's at Seán Ruadh's place two miles north of Carron. You know it, don't you? Ask him to come if he can possibly do so. Tell him that Niall is alive, barely, but he is alive.'

All three were gone instantly. They had all been trained from an early age into habits of instant obedience to their

Brehon. Mara sat back on her heels, quickly unpinned her mantle and wrapped it around the unconscious body. It was all that she could think of doing. She didn't think of praying. She didn't even think of Malachy. Everything depended now on how much the fourteen-year-old Nuala had managed to glean from her solitary studies of her grandfather's manuscripts.

Nuala was there almost before Mara had completely wrapped the body. She came in swiftly, made no outcry and asked no questions. She knelt by Mara's side, looked at the wound, at the ugly clots of blackened blood, and then lifted one eyelid and peered in.

'The wound is not a problem,' she said to Mara. 'He hasn't been badly cut. You can see that he has stopped bleeding a long time ago. That's why the blood is black. The problem is the skull. He had a terrible blow on the head. He may die quite soon. Feel how cold he is.'

She put her finger on Niall's wrist and then said decisively, 'There's very little life left. His blood beats too slowly. We need to get some warmth into him. Fachtnan, make a fire some way. As quickly as you can! There are some iron pots upstairs. You can heat up some water in them.'

'Here is my tinder box,' said Mara. She pulled the tinder box from her pouch and then took one of Niall's cold hands within hers and began to rub it gently. Nuala did the same, her face serious and intent.

'Should we give him a drink?' whispered Mara.

Nuala shook her head. She did not reply, but went on rubbing the cold hand. Then she released it, undid the latchets of the sandals and started to rub the feet. Mara took the two hands within hers.

'Pity we can't light a fire in here,' said Nuala in her normal voice, 'but that wood must be old and rotten for the millstones to fall like that. It's probably like tinder. The whole place might go up in flames.'

It seemed ages before Shane arrived with a small flagon of hot water. 'Fachtnan has more heating up, but he said to take this into you now,' he said with one quick, scared glance at the unconscious man. 'Hugh will bring some more as soon as it is hot enough.'

'Find a linen sack upstairs. I'll soak it in the hot water and wrap it around his feet,' said Nuala. 'Tread carefully, you don't want to fall through that ceiling.'

Shane went instantly. Mara glanced up. She was not sure that the timber, though old, was that rotten. The floorboards were far apart, but they seemed to be in good condition. What had made the shaft suddenly break, bringing down the two ton-weight millstones? Was it an accident, or was it another attempt at murder? What curse lay upon this ancient site that those lives which touched it recently should be lost?

'God bless us and save us, this is a terrible thing,' said a shocked voice at the doorway. 'What in the name of God has happened here?'

'Excuse me, Maol,' said Shane, pushing past the bald-headed man with scant ceremony. 'Here you are, Nuala. This is an old soft linen bag. I brought another one as well.'

Nuala dipped the bag into the boiling water, held it steaming in front of Niall's waxen-white face for a moment and then wrapped his two stone-cold feet in it. She left it there for a few minutes and then put it back into the water and immediately towelled Niall's feet in the dry bag, rubbing

271

them hard until a faint shade of pink appeared. No one answered Maol's question.

'Here's the next pot of water,' said Hugh.

'Good,' said Nuala. She took out the hot linen and then handed the first pot to Hugh. 'Tell Fachtnan to fill it up again. Tell him to keep on boiling water as fast as he can.'

'Why is he making that snoring noise?' asked Shane in a low voice.

'His skull is damaged. I've heard that before. He may die,' said Nuala. She went on soaking the linen, wrapping the feet, unwrapping, drying, wringing out the next hot cloth and then wrapping the feet again. Her concentration was immense but after a while she said in a low voice, 'When do you think Father will come, Mara?'

'Should be soon, now,' said Mara. 'You carry on. I think he is beginning to look a little better.' She wasn't sure whether that was true, but Nuala was beginning to look a little less like a competent physician and a little more like a frightened child. She deserved some encouragement. The possibility was that Malachy might not be able to come; the young mother might still need his assistance urgently and even if he did, he probably knew no more than Nuala. So Mara continued to warm the stone-cold hands and Maol continued to mutter an unending stream of prayers and querulous queries, whether addressed to her or to his God, Mara did not know. Nor did she bother answering. Shane knelt down beside her and started to rub the other hand. Hugh came to and fro with small pots of boiling water and once seized some broken timbers from the ceiling and took them out, for the fire no doubt.

'A terrible thing,' said Maol ponderously. 'Father and

son to die on the same spot: you would think that a curse had been laid on this mill.'

'Maol, you go back to your house and get a good fire going and a warm bed ready,' snapped Nuala. 'That would be some use at least. I think if Father doesn't come soon, I'll take a chance and move him. When you have everything ready, come back here with some sort of litter to carry him on. You and the lads will be able to carry him to your place.'

'Yes, that would be wonderful if you could do that, Maol,' said Mara diplomatically. 'If you need any help, then Aidan or Moylan would love to be of assistance. Where are Aidan and Moylan?' she asked as Hugh came back with more water.

'They're getting dead wood from the hedges for the fire,' said Hugh.

'That's good,' said Mara, feeling proud of all of her scholars. Each one of them was behaving in a practical and sensible way.

'Do you think it would be a good idea to move him?' she said in a low voice to Nuala.

'I've been trying to remember,' said Nuala, a frown of concentration etching itself across her smooth forehead. 'The trouble is that I know so little. I think, though, that it is only in the case of broken bones that you don't move them. I've never seen anything about the head. We could tie him to the litter and Maol, Fachtnan, Aidan and Moylan can carry him carefully. It's not far to Maol's house.'

'I'll go and send Fachtnan down with Maol,' said Mara. 'We'll do it straight away. We won't wait for your father to come back.' Privately she thought that Nuala was well on the way to being as good a physician as Malachy. She had such a deep interest and she continually studied and thought about things.

❊

The abbey bell had rung for the noontime recitation of the angelus by the time that Malachy and Enda arrived. By then, Niall was warming gradually, well tucked up in Maol's bed, snug beneath a pile of sheepskins and with a roaring fire fed enthusiastically by Moylan and Aidan. Nuala sat beside the bed, feeding small drops of hot mead into Niall's mouth; he had just swallowed something as Malachy came into the room.

'Sorry,' he said to Mara. 'I couldn't get here any quicker. The baby was just arriving as Enda came.'

Nuala looked a question and he gave her a reassuring glance. 'Yes,' he said, 'by the grace of God, they're both alive, but it was a hard birth. I had to pull the baby out with the birthing tongs that Fintan made for me. Let's hope that the mother survives, but the little boy is well and feeding hungrily. What happened here?'

Mara allowed Nuala to tell the whole story. Malachy nodded silently, felt the pulse in Niall's wrist and still said nothing.

'What do you think?' asked Nuala impatiently.

'He's bad,' said Malachy. 'He'll probably go on like this for days.'

'And then?'

'And then he'll die,' said Malachy impassively. 'Or else, he might just recover,' he added.

'I'll go and check on Hugh and Shane,' said Mara, rising to her feet. 'We left them there in case we didn't see you coming. I'll take Enda, Moylan and Aidan with me and leave you Fachtnan in case there is anything you need. Nuala will tell you all that she has done to keep the life in the man.'

She hoped that Malachy would be appreciative of Nuala's efforts. He was a silent man who appeared perpetually tired, a man who seemed to lose all love of life when his wife had died. He loved his daughter, but he put no enthusiasm into teaching her to become a physician. Mara remembered her own father, Séamus, Brehon of the Burren, and how proud he was of his clever daughter and how he made everything about learning the law seem such a wonderful game. Nuala's interest in medicine was so intense that she would respond enthusiastically to any little bit of teaching. Mara resolved to have a word with Malachy and then followed Enda out of the little house.

'Brehon, you know, I think that Niall stayed at Oughtmama all night,' said Moylan, as they walked up the steep lane towards the mill. 'There's a pile of sheepskins in the old house up there, the one with the stone roof – it looks like someone made a bed there, and Maol said he saw a light shining from the window last night.'

'But Fintan said he went back,' argued Aidan, 'don't you remember? He told Enda that he passed the forge a few hours later.'

'Doesn't mean that he didn't go back later on,' said Moylan.

'That makes sense.' Moylan looked flattered. For once, Enda was agreeing with him. He gave Aidan a scornful glance.

'He must have stayed the night, bird brain,' he said with

275

conviction. 'He wouldn't get up in the morning and go off to Carron without milking his cows and letting his dog out of the shed. Niall would never do a thing like that. He loves that dog.'

'I don't like that expression, "bird brain", Moylan,' said Mara mildly. 'Why don't you say something like: *well, let me put the case.* That would sound more lawyer-like.' This produced a stunned silence, welcomed by her because she needed time to think. Moylan's words had given her an idea. Suddenly all the puzzles about these two murders, which had seemed to be like a tangled length of rope, had begun to unravel and everything had started to fall into place.

❖

Shane and Hugh were happily engaged in sending boats, made from twigs, through the chute of the mill. Mara joined them.

'Just fetch me a mat, or a couple of old sacks from the mill, Aidan, will you,' she said, and when they came she knelt down and peered into the murky depths of the mill race.

'What are you looking for, Brehon?' came Hugh's voice.

'I'm not sure,' said Mara truthfully. 'I'll know it when I see it, though. I'm looking to see what Niall was looking for.'

She could hear Enda saying something but she did not listen. Right under the paddle wheel there was a gleam. A stray beam of autumn sunshine slanted in there and lit up something shining, something of silver and burnished iron. She pulled her head out and stood up.

'Sorry, Enda, what did you say?'

'I was explaining to Aidan why you thought Niall must have been looking for something in the water.'

Mara looked at him with respect. 'And what was your explanation, Enda?'

'Well, of course, he must have been lying down with his head just where the shaft is. I worked that out. Otherwise he would have been able to dodge the stone when it came crashing down. If he were lying down, peering into the water, then he wouldn't have had time to move out of the way. In fact,' said Enda, his voice suddenly rising, 'that was probably why the shaft broke. He was trying to move it so as to see something.'

'Or the murderer was up on the floor above and saw him and decided to murder him by bashing a hole in the floor and letting the millstones come crashing down,' suggested Moylan enthusiastically.

'Hmm,' said Enda sceptically. 'There are easier ways of killing a man than that. Anyway, why didn't he finish him off? He must have known that he was still alive.'

'Perhaps he was hoping that we would think it was an accident.' Moylan's voice began to lose conviction. Enda was very respected by Aidan and Moylan for the ease with which he learned everything.

'And did you see anything down there in the water, Brehon?' asked Aidan.

'I think,' said Mara, 'that there is a knife down there.'

'A knife!' breathed Moylan.

'I'll get it,' said Shane. 'I'll be the best. I'm the smallest. I'll fit under the mill the easiest.'

In an instant, he had kicked off his sandals, torn his *léine* over his head and was under the mill before Mara could protest.

'Be careful,' she called. She knew that he was neat and supple, and too clever to take unnecessary risks; nevertheless, it was a long minute before he crawled back out from under the wood. In his hand he held a knife.

'Dry yourself with one of those sacks before you put your *léine* back on,' she said, but her eyes were on the knife.

It was a long knife, a hunting knife, very finely made with a silver handle and a long blade, finely tapered to a point. The blade was not what she looked at, though. There would be nothing to see on the blade if it had spent a week in the turbulent waters of the mill race. She held the blade in her hand and studied the handle. It was made from silver and in its centre, surrounded by an oval line of small jewels, was a medallion made from dark blue lapis lazuli and set within the blue were three small lions carved from rubies. It was the crest of Brian Boru, the three lions. Only one of the *derbhfine* could have owned this knife. Her mind went immediately to that other knife, now safely locked away in the big press in the schoolhouse. That also bore the crest of Brian Boru, but it was not as fine as this one.

'Brehon!' Fachtnan came up the steep slope with long easy strides, and gave a quick, surprised glance at Shane pulling a *léine* over his bare torso on an October afternoon. 'Malachy and Nuala are going home now. Malachy says that there is nothing more that he can do for Niall. Just rest and warmth now and he may recover. Malachy wants to know if you need to see him.'

'No,' said Mara thoughtfully. She saw his eyes go to the knife and knew that he had recognized it as an O'Brien *derbhfine* knife. His dark bushy brows knitted in a puzzled frown. He would know the crest. After all, he and young Donal were friends and had often gone hunting together. She said no more, just watched him and saw that his lips paled and then set in an expression of firm resolution.

'The knife was under the mill; I got it out,' said Shane.

'It probably slipped through the floorboards,' said Hugh.

'That was why Niall was injured,' said Enda. 'At least, that is a possible hypothesis,' he added in a learned way.

Fachtnan said nothing. He continued to gaze at the knife, and then looked at Mara. There was a question in his eyes and she nodded gently.

'Yes, get your horse, Fachtnan, you can ride on ahead with Malachy and Nuala, we'll follow very soon. I just want Aidan and Moylan to show me something first. Don't hurry back, Fachtnan. As long as you are back in the law school for supper that will be time enough.' At least, Nuala would have someone to go over the events of the past few hours and to share in her relief and triumph.

'Is it the sheepskins, Brehon?' asked Aidan eagerly as Fachtnan clattered away down the stony lane. 'They're over here in the old abbot's house. Come on and I'll show you.'

'Do you think that Niall was waiting there, looking out for the murderer?'

'*Lying in wait* sounds better, Hugh,' said Shane judicially.

'Yes, *lying in wait*,' agreed Hugh. 'But who is the murderer, Brehon? Do you know?'

'Yes,' said Mara heavily, drying the knife and placing it in her pouch. 'I'm afraid I do know now who the murderer was.'

EIGHTEEN

CÓIC CONARA FUGILL

(THE FIVE PATHS OF JUDGEMENT)

There are five paths along which a case must be pursued:

1. fír, *truth*
2. dliged, *entitlement*
3. cert, *justice*
4. téchtae, *propriety*
5. coir n-athchomairc, *proper enquiry*

&

HARA, BUSY WITH HER THOUGHTS, rode slowly back down the road from Oughtmama, then up towards Carron and across the valley to Caherconnell and then to Cahermacnaghten. She took little notice of her scholars on the journey. It was, perhaps, regrettable that Enda had opened a sweepstake on the possible murderer and was briskly giving odds on the suspects. However, Mara normally operated a policy of tolerance towards the boys unless the occasion was serious and, in any case, she had plenty to think about.

At that moment, her thoughts were on Fachtnan, rather than on Enda. He had been with her since his fifth year. She remembered him well at that age: a small, squarely built boy with a mop of dark hair, wide eyes and a warm smile. Even at the most turbulent stages of adolescence, he had never given her any trouble and her only anxiety was about the slow progress of his studies. There was a time when she wondered whether she should suggest to his parents that they take him away and let him be a farmer like his brothers, but something always held her back. It was his judgement, she thought. Even as a child he always made the right decision. Yes, she could rely on him now. This matter would be conducted correctly.

The sun was beginning to set by the time that they arrived back at Cahermacnaghten. The sky above the Aran Islands was streaked with red, gold and dark blue and the ash tree outside the law school cast a long black shadow across the road.

'Have a game of hurling while Brigid is getting your supper,' she said to her exuberant boys when they reached the law school. 'Thanks, Cumhal,' she added, as she slid down and handed the reins to him. She walked across to the kitchen house.

'You'll find the lads as hungry as wolves, Brigid,' she said, as she went in. 'They had a great ride and they are all very pleased with themselves. I must say that they were quite a help to me today.' She told Brigid all about Niall and about Maol.

'Do that Maol good to do something for someone else for once,' sniffed Brigid. 'What about your own supper, Brehon?'

'Just give me a platter of oat rolls and some buttermilk,' said Mara. 'I have some work to do in the schoolhouse. I'll eat in there. You might add some honey cakes, as well. Fachtnan will probably join me there and you know how he eats!'

In the end, she went off with a whole basket of food, some drinking cups and some ale and left Brigid open-mouthed with surprise. She knew how much Mara disliked ale and yet she had taken a large flagon as well as the buttermilk.

The red light from the sunset was slanting in through the window of the schoolhouse, lighting up the white wall opposite. Mara placed the basket of food and the flagons in a cool spot near the doorway and sat down with a leaf of new vellum in front of her. She wrote steadily for some time, putting her thoughts into words, outlining her reasons. As she read it through, the weight of proof seemed to her overwhelming. She hoped that the king would be convinced by it. There could be no ignoring these murders, no hushing them up for the sake of a clan. The people of the Burren would have to know the truth and the fine would have to be paid. From time to time she lifted her head and listened, but she could hear nothing except the shouts of the scholars and the whack of the stick against the hurley ball. After a while Brigid called them in for supper and then everything was very quiet.

❀

There were three of them when they came. Mara heard the gentle clip clop of the horses' feet on the stone flags and then the murmur of voices, two deep-toned, and one light and feminine. She went to the door.

'Come in here when you've seen to the horses, Fachtnan,' she said quietly. She did not wait for a reply, but went back inside leaving the door open. First she went to the wooden press and took the knife from the back of its top shelf and placed it on her desk. Then she sat down and took up the leaf of vellum again. She read through carefully what she had written.

Mara, Brehon of the Burren to Turlough Donn, King of Thomond, Corcomroe and Burren.
    Here are the results of my investigations into the two cases of secret and unlawful killing which occurred here in your kingdom of the Burren.
    The murder of Ragnall MacNamara took place at Noughaval churchyard around sunset on Michaelmas Day in the Year of Our Lord 1509. I believe that . . .

'Brehon,' said Fachtnan, putting his head in through the door, 'Donal O'Brien would like to have a word with you.'

'Come in, Fachtnan,' she said cordially, rolling up the sheet of vellum and tying it with a strip of pink linen tape. 'Come in, Donal. Maeve, come and sit by the fire. You look cold.'

Indeed, the girl was shivering, her heart-shaped face blanched, her blue eyes enormous.

Mara heaped some more sods of turf onto the fire, then

took one of the wooden cups, poured into it a little mead from a flask in the press and held it to Maeve's lips. She drank obediently, but her eyes never moved from the knife on the desk and they were wide with fascinated horror.

'Pour yourself and Donal some ale, Fachtnan,' she said. 'Yes, do eat a honey cake, Maeve. The sweetness will make you feel better.'

Mara busied herself hospitably for several minutes. Donal made a few attempts to speak, but she kept pressing more oat rolls and honey cakes on him and, in the end, it was Fachtnan who spoke first. His eyes, also, had been attracted to the knife, but he showed no surprise and no unease.

'I hope you don't feel that I have done wrong, Brehon, or betrayed your trust in any way, but I went to see Donal this afternoon, just after taking leave of Nuala and her father.'

Mara turned an enquiring glance at him and then at Donal, who stood up, crossed over to the fireplace and knelt on the floor beside Maeve. The adoration on his face brought a lump to Mara's throat. She looked back at Fachtnan.

'I told Donal that if he had anything to do with these murders that he should come and tell you, and that was all that I said to him,' continued Fachtnan bravely. His eyes, again, rested on the knife with its revealing *derbhfine* crest, but then turned back to Mara with an expression of confidence.

'Good advice,' said Mara mildly. Now everyone in the little room was looking at the knife. It was a long moment before Donal spoke.

'What do you want to know?' he asked, looking very directly at Mara.

She looked back at him. 'Just the truth,' she said firmly.

'No holding back of anything and no altering of any facts; just tell me exactly what happened at Michaelmas.'

Donal put Maeve's small hand to his lips for an instant, more like one who clears his mind than one who gives a caress, and then he spoke.

'I did kill Ragnall,' he said slowly. 'I didn't mean to. He . . . he insulted me. He said I wasn't good enough for Maeve.'

Mara said nothing. He gave her an enquiring, slightly bewildered look, but then seemed impelled to fill the silence.

'I told him that he should think of his daughter's happiness and he said her happiness wasn't worth a stone to him, so I killed him,' he finished defensively.

Again Mara said nothing. She watched him carefully. He met her eyes defiantly. Maeve buried her face in his shoulder and he put a comforting arm around her tiny waist.

'I am willing to acknowledge my crime and I will talk to my father tonight; I will tell him the whole truth. The fine will be paid in full to . . . to Ragnall's daughter.' He gave a small tender smile, but Maeve did not respond. She had lifted her head from his shoulder by now, but her violet-coloured eyes were still full of terror.

'So you will tell your father the truth,' said Mara thoughtfully. She allowed him to relax for a moment, before adding quickly: 'What about telling me the truth, first?'

Fachtnan turned to look at her and then turned his gaze back on Donal. His dark eyes were reproachful, and young O'Brien looked away.

'Let's start at the beginning,' said Mara encouragingly. 'I always find that is best, myself. Start at Michaelmas Eve. You were there in the alehouse. Aengus and Ragnall started arguing. It developed into a fight. Liam, the O'Lochlainn steward, told me all about it. You took Ragnall's part and when Aengus, eventually, left the alehouse, you followed him. Tell your story from there.'

'I went to see Maeve, I told you,' said Donal sulkily.

Mara shook her head. 'You told me, but it wasn't the truth,' she said firmly. 'You went right up to Oughtmama that night. Don't deny it. There was a witness. Maol saw you.'

Donal stared back at her. He was young for his age, thought Mara. In some ways, he reminded her of Enda when he was fifteen. He had that mixture of truculence, offended dignity and at the same time a lack of confidence. She gazed at him in a friendly fashion, inviting him to trust her.

Suddenly Maeve raised her head and turned a tear-stained face towards the young man.

'You'll have to tell her everything, Donal,' she said. 'This thing is not going to disappear. We must face it.'

Mara beamed. 'That is the most sensible thing that I have heard here today. You have to tell me the whole truth and then we can decide what to do. Tell me about Aengus.'

Donal sighed, looking first at Fachtnan and then at Maeve. Both looked encouraging: it was obvious that Fachtnan, as well as Maeve, now knew the truth.

'I followed Aengus home from the alehouse,' said Donal. Now he was speaking quickly. 'I was drunk and he had sneered at me so I got on my horse. I thought I would catch up with him in a few minutes but my horse threw a shoe just next to Fintan's forge. Balor was there and he did the job for me, but by that time Aengus was well out of sight. I was still boiling over and I . . . I was . . .'

'Tired of being treated like a child,' suggested Maeve.

He took this up eagerly. Obviously it was a phrase that he had used frequently to her. 'Yes, that was it. I decided to follow him. There was a full moon and it didn't take me too long. I could hear him in the mill pulling sacks around. I burst in on him, gave him a fright, poor old fellow.' He gave a shamefaced grin and then his expression grew serious.

'It's terrible to think that he is dead, that they are both dead,' he said, looking at Mara, his dark eyes full of remorse.

'And what happened then?'

'Well, he grabbed me by the mantle and knocked me off balance. I fell on the floor with a thump and my mantle was torn off . . .' Now he had lost his reluctance and words poured out of him. From time to time he looked at Maeve and she gave him an encouraging nod.

'So that was it,' Mara said when he had finished telling her the whole story. 'I guessed that. Your brooch was torn off when the mantle was pulled from your shoulders.'

'Oh,' he said, taken aback. 'So you found it at Oughtmama? I thought you said that you found it at Noughaval churchyard.'

'I did,' she said gravely. 'Now tell me what really happened in Noughaval churchyard on Michaelmas Day. Why did you strike Ragnall? Not for a few hard words. You had heard plenty of them from him before.'

He flushed a dark red. 'I was frightened,' he said abruptly, with a sort of fierce honesty. 'I had spent the day feeling terrified. I thought everyone who looked at me could see what happened up there at Oughtmama. When Ragnall came to the fair, I forced myself to follow him. He seemed just as usual so I reckoned that he knew nothing. I thought I would talk to him. I followed him into the churchyard. I just chatted for a minute and then I said something about the flour in the cart and still he said nothing, so I was pretty sure that he hadn't seen me that time up at Oughtmama. I thought that I was safe.'

Donal would be like that, thought Mara. He would immediately blot out any unpleasant facts and hope, vaguely, that they would never resurface. As she thought, he was young for his age. Almost as young, in some ways, as her small grandson in Galway. Little Domhnall was always certain that no one could see him as long as he hid his eyes and this Donal seemed to share the same optimistic view of life. She could just imagine how he had persuaded himself that no one would ever guess what had happened up there in the mill house of Oughtmama.

'So then I decided that I would ask him again about Maeve and whether we could get betrothed. I thought that because I had taken his part against Aengus on Michaelmas Eve, that he would be more favourable to me. We spoke together. I told you the truth about what I said and what he said.'

'But what happened then?' asked Mara. 'You didn't lash out just because he said no, again.'

Donal hesitated and then began to speak in a rush: 'I was just turning to go away when he said, "I found something belonging to you." And then he got down off his horse and put his hand into the satchel. And then he said in a gloating sort of voice, "I found it in the mill up at Oughtmama." And of course, I immediately thought of my knife. I had missed it as soon as I went home, but I had hoped that it would not be found. I was terrified when he said that. I thought everything was finished for me. I felt that my family would be disgraced and that I would never be allowed to marry Maeve.'

'So you killed him?'

He nodded and then shook his head. 'No . . . well, yes . . . well, I don't know. I lifted my fist and I hit him on the head with it. I don't think I really meant to kill him. I just got into a rage with him. I hit him in the same way that Aengus hit me with his stick.'

'And your knife?' queried Mara. 'Did you take the knife from his pouch?'

He frowned. 'No, at that minute I saw Guaire O'Brien, the linen merchant, coming in through the gate. I slipped behind a tree and then managed to get out through the back gate when he wasn't looking. I went straight down to Shesmore. Maeve saw how upset I was. In the end, I told her everything. I didn't know that I had killed him then, but I thought it would be the end of everything for us. I thought that he would never forgive me for knocking him out. I was furious with myself for losing my temper like that.'

'And when did you find out that he was dead?' asked Mara.

'Well, when he didn't come home after a few hours, we got worried. And then we found his horse out on the lane by the house. I went back to the churchyard and I found him lying there. I started to cover him with earth and then I heard the old priest coming so I ran away again. I went back to Maeve. I asked her what I should do. She thought we should say nothing. She believed me that I did not mean to kill him.'

His eyes lingered fondly over Maeve's tiny face, and with no trace of self-consciousness she held out her arms to him. Suddenly she seemed to have acquired a new maturity. It was as if she were his mother. They held each other for a moment and then Donal released her. He looked over at Mara. She looked back at him, trying to assess whether he had told the whole truth.

'You've left out something, I think,' she said, watching him closely. 'Ragnall was hit on the forehead with a small stone cross.'

He frowned. 'No,' he said. 'I didn't hit him with a stone cross. And I hit him on the side of the head, not on the forehead. I remember that. I hit him just above the ear. I just thumped him. I couldn't believe it when I came back and found him dead. After all that had happened up in Ought-mama, it just seemed like a nightmare that was going on and on.'

It was as I had pictured it, thought Mara. That evening she had remembered the blue-black bruise above the ear and then the disfiguring gaping mess in the centre of the forehead. At the time it had not seemed important, but now tonight, thinking of those injuries, and of the missing pouch, she had realized that there had been two blows and two attackers. A rich young man like Donal, reared in the strict honour code of the O'Brien clan, would never have stooped to steal a pouch of silver from the MacNamara steward.

'I believe,' she said slowly, 'that you were not the man who killed Ragnall. I think, Maeve, that your father was killed after Donal left him.'

To her surprise neither asked any questions, though Fachtnan looked at her with a startled query in his wide eyes. She gave him a nod and then a slight indication of the head towards the door. He slipped out immediately, leaving her with the two lovers. The boy was more moved, more relieved by her words than the girl, she thought as she watched them embrace again. Maeve, despite her kittenish looks, was probably a pragmatist, who took the practical viewpoint that her living lover was of more importance than her dead father. Her father had probably never been much of a father to her. He had been a dour, stern man, not a man to rear a young girl. Maeve would not miss him much. It was good, though, that no cloud would remain over this young couple. She would have a talk with Donal later about keeping his temper, but she would not spoil this moment of delirious happiness for them now.

'You had better take Maeve home, now, Donal,' she said gently after a few minutes. 'Fionnuala will be waiting for her. I'll come and see you in a few days, Maeve, and then we'll have a talk together about your future.'

Maeve nodded demurely, but her glowing eyes showed that she had no doubt about what would be said. Donal, however, hesitated at the door for a moment, looking back in a troubled way.

'But what about Oughtmama, Brehon?' he said.

'I think you can leave that matter to me,' said Mara soberly.

NINETEEN

GÚBRATHA CARATNIAD
(THE FALSE JUDGEMENTS OF CARATNIA)

A tighernae, lord, *may lose his honour price, lóg n-enech, for many serious offences and failings. The king and the Brehon will decide together whether this punishment is merited. Among the offences are:*

1. *Betraying his honour*
2. *Casting blame on the innocent*
3. *Failing to fulfil his obligations to his clan*
4. *Eating stolen food (because a tighernae has the means to purchase his own food)*
5. *Tolerating satire*

౧౦

'LET ME START BY saying that your name will never pass my lips until I speak of this to your lord and mine:

King Turlough Donn O'Brien,' said Mara gravely. She looked at the sullen face of the man opposite to her. She had summoned him to her law school; had sent Cumhal for him once day broke that morning, and he had come, but not for seven hours. There had been a time, that morning, when she found herself half wishing that he would not come, that this ordeal would pass away from her, but she had reproached herself instantly for that thought. The secret and unlawful killing of Aengus the miller had to be acknowledged and recompense made.

If he did not come to her by the end of the school day, she decided, then she would have to go to him.

In fact, school had ended and the scholars were crossing the yard, jostling each other cheerfully, full of repressed high spirits and hungry for their supper, by the time that he had appeared silently at the door.

He looked at her warily now.

'Speak of what?' he asked. He tried to make his voice sound light and unconcerned, but his eyes betrayed him.

'Of Michaelmas Eve and of the murder of Aengus the miller,' she said.

He raised an eyebrow. 'What's that to do with me?' He tried to sound carefree, but she knew that it was a front. 'If you want to solve that mystery, and, of course, we are all waiting for you to do that, then you should talk to Maol MacNamara. Slaney says that Maol saw young Donal O'Brien passing his house late on Michaelmas Eve.'

'I've already spoken to Donal O'Brien,' said Mara. 'He swears that he is not responsible for the murder of Aengus.'

He sneered openly at that. 'Of course! He is the favourite of the king. I had forgotten that. *Your king and mine* will elect his father, Teige O'Brien, as *tánaiste* and then, I suppose, the plan is that son will follow father. No, of course, your murderer can't be Donal O'Brien. You have to find someone else to bear the blame.' His voice was heavily sarcastic.

'I do know that Donal O'Brien was at Oughtmama on that evening. I've known that for some time. I know, also, that he and Aengus struggled together. Aengus injured Donal, knocked him out with that stick of his and then went off, leaving him lying unconscious on the floor. No doubt, he thought, as was probably true, the young man had collapsed as much because of the amount that he had to drink, as because of the blow. It was unlucky for Aengus that he did not stay with Donal and bring him back to his senses. If Aengus had done that then he would not have met his murderer.'

'So what have I to do with all that?' He tried to sound bored, but he watched her in the way that she had once seen a fox watching a farmer who approached near to his den among the shattered limestone slabs.

'Because you were the one who cut the miller's throat and stretched his body out on the floor beside Donal,' said Mara.

'That's just a guess on your part.' He sounded triumphant and Mara gave him a minute to enjoy the sensation.

'You don't correct me,' she observed quietly, then.

He frowned, puzzled, still not seeing his mistake.

'You are not surprised to hear that the body of the miller was originally found in the mill, not in the millstream?'

He flushed a dark red. His mind was quick and cunning though, and in a second he regained his composure.

'I bow to your judgement, my lady judge,' he said. 'If you say that the body of Aengus was originally found in the mill, then that's the way it was. We all know how clever you are and what trust the king places in you.'

'You mentioned Slaney a minute ago,' said Mara evenly. 'I believe that she is the key to this murder. Without Slaney, without her greed, her passions and her desire to better herself in the world, there would have been no murder at the mill on the night of Michaelmas Eve.'

That shocked him. His face went red and then white. His eyes narrowed. For a moment Mara felt slightly alarmed. This man was ruthless; he had murdered Aengus just to ensure his worldly position. A man who would take a life for something like that was a man who would not baulk at further violence. She cast a quick glance at the window. She could hear Seán's voice as he brought the cows in for milking and, more reassuring still, the heavy strokes of a mallet. Cumhal, she knew, was repairing the high wall of the law school enclosure, just to the back of the schoolhouse. The man's eyes followed hers and she could see that he had noted the presence of her servants. In an instant he had recovered his composure.

'Slaney?' he queried with a puzzled frown. 'What can Slaney have to do with this matter?'

Mara did not answer, but looked at him with narrowed eyes, trying to understand the depth of his ambition and the extent of his ruthlessness. What solution would be best for the kingdom? The result of her investigations would have to be made public at Poulnabrone, but once the truth was known by the people of the Burren, then what could be the future for the murderer? She considered the matter carefully for a while, but decided that the next step had to lie with the man who sat silently opposite her.

'Let me tell you what happened on that night,' she said. She now felt full of confidence. She knew how to handle the affair. There was only one way in which this matter could end.

'Well, tell your story,' he said, crossing his legs and throwing a log onto the fire. 'Don't make it too long, though. It'll be dark soon, and I have to ride back to Carron tonight, unless, of course, you are going to offer me hospitality. I hear your guests get wonderful meals at Cahermacnaghten.'

She ignored that. 'This is how the story goes. You went to kill Aengus. You had a knife in your hand. You went after him. You are a fit, active man and he was a man well advanced in years. He ran back towards the mill, perhaps because he knew that another young man was there and might, if he had recovered, protect him against you. Or perhaps he just wanted to put a door between you and himself.'

'And, of course, you were there and you saw all of this!' His tone was scornful and his expression confident. He had had time to think and he had reckoned that his position would make him unassailable.

'The evidence is clear,' she said sharply. 'You grabbed Aengus, cut his throat, probably just inside the door of the mill, and then you had an unexpected piece of luck.'

Mara half closed her eyes, peering through them into the fire as if she could picture there that small wooden room filled with the sound of gushing water and the smell of blood beginning to overwhelm the scent of warm grain. She almost felt as if she had, indeed, been a witness. When she spoke again her voice was assured and decisive.

'Aengus had lit a candle earlier so once you had cut his throat you could see everything. You saw young Donal O'Brien lying unconscious on the floor and you realized immediately that he could be the scapegoat to carry your sin. You took his knife from his pouch and you plunged the blade into the wound. Then you placed the knife, with its O'Brien crest, not on the floor where Donal might see it when he roused himself, but on the shelf where it could be discovered once the murder was being investigated. And then you left Oughtmama. Donal O'Brien found the body when he recovered the following morning. He panicked; he put the body in the stream and tried to make it look as if Aengus had committed suicide. He told me the full story of how he scrubbed the boards and had everything clean by the time Niall arrived on the Monday morning to collect the tribute.'

'You haven't accounted for one matter yet,' he said calmly. 'You have told me the story of *how* you think this murder was committed, but you haven't told me *why*. I could have no sensible reason to murder that old man.'

'You had,' she said.

'Tell me it, then,' he challenged.

And so she told him.

And after she told him there was a short silence, which she broke by saying: 'You have two choices now. You can stay here tonight and ride to Thomond with me tomorrow and together we will tell the whole story to the king . . .'

She gave him a searching look, but his face was locked into an expression of indifference, the eyes stony, the mouth compressed, so she finished her sentence.

'. . . or you can leave here now and go back to Carron and from thence to where you wish.'

Then he rose to his feet, went to the door without a backward glance. She heard him call peremptorily for his horse, but she did not stir. She had finished her written statement to the king – no word of that would have to be altered, but she had to think of what to say to him. She had to think, not just of Turlough, but also of the effect on the whole kingdom. She sat for a long time and, although one part of her mind registered the quiet knock on the door, she did not move nor call out.

'Brehon,' Fachtnan's voice was apologetic and she realized that this was at least the second time that he had called to her.

'Sorry, Fachtnan, come in,' she said, rolling up the leaves of vellum again, tying them neatly with a piece of pink linen tape from her pouch and then turning towards him.

'Nuala and Malachy came by a while ago, Brehon. Malachy said that he wouldn't disturb you. They had just come from Oughtmama. Malachy said to tell you that Niall had recovered his wits, but that he has ordered that Niall should stay where he is for the next few days. Fintan has sent Balor to look after the farm and Malachy says that Niall just needs some rest and perhaps a few short walks now. Nuala has made him a strengthening tonic from her herbs.'

'That will do him a lot of good,' said Mara cheerfully. 'Nuala does great things with that herb garden of hers.' There

was something touching about the pride with which Fachtnan spoke of Nuala.

'But that's not all, Brehon,' continued Fachtnan. 'Niall
wants to see you. Malachy said to be sure to tell you that.
He's gone home now, but Nuala is still here. Would you like
to see her?'

❧

Cumhal was burning branches and twigs from the ash logs
in the centre of the yard and the scholars were roasting
apples dipped in honey and then skewered onto peeled rods
of alder wood. From time to time a shower of sparks set
them all shrieking and running back into the gathering
shadows. Nuala was amongst them, more daring than most,
as she slipped her apple into the glowing centre of the fire
and then quickly snatched it out again.

'We'll have no apples left for *Samhain* if you eat them all
now,' observed Mara, but no one took any notice of her
words and she was perversely glad of it. Why should they
worry about the future at their age? The festival of *Samhain*
was a good twenty days away and this evening with the sun
just setting in a sky filled with soft blues, yellows and reds
and the air crisping up towards a night of frost, this was the
time for fun and laughter and the sweet scent of roasting
apples.

'The physician will be back to collect the little lady in
a while, Brehon,' said Brigid. 'He has to dress the hand of a
shepherd on Baur North. I told him to leave her.' Her eyes
were fond as they rested on Nuala. 'Fachtnan said that you
might want to talk to her,' she added.

'I won't bother her now,' said Mara. 'Let her enjoy herself.' She knew what Niall would have to tell her and she was fairly sure that he had said nothing to either Malachy or Nuala. She waited for a moment, watching the fun and turning her plans over in her mind.

'I'll give the lads tomorrow morning off, Brigid, as they will have to be at Poulnabrone by vespers. I must see Niall at Oughtmama and I'll go on from there across the Shannon to Arra to see the king. Could you and Cumhal see that they all get there in time and that they are as neat and tidy as possible.' She hardly needed to say that, she knew, but chatting idly with Brigid and watching the merry young-sters around the fire distracted her from the thoughts of that moment when she would have to stand at Poulnabrone and tell the people of the Burren, the O'Lochlainns, the O'Connors, the O'Briens and the MacNamaras, the terrible truth about the two murders in their community.

TWENTY

AN SEANCHAS MÓR
(THE GREAT ANCIENT TRADITION)

No Brehon is able to abrogate anything that is written in the Seanchas Mór. In it are established laws for king and vassal; queen and subject; for taoiseach and liegeman; for the man of wealth and the poor man.

In the Seanchas Mór are promulgated the four great laws:
The law of social relationships
The law relating to tenants
The law of fosterage
Also the binding of all by verbal contract, for the world would be in a state of confusion if verbal contracts were not binding

&

'SO YOU SPOKE to her, Niall, you told her what you knew?'

'Not about the killing, Brehon, I never thought about that, then. It was the way she flew into such a rage with me that made me think of that.'

'So she was furious?'

'Frightened, too, Brehon. I could see the way she turned yellow and I could see the whites of her eyes.'

'And what did she say?'

'She screamed at me to get out. She called me every name that she could think of. Bastard was the least of them,' said Niall brooding. 'I didn't expect that sort of treatment. I just wanted her word to help to get what was only my own. I thought she would talk to the *taoiseach* and make him see reason. I wanted to uncover my father's hearth and to enter into possession of what was rightfully mine.'

'Don't worry about all that now, Niall,' said Mara gently. 'Don't go over these things.' She cast a worried glance at the thick soft linen bandage that swathed his head. His eyes were clear, but his face was very white and his lips bloodless. 'Just tell me about what brought you over to the mill after you had been to the abbot's house,' she said.

'Well, I suddenly realized what had happened to my father,' said Niall. 'You see, it was he that told me about it all in the first place. I guessed who killed him. I hadn't thought of it before. But I went over to the mill and I lit a candle. Well, I don't know if you noticed it, but those floorboards are very wide apart. It's built like that on purpose so that the miller can look down and keep an eye on the mill race as it turns the paddles.'

Mara nodded. She had noticed the gaps between the boards, but had not guessed the reason.

'Well, I was looking around, holding the candle, and you know the way it is when you are in the dark and suddenly you see things by candlelight that you would never see by daylight.'

Mara nodded again, with an anxious glance at the weary face. His voice seemed to be getting weaker, too.

'Well, the water picked up the light and suddenly I saw it shining there. I went down to the lower floor and I knelt down and I could see it clearly. I think I tried to move the shaft, but then . . .' His voice faded away and Mara got to her feet.

'You lie down now, Niall. You have told me all that I need to know. Just close your eyes and try to have a sleep. I'll send Maol in to you now and Fachtnan and Nuala will be riding over later in the morning to see you. Don't worry about anything, Niall. I will see that justice is done.'

❀

'So it wasn't young Donal that was the murderer after all,' said Turlough happily. 'Well, that is wonderful news. I could do with cheering up this morning and now you have done it for me. It's always wonderful to see you, but this news makes your visit doubly good.'

'What's the matter?' she asked. She had been so full of her own affairs that she had not noticed until now how drawn and weary he looked.

'It's Conor,' he said lowering his voice. 'I've been up all night with him. He's here, you know. His wife has gone back for a holiday to her own people. She says that it is upsetting to see her husband like this. My physician holds out little hope for him. He is wasting away. It's almost impossible to get him to eat. And then he gets these fevers and you can see the flesh melting off his bones. I don't know what to do about him. I try to stay hopeful, but I think that by Christmas I may have only one son left.'

Mara gazed at him compassionately. She did not know what to say. She wished she could comfort him, perhaps put the bad news aside, but that was not possible. She could delay it for minutes, but not for hours, and certainly not forever. He patted her hand and poured them both a cup of wine.

'Anyway,' he said, 'let's not talk about that. Tell me all the news from the kingdom of the Burren and how you have managed to solve these two cases. My mind needs diverting, so go on, tell me everything. The main thing is that Teige's boy, Donal, is not a murderer. I'm very fond of Teige; he and I are the same age and we were great friends from the time that we were both babies.'

'Yes,' she said lightly. 'I do believe Donal was not the murderer in either case. I myself examined the body of Ragnall and I saw the mark over the man's ear. What I am sure happened was that Donal struck him over the head and then went off. Guaire, the linen merchant from Corcomroe, came into the churchyard, saw the pouch, cut it off, and then Ragnall probably came to his senses and Guaire panicked. He was a very small man in comparison with Ragnall and he would have been no match for him. Ragnall would have been in a towering rage – at the best of times, he was not a good-tempered man and at that moment, with an aching head and a thief with his pouch full of silver in his hand there in front of him, Ragnall was possibly homicidal.'

'So you think that the linen merchant may have killed Ragnall?' asked Turlough.

Mara nodded. 'That's the way that I see it. Guaire seized the stone cross and hit Ragnall over the head – he may not have meant to kill him, but that was the outcome of the blow. These stone crosses, even the smallest of them, are very heavy. Guaire fled, and then Donal, when he returned later on, found Ragnall dead, and immediately assumed that everyone would think that he was the murderer. He is a very impulsive, impetuous young man who acts first and thinks later. I do hope that Maeve has a brain behind that pretty face as this young cousin of yours has few brains of his own.'

'So you're going to allow them to marry,' said Turlough smiling. 'I thought you would. You have great sympathy with young people. And you tell me Donal wasn't responsible for the murder of the miller, Aengus, either. In spite of the evidence of the knife?'

'The knife,' said Mara heavily. 'Yes, of course, the knife.' He had come to this second murder more quickly than she was prepared for. She said no more for a few moments while she organized her thoughts. The bad news about Conor was making all this doubly difficult.

'I'm afraid,' she continued, speaking slowly and carefully, 'there were two knives.'

'Two knives,' echoed Turlough, looking at her with a puzzled expression.

She nodded. 'Two knives,' she repeated. 'And each bore the *derbhfine* crest of the O'Brien clan.'

She put her hand into her pouch and felt the weight and the shape of the two knives. However, when she took her hand out, it was empty. The knives would have to wait for their place in the story.

'And what was it that Niall saw in the water, then?' asked Turlough. 'Go on, have that cup of wine. Yes, do, you've had a long ride, and an early start. I bet you were up before dawn. I was barely out of bed myself when I was told that you were waiting downstairs.'

Mara took the cup and sipped a little to satisfy him. She would have to educate him into a liking for French wine, she thought as she put the cup down. Spanish wine was not to her taste. It was far too rough and the flavour in her mouth was sour.

'Niall saw a knife in the stream,' she said. 'He saw the blade and the crest. He could see that it was the O'Brien *derbhfine* crest. The knife had dropped down through the wide gaps in the floorboards and into the stream. The flow of the water had washed it just as far as the paddle wheel and it had stuck there. Niall was trying to recover it. He moved the shaft and it split, bringing the two millstones down and hitting him a glancing blow on the forehead. So at least his injury was an accident.'

'But the knife?' asked Turlough, looking puzzled. 'Was this the knife belonging to young Donal O'Brien? I thought you told me that the little girl, Nuala, had found Donal's knife on the shelf.'

'So she did. And that knife was stained with blood. And of course I suspected Donal O'Brien. The evidence against him was overwhelming. He had followed Aengus home in a drunken rage. Ragnall had gone to the mill in the morning. He may have surprised Donal in the act of putting Aengus's body in the stream. I always guessed that was a clumsy attempt at giving a murder the appearance of suicide. This second knife, of course, had no blood on it because it had spent more than a week in the water. Nevertheless, it did have the blood of Aengus MacNamara on it, because this was the knife that killed him.'

'I'm getting muddled up,' said Turlough good-humouredly. 'Start at the beginning! What happened about the miller?'

'Well, to start at the beginning,' said Mara patiently, 'Donal O'Brien followed Aengus the miller to Oughtmama on the night of Michaelmas Eve. He punched Aengus; Aengus hit him with his stick and knocked him out.'

'So, did Aengus drown himself then out of remorse?' said Turlough flippantly. She could sense that part of his mind was still concentrated on his very sick son.

'No,' replied Mara. 'Aengus did not drown himself. He was not, perhaps, a very pleasant character. He left Donal lying there unconscious from a blow from a very heavy stick and he went off to amuse himself in the way that he often spent his evenings. After he returned from vespers at the abbey, of course,' she added lightly.

Turlough grinned. 'A secret drinker, eh?'

'No, I think sex interested him more than drink,' said Mara dryly. 'There is an old stone building there at Oughtmama. It belonged to the abbot in the days when Oughtmama was an abbey. It's in a pretty good state of repair; my lads discovered a little love nest there with its pile of sheepskins and a couple of rather fine wine cups.'

'Tut, tut,' said Turlough, tossing back his wine and pouring himself another cup. Mara wished that he would listen more seriously, but she had begun her story now, and she could not change its course.

'The lovers had met there very often,' she continued, 'but this was, I'm sure, the first time that they were aware that they had been seen. The woman probably stayed in the house, but the man went after Aengus. Aengus fled to the mill house. He managed to get through the door, I reckon, but not to shut it, before his pursuer drew his knife and cut the miller's throat. You see,' she said simply, 'this man was in a position where he dared not have his wife hear of an affair with another woman.'

Turlough stared at her with a puzzled expression on his face. He replaced the wine cup on the table. Divorce and relationships outside marriage were common in the Gaelic society, although very frowned upon among the English and Anglo-Irish portions of the country. Mara waited. She could see that he was beginning to understand. Eventually he spoke.

'You said two knives.' The smile had gone from his lips and his face was taut with tension.

Mara reached into her pouch and took out first one knife and then the other. Both bore the crest of the O'Brien *derbhfine*. The first was a hunting knife with a few jewelled stones embedded in the hilt and an enamel oval set well into the handle. In the centre of that oval were the three lions of the O'Brien crest. The second knife was more ornate. The hilt was made from silver and in its centre, surrounded by an oval line of small jewels, was a medallion made from dark blue lapis lazuli, and set within the vivid blue were the same three small lions carved from rubies.

Turlough leaned over and picked up the second knife and held it in his hand. He looked at it for a long moment and then raised his eyes to hers. For the first time in their relationship, she found it impossible to read those eyes. Normally she had seen them blazing with fun, or with tenderness, though occasionally they had been alight with anger, but never had she seen them as today, dulled over and unreflective like the surface of the brown peat water on a foggy morning.

'Is that knife belonging to your son, Murrough?' she asked, looking at him very directly.

He made no reply, just looked at her and signed to her to go on.

'Murrough has been hanging around Carron, flirting with the MacNamara's wife, Slaney, as you know,' she said bluntly. 'We talked about it, you and I, you remember? We laughed about it. Neither of us took it very seriously. You probably said to yourself something like: *"restless are a young man's desires"*, as Fíthail puts it. We thought of it as just a little fling – a certain attraction on his side and perhaps on hers, also, and certainly desire for a higher position on the part of Slaney.' She smiled at him, but he did not respond. His face looked dead. She put out her two hands and took one of his between them.

'The thing is, Turlough, that it was serious. Looking back on it, I realize that Slaney was completely enamoured of him, and perhaps he with her. I don't know. All I know is that they were meeting, perhaps on a daily basis. I should have guessed when I met her, one day, outside Carron Castle, that she was returning from Oughtmama, and Cumhal had met Murrough less than an hour previously coming from the same direction. I thought nothing of it at the time, but afterwards it came back to me. When I began to puzzle it all out, I realized that they were continually meeting – not at Carron, of course, except for public occasions, but at Oughtmama, somewhere among those ruined stone buildings. And then everything began to become clear to me. You see, I lost my way for a while in the solving of these crimes, by spending too long trying to find a connection between the two murders.'

She thought back to that moment at Lemeanah when Shane and Hugh were pretending to search for baby swallows. She smiled slightly at the memory of Donal's uncomprehending face when she had voiced her thoughts, saying: *It's a mistake to spend too long searching for something that doesn't exist.* She looked back at Turlough. His face bore the look of a man who had suddenly received a bad shock. She let go of his hand, waiting patiently for him to speak, looking at him with pity in her glance.

There was a sound of loud laughter from out in the courtyard where some carefree young men were burnishing their swords. It made the silence in the room seem by contrast to be especially heavy. If only I did not have to do this to him, thought Mara. Perhaps I could have allowed this murder to go unsolved. After all, Donal had no idea of who had killed Aengus; Niall did, but he would have been prepared to keep silence if the mill had been given to him. That could have been the solution. Go to Poulnabrone; say that I found Niall to be the true son of Aengus the miller, and that Guaire, the linen merchant from Corcomroe, had killed Ragnall and that perhaps Ragnall had killed Aengus. Would that have satisfied everyone? Probably, it would have. And then I would not have to inflict this pain on a man that I esteem so much, for whom I have so much affection. No one would have cared.

But I, she thought, I would have cared. I could not keep silence. She leaned forward and once again took one of his immense hands between hers.

'Turlough,' she said steadily, 'Murrough, your son, killed Aengus the miller. He killed him because Aengus saw the two of them, Slaney and Murrough. They used the abbot's house at Oughtmama for their meetings. I saw the room, with the sheepskins piled high in the corner and the brazier filled with charcoal. I saw the quality of the wine cups there, hidden beneath the sheepskins. They were made from silver. No miller ever had wine cups made from silver. Aengus went there on Michaelmas Eve and found the lovers. Whether he meant to be seen this time, whether he even thought of some blackmail, that I don't know; but I do know that he had seen them before. You see, Aengus had previously told Niall of his suspicions. He was an inquisitive old man who meddled with what did not concern him, but he did not deserve to die, Turlough.'

'You say all this to me,' said Turlough, through dry lips, 'but you haven't given me any proof. Where is your evidence?'

Strange how father and son used almost the same words, thought Mara, thinking back to the young man who had sat before her yesterday evening.

'Let me just finish, first,' she said. 'Slaney would not have wanted Garrett to find out, but, more important, Murrough could not afford to have news of this affair with Slaney get back to his wife. You yourself told me that. Murrough is ambitious and he needed to keep the Earl of Kildare sweet, and the Great Earl, as they call him, would not be a man to forgive an insult to his daughter. Murrough had to silence the miller. Probably Aengus fled back to the mill, Murrough pursued him, killed him, probably put his own knife down in order to clean it, and then, perhaps, saw young Donal stretched unconscious on the floor. He is quick-witted, your son, because he immediately saw how he could turn this to his advantage. He put down his own knife – either then or later on, it fell through the floorboards into the millstream. That is not important now, but what is important is that he took Donal's knife from his pouch, smeared blood on it and on the torn grey mantle. And then he and Slaney departed immediately. What part she played in it, I don't know, but she undoubtedly knew.'

'And then?' asked Turlough. His voice was so low that she had to half guess at the words. He looked like a man suddenly stricken by a fatal fever.

'And then, Donal came to his senses in the morning, saw the body, decided to try to make it look like a suicide, dragged it out and put it under the sluice gate. Probably Murrough's knife was dislodged then and fell through the floorboards into the millstream. I don't think that Murrough would have deliberately dropped it in there. Why throw it away when the knife could be easily cleaned and replaced in his pouch?'

Mara paused and looked at Turlough. His face was now hidden in his hands. She had no way of guessing what his thoughts were, but she continued resolutely.

'Donal told me that he had seen his own knife on the shelf, but had left it there, meaning to wash it afterwards.

However, when he heard the cart coming up the lane he panicked and took himself off. Niall saw nothing, but when Ragnall returned with the damaged sack, he picked up, not the knife – he didn't notice that lying on the shelf – but Donal's brooch, still attached to the piece of cloth. Unfortunately for Ragnall, he decided to return it to Donal – he knew nothing about the death of Aengus at the time, but Donal thought he did. So Murrough killed Aengus, for fear of betrayal, and Donal knocked Ragnall unconscious from sheer terror and, though he did not murder Ragnall, indirectly he caused his death, because he left him lying in the churchyard at Noughaval with his pouch full of silver.'

Mara waited for a moment but Turlough said nothing, so she added: 'And that is the solution to the two Michaelmas murders. I am as sure of it as if I were there at the time.'

'And what happens next?' asked Turlough. His voice was very low and his eyes were fixed on the floor.

Mara drained her wine and rose to her feet. The king did not follow her, but stayed sitting down. She took her mantle from the back of the door and slung it over her shoulders. From outside she heard the sound of a church bell tolling for the midday celebration of the angelus. If she left now, she would have plenty of time to get back to the Burren to meet the people of the kingdom at four o'clock.

'What happens next?' repeated Turlough.

'At the hour of vespers today, Saturday, 11 October,' she said quietly, 'I tell the truth about these two murders to the people of the Burren.' She waited for a moment, but now he had turned towards the window and his face was closed and without expression.

'And you?' she said. She wanted to reach out to him, to

tell him how sorry she was, but his stony face stopped her. She almost wanted to promise to keep the wrongdoing of Murrough to herself, but she knew that she could not do this. From the time that she was five years old she had been trained to respect the law and to know that it could never be bent or evaded. *No Brehon is able to abrogate anything that is written in the Seanchas Mór*, she repeated to herself, but found little comfort in the words.

He said no more. He did not lift his head, nor did he look at her. And so she left him and returned to the Burren.

TWENTY-ONE

MÍASHLECHTA (SECTIONS ON RANK)

The king's justice is the most important thing in each kingdom. If the king is just, his reign will be peaceful and prosperous, whereas if he is guilty of injustice, the soil and the elements will rebel against him. There will be infertility of women and cattle, crop-failures, dearth of fish, defeat in battle, plagues and lightning storms throughout the land.

∞

MARA THOUGHT THAT POULNABRONE had never looked so beautiful as it did on that afternoon of 11 October. There had been a shower of rain and the pavements shone as if they had been polished. The low sun of an autumn afternoon etched sharp black shadows of sculpted rock over the smooth surface of the clints; and the water-worn grykes, between the slabs of grey stone, were filled with the glowing plum colour of the burnet rose leaves and the silver latticework of the carline thistles.

She took her place silently beside the great dolmen and ran her hand for a moment over the rough edges of the giant capstone. How long had it been here, she wondered, and how much longer would it last? It had seen so much in its lifetime. Would anyone ever be able to unlock its secrets?

The six scholars arrived and bowed to her. She bowed back gravely, but did not speak. Normally she moved amongst the crowd before the court began, but today she did not. She just stood there impassively, holding the scroll of vellum in her hand. There were three large leaves rolled up inside it. She would deal with the cases one by one and she would do justice to all.

Turlough came just as the bell sounded for vespers. He was alone except for his two bodyguards. She looked keenly around after him, but Murrough was not there. She had half hoped, half feared that he would come. Would Turlough have felt humiliated if Murrough had made full confession, she wondered, or would he have been proud of his son? The king made his way through the crowd, who drew back to allow him past. He ignored the four *taoiseachs*, the O'Lochlainn, the O'Connor, the O'Brien and the Mac-Namara. They all had advanced towards him to meet and greet him as usual, but then they withdrew, seeing that he had no mind for conversation. Turlough bowed to Mara stiffly and she returned the courtesy. His face was set in strong, heavy lines. Suddenly he looked old.

Mara moved forward, greeted the crowd, paused for a second while the traditional blessing came back from them, and then unfurled the scroll. She selected one leaf and handed the other two back to Fachtnan.

'The first case today deals with the inheritance of Niall MacNamara. The case is that . . .'

As she read from the scroll, she glanced occasionally at Garrett MacNamara's face. He looked ill at ease and from time to time he licked his lips nervously. Slaney was nowhere to be seen.

'Niall can not be here today as he has had an accident,' finished Mara, rolling up the scroll again. She slightly emphasized the word 'accident'. No doubt there would be all sorts of rumours circulating about Niall's non-appearance. 'However,' she went on, 'on his behalf, I will call the witnesses. Who here can give evidence that Aengus MacNamara, the miller of Oughtmama, recognized Niall as his son?'

Instantly Ardal O'Lochlainn moved forward.

'Aengus MacNamara bought land from me a few years ago. He bought it to give to Niall on his eighteenth birthday. It was land sufficient to give Niall the status of an *ocaire*, such as a father would give to his son on attaining manhood. I certainly understood that Aengus was buying it for a son.' Ardal's voice was clear and full of authority. Mara glanced from him to Turlough, but the king's face bore no trace of interest. She looked back at the crowd.

'The O'Lochlainn has given his evidence. Is there anyone else wishes to say anything to support or to deny the assumption that Aengus acknowledged Niall as his son, born of the union between the miller and his servant, Cliodhna, now dead?'

There was no movement from any of the MacNamara clan and Garrett, their *taoiseach*, just gazed ahead as if he had little interest in the affair. Had he found out about Slaney? wondered Mara. If so, he would be quite within his legal rights to divorce her. Would he dare? Mara was so interested in this thought that for a moment she hardly heard a voice saying: 'I have some evidence to give.' And then her eyes were caught by the stocky figure of a young man pushing his way to the front.

'Yes, Brian?' she said encouragingly. Brian O'Lochlainn was one of the shepherds that worked for Ardal. He was a young man, only about nineteen, she thought. He was blushing furiously now with the eyes of the crowd upon him and she hastened to put him at ease by moving slightly so now he faced her and had his back to the crowd.

'You tend the sheep for the O'Lochlainn?' she asked. 'Do you work on the mountains above Oughtmama?'

He seized on her words gratefully. 'That's right, Brehon. We run the sheep on the mountain and just bring them down to the valley at shearing time. About a year ago, in early June, I was bringing down the sheep and I wanted someone to lift the sluice gate by the stream at Oughtmama, just where it enters the mill race. We always do this when we bring down the sheep. It saves breaking down the walls and having to build them up again, you see, Brehon,' he said earnestly.

Mara nodded. 'I can see that,' she said. 'And of course, at that time of year the water would be flowing slowly, so the sheep would easily be able to walk down the stream bed. So what happened then?'

'Well, I went in to ask Aengus and he was busy weighing sacks of flour so he said to me, "Ask my son, he's here today. He'll help you." And then he shouted down for Niall and Niall came up from the yard and held the gate for me.'

'And these were his very words?' asked Mara carefully. 'He said: "*Ask my son, he'll help you.*" And he shouted for Niall, not Balor? There was no chance that he might have meant Balor?'

'These were his very words, Brehon,' said Brian emphatically. 'Balor was nowhere to be seen. He had gone to work for Fintan, the blacksmith, by this time.'

'I see,' said Mara. Once again she cast a glance over towards Garrett, but he did not look at her, or even seem to be interested in the evidence.

'Thank you very much, Brian,' she said. 'That is very valuable evidence.' She turned away from him quickly. She would prefer it if he did not blurt out any unwise disclosure such as that he had been asked by his *taoiseach* to do this. Ardal, of course, was the soul of honour, he would never ask a man to lie, but it had been quick-witted of him to think of Brian. There was no doubt that the shepherd would have had plenty of contact with the mill. It was typical of Ardal's efficiency that he would have gone up the mountain one day during the week and interviewed Brian, arranged for a substitute shepherd and made sure that Brian was present at Poulnabrone at the correct time. In her mind, Mara saluted his enterprise but she did not want any link between himself and Brian to be uncovered, so she spoke rapidly now.

'Has anyone got any more evidence to put forward on this case?'

Once again she looked at Garrett, and once again he avoided her eyes. It was obvious that he had decided not to contest this case. She looked towards Turlough; as king, he should now at least be giving a nominal sign of having come to a conclusion, but he still seemed wrapped in his own gloomy thoughts so she concluded the matter, saying briefly, 'Well, in that case, I find that Niall MacNamara was recognized as the son of Aengus the miller and that he inherits his father's goods and he has the permission of this court to uncover his father's hearth.'

Mara turned towards Fachtnan, holding out her hand, and he gave her the second leaf of vellum. She unscrolled it, read it through briefly and then rolled it up again.

'This matter deals with the murder of Ragnall, steward to the MacNamara, in the churchyard at Noughaval on Michaelmas Day, at, or around the time of, sundown. Ragnall was killed by a blow to the forehead, from a small stone cross. Has anyone any knowledge of this affair?'

'I have, Brehon,' said Donal O'Brien, coming forward steadily and taking his place beside her. His colour was high, but his eyes were steady with courage. His father, Teige, stood up and deliberately moved closer to his son and then sat down on a low boulder nearby. He said nothing, but the show of unity was unmistakeable.

'I hit Ragnall on the side of the head with my fist,' said Donal. 'I knocked him unconscious and I went away and left him there. I admit the crime of assaulting an old man and then abandoning him.'

'Was Ragnall still alive when you left him?' asked Mara.

Donal met her eyes. 'He was, Brehon,' he said. 'He was unconscious, but he was definitely alive. He groaned just before I left. I thought he was coming to and I left quickly so that I would not lose my temper again.'

'So you are telling me that you were not the man who struck the blow with the stone cross?' asked Mara. She tried to make her tones sound both probing and sceptical, but already her mind had left this case and had gone ahead to the second murder.

'I am sure that he was alive, Brehon,' said Donal respectfully, 'and I am sure that I only hit him with my fist. He was an old man and he was the father of the girl that I love. I deeply regret what I have done and I am willing to pay whatever fine you impose, but I did not kill the man.'

'Has anyone else anything to say?' asked Mara looking around.

'I would like to say that Donal came to me immediately and told me what he had done,' said Maeve, stepping forward bravely. 'I believed what he said and several times, during the next hour or so, we kept listening for my father. When he didn't come, Donal went back. If he were still unconscious he was going to carry him back and help me to tend him. When he found that someone had killed my father, I was the one who persuaded him not to say anything. I was afraid that he might be blamed. The fault is mine as much as his.'

'No, the fault is mine,' insisted Donal, looking fondly at his beloved.

I'd better put a stop to this, thought Mara. Aloud she said, 'Thank you, Maeve, you may return to your place. Has anyone else anything to say?' She looked around but no one moved.

'Donal O'Brien,' she said, 'I find you guilty of assaulting Ragnall MacNamara, steward, and causing him grievous injury on the evening of Michaelmas Day. I find you not guilty of Ragnall's murder. I examined him myself and I saw that two blows had been struck: one was probably with a fist and the other, the blow that killed him, was struck with a stone cross. This crime was the work of another man and it appears very likely that the crime was committed by a man who is now dead.'

All the time that Mara was allocating the fine to Donal and listening to his formal expression of regret, her mind was on Turlough. His behaviour was strange. What was going to happen? Was Murrough going to turn up and defend himself, or was Turlough hoping that the case would not be mentioned, or that he could forbid the discussion of it? And then the matter was finished. Donal returned to his place and still there was no move from the king.

Mara waited for a moment. There was an audible murmur of appreciation rippling through the crowd. Donal's open confession and expression of regret would stand him in good stead in the future with the people. There were many smiles of sympathy as Maeve slipped her hand into his as he returned to his position by her side.

Mara allowed the murmur to die down before signalling to Fachtnan. He handed the final leaf of vellum to her. She glanced through it for a moment, less to familiarize herself with its contents than to give herself an extra moment before facing her ordeal.

'Last case,' she said then, her voice crisp and unemotional. She rolled up the vellum and held the scroll lightly in her right hand. 'Aengus MacNamara, miller, of Oughtmama, was slain on the eve of Michaelmas.' She paused and looked around at the crowd. All eyes had now left hers. Startled, she followed their direction and saw that Turlough had risen to his feet and was striding towards her. He bowed stiffly to her, but did not meet her eyes.

'My lady judge,' he said formally. For the first time since she had met him, his tone had all the regal tones of a king of three kingdoms. 'With your permission, I would wish to speak on this matter.'

'Of course, my lord.' Her tone was as steady and formal as his own. Her eyes met his and they did not waver. She hoped that she had conveyed to him the strength of her purpose. Then she moved away and sat on the boulder from which he had risen and turned her face attentively towards him. There was a long moment before he spoke, but when he did, his voice rang out like that of a chief on the battlefield.

'My friends, for almost ten years I have been coming here to judgement days at Poulnabrone on the Burren. During all of these ten years, I have just sat here and listened to your Brehon. Throughout the whole of that time, I have never felt that I needed to intervene, that I needed to take matters into my own hands. Every case has been dealt with by Mara, the Brehon of the Burren, showing the wisdom that understands the law and the compassion that understands the person.'

He stopped for a moment and looked around. His eyes did not meet Mara's, but she knew that he had made eye contact with many of the crowd. Every face was intent upon him.

'So you will ask me why I am intervening now, why I am speaking to you about this second murder in your community, the murder of an elderly man on the eve of Michaelmas.'

Again there was a pause, but no one moved and no one spoke. Turlough turned over one large hand and examined the palm as if to read something from the lines engraved upon it.

'I come from a warlike race,' he said suddenly, raising his

head proudly. 'My great ancestor, Brian Boru, named Brian of the Tributes, slew many men in his time, and so did the sons and the grandsons and the great-grandsons that came after him. Their names and their deeds will be well known to you; the bards and the *files* have repeated them in song and stories. And so have the names of the other O'Briens been renowned: my namesake, Turlough of the Triumphs, son of Teige-of-the-Narrow-Waters; Dermot, son of Turlough; Brian-of-the-Battles, his grandson; Donough-of-the-Chess-board; and then there was Teige the Bone-splitter; his grand-son, Teige of Coad, my own father, son of Turlough Beg; and then my father's successors, my uncles, Conor na Sróna, he of the big nose; and The Gilladuff – all of these men have fought with sword in hand from the age when they could first heft the weight of a weapon, but none of them . . .'

Here he smashed down a large fist on the capstone of the dolmen and raised his voice from the low steady tone to a warlike shout.

'Not one of them, I say, would have murdered an old man who had seen him bedding a harlot. Not one of them!'

Mara tried to look at Garrett MacNamara without turn-ing her head and then realized that everyone else in the large assembly was doing the same. It appeared that Niall had confided in Maol and the word had spread rapidly through the Burren. This accounted for Slaney's absence today. Hasti-ly, Mara turned her eyes back to Turlough. He had paused to wipe the sweat from his forehead and now his voice was very low.

'And not one of them,' he repeated, but this time so quietly that the crowd strained to hear his words, 'not one of them would have tried to place the guilt of his crime upon the innocent shoulders of his young cousin.'

Suddenly came the bell-like beating of the wings of ten great white swans, flying east above the heads of the crowd. Everyone looked up. Those swans would not be seen again until spring. Turlough watched them for a moment until they disappeared and when he spoke again his voice was still low, and now broken with sorrow.

'Now I name him to you, I name this man who is the secret and unlawful killer of Aengus MacNamara, the miller of Oughtmama: it is Murrough Mac Turlough, Mac Teige, Mac Turlough Beg, descendant of Brian Boru, once my son, but now a son no longer. He has fled to England, and the kingdoms of Thomond, Corcomroe and Burren will know him no more. Today here, before you all, I declare him to be a man without honour.' He paused for a moment, his eyes bent on the ground and then he raised them and said slowly and heavily: 'That man has lost his honour price.'

Then there was a murmur from the crowd. It was a terrible thing for anyone to lose their honour price. The *lóg n-enech*, the price of his face, was the most important possession of any man in the Gaelic kingdom. Without that, he was as nothing, just a *cu glas*, a homeless and landless cur. The people of the Burren glanced at each other with horror on their faces. There was compassion in their faces, also, but the compassion was for the father.

'Now go in peace,' said Turlough in broken tones. 'And in your charity, pray tonight for your king who has one son dying and the other lost to him forever.'

He watched them as they went, moving quickly and

silently as if they sought the shelter of their own homes and fireplaces as a refuge from such heavy sorrow. Rapidly they left the townland of Poulnabrone, walking across the great stone slabs in twos and threes, heads together, no loud voices, just the swelling of a shocked murmur, and the king watched them until the sound of their words ceased and all were gone. Then Turlough crossed over and sat beside Mara.

'Say something to comfort me,' he said with all the childlike simplicity which was so much part of the man. He held out his large hand to her.

Mara took his hand and laced her long fingers in between his.

'With the help of God and of the Blessed Mary, Mother of the Holy Child,' she said, 'I will give you a son to be proud of.'

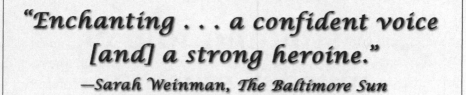
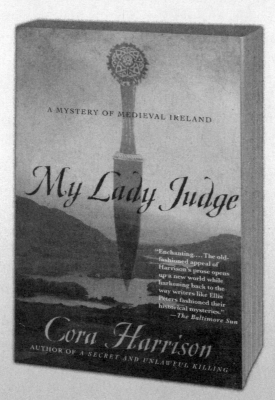